Praise for *Fatal Hearts*

"Norah Wilson does it again! *Fatal Hearts* is suspenseful, sexy, and satisfying."

— Theresa Ragan, *New York Times* bestselling author

"Norah Wilson weaves sizzling romance and deft pacing for a killer suspense you can't put down."

— Dianna Love, *New York Times* bestselling author

FATAL
HEARTS

Also by Norah Wilson

Every Breath She Takes
Haunted by Dreams

Serve and Protect Series
Protecting Paige
Saving Grace
Guarding Suzannah
Needing Nita

Vampire Romances
Nightfall
The Merzetti Effect

Casters Series
Embrace the Night
Enter the Night
Comes the Night

Written with Heather Doherty
Ashlyn's Radio

Dix Dodd Mysteries
Death by Cuddle Club
Family Jewels
The Case of the Flashing Fashion Queen

Gatekeepers Series
The Summoning

NORAH WILSON

FATAL HEARTS

Montlake
Romance

The characters and events portrayed in this book are fictitious. Any similarity to real persons, living or dead, is coincidental and not intended by the author.

Published by Montlake Romance, Seattle
www.apub.com
ISBN-13: 9781477824696
ISBN-10: 1477824693

Cover design by Anne Cain

Library of Congress Control Number: 2014904442

Printed in the United States of America

CHAPTER 1

Boyd McBride's stomach was empty, but it still managed to churn as he climbed into his rental car, exited the tiny airport's parking lot, and headed toward the city of Fredericton.

This wasn't the first time he'd traveled this road. The memory of the last time made bitter bile rise up in his throat.

Two weeks ago, he'd come to Fredericton to claim the remains of his twin brother.

Remains. Jesus, what a word. What a useless damned euphemism. He'd collected a body.

Josh's body.

As a fifteen-year veteran with the Toronto Police Service— three of those years in homicide—he'd used that word plenty of times when talking to a victim's next of kin. Had they hated the term as much as he now did? God only knew he'd heard it often enough in the past weeks as he'd dealt with the Fredericton cops and the New Brunswick Coroner's Office, not to mention the funeral director and the priest back home in Toronto.

Boyd's hands tightened on the rental's steering wheel. Josh's unexpected death had absolutely gutted their parents, leaving them barely able to function. So Boyd had stepped in and taken charge of the funeral arrangements, something he had never figured he'd be called upon to do.

He'd never dreamed his twin would die first, given their respective occupations. Josh was a journalist in a tiny, squeaky-clean, white-collar community, for chrissakes! Boyd was the one in danger every day. Not Josh.

The GPS's voice cut into his thoughts, instructing him to merge onto the Vanier Highway.

His brother was the one who was good with people. He'd always known what to say in every situation, how to be gracious, and how to put people at ease. Comfort them and allow them to comfort in return.

If people had expected those touches from Boyd at the funeral, they must've been disappointed. Oh, he'd gotten up and delivered a eulogy, but public speaking wasn't his forte, and certainly not under these circumstances. His comments had been short, raw, and had wrecked him.

His stomach added a rumble to its churning, reminding him it was almost noon and he hadn't had anything but two tiny cups of coffee on the plane. He should drop his stuff at the motel, then see about getting some lunch. Except it was probably too early for check-in.

Straight to lunch, then? *Nah.* Despite his body's signals, he really had no desire to eat. Everything tasted like cardboard these days.

He might as well get down to what he'd come here to do, starting by checking in with the Fredericton Police and seeing where they were in their investigation.

Initially, the local cops had treated the case as a straightforward sudden death investigation, not a suspicious death. Not that Boyd faulted them for that. That was SOP in the circumstances, until and unless they had reason to believe it was suspicious.

He actually couldn't fault them for anything. They'd done a thorough job processing the scene—Josh's car and the surrounding area. They'd also ordered a level-two forensic autopsy right off the bat, instead of a level one, and they had a pretty good start on the background investigation and working up the timeline.

But the fact was, his brother's death was *damned* suspicious, and Boyd had told Detective Ray Morgan as much the day after Josh died.

Josh had left a brief but excited message for Boyd, saying he'd cracked the investigation into their birth parents wide-open, but that the situation needed to be handled delicately. *Extremely* delicately. The next day, his twin had been found dead in his vehicle. Boyd's gut told him the two events were connected. Fortunately, Morgan and his supervisor, Sergeant John Quigley, weren't big believers in coincidence either. They'd upgraded the file to a suspicious death and promised to look into it while Boyd went back to Ontario to deal with the funeral and lawyers and such.

Ten days later, forensic toxicology was still pending, and the cops hadn't found any smoking guns, so it was still just a suspicious death. Now that the funeral was over, Boyd had come back to look into matters himself. He'd hated to leave his parents, but he was terrified the coroner's office was going to put a "Death by Natural Causes" stamp on the file and effectively shut the investigation down before it even got started.

But dammit, Josh had been only thirty-five. Men that young didn't tend to expire from sudden cardiac arrest. Not ones who were as fit as Josh had been anyway.

He just couldn't—wouldn't—wrap his head around the idea of natural causes. Not when his gut was screaming that this was connected to whatever hornet's nest Josh had stirred up with that damned investigation.

He decelerated the rental car as he approached the intersection of Regent and Prospect, and the big *H* sign for the regional hospital caught his attention. Since he was so close, he decided to go there first instead of the police station. The hospital was where the declaration of death had been made before Josh's body was shipped to Saint John for the forensic autopsy. Boyd had a power of attorney in his bag, as well as a certified copy of the will appointing him executor of Josh's estate. Boyd might have been the older brother—by all of seventeen minutes—but Josh had always been the organized one, prepared for any eventuality.

Even dropping dead, as it turned out.

The point was, armed with all that paperwork, he would have access to Josh's medical records. He also had the name of the ER physician who'd declared Josh. Maybe he'd stop by the ER to try to catch him. It was a long shot, but maybe something stuck out in the doc's memory that might be helpful.

And on that happy thought, he pulled into the hospital's paid parking area, killed the rented Altima's engine, and climbed out. Time to start this investigation.

~

Hayden Walsh chewed the inside of her lip as she studied her patient's lacerated hand. To call for a plastic surgeon or not? There didn't look to be much nerve involvement, if any. And if there wasn't, she'd get reamed out for calling for a plastics consult. Last time, she'd been told in no uncertain terms that they weren't a suture clinic and to learn to do her own damned stitches.

She could suture just fine, thank you. She stitched up most of the lacerations that came her way. But this one wasn't so straightforward. She'd feel better about getting the go-ahead from plastics.

Because if there *was* nerve involvement and she just sewed her patient up and sent him home, and he later alleged the hand was compromised because of her treatment, she'd be screwed. She would also no doubt get reamed out by the very same plastics guy for *not* calling for a consult.

She studied the man's rough, calloused hand some more. He was clearly a laborer. Drywall installer, she'd guess, from the deep cracks on his fingers and the white dust on his hair and work clothes. Not a young one either. Fifty-one, his chart said. Probably not a lot of alternative careers for a laborer his age.

"So what do you think, Doc? Can you stitch me up? Maybe hook me up with some good meds so I can get back to work tomorrow?"

"We're going to get you stitched up all right, Mr. Martin," she assured him as she rewrapped his hand. "But I'm going to call a plastic surgeon to have a look before we do. Better safe than sorry."

"Damn." He looked crestfallen. "I thought you were fixin' to do it."

She grimaced. "I know it's been a long wait to get seen, and now you have to wait some more. But you need both hands in your trade, I imagine. Better do everything we can to keep them both operational."

He grinned, the smile making his lined face look younger.

"Not complaining about the wait. I was just hoping you'd be the one doing the sewing."

She lifted an eyebrow in mock sternness. "Mr. Martin, are you flirting with me?"

"Depends. Is it working?"

"Sorry, but you're too late," she said, returning his smile. "I just gave my heart to the two-year-old charmer in Exam Room One."

"Wow, I feel really old suddenly."

Hayden laughed. "You'll bounce back, I think. In the meantime, I'm going to go page a plastic surgeon. If he gives me the okay, I'll do it myself, but if there are complicating factors, he'll want to do the suturing."

"Doubt he's as pretty as you."

She laughed again. "You're right there, but he does very pretty work. So hang tight, okay?"

With that, she headed to the desk to make the dreaded call.

She'd just finished paging plastics and updating Garth Martin's chart when she heard the voice.

"Excuse me, could I talk to someone, please?"

Hayden whirled. "Josh?"

The chart slipped from her fingers and clattered to the floor. Impossible. Josh was dead. The aching loss she'd carried around for these past weeks grew new claws, shredding her composure.

How in the hell can a dead man be standing in my hospital?

Through a haze of sudden tears, she barely registered him bending to pick up the chart and placing it on the ledge of the desk.

"I'm sorry. I'm not Josh," he said in that achingly familiar voice. "I'm—"

"Boyd." *Oh God. Not Josh. Not his ghost.* This was his identical twin. But what was Boyd McBride doing here? She'd met

6

him briefly when she'd traveled to Ontario for Josh's funeral, but she'd never expected to see him again. And never in a million years had she expected him to walk into her ER in Fredericton.

Their encounter had been *very* brief, just long enough to shake his hand in the receiving line at the public visitation and express her condolences. He'd looked so much like Josh, she'd wanted to hug him, but the marked coolness in his eyes had dissuaded her. She hadn't had time to dwell on it, because Ella McBride had recognized her and pulled her into a tight hug.

"And you're Hayden." He didn't sound pleased to see her, but he closed a hand on her elbow, as though he thought she might need his support. Maybe he was right. "I'm sorry to have startled you."

"No, don't apologize. It's just . . . you caught me off guard." Thankfully, her voice emerged relatively normal sounding, if a little croaky. The touch of his hand felt protective, almost sheltering. So naturally she stepped back. He let his hand drop to his side. She cleared her throat. "We met at the funeral. Or rather, the visitation. But you probably don't remember. There were a ton of people there, and—"

"I remember." His mouth turned down. As though remembering his manners, he said, "Thank you for making the trip. My parents told me afterward what a comfort it was to meet you in person."

Hayden blinked rapidly. "I'm glad. They're just as lovely as Josh said."

"He talked about you a lot."

She knew as much. Josh used to mention when he'd shared stories about the two of them with his family.

The triage nurse guided a patient past them, and Boyd's eyes followed them for a few seconds before returning to meet her gaze. Eyes that missed nothing, she sensed. So like Josh's with those tawny-gold irises, yet nothing like them. Boyd's were cool, and so much more guarded. They didn't show even a shadow of the grief he must be feeling.

Josh had always said his brother had mastered the art of the poker face. She now understood what he meant.

"Is there someplace we can go to talk?" he asked.

Of course. He'd want to talk about his brother. Find some closure. And unless she missed her guess, he'd want the medical files to pore over. Hayden sure would if she had a sibling. Actually, Josh had been the closest thing she'd had to one.

She glanced up at the ER secretary, Marta, whose sympathetic expression confirmed she'd seen the whole encounter. Marta had often chatted with Josh while he'd hung around waiting for Hayden to get off shift, and she knew how devastated Hayden was by his loss.

And how shaken up she was now to see the spitting image of him turn up in the ER.

"Go," Marta said. "Take a break."

Hayden glanced at Josh's brother.

"Okay, thank you, I will." She checked her pocket, reassured by the feel of her pager. "Page me if my plastics consult turns up?"

"You got it."

She led Boyd out of the ER and wended her way through the halls. After locating a quiet room that was not in use outside the intensive care unit, she opened the door and gestured for him to enter. She took a seat on a low couch and made a motion indicating he do likewise. There was a second's hesitation, then he complied, picking a chair opposite her across the coffee table.

She couldn't get over how like Josh he looked. Same height—a few inches over six feet. Same skin tone. Same glossy dark-brown hair with the hint of a widow's peak at the front, though

Boyd's was cut shorter. Same broad, slightly bony face with those high cheekbones and thick-lashed golden eyes.

"I'm so sorry for your family's loss," she offered.

"Thank you." He looked uncomfortable with her expressing her sympathies. She could understand that. She'd received the same kind of condolences after Josh's death from people who'd known how close the two of them had been. The words never made her feel any better either, but given the circumstances, what else could be said?

"So you and Josh were pretty much best friends, huh?"

She tucked a strand of hair behind her ear. "Yes."

"*Just* friends?"

"Yes, just friends."

He lifted a skeptical eyebrow. "Josh never . . . ?"

"What? Hit on me?"

"Yeah."

"Of course he did." Hayden smiled at the memory. "Until he figured out I meant it, about not dating. By then, we'd discovered how much we had in common and started hanging out."

"He accepted that? He never tried again to shift it out of the platonic zone?"

"No." She shook her head. "I mean, we weren't invisible to each other. I was perfectly aware he was a nice-looking guy, and I'm sure he noticed I had breasts, but it wasn't weird or awkward." She looked at Boyd's face, but she had no clue what he was thinking. "For what it's worth, I was a little skeptical too going into it. I'd never attempted that kind of close friendship with a hetero guy before. But it . . . worked. I loved him so much."

Boyd made no reply, but regarded her steadily, his gaze still giving nothing away.

Poker face, indeed.

She sighed and rubbed her temple, suddenly conscious that the slight headache she'd been beating back all day had pulsed into full-blown life. "Josh said you worked in law enforcement. Is that silent routine a cop trick? Do people rush to fill the void?"

Again he said nothing.

She groaned. "Right. I just did it."

The corner of his lips quirked in the smallest of smiles. "Sorry. That wasn't intentional. Habit, I guess."

That half smile made her stomach do a queer little flip. Which was weird. He looked like Josh. *Exactly* like Josh, to be precise. They were identical twins. And Josh's smile had never done that to her. Maybe because a smile was practically Josh's default expression. She had a hunch Boyd McBride didn't smile so easily or often, even when he wasn't grieving.

It made her happy to think she'd made him smile, maybe even made him forget his grief for a second. And because she didn't want to dwell on that feeling, she started talking again.

"Josh and I met when he was working on a story that involved the hospital. I couldn't really help him find the details he was looking for, but I enjoyed talking to him. Josh told me about some of the journalism jobs he'd had in Vancouver and Toronto. Of course, I just had to ask him why he'd leave a fantastic job at a big daily newspaper—a *national* one—to come here to work for a small paper. That's when he first told me about searching for his birth mother."

Boyd's face tightened again. He probably wished his brother hadn't followed that particular story. If he'd never come to Fredericton, maybe he'd still be alive . . .

"So that's how you met. What kept you seeing each other?"

"There's some overlap in our circle of friends, so we wound up bumping into each other once in a while." She shrugged. "Living here in Fredericton—it's very claustrophobic. Neither Josh nor I had been here very long and it seemed like everyone we knew was married. We were the only two who hadn't settled down, and we didn't really appreciate everyone trying to 'encourage' us to do the same, with each other or otherwise."

"I know exactly how that goes."

Hayden didn't doubt it. Josh had described his brother as the classic confirmed bachelor.

"I guess we felt like natural allies. He was just easy to talk to, you know?"

"I do. Josh always had that way about him." He cleared his throat, as if trying to hide the emotion that had crept into his voice. "So, what was the story he was working on? The one where you guys met?"

Hayden's stomach lurched at the memory. "There'd been a suicide on the premises. A patient released from the ER, actually. He slashed his wrists out on the side lawn. By the time security found him, it was too late."

Boyd's eyes darkened. "I'm sorry. That must have . . . been traumatic."

"Yeah." She heard the emotion in her own voice.

Boyd must have heard it too. "Were you the doc who saw him?"

She sent him a narrow-eyed glance. "Did I cut him loose to kill himself, you mean?"

He just held her gaze and waited for her to continue.

"No, I wasn't even working that night. But even if I had been, the decision to admit or release would have been called by the psych consult."

"But it could have been you on duty that night, and that scares you."

"Hell yes, it scares me."

"Not much you can do when they present with such calmness and composure and assure you they're feeling better."

She shot him a look. "How'd you know that? Everyone assumed he begged to be admitted and we turned him away."

"I've seen it. It's easy to misread the calmness that comes over them. A peacefulness. It can seem like they've changed their minds, but sometimes it's them coming to the final decision."

He was right, of course. "And you know this how?"

"My years on patrol," he said. "I've had occasion to try to talk suicides down while we waited for a trained team to arrive. I'll never forget that first one. A jumper." He looked down at his hands, adjusted the watch on his wrist. "The softening of his face, the relaxation of his posture . . . I thought I'd reached him. He didn't look tormented anymore, you know?"

He glanced up but dropped his gaze quickly, no doubt at the sight of the sympathy she couldn't hide. Part of her wanted to reach out and comfort him—and maybe get some comfort in return. Although she and Josh weren't related by blood, he'd come to feel a hell of a lot like the big brother she'd always wanted. Finally there was someone here who might understand what she was going through having lost her best friend.

"He jumped?"

"Yeah." His voice was grim. "Turned out it was just relief I was seeing. The relief of having resolved his conflict. He got all calm. Serene. I totally misread it."

"I'm sorry."

He rubbed his eyes wearily. "God, I must be more tired than I knew. I haven't thought about that case in years."

They were both silent for a few seconds. Boyd sat up straight and, in a much brisker voice, said, "So, Josh used to text you a lot."

His shift of tone and direction stiffened her own back. Another characteristic Josh had told her about: the sudden subject change to avoid things getting too personal. His eyes were now cool and remote again, as though that moment of shared understanding had never happened.

"Yes, he did," she said crisply. "He also used to meet me frequently for dinner and a movie. Sometimes he cooked for me, and sometimes he came over to my place, where we watched shows that I'd DVR'd. Once, I got him to take my car to the garage when it needed repairs to make sure I didn't get highballed on the estimate. And once I cleaned and dressed a scrape he got on his calf from his bike pedal when he left the trail to avoid running over a pair of squabbling chipmunks." She shook her head. "Why are you making a federal case out of my relationship with your brother?"

"I'm interested in all Josh's relationships, not just the one you and he shared."

"But *why*?" She frowned, trying to understand. "Josh is gone now. What's the point? Why are you even here in Fredericton?"

"I'm conducting my own personal investigation into Josh's death. I refuse to believe for a minute it was natural causes."

Not natural causes? As in homicide? Someone might have murdered *Josh?*

Hayden shot to her feet, then realized her mistake as the world started to reel.

Boyd was on his feet instantly, easing her back onto the couch. Before she could do it herself, a big hand on her back pressed her forward, urging her head down toward her bent knees. "Take it easy," he said. "Slow breaths."

She pushed his hand away. "I'm a doctor. I know what to do."

She kept her head down, regulating her breathing. It took just a few seconds to recover her equilibrium. Then she felt the

13

cushions next to her depress with his weight, followed by the warmth of his hand on her back.

"Better?"

No, not better. The sound of his voice, his scent, the comfort in his touch . . . It was almost as if Josh were right there with her. But he wasn't. He was dead, possibly murdered. She sat up, forcing herself to do it slowly this time, and raked her hands through her mass of hair. "Sorry about that. Obviously, I jumped up too fast. Didn't give my blood pressure a chance to compensate."

"Of course." He got up and filled a tiny paper cup with water from the cooler in the corner. "Here," he said, pressing the cup into her hand. "Drink."

His thoughtfulness had her throat suddenly aching. That was something Josh would have done.

No, Josh would probably have sat down beside her and pulled her into a massive bear hug. For a brief moment, she tried to imagine this man, who looked so like his brother, doing the same thing.

He wouldn't do it. She was sure of it.

And if he *did* put his arms around her, she doubted it would be platonic. Not that he'd put moves on a distressed woman; she felt confident about that too.

There had been something about Josh that said "protective big brother." But nothing about the way Boyd threw her off center felt brotherly.

"Thank you," she managed.

She drank the cold water, letting it soothe her emotion-tightened throat, then put the empty cup on the coffee table. "So, about Josh . . . I thought it was cardiac arrest? You think there was some foul play involved? That he didn't die from natural causes?"

"I don't know what to think." A muscle leapt in his jaw, but he didn't say anything else.

"Come on, Boyd. You can't drop a bombshell like that on me and then hold back the rest." When he remained silent, she added, "Josh was like family to me. I'm *heartbroken* that he's gone. If there's anything about his death that you think is suspicious, I need you to tell me. For God's sake, I'm a doctor. That makes me a good person to test your theories on, right?"

His tight expression eased, and she knew she'd gotten through to him.

He sighed. "I'm concerned the coroner won't find anything obvious and will call it natural causes, and the cops will close the file. We already know there was nothing remarkable about the hospital toxicology tests." He rubbed the back of his neck. "And, yes, I know a standard hospital tox screen doesn't mean a whole helluva lot and it's the forensic toxicology report that'll tell the tale. But even so, it seems like folks are getting cozy with the idea that this was natural causes. Maybe that's paranoia on my part," he allowed, "but I've had almost two weeks to try to swallow this, and it's still not going down."

His hand went to his chest as though the coroner's probable ruling were literally lodged there in an indigestible lump. Hayden suspected the gesture was purely unconscious.

"But why do you think someone would want to kill him?"

"I think he stirred something up, discovered something someone didn't want brought to light."

She was about to ask which investigation when he hit her with a question.

"What about you? What was your first reaction—your *gut* reaction—when you heard the news? What did you think had happened?"

"As a friend or as a doctor?"

"Both," he replied.

"Congenital defect." She leaned back into the cushions. "I figured he must have had some kind of abnormality, a rhythm or conduction disorder that had gone undiagnosed. Unfortunately, tragedies like this happen more often than you'd think. Sometimes the first symptom the patient has is sudden death."

"Yeah." Boyd shifted beside her. "But I've been researching medical journals and online articles and, from what I've read, if that was the case, it should have shown itself earlier. Much earlier. Did you know Josh played hockey through high school and university?"

She frowned. "He did?"

"Yes. He was a forward. A right winger. That kind of activity, requiring sudden, intense bursts of exertion, should likely have uncovered a problem. How could he survive competitive hockey without a blip, then drop dead in his car right after completing an easy noon-hour jog?"

He was right. The kind of anaerobic activity involved in hockey should have disclosed any such problem.

"You're right. He jogged almost daily too. It's not like he was a couch potato who got a wild impulse to run a half marathon. I even joined him sometimes when my schedule allowed, and I saw no sign of anything." Grief engulfed her afresh at the memory. "I mean, he slowed his pace for me, I imagine, but still . . ." Hayden paused briefly. "You know, if Josh had a congenital issue, there are medications that can exacerbate it," she said. "Maybe he was taking something that—"

"You're thinking long QT syndrome? And that he might have been taking antihistamines or antidepressants or even antibiotics to trigger the event?"

She lifted an eyebrow. "You *have* been doing your research. Except I never saw him take medication, ever, for anything. No, that's not true," she corrected herself. "He did take amoxicillin once for a strep throat infection a few months after he arrived here. But other than that, I don't think he was on any meds."

"That bears out what I found," Boyd said. "When I came down here the first time to see to things, I cleared out Josh's room at the bed and breakfast, boxed it all up to take home. My line of work, it's second nature to look for drugs, so I paid attention. But nothing really stuck out as I packed up his stuff. After the funeral, I dug the boxes out and gave everything a hard second look. I can confirm he took a few supplements—vitamin D and fish oil—and he had some regular-strength ibuprofen on hand. That's it. There were no other medications or supplements in his room, and the cops didn't find anything in his car or at his office."

"So not drug induced then."

"Unless someone doped him up somehow."

Her stomach knotted. "You think someone helped induce the arrest?"

"That's my theory. And before you ask, yes, I've been checked out by a gaggle of heart specialists. I've submitted to all the tests, and they can't find any evidence of cardiac issues, anatomical, electrical, or otherwise."

Hayden wasn't surprised to hear about the full cardiac workup. In fact, when she'd talked to Ella McBride at the visitation, she'd planted the suggestion that Boyd do just that. If Boyd had no issues, Hayden doubted his genetically identical brother would have either.

Except hadn't she read some genetic issues weren't always detectable?

"We're talking about a very specialized field here," she said, "but if I remember correctly, I think it's possible to have certain heart conditions that aren't readily detectable."

"So they tell me," he agreed. "Which is why they're doing genetic testing."

She lifted an eyebrow. "And?"

"And I just had it done last week. I'm still waiting on results. They told me to be patient and to avoid taking any drugs or running any marathons in the interim, just in case."

She nodded. "That's good advice." After a pause, she asked, "So, do the local cops know you're here?"

"That's my next stop when I finish here."

"And how are the local police going to take the news that you're conducting your own investigation?"

"I don't actually plan to frame it like that," he said. "But they're very much aware of my concerns. I met with them as soon as I hit town last time, the day after Josh died. They agreed several things looked suspicious—a message Josh had left for me, coupled with the fact that nobody can seem to find his cell phone. They upgraded the file from a simple sudden death investigation to a suspicious death and have been doing some poking around."

"I know. About the poking around, I mean. Detective Morgan came to speak to me last week."

"Of course. Because you guys were so close. You were probably one of his first calls."

"But I don't understand. He didn't say anything about foul play. I got the impression his questions were just part of the standard procedure for a sudden unexpected death of someone so young and apparently healthy." She frowned. "He *did* ask me about Josh's relationships, how he got on with people, and that kind of thing, but I thought he was just trying to construct a fuller picture of Josh. It never even occurred to me they thought he might have been murdered."

"I wouldn't go so far as to say they think Josh was murdered," Boyd said. "Only that the concerns I raised were enough to make the death suspicious. I imagine Detective Morgan would have kept it pretty low key, getting the answers he needed without upsetting you any more than he had to."

She grimaced. "I can believe that. I was a wreck as it was."

"So Morgan asked you about Josh's relationships?"

"Yes. And about his personal investigation, of course. I wasn't able to tell him much about that. I mean, I knew Josh was trying to find your birth parents, but beyond a couple of conversations early on, he never really talked about it to me."

"Really?" The look he gave her was skeptical in the extreme.

"Really." She reined in her irritation. "I tried to give him openings. I'd ask him how it was going from time to time, and he'd give me the general lay of the land. You know, 'making progress' or 'not much progress,' that kind of thing."

Boyd frowned. "That doesn't sound like Josh."

"Yeah, he did like to talk," she agreed. "But in this case, he figured there was some medical malfeasance involved, and he wanted to keep me far away from it."

"Okay, now that bit *does* sound like Josh." He rubbed the spot between his eyes as though he had a headache. "Although it seems a bit of a stretch that something that happened thirty-five years ago could impact your career today."

"That's just what I told him. I also pointed out that it was no secret we were bosom pals. Even if I didn't help him with his investigation, they might assume I had. Of course, he countered that I hadn't been in town much longer than he had, and I couldn't add enough special knowledge to warrant involving me in the investigation."

Boyd nodded. "He cared for you a lot. Even though the risk of any blowback on you was small, he'd want you to have deniability."

The thought made her chest tighten. She took a deep breath and released it. "So what else are the cops doing? Looking into Josh's phone records, credit card trail, stuff like that?"

"Not exactly. That kind of thing requires warrants, and at this stage, they don't have enough information to convince a judge of reasonable and probable grounds. But they've been poking around."

"And now you're going to do some poking around too?"

"Yep."

"And maybe they'll look at it a little harder, with the big-city detective peering over their shoulders?"

"Maybe."

Hayden smiled, but what she really felt like doing was crying.

It was hitting her now, really sinking in—Josh might have been *murdered*. The wound of losing him had barely begun to heal, and Boyd's words, his coming here, had ripped away that thin beginning of scar tissue. None of it made sense. She needed time to digest this. Most of all, she needed this conversation to be done before she broke down and started sobbing.

"I imagine you've come to requisition the medical records?"

He drew a folded manila envelope from the breast pocket of his sport jacket. "Got the papers right here."

"Well, you'll need to check in with the corporate office upstairs. They'll direct you accordingly."

"Yeah, I figured," he said, tucking the envelope back in his pocket. She checked her watch. "I have to get back to work." She levered herself to her feet. He stood and followed her to the door. As he held it open for her, she paused, looking up into those features that were so familiar, yet so strange. "It was good talking to you, Boyd. I wish it had been under better circumstances."

"Yeah. Same here."

"I just want to say again that I'm so sorry for your loss." She pushed the words out through the sudden lump in her throat. "It's got to be hard. Josh was a great guy. The best."

"Thank you. And I'm sorry you lost a friend."

"I still can't believe he's gone. I find myself checking my phone for one of his messages the moment I turn it on."

"God, yes, the messages. We used to talk maybe once a week, but I don't think a day went by when I didn't get at least one text. He used to drive me crazy with them. Now I wish I could have just one more."

She put a hand on his arm. When he glanced at her, she glimpsed raw grief and sorrow in his eyes. "I'm so sorry," she said, her voice husky.

"Me too." He schooled his features back into that composed mask.

Her heart aching, she just nodded. Tears stung the backs of her eyes as she headed back to her post.

"Dr. Walsh?"

She stopped, blinked a few times, then turned back to him. "Yes?"

"Can I take you to dinner when you get off?"

Her eyes shot open wide. "Dinner?" The idea filled her with dismay. No, not dismay. Disquiet. There was something about Boyd that unsettled her equilibrium. Maybe it was the coolness in those eyes sometimes, as though he didn't much like her. Not that she needed or expected everyone to like her. But to have that coolness directed at her by eyes that were so like Josh's was just . . . wrong. "Oh, I don't think—"

"Please?"

She met his gaze again. He wasn't giving her the cool-eyed treatment right now. Right now, his expression was fierce, intent.

"You and Josh were good friends. Best friends, from the sound of it. I could use your help piecing things together. For Josh."

For Josh.

The absolute last thing she wanted to do was sit down across an intimate table from Boyd McBride with this strange vibe going on. A vibe that had nothing to do with grief. But she couldn't refuse. She'd do it for Josh.

"Okay," she agreed, naming a busy downtown pub and a time.

She hoped she wasn't going to regret it.

CHAPTER 2

Boyd signed in at police HQ almost two hours later. It had taken an hour to get the slim medical file from the records department, which he counted as a minor miracle. That kind of request often took days, if not longer. Twenty minutes for lunch while he took an unrewarding cruise through the hospital records, which were very minimal, and another half hour to get out of the busy hospital parking lot and downtown. Ten minutes after that, Detective Ray Morgan strode across the police station lobby toward him.

If Boyd hadn't met the guy already, he wouldn't have pegged him for a cop. He'd probably have figured him for a lawyer, given the setting. For starters, that custom tailored suit looked like it belonged on a model, as did that hundred-dollar haircut. Morgan was early to midthirties by Boyd's estimation, but it was hard to say with guys like that. The first time they'd met, Boyd had been ready to write him off as a dandified lightweight. But that was before the guy got close enough for him to get a look at his eyes and the deep grooves on either side of his mouth. That and the handshake convinced him there was a real cop under the elegant packaging after all.

"Detective McBride," he said, his voice as smooth and perfectly pitched as the rest of him. "Sorry to keep you waiting. Took me a while to get off the phone."

"Morgan." Boyd stood and grasped the other man's outstretched hand. "Thanks for agreeing to meet with me."

Morgan led him back to the detectives' bull pen. This was Boyd's second visit, but it struck him again how small it was. A mind-blowing thought, considering that this detective squad was the sum total for the whole city. Of course, there were more citizens in the city of Toronto than in the whole province of New Brunswick. A whole hell of a lot more. So it made sense that it would be small.

For his brother's sake, he hoped *small* didn't translate into ill equipped. Or, worse, incompetent.

They passed several desks, some manned, some empty, but all stacked high with paper and files and sticky notes and colored phone messages. The organized chaos made him feel right at home. A detective with a phone pressed to his ear nodded at them as they passed without missing a beat of his conversation. When they reached Morgan's desk, Boyd sat in the chair Morgan indicated.

"Coffee?" Morgan offered.

"No, thanks. I'm good."

Morgan gave a wry smile. "Good decision," he conceded. After taking his suit jacket off and carefully draping it over the back of an empty chair, he took a seat. Then he reached into a drawer of his desk and withdrew a folder, which Boyd assumed to be Josh's.

Boyd's gaze fell on the file on the desk between them. "So, what can you tell me about my brother's death?"

"Since we last talked on the phone? Very little more. I told you the coroner found no obvious problems with your brother's heart?"

"You did. And if I understand what you told me, that's not common, but it's not unheard of either. What was the stat you gave me? Up to five percent of sudden cardiac arrest victims display no discernible anatomic problems on autopsy?"

"Correct. The forensic toxicology report is probably still weeks away."

Boyd raised an eyebrow. "Weeks?"

"You know the drill, McBride. They test for probably three hundred substances. And you know there are new experimental drugs being introduced all the time and new designer crap hitting the streets. It takes time to test for all that stuff. And then if they find something, the result has to be replicated independently. If we find there was foul play, this shit has to hold up in court."

"I know. I'm just . . . anxious."

"We do have the hospital's standard tox screen, as I've already reported, so the really obvious ones—alcohol, cocaine, yada yada—can probably be safely eliminated."

Boyd wanted to say the illegal stuff could be eliminated without the benefit of testing, because this was Josh they were talking about, dammit. The man barely even took the occasional Advil. But he knew all too well that drugs sometimes wound up in a vic's system through no conscious choice of their own. Just ask all the roofied girls he'd talked to in ERs while a forensic nurse prepared to give them a sexual assault kit. Boyd drew a deep breath and exhaled slowly.

"We're also waiting for the genetic tests the coroner's office ordered." Morgan's eyes were sympathetic. "Maybe those results will shed more light."

"Right." He dragged a hand over his face. "So, what kind of wait are we talking about for the genetics? Weeks? Months?"

"Months would be my guess. The backlog is hellish."

Boyd nodded his understanding. He'd had to explain similar delays to many a bereaved mother or father or wife who'd just wanted to understand what had happened to their loved one. "Maybe my results will come back first."

"You had genetic testing done on yourself?"

"After what happened with Josh, I had *everything* done. I've been imaged, had ECGs, EEGs, cardiac ultrasound, stress tests. I've worn a Holter monitor for forty-eight hours. They couldn't find even a whiff of abnormality, with the electrical system or otherwise."

"Interesting." Morgan scribbled a note and put it in the folder.

Boyd gestured to the file. "Any chance I can get a copy of that?"

"The file?" Morgan snorted. "You're welcome to look at it, but I can't be giving out copies. Which I think you knew before you asked. But I'll keep you abreast of developments. Like I said on the phone, I'm happy to do another sit-down with you further down the line, if it seems like it would be useful."

"I guess that'll have to be good enough."

The other detective's handsome features hardened. "I've already assured you that when I get toxicology back, you'll know about it. When I have the genetics report, you'll hear from me. Short of deputizing you and handing you the case, I don't know what more I can do."

"Sorry." Boyd held up his hands in a conciliatory gesture. The man was right. And the last thing Boyd wanted to do was piss off his best window into Josh's case. "I know you're bending over backwards here. I didn't mean to imply otherwise. I'm just—"

"I know." Some of the ice went out of Morgan's eyes. "Don't sweat it."

Boyd cleared his throat. "Look, I know you told me a lot of this stuff on the phone, and I appreciate that. I really do. But can you walk me through the timeline again? I just need to understand what happened."

Something stirred in Morgan's eyes now. Pity, he realized. Ordinarily, that would sting. Nobody pitied Boyd McBride. But under the circumstances, he'd take it. Take it and exploit it if he could.

Anything to find out the truth about Josh's death.

"Sure." Morgan pulled the file closer, opened it, rifled through a few papers. "Josh got up early that day. He responded to emails around six a.m. As you know, he was living at Stratton House B&B—Dr. Sylvia Stratton's place on Waterloo Row—rather than renting an apartment. The housekeeper there reported that he had breakfast at about six fifty, same as usual. He had his laptop with him at the breakfast table. Said he was putting the finishing touches on an article he was going to file that day with his editor at the paper." Morgan glanced up. "I probably told you all this last time you were here. We'd pretty much had this timeline worked up."

"Yeah, but keep going. Maybe I'll hear something I missed last time. I wasn't at my best."

"Okay." Morgan scanned the page in front of him again. "Sylvia Stratton and two of her staffers, including the aforementioned housekeeper, saw Josh at breakfast and attested that he looked fine. The housekeeper remarked she thought he seemed especially upbeat, although she concedes he was always in good spirits. Dr. Stratton didn't notice anything different."

"Judging by the voice mail he left for me, I'd say he probably *was* upbeat. Excited."

Morgan nodded. "Right. The message he left you saying he thought he'd made a major breakthrough in discovering the identity of your birth parents. That search, of course, being the whole reason he moved to Fredericton in the first place. But damned if we could find any evidence of what he'd learned."

"What about the laptop?" Boyd had explored the computer himself, had opened and read every last file. But his skill level in IT matters topped out at using a password recovery tool to get into Josh's various accounts and software programs. When he'd found nothing on Josh's search for their birth parents, he'd turned the laptop over to the police for a deeper look. "Your tech crimes guys weren't able to find anything? No hidden files or deleted files that might still be recoverable?"

"I'm afraid that's exactly what I'm saying. I just got the report yesterday." Morgan flipped through a few pieces of paper until he found the one he wanted. "Our guy resuscitated everything he could, and still nothing about the investigation. Just the casual mentions in emails to you. That includes a search of your brother's Internet-based web mail addresses and"—he paused to scan the report—"the automated online backup service he subscribed to, his Dropbox, and a dozen other places he might have stashed a file." Morgan looked up again. "Apart from the exchanges between you and him, we found a big fat nothing."

"What about the physical notebooks?" Boyd had found dozens of them in Josh's room at Dr. Stratton's. From his own perusal on his last visit, he was certain they were all work related. However, on the remote chance that Josh had used them as some bizarre way of hiding or disguising the notes from his personal investigation, he'd asked Morgan to see if one of Josh's coworkers could corroborate that.

Boyd was a damned good cop, but, in his state of grief and shock, he hadn't trusted himself to have a critical eye on Josh's things. Turning the laptop and notebooks over had seemed like the best next step after his initial search yielded nothing.

"No joy there either," Morgan said. "Everything in them corresponded to articles which were subsequently published or scheduled to be published. No cryptic messages or hidden codes."

"Dammit. I was hoping there'd be something there."

Morgan grimaced. "My money was on the laptop. But unless your brother was the kind of guy who was obsessive about secure deletion, it's pretty safe to say the file never existed on that computer. At least not on the hard drive or the flash drives you gave us."

"Secure deletion?"

"Yeah. A tool that overwrites all the clusters where the data was originally stored with a bunch of random data."

Boyd frowned. "Josh was careful with data. He was an investigative journalist; he had to be concerned about the security of his files. But I'm talking more about relying on firewalls, complex, frequently changed passwords, and using only secure Wi-Fi. I doubt that concern extended far enough to prompt him to use deletion tools designed to thwart a forensic computer specialist."

"Did he have any other electronic storage devices?"

"His iPhone. But as you know, that was never found. Unless . . . ?"

"No, nothing's turned up."

Boyd nodded grimly. Without a warrant from a judge, the phone companies weren't prepared to try to triangulate it for them. They only did that kind of thing without a warrant if a life was in immediate danger. Since Josh was dead, the urgency—or *exigency*, as the lawyers liked to call it—required to obtain that cooperation was absent. Personally, Boyd figured it would be a waste of time anyway. He was convinced someone had taken Josh's cell phone. And the first thing they would have done was yank out the battery, destroy the SIM card, and pulverize the phone.

When Boyd had alerted Morgan that Josh's phone was missing—another factor that had tipped them from sudden death investigation to suspicious death—the cops had used the police K-9 to do an article search of all the walking trails, in case Josh had simply dropped it on his jog. The search had netted lots of interesting items, none of them belonging to Josh.

"No iPad or Android tablet? Anything like that?"

Boyd shook his head. "I highly doubt it. I gave him a PDA once, thinking he might prefer to use it for notes instead of those notebooks, but he never really took to it. He just preferred pen and paper. Said they never crashed or got hacked."

"You still think he kept a physical notebook on the birth investigation?"

"More than ever. This investigation was so personal to him, I can see him not trusting his research notes to digital. The forensic sweep of the laptop pretty much confirms my hunch. Which leaves a couple of possibilities. Either his notes were stolen along with his phone when he died or he might have hidden the notebook somewhere."

Morgan tilted his head. "You really think he might have hidden it?"

"If he didn't have it on him, yes. I'm pretty sure he'd secure it somehow. He'd never just leave it lying around."

"Hidden it where?"

"His room at Stratton House is the most obvious place."

Morgan nodded. "His personal belongings were all removed, weren't they?"

"Yeah, I packed up the room myself on my first visit to collect my brother's body. I didn't get around to doing a deep search of it at that time." Between cracking passwords and reading everything on Josh's computer, scanning those notebooks, meeting with police, dealing with the Fredericton funeral director on the logistics of preparation for transport, and checking in frequently with his parents, he hadn't had time for that kind of search, even if it had occurred to him to do so. Which it hadn't. "I plan to go by there soon, see if they'll let me have some time in the room, if it hasn't been rented to someone else."

"Good plan." Morgan nodded approvingly. "I can't see them denying your request, if the room is still empty." He looked down at the file. "Shall we get back to Josh's day?"

"Please."

"He was at his desk at the paper by seven fifteen and filed his story. He worked until eleven." Morgan's finger trailed over the printed report as he scanned it. "Then he went for a lunch-hour jog at Odell Park, which he did on days when he didn't get in a morning jog. When he got back into his car, he suffered a fatal cardiac arrest. Another park visitor discovered him toward late afternoon. The sun had moved and your brother's car was no longer in the shade. The guy thought it was odd someone would choose to doze in a hot car in the direct sun and went to check on him. He called nine-one-one, and there was an officer on the scene in four minutes. That's what we know."

"Right." Boyd's hands fisted despite himself. "Because there's no security camera in the parking lot."

Morgan pinched the bridge of his nose. "It's a park, McBride. People go there to sit on benches and eat their lunch or feed the ducks or walk or run. I can't remember the last crime committed there. Besides, you know how expensive it is for a city to install cameras in all of their public locations. I doubt this would be seen as a high priority for City Council."

Boyd took a deep breath and exhaled, unclenching his fists. "What about other people at the park? You say lots of people eat their lunch there and it must have been pushing eleven thirty or quarter to twelve. No one saw anything unusual?"

Morgan shook his head. "Nothing. Which suggests if he was in distress, it couldn't have been too acute or he'd have attracted attention. Seems like it might have happened once he was in the car. Of course, maybe something started outside the car, but, being a man, he didn't want anyone to witness him having a weak spell or something, and he hid it until he got in the car."

"That's possible," Boyd acknowledged. "Have you gone back to the scene around that eleven to twelve time frame to try to catch the people who frequent the park?"

"Every day for a week," he confirmed. "We talked to everyone coming or going or just hanging around during that hour, hoping to find someone who saw something."

"It came to nothing, I guess?"

Morgan shook his head. "Nothing. Unless you count the tip about the man who is supposedly practicing mind control on the ducks."

Boyd snorted. That was a new one on him. There were always a few reality-challenged folks who surfaced when you talked to a broad cross section of people like that. He knew better than to dismiss them, as did Morgan, no doubt. Just because they saw things a different way didn't negate that they saw things. But it sounded like the guy's attention was firmly fixed on the duck pond, not the parking lot or the trails.

"What about Josh's car?"

"Like I told you in one of our earlier conversations, we had it examined to make sure there was nothing wrong electrically, but everything checks out."

"What about friends, associates, coworkers? Have you talked to them?"

"A few key people," Morgan said. "His landlord, Sylvia Stratton, some friends, coworkers who shared adjacent space. No one saw any hint of a health issue."

"Anyone think Josh had made enemies here? Or that his search for his birth parents might have stirred up a hornet's nest?"

"No known enemies. But the other thing—the fact that he was trying to find your parents—doesn't seem to have been a secret. I think just about everyone we interviewed knew that. Nobody raised it as something potentially risky. Since we're not working a homicide per se, we didn't go too hard after people. We asked if they knew about his investigation, and, if so, had he told them anything about recent developments. No one seems to have known he figured it out."

"Or if they did, they're not saying."

"Right."

Boyd tried to relax his jaw before he cracked a molar. "Did any of them know our adoption was an illegal one?"

"A couple of them know about the . . . uh . . . irregularities."

"Irregularities? I'll say. As in no actual record of our birth having been lodged with vital statistics, at least not in the name of Holbrook, which was the surname on the birth certificates our adoptive parents were given."

"I still can't get over that," Morgan said. "Kinda defeats the idea of a closed adoption."

"Exactly. Ella and Frank McBride should never even have *seen* those documents, let alone been given copies of them. And when Josh petitioned the courts to open any sealed adoption records pertaining to the infants Holbrook, there was no record to be found under that name. Presumably because those birth certificates were forged in the first place."

"Why do you suppose your parents were given those birth certificates? They certainly wouldn't have needed them. New birth certificates would have been issued in the McBride name when the adoption was approved, and the original birth record sealed, right?"

"My best guess is that it was to misdirect us, to prevent us from ever finding our birth parents if we decided to look."

Morgan shook his head. "Either some horribly incompetent civil servant made the mother of all screwups or the adoption was outright illegal."

"The latter, I'm sure." Boyd's jaw tightened again. "And I appreciate your department's discretion. The last thing I want to do is embroil our adoptive parents in a serious investigation three and a half decades later, one they don't deserve to be subjected to. No matter how shadily—or maybe incompetently—the adoption might have been handled from this end, I can promise you that Frank and Ella believed it was completely aboveboard."

"I do believe that. And I also take the point I presume you were making, that someone might not have wanted his investigation to succeed. If someone went to great lengths to bury the adoption years ago, who knows what lengths they'd go to now?"

"Exactly." Boyd massaged his temple. "I'm sorry, I kinda sidetracked the conversation. You said a couple of folks knew about the irregularities?"

"Yeah, two of them. To one extent or another. That would be Dr. Hayden Walsh and your brother's landlord. But that makes sense. I gather he was pretty close to Dr. Walsh, and, of course, he met Sylvia Stratton in the course of his investigation, so she's known from their first contact, before Josh ever took up residence."

"Of course. There have to be others out there who know, though. Josh has been investigating this for almost six months. Somewhere along the way, he had to have told other people."

Another nod from Morgan. "Seems he couched it as a clerical mistake, not a flat-out illegal adoption, or so I gather as I quietly work my way through the list of obstetricians in the city in an effort to reconstruct Josh's search. Your brother's standard line was that he thought the ob-gyn in question had delivered you guys, but that the birth record was inexplicably mixed up with another set of twins. That was apparently good enough for most of these guys, who had their staff check their records for the period in question. So far, they've all told us they didn't deliver any twin boys who could have been you or whose records could have been confounded with you."

Boyd's lips thinned. "And a doctor would never lie."

Morgan sighed. "There's that. But for what it's worth, I've been talking to these docs myself. I'm not holding myself out as a human polygraph, but I do tend to have a pretty good feel for when I'm being bullshitted."

"And you believe them?"

"So far."

"You know I'm going to be out there talking to people too, right?"

"I figured. And more power to you. If you can bring me something that lets me ramp up reasonable and probable grounds, we'll be all over it," Morgan said. "So long as you're not out there showing us up."

Boyd nodded. "Shouldn't be a problem." He almost added "as long as you're doing your job right," but he thought better of it. From the glint in Morgan's eyes, it appeared he didn't have to say it out loud.

"I hope you know what you're doing, McBride."

"Well, if I don't know what I'm doing by now, I'm in trouble."

"I mean, have you considered that if you go poking around, you might not like what you find?"

Boyd just raised an eyebrow.

"Off the top of my head, the person who might have the most to lose from your brother's investigation might be your birth mother."

"The thought had occurred to me."

"But you're not going to leave it alone?"

"Would you?"

Morgan ran a hand through his hair, which fell back into perfect place. "Just remember, be discreet. Because if I get any complaints, your officer in charge back home is going to hear from my boss. Got it?"

"Got it."

Morgan flipped the file closed and stood.

Boyd rose and extended his hand. "Thanks, man."

"No problem. For what it's worth, I really want to help you out. My wife, Grace, works for the same local paper as Josh did, and she really liked your brother. Says she learned a lot from him over these last months, and she's still really broken up about his death. Hell, I met him a couple of times over drinks, and I liked him too. Even had him and Hayden over to the house for dinner. It was a damned shame."

Boyd blinked. "I didn't know. That he worked with your wife, I mean. You didn't mention it last time."

Morgan shrugged. "You had enough on your mind. And I'm telling you now so you'll know that even if I didn't have you breathing down my neck, I honest to God could not go home at night if I wasn't busting my hump to get to the bottom of this. I couldn't look Grace in the eye if I wasn't doing everything I could."

Boyd looked at Ray Morgan and saw the fierce love he bore for his wife blazing in his face. The kind of love Josh had believed in and had been holding out for. The kind he had hoped he'd one day find with Hayden. It still pained Boyd to remember that months-ago conversation with Josh and his confession that he loved Hayden. But she was married to her career. She'd shut him down just like she apparently shut down everyone else, but Josh had never been a quitter. He'd said it was a matter of timing for Hayden. She needed to achieve her goals and feel more secure before she could open herself up to romance. He'd been banking on her eventually coming to love him back, when the timing was right. But now his brother would never have that chance, never have a woman he could love as ferociously as Ray Morgan loved his wife.

He nodded. "Understood. And thank you."

CHAPTER 3

Hayden spotted Boyd at a table near the back of the restaurant. He sat studying papers he'd spread across the tabletop, and she caught her breath at the wave of grief that washed over her. God, he looked so much like Josh. Then he glanced up.

There was nothing of Josh in those eyes as he watched her. Her friend's gaze had been warm and welcoming. His brother's, however, cut through her like a laser beam, as if he could see straight to her soul.

She couldn't remember the last time someone had had such a profound effect on her. She couldn't deny there was something about Boyd that drew her to him.

It's just because he's Josh's brother and both of you are grieving. Squelching her nervousness, she made her way to his table. He stood, pulling out a chair for her. Apparently Mr. and

Mrs. McBride had raised their sons to display good manners. Something that had been severely lacking in other men she'd dated.

Not that she and Josh had dated. And her dinner with Boyd certainly wasn't a date.

"Thanks for coming, Hayden."

"Happy to help if I can."

She took her seat, and he started gathering up the papers. Medical records, she saw.

"You got the records already?" She gestured to the material. "They must have bumped your request right to the front of the line."

He pushed the papers back into the envelope bearing the hospital's logo and set it on the unused chair to his right. "Charlotte was very accommodating."

"Wow." Her brows shot up. "You're on a first-name basis with Mrs. Trecartin?"

He smiled, lifting his shoulders in an easy shrug. "I work fast."

Apparently the man was capable of being charming when he chose to be. Not that she'd seen any evidence of that herself. Pretty much all she'd seen from him so far was serious intensity. "It must be hereditary." She laughed, shaking her head. "Josh could charm the birds out of the trees too."

His face sobered immediately, and she regretted raising Josh's name. And how stupid was that? Josh was the reason she was here after all.

A waiter appeared to take their drink orders, and she asked for her usual, a Picaroons Blonde Ale.

Boyd quirked his brow. "Picaroons?"

She nodded. "Local microbrewery. It's good."

"Then bring me one too."

When the waiter left, Hayden picked up the menu and started studying it, even though she pretty much knew it by heart.

"Do you eat here often?" he asked.

"More often than I like to admit," she confessed. "I hate cooking just for myself."

He looked up from his menu. "So no boyfriend, then?"

"Lord, no. I don't have time for romance."

"But you had time for my brother?"

She closed her menu. "Like I told you before, Boyd, I don't date. I've seen too many med school students and residents wind up dating someone in the city where they're training. Next thing you know, they're getting married, buying a house, adopting a dog from the local rescue, and settling in. I've seen it again and again, and I promised myself that would never be me. I just won't do that—won't constrain my career choices that way. Josh and I were friends, but that was it."

"Interesting." He studied her with those tawny eyes.

She felt a flush creeping up her neck, but she held his gaze. "Very *un*interesting, actually," she said. "But it's the way it has to be. I have plans."

"Of course you have plans. Medicine isn't the kind of career you fall into. But no dating? No romance? No sex? Isn't that a rather radical choice for someone so young?"

"I'm not nearly as young as I could have been."

"Excuse me?"

"For this point in my career, I'm almost two years behind the cohort I started out with. Two years that I threw away on a relationship. I let myself get dragged off course. When I dusted myself off and got back into a medical program, which I was damned lucky to be able to do, I swore it wouldn't happen again. I'm not going to throw away my tomorrow for a relationship today. A relationship that would only tie me down to someone else's expectations."

"Did Josh know that? I mean, about you dropping out of med school?"

"Of course." She frowned. "He was a great guy, my *friend*, not some jerk in a bar. I owed him more than just the standard I-don't-date line. You think I'd have rebuffed his overtures without explaining?"

"Of course you wouldn't. Sorry."

She sagged in her chair. "No, *I'm* sorry. It was a simple question. I shouldn't have jumped down your throat." She pushed the weight of her hair back. "I told him the whole sad story. We actually talked about it a few times, how not all men were controlling jerks and that when the time was right, the perfect guy would turn up, et cetera. Of course, I told him the same would happen for him. He'd solve the riddle of your birth parents, go back to the big city, meet an amazing woman who wouldn't be nearly good enough for him, but he'd fall in love with her anyway, and that would be that."

She glanced up to see that his face was contorted with pain.

"Oh, Boyd, I'm sorry. You don't need reminding of all the things he'll miss out on."

"But it's true, isn't it? He never got to hold the woman of his dreams, make love to her. Never got to marry, have children, grandchildren."

Her chest constricted with grief. *Poor Josh!* If ever a guy deserved those things, it was him. For all the pushback he'd given their happily married friends about not wanting to join their ranks just yet, he'd have made a wonderful husband and a loving father. Maybe she should have been pushing him too, urging him to find that woman. Instead, the two of them had banded together to fight off their matchmaking friends.

God, she missed him. How much worse Boyd must feel, losing his only brother. His twin. The thought had her on the verge of tears, and she had to blink rapidly to clear them.

She heard him stifle a curse.

"I'm sorry." His voice was low, gruff, vibrating with his own grief. "I've upset you."

She gave him a gentle smile. The softness—the sadness—in those golden eyes had her reaching across the small table to place a comforting hand on his forearm. She felt his muscles tense under her fingers and withdrew her hand.

"It's not your fault. And I started that line of discussion, if you'll remember." She hugged her arms around herself. "Besides, I agreed to come here. I agreed to talk about Josh. It's just still so . . . fresh, you know?"

"I know."

The waiter approached the table with their beers. "Are we ready to order, or do you need a few more minutes?" he asked.

"I'm ready." Hayden handed him her menu. "I'll have the New Orleans salad."

Boyd closed his menu, having given it the briefest of glances. "Grilled salmon, but can you give me extra vegetables instead of a starch?"

"Certainly, sir." The server took the menus and disappeared.

After a fortifying sip of beer, Hayden returned to the subject of Josh. "So, what is it you think I can do for you?"

He picked up his beer and took a drink, then a larger one. "Nice. Great recommendation," he pronounced. Then he put the mug down and met her eyes. "I want to know more about his life here. You said you two gravitated toward one another? How so?"

"Well, at first, it was over little things. TV shows we both liked. Movies we both wanted to see. We both liked jogging. Then the more we talked, the more we realized we liked talking."

"Talking." He smiled wryly. "Of course."

"Also, like I told you earlier, all of our married friends kept trying to throw us together for different reasons. The whole matchmaking thing."

He raised his eyebrows. "I bet."

"We both thought it was funny. I mean, Josh was a good-looking guy, so it's not like I couldn't see why a girl would be attracted to him."

His eyebrows went up even higher. "Really?" That's when she realized that by saying Josh was good-looking, she was also saying Boyd was good-looking. She felt herself blush and took a quick sip of her beer to help hide it.

"Well . . . yes. I guess."

"When did he make his move on you? Before or after you became friends?"

"After," she said. "If he'd done it up front, without knowing anything about me, I doubt we ever would have become friends. I have a low threshold of tolerance for men who see a woman and try to 'hit that' right out of the gates."

"Understandable."

She called up the memory. "We'd had a few of drinks—one of the few times I'd seen him have more than two—at a friend's engagement party. I think it wasn't a serious pass so much as one of those reflexive things you do when you're slightly drunk. You know, like those people who pat their pockets for a cigarette, even though they gave up the habit months ago."

"You're sure?"

His intense scrutiny made her shift in her chair. "That it wasn't serious? Yeah, pretty sure. We laughed it off, and every-thing went back to normal."

"And normal was . . . ?"

"He was like the big brother I never had, helping me around

my apartment with the handyman stuff and keeping an eye on me. I always got the feeling that your brother was looking for something—some*one*. Not actively, but, you know, keeping his eyes open. I just knew his heart would be wide-open to her when she came."

"And you?"

"I wasn't looking for anyone at all. I'm still not."

He looked as if he was going to ask her more about her declaration, but instead he took another sip of beer. "Fair enough. You said Josh didn't really keep you abreast of his investigation?"

"Only in the most general of terms. It was the one thing he didn't talk to me about."

"I doubt it was the *only* thing."

She blinked. "I'm sorry, what?"

He lifted a shoulder in a shrug. "I'm just saying no one is ever a completely open book, no matter how much they might appear to be. We all have things we hold back."

His words were casually spoken, but when she met his eyes, they were filled with a strange intensity. Almost . . . was that *accusation*? Did he think she was holding back on him?

She lowered her own gaze quickly. "I suppose you're right."

An awkward silence fell between them. *This* was why she hadn't wanted to dine with him. She picked up her beer and took a swig of it. "So, what more do you want to know, Boyd?" She placed her mug down carefully instead of thumping it down like she wanted to. "I'll try to answer as honestly and completely as I can. You know, be that *open book*."

"Now I've offended you."

She looked up to find him studying her, but he'd tamped down whatever that was she'd seen in his eyes.

"Not at all," she lied. "People *do* hold things back, tell each other white lies. It's the social lubricant that makes the world go round, right?"

"Right."

"He did mention that you weren't as interested in finding your birth parents as he was." Hayden picked up her beer mug again, more for something to do with her hands than because she wanted another sip. "He said you didn't approve of the investigation."

Boyd stared hard at her. Ignoring her comment, he said, "So he didn't tell you he thought he'd had a major break in the case? That he'd found the identity of our birth mother and was pretty sure he knew who our father was too?"

"No." She clumped the heavy mug back down on the table. "No, he didn't. Is that speculation, or did he tell you that?"

He rubbed at his temple again. "He sent me a series of text messages asking me to call, but my cell phone had run out of juice, and I'd forgotten my charger at home. So he left me a voice message saying he'd had a big break and thought he knew not only who our mother was but possibly our father. I didn't get the message right away, or even the next morning. By the time I plugged in my phone, saw the texts, and called back, Josh was freshly dead." A muscle leapt in his jaw. "When I couldn't reach his cell, I tried to reach him at the paper. They told me he hadn't come back from lunch. I tried him at Dr. Stratton's, but they hadn't seen him since breakfast. I made a mental note to try his cell again in an hour or two, but before I could, Sergeant Quigley called me with the news."

"I'm so sorry." Hayden forced the husky words through a throat tightened to the point of pain. "That must have been horrible."

He dragged a hand across his face. "It was a complete shock. I mean, when he worked at the bigger papers and was still building his reputation, he'd been involved in a handful of dangerous investigations over the years. Biker gangs, political corruption, corporate wrongdoing. Any one of those investigations could have gotten him killed if he put a foot wrong. But with him in Fredericton, covering small-town news and searching for our birth parents, I thought he was safe for once. Compared to his other assignments, searching for our biological parents didn't even register on the danger meter. I just . . . I wasn't prepared to hear that he'd died. If only I'd been home when he called, maybe things would have been different."

Her hands tightened around the cool mug as she realized what he was saying. He'd intimated before that he thought Josh had stirred up a hornet's nest, but she'd somehow assumed it was a work-related investigation. "You think he was killed over the investigation of your birth parents?"

"I don't know what to think. All I know is that he's now gone, before his time, and I'm here trying to piece together how in the hell it could have happened."

"Did he give you a name? Tell you what the big break was?"

His laugh broke. "Of course not. This is Josh we're talking about. He just gave me the teaser. He was saving the full story for when I called back. But he never got a chance."

Hayden heard the self-blame in his voice. She wondered what had kept him away from home overnight. Work? Or a woman? The latter thought came complete with visuals, shockingly vivid in their details. She shook them away.

"You said you were going to meet with the police when you left the hospital earlier," she said. "Did you learn anything more? Are they closer to knowing the cause of death?"

"Unfortunately not. I already knew the pathologist found nothing untoward on the autopsy—no anatomical evidence of a heart problem—and that the standard hospital tox screen showed nothing. The forensic toxicology report is probably weeks away still, and the genetic report will no doubt be months coming. My results from the private lab will probably be back quicker."

She licked suddenly dry lips. "So do you have reason to suspect anyone?"

"No, no one specific." He lifted his shoulders in a shrug. "But it just doesn't smell right. The message he left me, then his phone going missing . . ."

"To play devil's advocate here, that could be coincidence, couldn't it? The timing, I mean."

"I'm a detective. I don't have the luxury of believing in coincidence."

"Fair enough, I guess." She watched him take a sip of his beer. "What about the phone. Isn't it possible that he could have just lost it?"

He slanted her a look. "Again, this is Josh we're talking about. I can't see him letting carelessness separate him from that phone. It was like a damned appendage."

She shrugged. "It happened once before."

His eyes widened. "He lost his phone? How?"

"While he was gassing his car up, he thinks. He finished his call, put the phone on the roof of his car while he recapped his gas tank, went inside and paid, then hopped in the car and drove away without pocketing the phone. He completely forgot about it once he set it down. It must have fallen off the roof somewhere along the way. He retraced his route, but he never did find it, or even pieces of it. When he tried calling it, he got that 'customer out of range' message, and figured it must have been smashed when it hit the asphalt, or maybe gotten run over."

"Or someone stole it while he was in paying for the gas," Boyd put in. "There's a huge market for stolen phones."

"Really?" She arched an eyebrow. "Then maybe someone

stole it this time too. Maybe he left it in the car while he went for his run and someone stole it."

He shook his head. "No evidence of a break-in, and you know Josh. He'd never forget to lock his car."

"Maybe they used one of those mystery devices we've been hearing about that can unlock a car remotely. Then there wouldn't be any broken windows or scratched paint."

"And they only used this rare high-tech break-in tool on Josh's car? None of the other cars that were parked there?"

"Okay, so probably not." She tapped her finger on her glass. "So basically, you're in a holding pattern, waiting for those reports?"

"Not quite," he said. "Detective Morgan has been checking in with obstetricians, trying to discover which ones Josh had talked to, what they'd told him. But he's one guy, and he has other cases."

"What are the chances they're going to voluntarily tell the police if they were involved, even peripherally, in a shady adoption?"

"I know!" A few diners turned their way. His face strained, he continued more quietly. "Sorry. I'm just a little frustrated. I know we don't have much to work with. Maybe when the toxicology report comes in, it will point to something that can help. Or maybe there'll be nothing there at all. Maybe the coroner will call it natural causes, and the guys won't be able to sustain the file. But I can't sit still doing nothing, waiting God knows how long on the damned tests to come back when I feel in my bones something isn't right about his death. And if our situations were reversed, if I were the one discovered dead in my car, I know Josh wouldn't rest until every stone had been turned, every lead exhausted, every theory—no matter how implausible—run to the ground. And that's what I'm going to do for him."

The waiter arrived just then with their meals. Grateful for

the interruption, Hayden leaned back in her chair to allow the young man to place the plate in front of her. The gorgeous salad failed to tantalize her as it usually did. Not surprising, since her stomach felt like a leaden ball.

After placing Boyd's plate in front of him, the waiter said, "Enjoy your meal," and left them alone. Hayden noticed Boyd seemed even less interested in his meal than she was in hers. Then she remembered how pale he'd appeared earlier. He needed to eat.

She picked up her fork and dug into the salad. "Mmm, just as good as I remembered." She gestured with a fork at his untouched plate. "How's the salmon?"

The look he sent her told her he knew what she was doing, but, dutifully, he picked up his knife and fork, cut off a piece, and ate it. "Pretty good," he said, sounding surprised. "Pretty damned good."

They ate in silence, which was probably a good idea considering the subject matter of their conversation thus far. Forensic talk, grief, and guilt were not good dinner companions.

Guilt. Yes, he felt plenty guilty. She'd heard it in his voice, in his words. He really thought if he'd been home to take that call, Josh might not have died. But she doubted that. On the other hand, he now would have had the name of the woman Josh thought was their birth mother. She put down her fork.

Across the table, Boyd put his own utensils down and leaned back. His plate, she saw with satisfaction, was bare.

"I guess I needed a good meal. Thank you, Doc."

"For what? I didn't do anything."

Instead of answering, he picked up his mug of beer and cradled it. "Did you ever go to Josh's place?"

"At Dr. Stratton's? Yeah, I used to go there to watch TV sometimes. It felt strange, at first, being in her house. She's sort

49

of medical royalty in this town, which made it kind of weird. Initially, I couldn't get why Josh didn't just go ahead and rent an apartment, but he seemed to like staying there."

"You must know how he wound up there?"

"Yeah. He told me. Apparently, she was one of his first stops when he got to town. He picked her because she's one of a handful of active docs who were practicing back then, and he figured she'd be a good resource to give him the lay of the land. When she realized the duration of his stay was contingent on his investigation, she suggested he take a room she'd just finished as a B&B rental." She laughed sadly. "He took her up on the offer for the short term, planning to get himself an apartment, but then he had his first gourmet breakfast there. The arrangement instantly became longer term."

Boyd grinned. "Classic Josh. Thinking with his stomach."

"Definitely."

"I imagine he was also influenced by not knowing how long he was going to be here." Boyd sat back in his chair. "If he'd solved his investigation within the first few months, he probably would've given his notice at the paper and gone back to his old job, or at least another big-city paper. By staying at the B&B, he wouldn't have to fuss with a lease or find someone to sublet when he left."

"All while saving a bundle. So I got used to it. It's not like I even saw Sylvia when I went there. Well, not very often."

"I haven't had the pleasure of meeting her—she wasn't around when I went there to clear out Josh's things—but she sounds intimidating."

"She is. Very old-school. It's *Dr.* Walsh and *Mr.* McBride. I don't think I've ever heard a person's first name pass her lips, not even her ailing husband's, whom she refers to as Senator Stratton or the Senator. I gather they were a serious power couple, back in the day."

Boyd frowned. "I remember Josh talking about the Senator. He's in a coma, right?"

"I'm not sure it's a coma, exactly, but he can't communicate. Or so I've heard."

"I'm going to head over there later, I think."

"To Stratton House?"

"Yeah. I'd like to give Josh's room a thorough search. The kind I should have done the first time around." He shrugged. "I just wasn't thinking."

She imagined him packing away Josh's clothes. Had he taken them back to Ontario? Or had he dropped them off at one of the many community donation centers around town? And his toiletries . . . Her heart hurt for him.

"What are you expecting to find?" she asked.

"Josh's journal. That has to be where he kept the details of his investigation into our birth parents," he said grimly. "There were no relevant notes on his laptop, which the cops did a forensic examination on, and no file to be found in his room. And, yeah, I know his phone is missing, but no way would he have kept his research notes on that. I bought him a slick hand-held PDA once, and he hated it. He preferred his notebooks and his laptop."

"He wasn't much for gadgets, that's for sure," Hayden agreed. "I tried to convince him he should buy himself an iPad when I saw all the notebooks he'd filled for work, but he said the only tablets he was interested in were the ones you could write on with a pen or pencil."

"Exactly. So I'm betting he kept the notes for this personal investigation in a physical notebook. I didn't come across it when I cleared his things out of his room at the B&B, but I wasn't thinking straight at the time. I should have looked harder. Josh was private about his personal journals. If they weren't on him, they were tucked away where prying eyes couldn't find them."

"You think he hid it because the information he uncovered was sensitive?"

"Yeah, that too, but I'm pretty sure he'd hide it anyway. Force of habit." At her lifted eyebrows, he explained, "Years ago I found one of his journals lying around. I teased the hell out of the poor bastard, quoting his deep thoughts back to him. You know, stupid teenage brother ribbing. Oh, man, he was furious. Wouldn't speak to me for the longest time. He eventually forgave me, but ever since then, if the journal wasn't on him, he made damned sure it was well hidden."

"So you're saying the journal—"

"I think there's a good chance he hid it in his room."

CHAPTER 4

Boyd trailed Hayden's black Subaru Outback through the light evening traffic with ease.

He hadn't meant to invite her along. Scratch that; he literally *hadn't* invited her. But once she'd realized his destination, she'd insisted on accompanying him. It didn't take a genius to see she was concerned about him. She hadn't wanted him to face that empty room alone. Now that he'd had a few minutes to think about it, he decided it was a good thing. Hayden knew more about Josh's life here than anyone else. He needed to keep her close, keep her talking, see what he could learn.

He had a GPS and could find his way back to the B&B on his own, but following a set of taillights was easier. She led him past a rear view of the provincial legislative assembly building and the towering steeple of Christ Church Cathedral. Then it was through the strange, convoluted intersection beneath an underpass that had confused him last time. Hayden didn't hesitate, though. She'd probably traveled this path dozens and dozens of times.

On his left flowed the Saint John River, flat and black and glistening with the reflected lights of the city. On the right, they passed a series of grand old houses until she signaled and turned into the driveway of one of them.

It was a large circular driveway constructed of paving stones. Boyd didn't know a lick about architecture, but the house was impressive, in a monstrous yet distinctly feminine sort of way. Victorian, he supposed, as he took in the rambling, asymmetrical shape of the whole, with its steep roof, gabled windows, and wraparound veranda complete with white rounded columns. And, yes, it even had a tower. A round one. Funny, he hadn't even noticed that on his earlier visit to claim Josh's stuff.

Instead of drawing up in front of the veranda, which Boyd had done on his visit, Hayden took a side road that sprouted off the driveway. Paved tastefully with crushed rock instead of cobblestones, it led around the house to a parking lot at the rear, also finished with crushed rock.

He parked his rental beside Hayden's car, climbed out, and looked around. "Wow, do they have enough parking?"

"They need it." Hayden closed her car door. "According to Josh, Dr. Stratton expanded it after Senator Stratton fell ill. She keeps a fairly large staff coming and going. Maids and gardeners for the house, LPNs and personal care workers for her husband."

"And B&B customers, of course."

"Yes, B&B guests too. Josh tells me—" She broke off, biting her lip. "Josh *told* me that's why she turned it into a bed-and-breakfast, to help defray the cost of keeping such a big staff. Although that probably points to a certain frugality, not a need to make ends meet."

"She doesn't look like she's hurting."

"She comes from old money, the kind that doesn't get wiped out by a market crash. And even without the Proust money behind her, she still has a healthy medical practice, and the Senator would have a generous pension."

She turned toward him in the lighted parking lot, and he found himself catching his breath. The light cast a halo around her curly golden hair and plunged part of her face into shadow, but the part he could see . . . God, she was beautiful. No wonder Josh had been so hung up on her. If only she'd loved him back like he wanted, instead of loving him like a brother . . .

He cleared his throat. "Will Dr. Stratton be around?"

"I hope so," she said. "I doubt we'll get permission to check Josh's room if she's not here. And remember—"

"I know. It might already be occupied by a new guest. I got it."

She led the way to the rear entrance, rang the bell, and stepped back. A moment later, an older woman dressed in black right down to her practical nonslip shoes, opened the door to them. Boyd recognized her as the housekeeper.

"Dr. Walsh," the woman said, her voice sounding younger and more melodious than her years. "Good to see you again. And who's that with you?" The woman leaned to peer around Hayden, caught sight of Boyd, then stepped back, her hand going to her chest.

"It's okay, Mrs. Garner," Hayden hastened to assure the distraught woman. "This is Josh's brother, Boyd McBride."

"Oh, dear, of course!" she said. "I hadn't thought to see you again after you cleared out Josh's room, Mr. McBride. And seeing you with Dr. Walsh . . ."

"I understand. Sorry to pop up like a ghost."

"I'm just helping him get a feel for Josh's life here, and he'd really like to see Josh's room," Hayden said into the awkward silence. "Do you think that can be arranged? I mean, if it's not rented again."

Mrs. Garner's features softened in sympathy. "It hasn't been rented. Come in, and I'll see what I can do for you." When they stepped inside the entryway, she said, "I'm going to have to ask you to wait here while I talk to Dr. Stratton." Her tone was apologetic. "She has strict rules about these things."

"Thank you, Mrs. Garner," Hayden said. "We'll be happy to wait here."

When the old girl bustled off, Boyd turned to Hayden. "Strict rules?"

"I think she's worried someone will try to see the Senator," she murmured, keeping her voice low. Even at that level, the acoustics of the vaulted ceilings made her voice echo around. "She's very particular about visitation. Josh said no one gets in to see the Senator except Dr. Stratton, their son, Jordan, who's an internist in Saint John, and the Senator's caregivers." She peered around to make sure no one was coming up the hall where Mrs. Garner had disappeared.

"And you felt comfortable coming here?"

Hayden shrugged. "Josh always met me at the door so I didn't have to run the gauntlet alone. But we still managed to bump into her once in a while." She gave an exaggerated shudder. Or at least he hoped it was exaggerated. The woman couldn't be that much of an ogre. She'd been working the day he'd come by for Josh's things, so he hadn't met her.

He heard the click-click of high heels on hardwood before he saw her. Then she turned a corner and entered the room. Beside him, Hayden straightened her back. Wryly, he realized he had too, in that come-to-attention response a soldier had to his officer in charge.

"Well, well, Mrs. Garner was right. You are the spitting image of our Mr. McBride. Identical twins, I presume?"

"Yes, ma'am."

She was thin and very fit looking for her age, but her dark hair was shot with silver. And she projected incredible command presence as she crossed the room, her carriage as upright and impeccable as any queen's. No wonder Hayden had described her as royalty. She drew up in front of him and looked him squarely in the eye. "I'm so sorry for your loss, Mr. McBride. We still miss your brother at our breakfast table."

"Thank you, ma'am."

She extended an elegant hand and he grasped it in a firm handshake. She released her grip quickly, turning to Hayden. "Dr. Walsh. Good to see you again."

"Thank you, Dr. Stratton. You too."

She turned her gaze back to Boyd. "And what's your first name, Mr. McBride?"

"Boyd, ma'am."

"Well, Boyd McBride, for all of your shared genetics, you are a harder customer than Joshua, unless I miss my guess."

She didn't add, "And I never miss my guess," but she might as well have. He heard it loud and clear.

"I understand you wanted to view your brother's room?"

"That's right, ma'am. I'm just trying to get a feel for his life here. I never got a chance to visit, and now . . ." He let his words trail off.

"I understand," she said, and he felt oddly pinned by those steely blue eyes that held his gaze so steadily. The Senator must have had brass ones to take this woman on. "But perhaps I can do you one better?"

One better? What the hell does that mean? "Ma'am?"

"Your brother had paid his rent to the end of the month, Mr.

McBride. If you're going to be reconstructing his life and death here in Fredericton, you're welcome to have his room. I had thought to prorate the unused rental and send a check along to his estate, but if you're in need of a place to stay, perhaps this will work just as well."

Yes! Legitimate, long-term access to Josh's room, handed to him on a platter. He could quietly tear the place apart until he found Josh's notes. Plus it would save him a bundle. He could cancel his reservation at the Comfort Inn. Nothing of his excitement showed, though, when he spoke.

"Thank you, Dr. Stratton. That's very kind of you. I'll take you up on that offer."

She waved his thanks away with a gracious hand. "No need to thank me. The room is bought and paid for. Breakfast is served between six and seven thirty, if you want to avail yourself of it. You may, of course, have to share the breakfast table with myself or my staff."

Better and better on the budget. "That's great with me."

"All other meals are on your own, and please, no music or television or other loud noises late at night." She aimed a look at Hayden as if that message were for her too.

Boyd's mind leapt immediately to a picture of him and Hayden in a bedroom upstairs and the kinds of noise they could make. Clearly, Sylvia Stratton's impersonation of a general must have put him more off balance than he'd realized. Time to get a grip.

"Thank you—that sounds very reasonable."

"Very well. Shall I show you to the room? The key is in there."

"Please."

She turned and click-clicked her way back along the tiled hall. With a gesture for Hayden to precede him, he brought up the rear of the procession.

Sylvia Stratton led them up a wide, elegant staircase with an intricately carved newel post. As they climbed the stairs, he let his right hand glide along the polished banister. The dark wood felt smooth as satin beneath his hands. She hung a left at the top of the stairs and led them along a high-ceilinged hall. If Boyd hadn't already seen it for himself, he probably would have stopped to gaze in amazement at the width of the planking on the floor, not to mention the wide, ornate baseboards and crown molding. The house had to be hundreds of years old. You couldn't get wood like that anymore.

"Your home is very lovely, Dr. Stratton."

"Isn't it?"

She stopped before a tall door framed in wide trim that matched the baseboards, but with extra hand-carved details at the top corners. If he added up the running feet of trim in this old house, the cost of reproducing it would probably exceed the value of his tiny condo back in Toronto. Hell, his condo *and* his car.

"This is it." Pushing the door inward, she waved them into the room.

He felt his chest tighten to be standing again in the room where Josh had lived for the past five-plus months of his life.

"So, have you just landed in town, Mr. McBride, or are you already established somewhere?"

"I hit town earlier today," he confirmed. "But I haven't had a chance to check into my motel."

"If you have your bags with you, you're welcome to take up residence tonight."

"That'd be great," he said. "My stuff is still in the car."

"Then, please, make yourself comfortable." She crossed the room to the bedside and pulled open the drawer of the night table. Turning, she held out a plain key ring with a pair of keys on it. "This one will get you in the rear entrance you just used, and the other is for the room. When you're ready, you can go fetch your things and let yourself back in without disturbing my staff."

He took the key from her. "Thank you."

She stepped back. "Well, if that's all, I'll go back to reading to my husband." She glanced at Hayden. "I trust you can see yourself out later?"

"Of course, Dr. Stratton."

With a regal inclination of her head, Sylvia Stratton turned and left. Boyd could hear the tapping of her heels as she retreated down the hall; then he heard them on the stairs.

He turned to Hayden. "I see what you mean. Seems like she'd have been more at home during this house's heyday, commanding a fleet of servants with an iron hand."

"Yeah, that whole lady-of-the-manor routine." Hayden gave a delicate shudder. "The scary part is that she's on the medical advisory board at the hospital. I try to minimize my contact with her, because I always come away from any encounter feeling as though I've been found lacking. I tell myself not to take it personally, since pretty much everyone comes away from her feeling like that, but it's a challenge some days."

"I don't know . . . Something tells me you can hold your own."

She smiled. "Thank you."

Oh, yeah, he could definitely see why this woman had captivated his brother. She was pretty damned stunning.

He realized silence had fallen, so he said the first thing that came to mind. "So, have you ever met the Senator?"

"No." She shook her head. "I don't think he ever gets out of his sickroom."

"That's a damned shame to see a guy like Lewis Stratton laid low."

She was watching him curiously. "You know him?"

His lips twitched at the idea. "Just by reputation. He took an interest in law and order."

"I guess that stands to reason. Josh said he was some kind of big deal lawyer before he went into politics."

Boyd snorted. "Isn't every politician a former lawyer?"

Her lips curved in a smile that was quick to come and go. "Seems like it, doesn't it?"

Her face sobered again, but Boyd found himself looking at her world-class lips, wondering what it would take to make that smile flash again. Or even better, to make her laugh. Would her laughter be throaty and sexy? Or clear and delighted as a child's? And what would it feel like if he were to catch that laugh on her lips, take it into himself?

He realized she'd caught him looking at her mouth.

"I'm sorry—I lost my train of thought," he offered. "Not enough sleep." That was certainly true. His eyes felt gritty and his head clouded with fatigue.

Her mouth softened again. "I can only imagine. It must be so hard."

His throat clogged with unexpected emotion at her words of sympathy. "For you too. I can see how much you miss him."

They stood there in the small, high-ceilinged bedroom, not touching but connected by their shared grief. He felt an even stronger pull toward her to comfort and be comforted.

The thought had him stepping back. "So what happened to the Senator? Was it a stroke? I think that's what Josh said. I know it was something catastrophic, since he had to vacate his Senate seat."

Hayden seized the change of subject, clearly eager to put the awkwardness behind them. "Yeah, the official statement said stroke." Hayden walked to the window and drew the curtain aside to look out. "Funny thing, all the media attention seemed to focus on his seat, not the Senator himself. If I hadn't been friends with Josh, I doubt I'd even have known he was here."

"Yeah, but you're from away, right?" Boyd joined her there, taking care not to crowd her, to see what view his new bedroom offered. The rear parking lot, as it happened. He hadn't even looked last time he'd been in this room. Or if he had, the view hadn't registered. "Maybe folks aren't as open if you're not third-generation Frederictonian."

She rolled her eyes at him. "That's a terrible stereotype about Maritimers." She let the curtain fall back into place and moved away. "Things haven't been like that for, oh . . . tens of years."

He laughed. "So they've adopted you?"

"They're campaigning hard to add me to their census roll, all right."

"Ah, the hard-sell recruitment?" He took her sigh as an affirmative. "Have you told them you're not sticking around?"

"Repeatedly. The recruitment officer doesn't let a little thing like my life plan deter him."

Boyd caught himself before he could ask her what her life plan involved besides disappointing his twin and robbing him of the chance for the kind of love he'd dreamed of.

Shit. The thought was unworthy of him. As much as it pained him to think about the unrequited love Josh had harbored for Hayden, it wasn't her fault. Emotions couldn't be willed or manufactured, something he well knew. But knowing that and getting past it were two different things.

He realized she was looking at him as though she expected him to say something. Oh, yeah. The overly optimistic recruiter. "So you're going to break the poor guy's heart and go where, exactly?"

"I'm not sure."

Not sure? After that speech about career plans and not letting relationships get in the way—dammit, after using it to shut Josh down—she didn't even know where she wanted to end up?

She snorted. "God, Boyd. I wish you could see your face. You look like I just said I was going to burn my diploma and walk away from medicine when I finish my residency."

"I'm sorry . . . It's just . . . How could you not know where you're going?"

Her smile faded. "Okay, I should have said I'm bound for a bigger center. Toronto, Edmonton, Vancouver, even Halifax. It depends on what offers I get. All I know is I want to work somewhere where I can help the people who have the biggest health challenges, the people who need intervention the most."

He blinked. "Junkies?"

That elicited another eye roll. "I meant the poor, Boyd. Which, yes, could include addicts."

"And there are no poor people here?"

"Of course there are. There's always poverty, wherever you go. But it's relative. I'm sure Josh must have told you what a white-collar town this is. Seat of government, home to two universities, culturally rich. Scores very highly on all of those best places to live polls. It has a very high percentage of people with postsecondary educations, and we rank fairly high on per capita income."

"I see your point. Why would anyone want to work here?"

That smile flashed again. "Okay, so it's a great place to live and work for most people. But Fredericton doesn't really need me. Rich, well-educated Canadians generally demand and receive high-quality care. They navigate the health system extremely well. They also tend to be healthier to begin with. They eat better, exercise, do all those things that reduce their risk of disease."

His irritation with her segued into a grudging respect. "Well, you'd certainly find your target populations in any of those cities you named. I can personally vouch for Toronto."

"Toronto would be great. But actually, my first deployment is going to be to Haiti."

"*Haiti?*"

"Yep. I'm going to do a stint with Doctors Without Borders there. I've always wanted to do something to help the people of Haiti. That's where my mother is from."

A Haitian mother? That must be where she got her slightly exotic looks. The wide, full mouth, golden skin tone, and masses of curly hair. Her father must have contributed the blue eyes and the blonde hair color.

"So is your mom still there, or is she here in Canada?"

"Here," she replied. "She emigrated from Haiti to Canada with her parents in the seventies. They settled in Montreal, as so many of them did. But she still has relatives back in Haiti, including two brothers. When I got to be old enough, we—my parents and I—started to go on mission trips with the church a couple of weeks every year. I've met all my Haitian uncles and cousins, and now those cousins have families of their own."

"And that's where you got the bug to do good deeds?"

"I got so much more than that out of it. What I saw down there . . . that's what gave me the passion to study medicine in the first place. It only seems right that I honor that, you know?"

Yes, he could understand that. "Have you explained this Haitian connection to the recruiter?"

"Of course. But it's his job to not take no for an answer. He's never going to let up."

"Guess he'll have to when you walk out the door after your last shift, huh?"

She laughed, and it was just as musical as he'd imagined. He must have been watching her mouth again, because she sobered quickly.

"I was going to stay and help you search, to save you from being alone in this room," she said. "But if you're going to be staying here, I guess there's not much point in that, is there? You're going to have to get used to it."

"I thought that might be what was behind your . . . uh . . . offer to come here with me."

"My insistence, you mean?"

"I'm glad you insisted. It was very kind of you."

She shrugged. "I just know I wouldn't have wanted to come back here alone." She glanced around the room. "I should go. You're probably anxious to start your search, and I should get home."

"Of course," he said. "Let me walk you to your car."

"No need for that. The parking lot is reasonably well lit, as you saw, and this isn't exactly a high-crime area."

He grinned at the idea of a criminal daring to invade Sylvia Stratton's world. "I'm sure you're right, but I'm still going to walk you out. I have to get my bag from the car anyway."

A moment later, they stood in the parking lot by her Subaru.

"So, you're good from here?" she asked, keys in hand.

He understood instantly what she was asking. "I'm further ahead than I was," he acknowledged, nodding his head toward the Stratton House behind him. "But I think there's more I can learn from you. Nobody knew Josh—the Fredericton Josh—like you did. I'd still like to talk to you some more."

She eyed him uncertainly. "You really think my telling you this stuff—what movies we saw together or which nights I came over here or he came to my place—is going to help you?"

He met her gaze. "Absolutely. One way or another, it'll help. If it doesn't lead me to understand more clearly what happened, maybe it can lead me to accept it." He shrugged. "To be honest, I could use someone to talk to about Josh. I can't say his name around my parents without one or the other of them breaking down. And everyone else . . . they just don't know what to say."

He saw her acquiescence in the slight relaxation of her shoulders.

"Okay," she said. "Just tell me what I can do."

"You can start by hanging around with me, just like you would with Josh."

Her eyebrows shot up. "Just like that, huh? We're going to be insta-buddies and we're going to text each other five times a day?"

He grimaced. "Okay, maybe not that part."

"Good. Because I don't think I could stand that." Her voice sounded thick. "I mean, you look so much like him . . ."

"I get it," he said flatly. "I'm not Josh. Believe me—I know that very well. I don't think there's any danger of either of us forgetting it."

"That's not what I meant to—"

"But it's the truth. I'm a fan of truth, Hayden. In that respect, at least, I'm a lot like my brother."

She gazed up at him. "But not *all* truths, I guess. Josh told me you weren't interested in knowing your birth parents."

She'd said something very like that to him when they'd talked at the restaurant, but he'd completely ignored her statement. This time, her words slid into him like a surgeon's scalpel.

In his defense, he could have told her what he'd told Josh— that this investigation could land the people who'd been their *real* parents in questionable legal waters. But it would have been a false defense. The truth of it was he just didn't care to know.

Their birth parents had given them up, and that's all there was to it.

Oh, it'd taken him a while to reach that conclusion. Frank and Ella McBride had been solid parents, but, knowing they were adopted, he and Josh had often speculated about their "real" mother. In their young minds, she was glamorous and beautiful, and had shed glamorous, beautiful tears about having to give them up. In their imaginations, there was always a compelling reason. Josh's favorite had been that she was a superhero and hadn't been able to take care of them herself because she was busy saving the world. Boyd preferred to think that she'd been knocked on the head and developed amnesia—or, even better, that she'd been magically enchanted and made to forget about them—but eventually the amnesia would clear, or the magic spell would be broken, and she would remember and come find them.

For Boyd, those childish fantasies had given way to the certain knowledge that their mother just hadn't wanted them. But for Josh, the dream had never really died. Not that he still believed their mother was a superhero or a secret agent or a fairy princess, but his conviction that their mother would want to meet them never faltered. It had irked Boyd that Josh continued to search into his adulthood, after it became painfully clear that their mother didn't want to reconnect. There were plenty of places she could have registered if she'd wanted to be found.

He smiled. "There's that magic word—*interested*. If I'm not interested, if I don't care about learning a particular truth, there's no point in the pursuit of it, is there? Unless, of course, it means discovering what really happened to Josh."

"You're right, and I'm sorry." She sighed. "Look, can we park this conversation until tomorrow? I'm exhausted, and if I don't get my sleep, the ER will be hell in the morning."

Damn, she did look exhausted. "Of course."

She hit the remote to unlock her car, and he reached for the door handle and opened it for her. She slid into the seat.

"When can we get together again?"

"You really want to walk in Josh's shoes?" she asked.

"As much as I can, yes."

"So be it," she said. "Tomorrow night, then. My place. It's *Burn Notice* night, and it's your turn to bring pizza." She produced her phone. "We might as well get each other's details."

He punched in her number and address, then gave her his phone number.

"What time?" he asked, when she'd finished programming her phone and tucked it back in her purse.

"Seven. And make it a veggie pizza."

"Veggie?" He made no attempt to hide the dismay in his voice.

"Yes, veggie." Smiling, she keyed the ignition and the Subaru's engine sputtered to life. "Now close my door."

"Yes, ma'am." He obliged, then stepped back as she reversed out of the parking space and drove away.

He glanced up at the old Victorian, his smile dying as his gaze found the lighted window of Josh's bedroom. *His* bedroom for the next couple of weeks.

I'm not giving up on you, Josh. If your death wasn't natural, I'll uncover the truth.

With that determination, he unlocked his rental, retrieved his leather travel bag, and trudged back toward the house.

∾

Hayden was three blocks away before she realized she was holding herself so tensely, something was likely to snap.

Easing her death grip on the steering wheel, she took a few slow, deep breaths and willed her muscles to relax. After a few moments, they complied.

Much better.

Small wonder she'd been tense. Between Sylvia Stratton's company and her increasingly acute awareness of Boyd McBride, she'd overloaded her circuits.

Boyd. Several times tonight, she'd caught him looking at her face. No, not her face—her *mouth.* Had he been thinking about kissing her?

God help her, she'd been thinking the same thing.

She didn't know what was more bizarre, that she was having this strong reaction to someone she'd met just that day—the handshake at the funeral was so brief and impersonal, it hardly counted—or that that someone was a genetic duplicate of the best friend she'd just lost.

Okay, that last part was definitely the more bizarre.

What would Josh think to see her worked up like this over his twin?

Her laugh emerged as more of a sob. He'd probably think it was hysterical.

No, he'd have warned me away.

The truth of that thought resonated deep within her. That's exactly what Josh would have done. Well, eventually, once he noticed her normal immunity to masculine charms was absent. Josh had clearly loved and admired his twin, but he'd once told Hayden he despaired of Boyd ever settling down with one woman.

Boyd had said it himself. He was no Josh.

For that matter, Sylvia Stratton had seen it too, on first sight. What had she said? *You're a harder customer than our Joshua, unless I miss my guess.*

And, yes, Hayden had seen it for herself. It was impossible to look into those gold-brown eyes and not see the walls, the reserve. Oh, she was sure there was good reason for that distance.

As a cop in Toronto, it was probably safe to say he'd seen some horrific things.

Unlike Josh, she suspected he'd have no problem compartmentalizing the pieces of his life. Job, family, sex. A woman would have to fit into one of those neat compartments and be content to stay there. Definitely not an attractive quality in a man.

Not that she was looking for a man. God, no! But if she were, she'd know enough to leave *this* one alone. Men like Josh were more her speed. Well-adjusted, emotionally mature, stable. If she were looking for a romantic relationship, she'd pick a guy just like Josh. Well, hopefully one she was more sexually attracted to. She'd seen friends go into relationships where they had great compatibility on almost every front but not much chemistry. They hadn't been much more successful than the ill-matched ones who had nothing *but* chemistry going for them.

So why did her stomach drop when she thought about spending tomorrow evening with Boyd?

"Duh. Because he thinks someone might have deliberately caused Josh's death, that's why. Of course you're unnerved."

Hearing her own words reassured her. That was totally it.

Feeling better, she turned left onto Regent. In about seven minutes, she'd be letting herself into her Priestman Street apartment. Ten minutes in a hot bath to raise her body temperature followed by twenty minutes to let it plummet—her favorite non-medicinal trick for sleep inducement. Then it would be sweet oblivion.

After learning Josh might have been murdered—and meeting his unsettling twin—she needed it.

CHAPTER 5

Boyd woke to the sound of birds chirping. He tried to ignore their insistent cheerfulness, burrowing deeper into the covers, but then it struck him—he never heard birds singing in his eighteenth-floor condo.

He jerked upright, scanning the unfamiliar room. Memory flooded back. Josh was dead, and Boyd was now occupying Josh's rented room at Sylvia Stratton's bed-and-breakfast.

Jesus, when would this stop? Every night, sleep wiped the grief away, and every morning he woke up blank but knowing somehow that a shoe was going to drop.

Throwing the covers off, he swung his legs to the floor. For a moment he just sat there, elbows on his knees, head in his hands. Grief had its own inertia, he'd discovered. It was a hundred-pound weight he had to carry, every moment of every day. His frail, aging parents had been crushed by it. In the wake of Josh's death, Boyd had had to push himself to do what needed to be done. The shock, the unreality of it, had protected him in the initial days.

But the insulation hadn't lasted. He dragged a hand through his hair and stood up.

Even though they hadn't seen each other in person in more than three months, Josh had been very much a part of Boyd's everyday life. A phone call at least once a week, and oh, God, those infernal text messages. Boyd had often bitched about Josh's talkativeness, textually speaking, but what he'd give to be peppered by them now.

Josh had also phoned their parents once a day, every day. By contrast, Boyd had been in the habit of calling them once a week. Sure, he visited them a couple of times a month, to take care of any odd jobs his father needed done around their old brick home in Glen Park, or at their lake cottage, but it was Josh who'd brought joy into their lives on a daily basis. When he got back, he'd have to start spending more time with them and calling them more often. Of course, the latter he could start doing now. He hoped to God they could spring back from this. They'd been fairly socially active up to now and still had a few longtime friends whose families had grown up beside each other in middle-class suburbia. Good friends who hopefully would help draw them back into their routines.

Pushing those thoughts away for the moment, he glanced around the room. Missing Josh was something he couldn't do anything about. And he certainly couldn't bring him back from the dead. But he could—and he *would*—get to the bottom of what happened. But first, he needed to eat.

Fifteen minutes later, showered and dressed in fresh jeans and a plaid button-down shirt, he headed for the breakfast room.

Sylvia Stratton was there when he arrived, seated at the table reading the newspaper. She glanced up.

"You look better this morning. Did you sleep well?"

"I did, thank you." And he had. Well, once he'd given the room a first cursory search. He'd known the notebook wouldn't be in an obvious place. If it had been, he'd have found it the first time around. He'd started in the bedroom, checking all the drawers, looking for false bottoms or backs, and checking to make sure nothing was taped to the undersides. Using his shaving mirror and a flashlight, he'd examined the undersides and backs of the other furniture—the bed frame, the night table, the wardrobe. He'd moved on to other obvious places in the living area of his suite—behind the big flat-screen TV, down the sides of the couch with its oversize cushions. Hell, he'd unzipped the cushions themselves and examined the interior.

Yes, his search had felt a little bit like something out of a 1980s crime movie, but he knew his brother was particular as hell about his personal journals. Having a twin meant having almost no privacy. Not that Boyd was a big snooper, but neither twin was above rifling through the other one's stuff if it was left lying around. And after Boyd had given Josh holy hell for his "feelings" notebook, his brother had sworn that Boyd—or anyone else—would never get his hands on it again.

It might be a stretch that Josh was still *Mission: Impossible* about hiding his stuff, but Boyd wasn't taking anything for granted. Not if it meant bringing a murderer to justice.

Eventually exhaustion had caught up with him. He'd crawled in between the sheets and went to bed, more frustrated than he'd been when he'd arrived.

"Help yourself to breakfast, Detective." She gestured to a sideboard, where several stainless steel chafing dishes gleamed, the kind caterers used to keep food warm. "The live-in staff have already eaten, but there's plenty left."

"Thank you, I'll do that," he said. "But there's no need for the 'Detective' business. I don't have any standing here."

"Oh, but there's every need. I doubt you stop being a detective just because you've left your jurisdiction, any more than I stop being a physician when office hours are over."

"If you prefer."

"I do," she said. "I believe I called you Mr. McBride last evening, though, and for that I apologize. Put it down to tiredness. Your brother mentioned your occupation a number of times. He was very proud of you."

Shit. Just like that, emotion tightened his throat. "Well, the feeling was mutual." His voice came out sounding amazingly normal. "We couldn't have been prouder of Josh." He looked around for something to sip to ease the ache. "Is that coffee I smell?"

"I'll pour it for you while you get your breakfast ready." She stood.

"Don't let me put you out. I can get it myself if you just show me where to find the mugs and the coffeepot."

"Very well." She subsided into her chair again. "The coffee urn is on the other side of the refrigerator. Mugs in the cupboard up above."

He poured the coffee into a bone china mug, added a couple of creamers, and carried it back to the table. Gesturing to the elaborate place setting, with bowl, saucer, and plate stacked on a woven charger, surrounded by silverware and juice glasses, he asked, "That for me?"

"Of course, Detective."

"Very fancy."

"Merely civilized."

She got up to refill her own mug while he helped himself to breakfast. Fresh cut-up fruit, fluffy scrambled eggs, and a heap of hash browns that looked to be made from scratch with fresh potatoes. By the time he sat down at the table, he was actually hungry.

She placed her refilled mug on the table. "You need fruit juice," she remarked, looking at his breakfast. "What's your preference? I can recommend the orange juice. It's fresh squeezed."

That sounded like heaven, and Boyd said so.

She took his glass and went to the refrigerator. A moment later, she placed the juice in front of him.

"Thank you."

"You're welcome."

She glanced at his breakfast again, and, seemingly satisfied he had all the food groups covered now, she went back to her crossword.

He ate quickly, until he felt Sylvia Stratton's gaze on him.

"What?"

"You really aren't much like your twin, are you?"

"Excuse me?"

She gestured to his plate, which was all but empty now. "Josh took a more leisurely approach to his meals."

"That's one way of putting it," he said, smiling at the memory. "Meals were events for him, whereas food is pretty much just fuel for me. Yes, I appreciate the high-test fuel if it's there," he said, nodding toward the food-laden sideboard, "but regular does nicely too."

"I see. Well, you're going to be running on high test while you're here. See if a few weeks of organic, non-GMO, antibiotic-free, nutrient-rich diet doesn't improve your sense of well-being."

He doubted a few breakfasts were going to mitigate the effects of a cop's diet, but he smiled. "I'll drink to that." Picking up his glass of OJ, he raised it in a toast to her, then drained it. Then he stood and stacked his dishes, intending to stow them in the dishwasher or carry them to the sink, at least.

"Leave them," she instructed. "Mrs. Garner will be in to clean up after us as soon as we vacate."

"Suits me." He put the dishes back on the charger. "Look, I thought I'd go out for a jog, and I was thinking I'd like to try some of Josh's routes. Can you tell me where he liked to run?"

She blinked at him. "I couldn't say."

"You know he died after jogging on a wooded trail in Odell Park, right?"

"Of course. But he also jogged a lot closer to home, on trails he could reach without getting in his car and driving to them."

"Such as?"

She waved a hand. "I don't know. Along the Green, I imagine."

"The Green?"

"The strip of land running along the river. He could have gone west or east once he hit that. You'll find there are a lot of walking and biking trails in the city, Detective. I suggest you go to city hall and pick up a map. In fact, if you decide to run upriver, it's really not that far. You could probably duck in and get one."

He thanked her for the suggestion, but he knew where he'd be heading this morning. He was going to Odell Park. The last place Josh had run. The place where he'd died, in his car in the parking lot.

He would start learning more about his brother's life at the very place where that life had ended.

CHAPTER 6

Boyd climbed out of his car and looked around. He could hear the trickling of a small stream in the tree-shaded area west of the parking lot. He turned on his heel, taking in the expanse of neatly mown green grass, the duck pond, and, to the east, the caretaker's house and a horse barn and paddock. His gaze swept over the driveway and parking lot until he'd turned full circle.

He'd been here before, on his first trip to claim Josh's body. He'd felt compelled to see for himself where Josh had died. Now, as then, all he could think was what an incongruously beautiful place it was to die.

Pushing the thought away, he did a few cursory stretches, then loped off toward the first trail he spotted. As soon as he started running, he stopped consciously thinking. That was the best thing about running—switching off his conscious mind.

When he ran, there was nothing but the breath sawing in and out of his lungs and the burn of muscles doing what they were meant to do. Nothing but the pound of his footfalls and the scents that wafted up from the sunny meadows and the more mysterious scents lingering in the shadowed forest.

He ran the first kilometer at an easy jog, then stepped it up. He wanted to keep his heart rate elevated. But not too much. Even the mental decluttering of running couldn't dislodge from the back of his mind the memory of what had happened to Josh.

Then he caught the train of his thoughts. Jesus, the heart doctors had worked him a lot harder than this on the freaking treadmill. He'd passed every test they'd thrown at him with flying colors. He damned well wasn't going to drop dead if he ran his usual pace. He'd keep it shorter than his usual run, though. A nod to the doctor's advice not to run any marathons. And it would better simulate what Josh had done on his lunch hour.

He cranked it up a little more. His breath came hard on the uphills and his shins felt the impact on the downhills, but he pressed on. He didn't even pause to admire the deer he spotted in their penned area, and only slowed periodically to drink from the water bottle he carried.

A little over fifty minutes later, he'd run twelve kilometers of the park's sixteen-kilometer trail—a good seven and a half miles—which he figured had to be nearly twice as far as Josh could have run that day on his lunch-hour jog. Not his best time by a long shot, but not an easy jog either. By the time he got back to his car, he was beat, but the normal kind of post-workout beat. His legs were tired, he was breathing hard, and he was ready for that second big bottle of water he retrieved from the car. Leaning against the rental, he drank deeply. In a few minutes, his breathing normalized and his heart rate came down.

Well, he had his answer. No goddamned way did Josh jog a

much shorter distance, over the same terrain, on an even cooler day, then climb into his car and die behind the wheel. Not without help.

After running considerably farther and with a minute's rest, Boyd had no distress at all. All he felt was runner's euphoria. And wasn't that fucking awesome? His brother was dead, and here he stood, his blood pumping, giddy with endorphins.

Grimly, he capped the water bottle. There was nothing more to be learned here.

It took him fifteen minutes in light morning traffic to get back to the B&B. Finding no sign of Sylvia, he went in search of Mrs. Garner. He located her in the walk-in pantry off the kitchen. She started when he spoke, but he wasn't sure whether he'd just surprised her or whether she'd mistaken him for Josh again.

"Mr. McBride." She came out of the pantry, holding what was obviously a grocery list in her hand. "I hope you're not looking for lunch. Breakfast is the only meal we set for guests. Although I suppose I could—"

"No worries. As fantastic as breakfast was, I'm not looking for you to feed me. I know you have your hands full, running this house." He gave her his most dazzling smile, and she blushed. "I was just wondering where Dr. Stratton might be found?"

"Not here, I'm afraid," Mrs. Garner said. "She keeps office hours Monday through Thursday. Shall I tell her you'd like a word with her tonight when she gets home?"

"No, that's fine. It'll wait until morning. I presume she'll be here for breakfast again?"

"Every morning, like clockwork."

That was good to know. With another smile, he thanked her, then headed for his room. At the kitchen doorway, a thought stopped him. He turned. "Mrs. Garner?"

She stepped out of the pantry again. "Yes?"

"Are there any other places in the house where my brother might have spent time? Besides his room, I mean?"

Her eyebrows soared.

"It's been tough letting go," he said before she could ask why on earth he'd want to know something like that. "Josh was my only sibling, my twin. I just want to find some peace with that. I'm hoping that being here—here in Fredericton, here in the place where Josh lived—might help me to find it."

Her face softened. "I can only imagine how hard it's been. Your brother was a very nice young man, and the shock of him going so suddenly . . ." She stroked the back of one hand with the other, he noticed, an unconscious self-comforting gesture. "I do hope you find your peace, Mr. McBride, but you'll have to find it in your brother's room. Guests are not permitted to wander. Apart from the kitchen, where he took his breakfast, he wouldn't have been anywhere else in the house. Well, except for Dr. Stratton's den when he was newly arrived in town, and the parlor, where they had a glass of sherry, but that was before he took up residence."

Well, that probably eliminated the other rooms in the house. Josh would never hide his notebook someplace he couldn't easily retrieve it. And not where it could be found by the diligent Mrs. Garner.

"Of course. Thanks, Mrs. Garner. I'll let you get back to work."

"No trouble."

Boyd climbed the stairs to his room, his legs heavy from the earlier exertion. First stop, a hot shower. Deciding to skip the shave, he stood under the high showerhead and let the steaming water beat down on tired muscles. Out of nowhere, he flashed on Hayden Walsh. Naked in the shower with him, naturally.

She was a damned good-looking woman. Even the lab jacket

and scrubs couldn't hide that fact. He'd bet there were a lot of handsome doctors who'd like to score with her. Except Dr. Walsh didn't date, as Josh had discovered too late, after he'd fallen for her.

And oh, God, here he was fantasizing about the woman his brother had loved. *Jesus*. Well, that killed the mood quicker than a jolt of cold water could have.

Poor Josh. When his brother had confided his predicament, Boyd had agreed it would suck to be in love with someone who saw you as a friend or a brother. But that was before he'd seen Hayden. Now he knew "sucked" didn't come close.

Boyd knew he could never have a platonic relationship like that with Hayden Walsh. Though she seemed completely oblivious of it, she was a walking sexual charge. It would be a damned lucky man who found himself on the receiving end of that pent-up sensuality when she finally decided she was ready to unleash it.

After showering and dressing, he resumed his search of the room. He worked quietly, searching each quadrant carefully and methodically. By lunchtime, he was reasonably confident there was no notebook hidden there. He'd stripped the bed and examined the mattress from every angle, checked every floorboard and wide windowsill. He'd felt under the wardrobe and examined every square inch inside it. The desk and chair got a similarly thorough treatment, as did the vanity in the small bathroom. And, yes, he popped the top off the toilet tank to make sure Josh hadn't sealed the notebook in plastic and dropped it in there. He'd felt the hem of every curtain and taken down the valances to inspect them. And although he could see there was nothing inside the floor vent, he unscrewed the cover and felt the walls of the air duct to make sure they were solid. All he got for his trouble was dusty hands.

He sat back on his heels and looked around the room. There *had* to be a notebook. There just had to be. But where was it?

Had someone here at the house removed it before he'd arrived in town and secured Josh's belongings? Doubtful. Never in a million years would Josh leave it somewhere it could be found by a cursory search.

It might have been in Josh's car.

Jesus. He'd been fighting that thought, but couldn't hold it off any longer. Josh's phone had disappeared somewhere along the line, presumably from the vehicle. Why not the notebook too? Except, dammit, if that was the case, it would have been shredded into a million pieces or reduced to a pile of ash by now. He felt his stomach lurch at the idea.

On the other hand, maybe Josh had stashed it somewhere at work. Yes, he normally kept his journal on or near him, but he'd been heading out for a lunch-hour jog. Why drag it with him, only to leave it in his car where it might get stolen?

His laptop had been left at work after all, and that was something he carried to and fro between home and work. If he hadn't dragged the laptop with him to the park, maybe he hadn't taken the journal either.

The cops had been to the newspaper early on, during Boyd's first visit. Morgan had interviewed Josh's editor about the types of investigations Josh had been involved with recently, to make sure there was nothing particularly dangerous among those assignments. He'd talked to some coworkers, as well, with the editor's blessing. But considering Boyd had already turned over the mother lode of notebooks he'd found in Josh's room, odds were they hadn't looked very hard for another notebook.

He pulled out his cell phone and called the paper. In a matter of minutes, he had an appointment with reporter Dave Bradley, a colleague of Josh's.

Instead of putting his phone away, he found himself thinking about calling Hayden. Except he had no good reason to. And she was probably working. His call would just go through to her voice mail. And he was going to see her tonight anyway.

Of course, if he could reach her, she could save him some time . . .

∾

Hayden pushed the remains of her chicken salad wrap away and picked up her phone again. No new texts. No messages. Not that she'd really expected any. Josh was gone, and all the friends she had left in Fredericton were right here at the hospital. They could pretty much find her anytime they wanted to. She didn't even know why she bothered to power the phone up for her lunch break anymore. She was just about to hit the "Kill" button when a call came in.

Boyd McBride. Her pulse leapt. "Hi, Boyd."

"Is this a good time? I don't want to take you away from anything."

"I'm on my lunch break still, so we're good. What's up? Have you learned something already?"

"I learned there's no notebook hidden in Josh's room, but that's about it."

"Oh, that's too bad. I was hoping you'd find it straight off."

"Thanks. I guess I should have known it wouldn't be that easy, huh?"

She pictured the wry curve of his mouth and smiled. "Things seldom are."

There was a brief silence. When it started to get awkward, Hayden filled it. "So, what now? What's your next move?"

"I've got an appointment to see Dave Bradley, at the paper."

"The reporter," she said. "I know him. Actually, I think I've met all of the reporters Josh worked with, if you count having after-work drinks with them as 'knowing.' I've seen more of Dave than the others, though. I think he must live in one of the apartment complexes close by."

"What's your impression of the guy?"

She closed her hand around her tea mug. "I don't know him well enough to say." Though not for lack of trying on his part. The man had attempted to strike up a conversation every time their paths crossed, which had seemed to be happening way more often than coincidence could explain. She'd suspected he'd been working up the courage to ask her out. When Hayden had mentioned it to Josh, he'd immediately volunteered to have a heart-to-heart with the guy, but she'd vetoed that idea. She could handle Dave Bradley, or anyone else who put the moves on her. She'd had a quiet word with him about her strict no-dating policy, and that had been the end of it. He'd stopped popping up everywhere she went. Hayden didn't tell Boyd any of that, though. She didn't want to negatively influence him, and, really, she couldn't blame a guy for trying. It had even been a bit flattering. "He did seem to idolize Josh, but so did most of the crew up there. Josh was a mentor of sorts, I think."

"Detective Morgan said something like that too," he said. "I gather his wife works at the paper."

"That's right. Grace Morgan. I really love her work."

He chuckled.

"What's so funny?"

"Are you sure this place isn't growing on you? Reading the local rag, following a columnist?"

"She's good, and I have to read *something* with my supper. Plus you can often predict the volume and type of traffic you're going to get in the ER based on what's happening in the community." She pushed away the mug of cooling tea. "Frosh Week at the two universities? Alcohol poisonings, hazings gone wrong, drinking-related accidents. High school graduation parties? More of the same, with some fights mixed in, plus a major trauma or two from motor vehicle accidents. I like to be plugged in."

"Your work sounds a lot like mine," he said.

"Oh, I imagine yours gets a lot grittier. Not to mention more dangerous."

"Yeah, well I don't have to try to put anyone back together. I just have to find out what happened."

"I'll still take my end of it, thank you."

He chuckled, and the low sound made her stomach do a funny flip.

She sat up straight. "You didn't say why you're calling. I mean, I'm going to see you tonight, right? Unless you've changed you mind." *Oh, hell, that didn't come out right.* It sounded like she'd be disappointed if he canceled. "Not that I'd mind. If you've changed your mind, I mean. I don't know what you could possibly learn from hanging out with me anyway, and—"

"Oh, I'm still coming over. I was just calling to ask where I could buy a good veggie pizza since I don't know the local pizza joints."

"Oh, of course!" She planted her face in her palm for a second.

"Left to my own devices, I'd just grab a pizza at the first place I spotted," he said, "but something tells me you might be a little more discriminating."

"Good call." Keeping her tone light, she gave him the name of the local mom-and-pop pizzeria she and Josh usually patronized. "Get the thin crust multigrain. It'll make a believer out of you."

"I expect it'll make me believe it would be really good with some Italian sausage."

She laughed. "We'll see." She checked her watch. "Whoops, gotta go. I have to get back to the ER."

"See you tonight."

His low-voiced words sent a thrill forking through her.

Before she could stutter out something stupid, she said, "'Kay, bye," and hung up.

Oh, man. She must be more tired than she thought. She resolved then and there to grab a nap after work. To face Boyd McBride at less than full strength would not be smart. The more she saw of him, the more her body hummed with sexual awareness. Which was totally weird. The guy was an exact duplicate, genetically speaking, of Josh, her best friend, a brother figure. While she'd have to be blind not to have seen that Josh was a great-looking guy, she'd never once reacted to him like she did to his brother, not even when he'd kissed her that time.

She'd been ignoring her reaction to Boyd, suppressing it. But denial was not her style. Well, not in recent years. She'd tried that once and had promised herself never again. Much better to acknowledge the problem.

Then she could go back to ignoring it consciously, in full self-awareness.

Yeah, she was definitely going to need that nap.

CHAPTER 7

Boyd was a few minutes early for his two thirty appointment with Dave Bradley, which was just as well. His appearance at reception caused a bit of a stir among the ladies behind the counter, to the obvious puzzlement of a young man who was trying to place his classified ad. Of course, the guy couldn't know that the ladies were looking at the spitting image of their dead coworker.

"I'm so sorry about your brother," the receptionist said when he'd introduced himself. "He was very popular here. The departments don't mix much, but he always had a cheerful word for us."

Boyd smiled. "That sounds like Josh." He glanced around. "Where would I find Dave Bradley? I'm a few minutes early, but he should be expecting me."

She gestured to the glass-walled cubicles to the left, where people worked in plain view of everyone else. "There. Far side, front end."

"Tan shirt and glasses, on the phone?"

"That's him."

"Thank you." He pushed away from the counter and strode purposefully toward the cubicles. The closer he got, the louder the voices got, as individuals tried to make themselves heard over other conversations and the pervasive background racket of some type of machine.

Bradley looked up and spotted him. He concluded his phone conversation and met Boyd just outside the entrance to his cubicle.

"Dave Bradley," he said, extending his hand. "And you, Detective McBride, don't need an introduction. Not in this building."

Boyd shook the man's hand, sizing him up. His grip was firm, but his hands were soft, as the rest of him appeared to be. Not overweight, but not gym material either. Curly dark hair, worn in a longish style that he probably hadn't changed since university, even though it was starting to recede on the sides. With his pale skin and dark-rimmed glasses, he definitely looked the part of the intellectual. More Geek Squad than sensitive artist, he'd wager.

"Sorry," Boyd said, releasing his grip. "I seem to be scaring the hell out of a lot of folks lately."

At Boyd's words, the conversation around them died abruptly, leaving just the noise of the unseen machine. A quick glance around confirmed they were all looking at him.

"No, *I'm* sorry," Bradley said, his eyes meeting Boyd's for just a second before skating away. "I should have warned people. I guess I forgot the detail that you two were identical." He turned to address the other reporters, all of whom were frozen in place. "Josh's brother," he called.

Like someone had thrown a switch, they went back to their conversations or keyboards. It was almost comical. Nothing like a deadline to bring focus, he supposed.

That's how Josh used to be. Boyd's chest tightened with the memory.

"There's an empty office we can use if you'd like a little privacy." Bradley gestured to a room almost directly opposite the reporters' station. While it had a window for a front wall, it was enclosed and had a door. "It's hard to have a conversation out here and not be overheard."

Interesting. Bradley was being friendly, but he seemed uncomfortable. His tone and his facial expression didn't match the message entirely. And he sure wasn't much for eye contact. In fact, he looked as though the last thing he wanted was a sit-down discussion. Was he just too busy? But if so, why had he agreed to the meeting?

Maybe it just freaked the guy out that he looked so much like Josh.

Or maybe he was nervous about something.

"This doesn't require privacy," Boyd said, watching for Bradley's reaction. "I just wanted to come by and collect any of Josh's personal belongings he might have left here."

Bradley's expression lightened. "Of course. I boxed up his things. His cubicle is still empty at the moment, but we've got interns coming and will have to shoehorn a couple of them in there soon."

"Can I see his space?"

"Certainly."

Boyd followed him around the corner to an empty cubicle. A banker's box sat on top of the desk. Boyd flipped the lid and looked inside. "This all there was?"

"There were some files on his desk, but they were all works in progress. They've since been handed off to other reporters."

"Nothing personal?"

"His laptop."

"Which the cops have." When Bradley's eyes slid away, Boyd added, "I turned it over to them for a forensic analysis. You never know, right? Best to make sure there wasn't anything sketchy on there, nothing that might lead someone to want to hurt Josh."

Bradley swallowed. "Right." His gaze met Boyd's again finally.

"No desktop unit?"

Boyd already knew the answer. He'd been the one who'd collected the laptop, not the cops, since they didn't have a warrant. The paper's editor had handed it over personally, noting Josh had been the only reporter to use his personal laptop as his work computer. Josh had maintained that his life as a journalist was on that computer, from bookmarks to browser history to contacts, not to mention reams and reams of research, and he'd argued he would be more effective using it than the desktop computer they'd provided. The editor had been more than happy to make that concession, especially since it freed up a computer for another intern.

"No. He preferred to use his own computer. Said he had a lot of shortcuts or something, and it would be quicker and easier."

"No personal files?"

"Nope, nothing like that." Bradley glanced away again.

Boyd wasn't certain if that was evasive behavior or whether his eyes were distracted by motion in the other cubicles. Damned glass walls. Boyd turned his attention to the box.

"I'll get out of here, give you some privacy," Bradley said.

"No need. This will just take a second."

Boyd quickly removed the larger items so he could see what was in the box. A pack of notebooks, all empty. Some dog-eared reference books, a digital photo frame, one of those tension-relieving foam balls for squishing, a digital camera. He got a little excited when he spotted the mini–digital recorder, but when he hit "Play," he heard nothing. He rewound and got the same. Fast-forward, still nothing. He'd give the whole thing a listen, but he was pretty sure there was nothing on it. He poked the remaining stuff around. A handful of expensive pens—Josh had loved a good pen. Some AAA batteries for the minirecorder, three energy bars, a pouch of trail mix, and some other odds and ends. Sighing, he put the cover back on the box.

"Didn't find what you were looking for?" Bradley asked.

Boyd glanced up. "Did the cops take anything when they were here?"

"No." He rubbed his temple. "Our editor let the detective have a look at the work space, but it was real quick, like he knew what he was looking for and didn't find it. Mostly, he spent his time talking to the editor and a few journalists."

"Were you one of those journalists?"

"To talk to the detective? Yeah. He was mainly interested in what Josh had been working on. I told them what I knew. By then, the files he'd been working on had already been reassigned."

Boyd wasn't surprised to hear that. By the time he'd driven to his parents to break the news, booked a flight, and got his ass to Fredericton, it had been nearly twelve hours later. Another hour to get to the police station to speak to the investigators. All of which meant it was late the next afternoon before Josh's file got bumped up to suspicious. It wasn't until the following morning that Morgan got there to do his interviews. That would be an eternity in the news world, where a new edition had to be ground out six days a week, no matter who died.

"Then you turned up shortly after and the boss turned over Josh's laptop and jump drives." He nodded to the box on the desk. "If we'd known you were coming, I could have had his desk cleaned out and his stuff packed up sooner. We were still in a bit of a state of shock."

"No notebooks?"

Bradley shook his head. "There weren't any here. Most of us keep our old notebooks and files in our cubicles or in those cabinets," he said, nodding toward a wall of cabinets that formed an artificial wall separating the reporters' area from the front desk. "But your brother was in the habit of taking his home."

"Yeah, there were a bunch there with his work-related notes and research. But he was also conducting a personal investigation. That's the notebook I haven't been able to find."

Bradley blanched, his gaze swinging back to Boyd. "What kind of investigation?"

Boyd kept his face expressionless. "I don't know if he mentioned it, but Josh and I were adopted. He was looking into our birth parents. Because of a problem with our birth registration, the usual methods for opening the adoption records weren't cutting it. So he was working that investigation in his spare time."

"Oh, of course." The relief on Bradley's face was evident. "I knew that, but I guess I'd sort of forgotten."

"Did he ever talk to you about it?"

"Not really, but we all knew. You see, when he first joined the paper, a group of us were speculating about what might have happened to make him leave one of the best jobs in the country for *this*. We figured he must have disgraced himself somehow."

"Josh?" Boyd snorted. "He'd be the last guy to do something journalistically unethical."

"I couldn't agree more," Bradley said. "But we didn't know him then. In fact, none of us had ever laid eyes on the guy. Which was why he was able to walk right up and join the conversation we were having about him." Bradley laughed. "Talk about some red faces."

Boyd grinned. He could see Josh doing that.

"Anyway, I never gave it much thought after that. Whatever he was doing in his spare time, it didn't impact what he did here at the news desk. He worked hard, learning the lay of the land, political sensitivities, historical background. He assimilated more information about us in the first two months than most New Brunswickers will ever know." He shook his head wonderingly. "I've never seen anything like it."

"Yeah, he was good at that," Boyd agreed. "And he'd changed jobs a few times, so it wouldn't have been the first time he had to come up to speed in a hurry."

"He really helped the rest of us up our game," Bradley said. "He'll be sorely missed, but he left us better than he found us."

That made Boyd's throat tighten. He cleared it. "So, would you mind if I give the cubicle a search myself?"

The other man's eyebrows lifted, but he said, "Not at all. Knock yourself out."

"Thank you." Boyd stood there, waiting for him to go.

Taking the hint at last, Bradley said, "Well, I'll leave you to it then."

With the reporter's departure, Boyd turned his attention to the cubicle. It was a short and fruitless search. Before five minutes had passed, he sat back in the chair, suppressing another sigh. *Dammit. No journal.* He'd looked in, under, and behind every drawer and every piece of furniture in the room.

He glanced up at the wall of cabinets beyond the warren of cubicles . . .

Nah, Josh wouldn't have stashed it in the cabinets. As Bradley had pointed out, he hadn't even used the storage space for the work-related notebooks. No way would he leave his personal notebook there.

"Detective McBride?"

Boyd glanced up to see a woman standing in the doorway. A beautiful woman. Late twenties, he figured. Maybe thirty. She was dressed demurely enough. In fact, apart from a few inches of slender leg below her cropped black trousers, there wasn't an inch of skin to be seen from her neck to her retro-looking heels. Yet the high-necked white blouse and the bright-yellow cardigan couldn't hide a knockout shape, and the shiny swing of precision-cut hair framed her face perfectly. She put him instantly in mind of the actresses in the old black-and-white movies his mother still liked to watch.

Belatedly, he stood and held out his hand. "That's right. I'm Josh's brother, Boyd. And you are?"

"Grace Morgan. I'm a reporter here. Josh was an inspiration and a mentor."

It clicked then. "You must be Detective Morgan's wife."

Her eyes widened. "You know Ray?"

"Just in the context of the investigation of Josh's death. But he mentioned you'd worked with Josh here."

"Of course." She blinked rapidly. "I just wanted to say how very sorry I am about Josh. He was an amazing reporter and an even more amazing person."

Seeing the sheen of tears in her eyes made his own eyes burn. "Thank you," he said gruffly.

She cleared her throat. "I also came to see if I could help. You seemed to be looking for something."

"A notebook. Specifically, the one I'm sure he must have kept in connection with his investigation into our birth parents.

I haven't been able to find it at his place. Everything there was work related."

Her brows drew together. "Is it a mininotepad with a sort of camel-colored leather-look cover?"

His heart rate bumped. "You know where it is?"

She shook her head. "Sorry, no. I don't even know if that's what he used it for. But I did occasionally see him pull it out. It was different than his usual preference."

"Yeah, he liked to rock a plain old steno pad," Boyd said, but his mind was spinning. A small leather-bound notebook! That had to be the one. It *did* exist.

Just then, Dave Bradley appeared in the doorway behind Grace Morgan.

"Hey, Grace," he said.

"Oh, hi, Dave."

Bradley turned his attention to Boyd. "No luck, I take it?"

"None," Boyd said. "But Mrs. Morgan was just saying that she'd seen Josh using a different notebook sometimes. A smaller pad, with a camel-colored leather or leatherlike binding. Do you remember seeing anything like that?"

"Nope," Bradley said. "But I can't say I pay a whole lot of attention to that kind of thing."

Grace laughed. "Come on, Dave. Just say it. I'm anal about details."

"A little." He chuckled, looking more relaxed than Boyd had seen him yet. "Do you really know what kind of notebook everyone uses?"

"Yep. Blueline Executive hardbacks for you," she replied. "Anselm likes those black, soft-sided pads that flip vertically, but smaller and thicker than a steno pad. I like my Martha Stewart black-and-white floral journal, and everyone else seems to pretty much rotate different kinds of pads."

Bradley whistled. "You called it right for me, at least. I'm Blueline all the way. But how do you *notice* these things?"

"Blame it on my husband. It started as an exercise to improve my observation skills, but now it's an ongoing challenge. I'm almost as good as he is, though he'd never admit it."

Boyd's ears perked up at that. "So, you've been honing your observation skills here at work?"

"Everywhere. And once you start noticing everything, you can't turn it off."

"Amen to that," he said. "No taking a holiday, is there?"

"Not even when you want to. It's useful and a blessing, I guess, but there are days when I notice things I wish I hadn't."

"Can you tell me if you noticed anything different about Josh the day he died? Or in the days leading up to his death?"

"I thought we might be headed there." She smiled sympathetically. "The thing I remember is what a great mood he seemed to be in that morning. I mean, he was always upbeat, energetic, enthusiastic, and all that. But he seemed especially . . . happy. Maybe even a little smug. That usually meant he'd found a new story and was really digging in. I even made a note of it." She lifted her shoulders in a half-embarrassed shrug. "I like to keep track of these things, so I can see how often my intuition steers me right. I wrote that I thought he was onto his next big story."

Boyd had to swallow before he could speak. "I think you were right again, Mrs. Morgan." And Boyd would lay odds what that story was. Proof of the identities of one or both of their birth parents.

Dave Bradley cleared his throat. "So, is there anything else we can do for you, Boyd? Grace and I are due in a meeting in a few minutes."

Boyd shook his head. "No, I think I've learned all I'm going to learn here. Thank you both."

And he had learned quite a bit, he reflected as he headed for his car with Josh's boxful of personal effects. As disappointed as he was at not finding the notebook, at least he now knew for certain that it existed and what it looked like.

He also knew his being there, searching the cubicle, and talking to Grace Morgan had unnerved Dave Bradley. Maybe it was as simple as the fact that Boyd was a cop. God knew the straightest, most stand-up citizen could get paranoid as fuck when they found themselves being followed by a marked squad car. Maybe Dave Bradley was that sort of guy.

Or maybe Mr. Bradley had something to be nervous about.

CHAPTER 8

Hayden found herself pacing—again—and planted herself on the couch with a huff of exasperation. God, what was wrong with her? You'd think this was a date, for God's sake. It was so not a date.

Despite the tough self-talk, she wanted to jump up and check her hair. With a grimace, she restrained the urge. Her hair was fine. She'd taken it down and shook it out like she did every night. And she'd never checked her hair for Josh.

Of course, she'd never put on her best Seven jeans and the dangly sea jasper earrings she'd scored at the market or slicked on a tinted lip gloss for Josh either.

Oh, crap! She needed to lose the earrings and the lip gloss. It sent the wrong message.

She leapt up to do just that, but the doorbell sounded. *Dammit. Too late.*

She opened the door with a quip ready on her lips about the veggie pizza and his macho image, but the words didn't come out. Instead, her breath caught. She'd been steeling herself against the man's sex appeal, but she'd forgotten to prepare herself for the shock of the similarities. He stood outside her apartment door dressed in jeans and a gray T-shirt, with a pizza in one hand and a six-pack of beer dangling from the other. God, he could be Josh, right down to the brand of beer—Molson Canadian in cans.

He caught her staring, and his eyes darkened. "We don't have to do this. It was probably a bad idea anyway."

Before he could leave, she grabbed his arm. "No, don't be silly. It was just the beer."

"Um . . . okay."

"Josh used to bring beer too. Same brand, always cans, never bottles. I had a little flashback is all." She stepped back. "Come on in."

He moved past her, and she caught the smell of some masculine grooming product. Not aftershave, judging by the slight stubble that darkened his face. Probably body wash. Before she could form any mental pictures, she closed the door.

"Is the pizza still hot or does it need to go into the oven for a while?"

"I guess that depends on how you like it."

She caught herself before she could say, "I like it hot." Instead she took the box from him, led him up the three steps to her kitchen, and plunked it on the counter. Then she popped the lid and checked the temperature.

"Still hot," she declared. "That means you must have made the beer run before the pizza run. Thank you for that."

"You're welcome. And I made a few other stops between the beer and the pizza, so the beer isn't as frosty as it should be. Maybe we could slide a couple in the freezer for a few minutes."

"Go ahead." She nodded to the refrigerator. "And put the others in the fridge. I'm good for two of them."

"I'll also be limiting it to two," he said. "The whole driving thing."

She was pretty sure a big guy like him could safely metabolize more than two alcoholic beverages over the course of a whole evening, especially with a pizza thrown in there, but she was glad to know he exercised moderation in that area. Like Josh. In all the months she'd known him, she'd rarely seen him have more than a couple of drinks.

He moved around her to stow the beer while she reached up into the cupboard for plates. Having him in her kitchen was *nothing* like having Josh there. She was too completely aware of him.

"Okay, if we're going to wait for the beer to cool, maybe I should stick this in the oven to keep it hot." She glanced up at him.

"Good by me," he said agreeably.

She turned the oven on, popped the pizza in, then leaned back against the counter. He did the same, several feet to her left. Her gaze slid sideways beneath her lashes, taking in the way his arms, which were folded across his chest, strained the sleeves of his T-shirt.

"So what are we watching again?" he asked. "A UFC match?"

Her head came up in horror. "No!"

He chuckled. "Sorry, couldn't resist. *Burn Notice*, right?"

She smiled. "Very funny."

"It's a good show. I watch it sometimes myself." He shoved both hands into the pockets of his low-riding jeans, an action that drew Hayden's attention to those long denim-clad legs. "I gather Josh liked it?"

"Liked it?" Hayden lifted her gaze. "That's an understatement. He just hated to see it end. We'd been rewatching season seven. You know, sometimes he used to narrate whole evenings, à la Michael Westen."

That drew a bark of laughter. "Really?"

"Really. He had the voice down pat. He used to crack me up with it." Heavy as her heart was, she couldn't help but smile remembering. There was something freeing about being able to talk about Josh. No one in Fredericton knew him like she did. His death had left her in such a state of shock, she couldn't talk about him. But now . . .

She understood why Boyd wanted to hear more about his brother's life here. It was a way to feel closer to him now that he was gone.

Tucking a lock of hair behind her ear, she continued. "And you never knew when Josh would whip the Westen voice out. 'The key to cutting up a cantaloupe is to cut it lengthwise first. Decisively.'" She gave her best imitation of Josh imitating the master spy character. "As with any job, you need the right tool if you want to come away clean. A carving knife, for instance. A cleaver will do in a pinch."

Boyd laughed. "You know, I can just hear him saying that."

Her smile trembled. "God, it's hard, him not being here. Sometimes I still reach for my phone when something funny happens or when I want to vent, but then I remember."

"I know." His voice dropped. "His death . . . it hasn't had time to integrate completely with that whole jumble of stuff that makes up my reality. I still wake up in the morning and have to remember it all again."

They stood there in silence for a few moments, apart but strangely together in this grief.

Hayden's throat ached with unshed tears. She swallowed a few times and cleared her throat. "So, how about that beer? Do you suppose it's cold enough now?"

"Definitely."

"I'll get the pizza."

She pulled the pie from the oven, dished a couple of slices onto each of the plates she'd laid out, grabbed a couple of paper towels for napkins, then led him to the living room.

"Nice," he said, taking a seat on the couch where she indicated.

She glanced around, trying to see her little apartment through his eyes. The furniture had actually been rented from one of those insta-home rental places so she wouldn't be stuck trying to sell it or move it when her residency was over. It was nice enough, she supposed. Very well coordinated and matchy and tasteful. Not at all what she'd do when she finally settled in one place.

"Thanks. It's rented."

"I kinda thought so, but I'm glad to hear you confirm it. It strikes me as a little . . . generic for you."

"Yeah. Home Decor 101." She plunked their plates down on the glass-topped coffee table. "So, Mr. Smart Guy Detective, what's my style, then?"

He shrugged, putting her beer down beside her plate of pizza. "I figure when you finally get where you want to be, you'll feather your permanent nest very carefully, very deliberately, with individual pieces. Some antiques, maybe. Some modern pieces. Stuff that speaks to you." He popped the top on his beer. "How'd I do?"

"Pretty damned good," she responded honestly. "And I can't *wait*. I've lived in dorms and rented rooms and apartments like this for so long, when I finally get a place of my own, I'm going to make it completely mine. It's going to have color and energy and joy, and it probably won't flow seamlessly, and there won't be a lick of beige anywhere. There'll be peaceful places too—the bathroom and the bedroom have to be tranquil. And, yes, I'll pick each piece of furniture, each lamp, each rug and faucet and fixture with a view to how happy it makes me to look at it." She picked up her own beer, snapped the tab, and took a sip.

His expression was slightly smug. And okay, he'd nailed it. But all that took was a little insight into human psychology.

"Shall I take a guess at what your place looks like?"

She put her beer down while he picked up a piece of pizza.

"Condo, I'm guessing, since Josh mentioned you'd been at this job quite a few years."

He nodded.

"Not totally Spartan but efficient. Militarily efficient. And nothing messy." She kept her eyes on his face, gauging his reaction, but he gave nothing away. *Great poker face.* "Big furniture," she continued. "Big flat-screen TV with theater-quality stereo sound. No houseplants, but maybe some art? Something really strong."

His brow furrowed momentarily, then relaxed. "Josh told you about it."

She grinned. "Nope. But he did talk about you a lot." She picked up her pizza and took a bite. "Mmm, this is so good. Thank you. Isn't that crust awesome?"

"It's good," he acknowledged.

"Told you."

"But it'd still taste better with some Italian sausage."

She rolled her eyes. "Okay, next time you can have sausage on your half."

Something stirred in those golden eyes, but then was gone before she could analyze it. Was it the mention of next time?

She cleared her throat. "So, what's this strong piece of art you figured Josh told me about?"

His expression was curious now. "He really didn't tell you about the Sam Shea?"

"What's a Sam Shea?"

"It's a giant photographic landscape of ominous darks clouds over a marsh. The photographer printed it out in huge panels, and the panels fit together to make a massive mural."

She shook her head. "That's a freaking gallery installation. I bet it's lovely."

"I like it." Having finished up his first slice of pizza, he picked up a second one. "So, what time's the show on?"

"Oh, it's DVR'd, not live. It's ready when we are." She glanced at him. "Are we ready?"

He shrugged. "What would you and Josh do?"

"We'd talk about our respective days."

"So you'd tell him about stuff that happened at the ER, and he'd talk about his investigations?"

"Pretty much, insofar as we could without naming names or breaching anyone's privacy."

"But not his personal investigation?"

"No." She shook her head. "He didn't talk too much about it, except maybe to say things were going well or certain avenues hadn't panned out. Just generalities. Sometimes he'd tell me stuff about you."

His left eyebrow lifted. "What kind of stuff?"

"You know, if you'd been involved in a particularly big or media-worthy bust. That kind of thing." She smiled. "He talked about some of the stuff you guys pulled as identical twins."

He actually blushed. "Oh, God, the hockey game."

She laughed. "The one on TV that you didn't want to leave, so you sent Josh to meet your girlfriend at the bar and keep her occupied until you could get there?"

"In my defense, it looked like the Leafs might actually make the play-offs. And how was I to know she'd pick that night to decide we should finally do it?"

"Poor Josh."

"Poor *Josh*? Thanks to his impassioned we-should-wait-for-our-three-month-anniversary speech, I had to wait. Two. More. Months."

She dissolved in a fit of giggling. "I'm sorry," she said as she wiped the tears from her eyes. "You got what you deserved, buster. Sending a stand-in."

"Yeah, you're right. I never did that again. But I did threaten to mess things up with his girlfriend-of-the-day. You know, committing to taking them jewelry shopping or something. He told me not to bother, because they had a code word she would ask him to say if she thought he was acting strange."

"Omigod! Is that true?"

"Probably, but I never tested it."

Her face sobered. "He told me about what happened when you guys were in grade two."

Boyd's smile disappeared. "Yeah?"

"He said it was really hard on you."

"Not just me." He raked a hand through his hair. "When I couldn't find him on the playground after school—we were in different classes, but we always met up to walk home together—I was sick. I didn't know enough to run into the school and tell the principal. Instead, I ran home and told our mother. She called the school, who confirmed he wasn't there, and then called my father's employer. Dad rushed home from the construction site. I'd never seen him look like that."

"You must have been terrified."

"Scared shitless." He turned the now empty beer can round and round in his hand. "Of course, the police were called, and they started a neighborhood search. They finally found him on a door-to-door canvass, but it wasn't until the following morning. I think my parents aged ten years in those sixteen hours."

"And all along, he was with the old lady with Alzheimer's, just a few blocks from the school."

"Yeah. She was confused. When she saw him outside the school waiting for me, she thought he was her son and took him home. Never mind that her son was then a forty-eight-year-old career officer in the Canadian army, stationed in Alberta."

"Josh said he was never really scared, even when he couldn't find a phone. He knew she was just confused and missed her son. And because she made him do his lessons, he knew she'd send him back to school in the morning. But the cops got there first, right?"

"Yeah. And Josh was so upset with them for arresting the old lady. But they were heroes to me. Those officers saved the day, saved my brother from a kidnapper."

"Is that why you went into law enforcement?"

He nodded. "Absolutely. From that day forward, that's pretty much all I wanted to do."

"Wow, one event, and it inspired two identical twins to go down two very different paths."

He frowned. "What do you mean?"

"Josh says that experience taught him that things aren't always as they seem. That lady wasn't a criminal, but a confused person suffering from dementia. He said that was probably the first event in his life that made him think about the story behind the story."

"He never told me that." Boyd looked down at his empty beer can. "I guess I probably should have figured it out for myself."

"Well, it's not as obvious as your epiphany. What boy wouldn't want to become a policeman after that?"

"Josh, apparently." He stopped fiddling with the can and put it on the coffee table. "I thought the whole desire to go into journalism was because of his affinity for the people who never really fit in. You know, championing the underdog, fighting injustice, showing people the other side. I swear, if there was a weird, ostracized kid on the playground, Josh would find them and befriend them. I had a full-time job keeping the bullies off his back."

"See? You were already playing your roles."

It made so much sense now, Boyd's worldview as compared with Josh's. Oh, personality accounted for a big part of it; she was sure. Just because they were genetic duplicates didn't mean their personalities should be identical, or even alike. But she could see so clearly how that traumatic event would have shaped them differently. Being on the inside and knowing he'd be free by morning, Josh had had it easier. His family would have thought the worst. She could see how Boyd would have emerged with a conviction that the world was a dangerous place, while Josh took something entirely different away from the experience.

"Yeah, I guess so."

Time for a subject change. Hopefully something not so heavy.

"He used to talk about your parents a lot too. I gather he spoke to them every day. I was there once when he Skyped with them. After that, your mother would always tell him to say hi to me."

"Why does that not surprise me?" he drawled. "I expect she was hoping Josh would present her with a daughter-in-law and eventually some grandchildren."

At his words, Hayden felt a hollow space open up in her gut. If anyone deserved to have children, to be a parent, it was Josh. Not with *her*, obviously, but with someone he was crazy about. He'd have been so good at it. What a waste. What a tragic, senseless waste.

"Shit, I'm sorry." Boyd's voice was a low throb. "I did it again. I'll just shut up now."

"Don't be silly." She tipped her head back and blinked rapidly. "We have to be able to talk about him or this won't work."

"True."

"Besides, it's hard . . . but it's also good. Does that make sense?"

He nodded gravely and held her gaze. "I know."

They stayed that way for a few intense moments. Breaking eye contact, she picked up the DVR remote control. "Let's watch the show now. It'll make us feel better."

It did. They ate their pizza, and Hayden drank her beer. Partway through, she paused the program so Boyd could get himself two more slices—the thin crust might be tasty, but he declared it not very filling, especially with no Italian sausage—and two more cans of beer for them. Afterward, Hayden clicked the TV off.

"This is where our night would typically end," she said. "Well, not this early, because we'd do the catch-up and just veg a little before watching the show. But that's basically it."

"And he'd just go home?"

"Uh-huh. Straight back to his room at Dr. Stratton's. He'd always text me when he got there, so I could stop worrying about him."

"Worrying about him?" That left eyebrow rose again and he laughed. "Hayden, from here to Dr. Stratton's would be . . . what? . . . eight or nine kilometers? In city traffic?"

"You sound like Josh now," she said. "He thought it was pretty funny too when I asked him to do that. Yet when I was at his place watching a show, he always insisted *I* call or text *him* to let him know when I got home."

"But that's different."

"Because I'm a woman, you mean?"

Boyd shrugged. "Well, yeah."

"That's what Josh said too." She sighed. "And, yes, it's true. It's grossly unfair and completely deplorable, but, yes, because

I'm a woman, I stand a much greater chance of being assaulted when I'm minding my own damned business than you do. But when it comes to an impaired driver blowing through a red light and T-boning your car, in my experience, it doesn't matter what sex you are. And as for accidents at city intersections, just two weeks ago we had multiple trauma—"

"Whoa, whoa." He held up a hand to stop her. "I get it. You don't have to convince me. I've attended my fair share of urban MVAs. And I'm sorry for laughing. I just wasn't thinking of how your front-row seat to all that trauma would affect the way you look at everything, including a crosstown commute. Josh could've told you I'm not sensitive that way." He smiled, but it looked sad. "Not particularly empathetic."

She wanted to put her hand on his where it rested on his leg and squeeze it. She wanted to see the sorrow chased from those golden eyes. A little freaked out at the impulse, she picked up her empty beer can and fiddled with it.

"No big deal," she said. "It's not like I look for things to worry about." She pretended to drink a last swig from the can and put it back on the table. "It really wouldn't have driven me crazy with anxiety if Josh hadn't agreed to check in. It's not like I'd have lost sleep or anything. I don't know how to describe it. I guess you could liken it to some kind of little program running in the background of my brain. It's just *there*. When he checked in to say he was home, it could shut off, you know?"

He rubbed his jaw, and the distinctly masculine rasping sound of a calloused hand running over beard stubble sent a shiver through her.

"I can't say I do," he admitted. "I guess we don't have the same software."

She laughed. "I think that's a safe bet, Detective."

His answering grin was her reward. Then his gaze dropped to her mouth, and she stopped smiling. So did he.

"Well, I should shove off and let you get your rest," he said, pushing to his feet.

She jumped up too, busying herself by picking up the plates and napkins. Boyd collected the four empty cans and followed her to the kitchen with them.

A moment later, she walked him to the door. He had his hand on the doorknob, ready to leave, when he turned back. Hayden's heart took a bounding leap, then fell to hammering in her chest. Was he going to kiss her?

"I almost forgot to ask," he said. "Do you recall ever seeing Josh with a leather-bound notebook? It would have been camel-colored."

Her eyes widened. "That's a very specific description."

"One of his coworkers, Grace Morgan, confirmed he carried one like that sometimes. I figure that's gotta be the journal he was keeping about his investigation into our birth parents."

She frowned. "I was going to say I hadn't seen it, but actually I might have. It was fairly compact and definitely leather-bound. Soft leather. Although the one I saw I would have described as more buttery yellow than camel. Of course, it was night . . ."

"That sounds like the one," he said, his expression tightening with eagerness. *Not such a poker face after all. At least not when it comes to Josh.* "Where'd you see it?"

"In the glove compartment of his car. We were coming back from supper on a holiday weekend and got stopped at one of those routine checkpoints. You know, where they look for impaired drivers, seat belt infractions, inspection stickers, and the like. Anyway, he asked me to dig the registration out of the glove box. That's where I saw it. I hauled it out along with road maps and the car's manual and napkins and everything else that was in there."

"Have you seen it since?"

"No, I never saw it again." She hated to have to say it, watching that new hope fade from his eyes. "Odd that the cops didn't find it." She didn't add, "Since he died in that car." She didn't have to.

"He wouldn't have stored it there permanently," he said. "Too easy to break into a car. Or steal the whole car, for that matter."

She blinked. "Someone would steal a *notebook* out of a car?"

"These are usually addicts. Typically, a 'car shopper' will grab whatever they can—loose change or anything small enough to shove in their pockets or put in a backpack. Stuff they can sell quickly. If it's small enough, they'll grab it, then evaluate it when they've put a little distance between themselves and the crime. We always tell people to search the immediate neighborhood when their car gets broken into. The bag the thief thought might contain something they can sell for drug money turns out to have a wet bathing suit and a soggy towel, or diapers and baby wipes. Or the stuff they scooped out of the glove box or console turns out to be a leather-bound notebook, not a wallet. The thief often dumps the unwanted stuff within a few blocks." He sighed. "Guess I'll go back to looking at Dr. Stratton's."

"You've checked his room?"

"As thoroughly as I know how," he said. "If Josh hid it there, he did a damned good job of it."

"You know, Josh might have locked it in his glove compartment that day, especially since he was only going for a short jog. And if he did, maybe his car got broken into while he was off jogging. That would account for the missing phone. You said there was a market for stolen phones, right? And maybe they thought the notebook was one of those wallets that hold a passport and wads of money or something. I know it's a stretch to think something like that happened at just the right time before his death, but I've heard of weirder things."

"There was no evidence of a break-in, though, and we know Josh always locked his car. While that probably rules out straight theft, it doesn't rule out foul play. Someone could still have killed him just as he got back inside his car, then made off with his phone and journal."

Hayden's heart contracted painfully. "Do you believe that?"

"That's what my gut is telling me."

"But how?"

Boyd sighed. "They could have come upon him when he'd unlocked the car and got in, but hadn't yet turned the ignition on or engaged the locks."

"Oh, God." She put her hand to her mouth.

"He probably reached for a bottle of water and a towel to mop his sweaty face. That would give them some time."

"To what? How could they cause him to arrest on the spot?"

His lips thinned. "Stun gun."

She flinched.

"Sorry," he said. "This is gruesome, I know. But I've been racking my brain and that's what I keep coming back to."

"They're considered a prohibited weapon here, aren't they?"

"Absolutely. But we seize more and more of them every year. They're easy to order online, and if they're not properly marked on the customs declaration, they can slip past the border."

Hayden blinked. "Wait . . . if they Tasered him, wouldn't it have left marks to be found on autopsy? I've seen exactly two Tasered patients come through, and they always have puncture wounds from the darts."

"Police incidents?"

She nodded.

"Most people who go in for these things tend to carry small, easily concealed stun guns, not police-type TASERs. Some are as small as a cell phone. None of them use darts. They're for close-up self-defense. You pull the trigger to make electricity arc between the metal prongs, then apply it directly to the attacker's skin or clothing. That kind of contact stun doesn't leave puncture wounds or bruises, and unless it's applied directly to the skin, it probably wouldn't even leave a mark."

"What kind of mark? A burn, I suppose?"

"Yeah, when it's used directly on the skin, it can leave a minor burn the same width as the space between the prongs."

"Because the electricity arcs between the two prongs."

"Exactly."

"But not if it was applied through clothing?"

He nodded. "I suppose there might be a bit of a red mark, but not necessarily. And unlike the TASER, it doesn't make the muscles seize up and immobilize the target, but rather relies on overwhelming pain."

"Omigod." She placed her hand on her chest, wondering what that kind of shock would feel like. If Josh were sitting in his car and someone opened his door and applied that shock to his chest . . . "Could the stun gun be fired repeatedly?"

"Oh, yeah."

"I know the literature is inconclusive on electroshock weapons, but I would think that a jolt like that, especially if delivered close to the heart, could easily cause a fatal arrhythmia in someone with LQTS or some other kind of electrical problem. Maybe even someone with a perfectly *normal* heart, especially if they'd been jogging. Josh would have been hot and tired after his run, needing to replace electrolytes . . ." She looked up at him, horrified. "That could really have happened."

"Yeah." He raked a hand through his close-cropped hair, leaving it standing up. "It's getting harder and harder to believe anything other than foul play. The missing phone is really troubling. And now there's been definite confirmation of the existence of a journal, which we've yet to be able to locate."

"Have you raised the stun gun possibility with Detective Morgan?"

He shook his head. "Not yet. Nor have I told him that both his wife and you can attest to having seen that journal. But I've got a call in to him."

"I'd so much prefer to think it was natural causes, and that someone stole that stuff out of his car. I know that can't be, because he'd have locked—" Hayden's eyes widened.

"What?"

"The back door on the passenger side—the lock wasn't working consistently. We noticed it not long ago when I opened the back door and threw my gear in the backseat before he clicked the locks open. He said he'd make an appointment to get that fixed, but I don't know whether he ever got it done."

"I'll have Morgan look into that, whether the lock works. The car is still at the impound lot."

She looked up at him, trying to decipher his expression, but she couldn't tell whether he thought that was good or bad news. "If it's still on the fritz, doesn't that mean someone could have stolen his things while he was running?"

"Or someone might have slipped into his backseat."

Her heart jumped. Oh, God, he was right.

"But it does raise the possibility that it was a simple theft," he said. "And if so, once the thief realized it was a notebook and not a wallet, they'd probably dump it before they got too far away. When Morgan calls me back, I'll see what they can do. They already used the police K-9 to search the trails for his phone in case he dropped it during his run, but they wouldn't have searched the park exits or treed perimeters. Maybe they'll agree to do another search to see if the notebook turns up."

"I hope that's what happened," she said, hearing the tremor in her voice. "It's bad enough thinking Josh might have died from natural causes. If someone killed him . . ."

Boyd swore softly. "I've upset you again. I shouldn't have brought that stuff up, especially just before bedtime."

"It's okay." She shook her head. "I mean, if someone killed him—"

"If someone killed him, I'll see them brought to justice. You can bet on it."

Looking at him just then, Hayden was inclined to believe him.

"Good night, Hayden. Try to think of more pleasant things."

"I'll try."

He held out his hand. Hayden automatically extended her own hand and it was swallowed in his larger one. He shook it once, then released it. She knew it was more than a good night. It was a promise. If someone were responsible for Josh's death, he'd find them.

"Good night, Boyd."

Fifteen minutes later, with her apartment tidied, face washed, and teeth brushed and flossed, she was ready to crawl into bed. Then her phone buzzed. Picking it up off the charger pad, she looked at it.

It was a text message from Boyd. And it read, *Home safe.*

She laughed out loud and texted back a *Thx!*

CHAPTER 9

"Thanks, Morgan. Meet you there in twenty."

As Boyd terminated the call and put his phone down on the polished walnut table, Dr. Sylvia Stratton came up by his right elbow. "Orange juice?"

"Please. That fresh-squeezed stuff is amazing. But you don't have to wait on me. I can serve myself."

"No problem. I was getting a refill myself." After filling his juice glass, she topped up her own, then sat. "Did you enjoy the eggs?"

"I did, ma'am. And you might be onto something with the free-range thing. Much tastier."

"No surprise that a healthy free-range hen produces a superior egg." She slipped on her reading glasses and picked up the newspaper, although she made no move to go back to reading it.

"And it's not just tastier, but more nutrient rich and antibiotic-free. Same with grass-fed beef. The beef is actually much richer in omega-3 fatty acids than its grain-fed counterpart."

"What about free-range pork?" he said hopefully, although he already knew there was no bacon, ham, or sausage available. Dr. Stratton probably frowned on those things. "Is that superior too?"

She lowered her head to slant him a reproving glance over the black-framed reading glasses. "No doubt, but I don't serve smoked or cured meats, Mr. McBride. The nitrates are very bad for one's health."

"Of course."

"Have you tried the fish? It really is excellent, and the punch of omega-3 gets you off to a good start."

He managed to suppress a grimace. "I haven't quite developed a taste for fish at breakfast yet."

"Yes, it's a bit of an acquired taste," she allowed. "Your brother wasn't much of a fan of it either."

Boyd went back to eating his breakfast, but he noticed Dr. Stratton still hadn't gone back to her paper.

"So, how's it going? Your ... investigation, for lack of a better word, of your brother's last days?"

"Fine." He tossed back the orange juice, then reached for his coffee. If he was going to meet Morgan on time, he'd have to haul ass. "I'm getting to know his friends and coworkers. And you, of course. This house. Sort of reconstructing his time here."

"And was the Morgan you were arranging to meet just now Detective Morgan?"

He looked up, surprised. "Yes." He put his coffee cup back down. "I guess he interviewed you, didn't he?"

"Yes, he did. He seems a very respectable sort."

She didn't add, "For a policeman," but Boyd heard it just the same. And he could see where she'd be favorably impressed by

Morgan's hundred-dollar haircut and tailored suits. And something told Boyd that Morgan could turn on the charm when he chose.

"Yes, he seems to be a good man," Boyd said. He thought about telling her what they were going to do this morning, then reeled himself back in. The fewer people who knew, the better. According to Ray Morgan, even the employees at the park had only been told it was a routine training exercise for the K-9. No point getting people stirred up. "He's indulging me by going over Josh's file again."

She smiled. "Well, don't let me keep you."

"Yes, ma'am." He swallowed the last of his coffee and stood to go.

"Detective?"

He turned back to the table.

"Would you care to take coffee to your meeting? I have takeaway cups, and I do seem to recall Detective Morgan was partial to my organic coffee with almond milk."

Ha! He was right. The lofty Dr. Stratton might be devoted to her ailing husband, but she'd obviously taken a shine to Pretty Boy Morgan. Not that he could blame her. Plenty of women went in for that refined, urbane look.

He grinned. "Are you kidding me? He'd love that."

"Then go get ready. I'll put on fresh coffee and dig out a pair of take-out cups."

"Could you stretch it to three?" he asked. "I think one of Morgan's colleagues will be there."

"Of course."

Her smile never faltered, but he sensed she wasn't pleased he didn't offer more explanation. Or maybe she wanted an explanation of who the third party was. Too bad for her.

"Almond milk for Detective Morgan, cream for you . . . And how shall I make the third one?"

Boyd suppressed a smile. Yep, she was dying to know who the other party was. Had Morgan brought someone else with him when he'd interviewed her? Well, someone other than a uniformed cop? Sylvia Stratton would never take notice of a mere patrolman. Maybe it was Morgan's sergeant, John Quigley. And if she had met Quigley, she'd have formed an entirely different impression about him than she had for Morgan. The sergeant's suits weren't just off-the-rack, they looked like they'd been trampled *under* the rack.

When Boyd came back downstairs seven minutes later, she had three coffees in cardboard cups with tight-fitting covers. In lieu of a take-out tray, she'd stood them in a tall plastic storage container, the kind Boyd used to store plastic lids in until he got so frustrated by never being able to find the right lid that he threw them all away and started again with new containers.

"Be careful with that," she admonished. "That's a lot of hot liquid."

Had Dr. Stratton fussed this way over Josh? And how had he received it? Graciously, no doubt. Boyd would make an effort to do the same. "Yes, ma'am."

Fifteen minutes later, he rolled into the parking lot at Odell Park. The K-9 unit, a big Ford Expedition, sat idling in the lot, air conditioner running for the dog, while Ray Morgan and a tall, lean woman in summer uniform stood several feet away in the shade.

"You're late," Morgan said.

"Yeah, but you'll forgive the five extra minutes when you see what I brought."

His eyes lit up. "Starbucks?"

"Better." Boyd opened the rented Altima's back door and retrieved the container with the coffees from where he'd propped them behind the driver's seat. "Sylvia Stratton sends her regards."

"Organic custom grind," he breathed reverently. "With organic almond milk?"

"Yeah, she remembered." Boyd handed Ray the cup with the lid marked *A* for almond. "You must have made an impression on her."

He shrugged. "She just appreciates people who appreciate quality."

"Quite," he mimicked Dr. Stratton's voice.

Morgan laughed. "That's a pretty good imitation of her." Then he turned to the officer at his side. "Anders, this is Detective Boyd McBride of the Toronto Police Service Homicide Squad. McBride, this is Constable Lori Anders, our K-9 handler."

She nodded at him. "Sorry for your loss."

"Thank you." He shook the hand she extended to him. Her grip was firm, lacking any bullshit. He liked her right away. "How do you feel about black coffee, Anders?"

"Only way to drink it. Especially if it's as good as he seems to think." She nodded her head toward Ray Morgan.

"Oh, it is." Boyd handed her the unmarked cup and took the last one, which Sylvia had helpfully marked *C* for cream.

"I'll just leave this for after," she said, parking the cup on the roof of the Expedition. "We should get right to this in case I get another call."

"Are you the only K-9 handler on duty?" he asked.

"I'm the only K-9 handler *on staff*," she replied.

Boyd's jaw dropped. "The only one?" Police Dog Services in Toronto was its own department with more than twenty handlers.

"Yup. But Max and I like being busy." She opened the door, clipped the dog to its leash, and let him jump out.

Boyd liked dogs but knew better than to touch this one while it was on duty. It needed to stay focused. This was a Belgian Malinois, he noted, not the classic German shepherd.

"What do you do for vacation?" Boyd asked, still astonished that there could be only one K-9 team.

"The RCMP K-9 unit covers for me," she said. "We do a lot of training together, back each other up." The dog looked up at her expectantly, and she scratched his ears. "So we're just going to do an article search. You're familiar with what that is?"

Boyd nodded. The dog would be directed to search a specified area and would alert on anything and everything that didn't belong. In a natural environment like this, that usually meant finding a lot of gum wrappers, discarded Tim Hortons cups, McDonald's wrappers, and the like. It was a task they drilled for endlessly, no doubt, so that the canine would find that knife dropped by a fleeing assailant, or a gun, or spent shell casings, or a discarded burner phone, or, in this case, a stolen journal.

Boyd and Ray stood back while Lori Anders put her dog to work. Over the next forty minutes, dog and handler had covered the most probable spots for a thief to have jettisoned the journal. Each time Max alerted on something, she praised him lavishly, but Boyd knew the "finds" were not what they'd been hoping for. When they finished, the handler congratulated the dog and rewarded him by tossing him a Kong. The dog snatched it up, gleeful as a puppy.

The handler joined them, handing Morgan a clear plastic bag full of mainly trash. Boyd's slim hopes faded.

Morgan took the evidence bag from her, turning it over in his hands. "A china plate and real forks?"

"I've seen odder finds." Anders shrugged. "My guess is some young Romeo was impressing his date, sweetening her up with a piece of cheesecake or something he nabbed from his mother's fridge, then left everything behind afterward."

"Afterward?" Boyd asked.

She shrugged again. "Max found a used condom within tossing distance."

Morgan shook his head. "No respect for fine china. Some woman is probably still looking for that missing plate."

Despite his disappointment, Boyd couldn't suppress a smile at Ray Morgan's doleful expression.

"If there's nothing more I can do, I'll take off. There's some paperwork I have to turn in."

"We're good, Lori. Thanks."

"Yes, thank you, Constable," Boyd said. "And thank you, Detective."

Anders said her good-byes, stowed her dog, rescued her coffee from the roof of the vehicle, and drove off.

Morgan turned to face him. "It was a good thought, McBride. Worth a shot. And I'm sorry we didn't pick up on that rear passenger door lock earlier."

"It was practically a new car. Who'd have thought?" Boyd rubbed the back of his neck. "It does open the possibility that the phone and the journal were simply stolen. But it also means someone could have slipped into that backseat and been waiting for him. Or maybe they approached just as he got into the car and before he keyed the ignition or activated the locks."

"And did what?"

"He might have been hit with a stun gun."

Morgan's eyebrows soared. "Now there's a thought. Although the jury's out on whether those little stun guns do anything more than piss off would-be assailants. They don't even stop people from struggling like a TASER shot does. From what I've read, he might have been just as likely to get out of the car and lay an ass-whooping on his attacker."

"I don't know. Dr. Walsh seemed to think it could be fatal if someone had an underlying electrical issue. She also said it might cause a fatal arrhythmia even in someone with a normal heart if they got multiple shocks to the chest area. And if they'd been running in the heat, like Josh, and their electrolytes were out of whack."

Ray Morgan eyed Boyd. "The problem with that theory is it's impossible to prove. No eyewitnesses, no camera footage, and no evidence on autopsy."

Boyd knew that, but his gut still twisted to hear it. "I know. I'll just have to keep digging. I'll bring you more."

"I'll keep digging too," Morgan said. "But frankly, if anyone can crack this, it's probably you. You know your twin like no one else could. Hell, you've already uncovered a couple of things we'd never have known. That faulty lock, for instance. And the journal. Nice work."

"Thanks. By the way, I met your wife yesterday. She's one observant lady."

"I know." His pride in her shone in his face, making him look suddenly younger, almost boyish. "She's a natural. Don't tell her I said this, but she might even be better than me."

Boyd snorted. "I think that ship's sailed."

Morgan's grin only widened.

"So where are you with talking to doctors?"

"Still working my way through the ob-gyns."

Boyd frowned. "How many can there be in a town this size? A dozen or so?"

"At this moment? Yeah. But you and your brother weren't bounced out yesterday. We're talking thirty-five years ago.

Doctors come and go, and they die too. Gotta figure out who took over the practice, where the records landed, and all that."

"And you're not just asking about twins with the surname Holbrook?"

Morgan cocked his head. "You're seriously asking me that?"

Boyd held his gaze.

The other man sighed. "Well, since you told me from the get-go that the birth record was probably falsified and Holbrook might or might not be your birth mother's name, the answer would be yes. I've been beating the bushes for anything that looks like it could be a match. All male twins born anywhere near your birth date, under any name, who were whisked away for adoption at birth. Satisfied?"

"Sorry. Just had to make sure."

"I know. I'm just cranky about my lack of progress."

"Know that feeling." Boyd drained the rest of his coffee. "I'm hoping I can get my hands on Josh's cell phone records any day now. I put in a request as next of kin last week, but you know how it can be."

Morgan perked up. "Good. You told me you'd do that when you realized the phone was missing."

"Yeah, took a while to get the paperwork in order with the lawyer back in Ontario, to prove I'm the trustee."

"Think they'll give them to you?"

"They have to, eventually. After they make sure all the i's are dotted and the t's crossed from a legal standpoint."

"What'll they give you for calling detail records in a case like that? Do you know?"

"Yeah, I talked to the privacy ombudsman. The CDRs I'll get will be limited to only outgoing numbers that Josh dialed, with no incoming phone numbers."

"So for the incoming stuff, it'll be basically date, time, and duration of the call?"

"Yup. Unless we can produce a court order, there's no way to get at an incoming caller's phone number or identity."

"Well, I'd call the outgoing numbers a damned good start. A fucking treasure trove, compared to what we have now. He must have made lots of outgoing calls in connection with his investigation."

"I'll keep after them and will share when I get it. Meanwhile, I intend to keep poking around."

"Great. I could use the help. And if the evidence is out there, we'll find it."

Boyd managed a gruff, "Thanks."

"Just remember what I said. If people start complaining about the hotshot Toronto cop doing our jobs for us, my ass'll be in a sling. And you know what that means."

Boyd knew exactly what he meant. One call to the mayor or the police chief from a citizen with ruffled feathers, and the crap would begin to roll downhill, gathering speed until it came to a splattering stop at the detective's doorstep. And from there it wouldn't be long before it landed on Boyd's boss's desk.

"Understood."

CHAPTER 10

Back at the house, Boyd found himself at loose ends.

He'd gone for a run shortly after leaving Detective Morgan. Since then, he'd had his second shower of the day and called his parents. Of course, when he'd come to Fredericton, he hadn't told Frank and Ella McBride what he was up to. He hadn't wanted to add to their pain.

They'd cried when he'd broken the news of Josh's death to them, a deed he hoped would stand as the hardest thing he would ever have to do. Despite their shock and shattering grief, they'd both soldiered through the visitations and the funeral. They'd been touched to see the genuine outpouring of grief from so many people and had been grateful to meet Hayden.

The days afterward had been very dark, though. His father, ever solicitous of Ella's comfort, safety, and well-being, had tried to keep some semblance of normalcy going, but his mother had been impervious to his attempts. In those days, she'd walked around like a ghost, hollowed out by the loss of her son. Of course, after a few days, Frank McBride gave up and retreated into his own silence. Fortunately, Ella had come around, at least enough to see to meals and make sure Frank took his medication. She was a nurturer at heart, always had been. When she'd seen her husband sinking under his own grief, she'd responded. She was needed, and therefore she would rise to the challenge.

Damn, he'd hated leaving them. Hated lying about where he was going too. But he'd had to. Knowing he was here, digging into Josh's last days because he thought he'd been murdered would definitely pain them. So he'd told them he was taking a long-overdue vacation. A fishing trip, he'd told them, since that was the only type of vacation he ever took.

Ella had answered on the third ring. Yes, he was relaxing. No, he hadn't caught anything really camera-worthy yet, but it was early days. No, they didn't have high-speed Internet, so he couldn't Skype, but cellular service was good, and he'd call more often.

He felt like crap when he finally hung up. They seemed so frail since Josh's death. They were both in their early seventies, having adopted him and Josh when they were just a few years older than Boyd now was. He'd never thought of them as frail before. Sure, Frank had degenerative disc disease and his joints complained now and then and he took meds to control his cholesterol and high blood pressure, and Ella had a thyroid condition, but somehow he'd never really even thought of them as *old*. But in their grief, they seemed so now.

Maybe he shouldn't have left them so soon. But to delay any longer . . . the trail was cold as it was. And they did have a home care worker who checked in on them three times a week, made up a few meals, and dealt with the laundry. Physically, they'd be all right.

He leapt up off the chair. Dammit, he needed to do something to get him closer to an answer. And he had to do it *right fucking now*! But what? Until he got those call detail records, he didn't have anything solid to work from. And the journal . . . it had probably gone the way of Josh's phone, but even if it hadn't, he'd already torn the room apart. He'd talked to Hayden. He'd talked to Josh's landlady. He'd talked to Josh's coworkers and put his head together with Detective Morgan.

He reached for his phone again. It was just past noon. Hayden would be working and would have her phone turned off. But he could still text her. Forcing himself to sit down at the table again, he pecked out a text message. *Can we do something tonight?*

No sooner did he put his phone away than it rang. He pulled it out. Hayden.

He hit the button to answer the call. "Wow, that was quick."

"I'm still on my lunch break," she said. "Has something come up? When I saw your message—"

"No." He bent forward, elbows on the table, one hand propping up his head, the other holding the phone to his ear. "Kind of a disappointing morning, actually." He told her about the K-9 search at the park and coming up empty. "The truth is, I just talked to my parents, who think I left them to take a vacation because I didn't want to tell them I think Josh was deliberately killed. And the investigation . . . I'm expecting the phone company to send me some call records from Josh's cell phone activity."

"That's good, isn't it? Really good."

"It probably won't hand us answers on a platter because it won't give us incoming numbers, but the outgoing numbers should help us retrace some of Josh's steps. Enough to point us in the right direction, hopefully. So there's reason for optimism that we can figure this out."

"But?"

"But at the same time, there's this unrelenting voice in my head saying if I don't make something break soon, it'll be too late."

"Sounds like you need to take a break."

"Maybe." He dragged a hand through his hair. "No, it's not even really that. I think I just want to feel closer to Josh, you know? For a while last night, when we were talking, I kind of did."

"Me too," she said softly. Then, in a stronger voice, "So what are we doing tonight? Want to come over to my place again? I'm not much of a cook, but I could probably rustle up—"

"No." He cleared his throat. "Let's do something different. Something else you and Josh used to do."

"But someplace we can still talk?"

"Yeah."

After a pause, she said, "Do you having swimming trunks?"

"No, but I can get some in a hurry."

"Then I think you should pick me up after work and we'll go to Killarney Lake for a swim."

"You guys used to get away to a lake after work on a *weeknight*? There might be something to this laid-back Atlantic lifestyle. I bet all the medical residents want to come here."

"Hey, I'll have you know I put in twelve hours most days. Today I'll have worked from seven to seven."

"So how do you fit in a jaunt to the lake? Wouldn't it be dark by the time you got there?"

"Ah, I get it."

His eyebrows drew together. "Get what?"

"It's not that kind of lake. It's more of a large pond, shall we say. Okay, not even really that large a pond. But it's really close.

Yeah, the water can be a little on the cool side by the time I get there, but on the upside, the crowd is thinner and you don't need to slather up with sunscreen."

"Do you work twelve-hour shifts in the ER every day?"

"They're not all twelves. Sometimes it's an eight-hour day, like the other night when I met you for dinner."

"So when you're done, you'll be what? An emergency room doctor?"

"I'm in an integrated family medicine/emergency residency, and when I'm done, I'll be a family physician who's equipped to do cover shifts in the ER. Right now, I happen to be doing an ER rotation, but I'm actually splitting my time between the ER and a family medicine clinic."

"That sounds exhausting."

"Frankly, I've had worse rotations."

He frowned. "But if it's family medicine/emerge, aren't you getting what you need right there? Why would you have to do other rotations?"

She laughed. "Oh, man, I wish. By the time I'm done, I'll have rotated through just about every department you can name, anywhere from four to twenty weeks. Community family medicine, core family medicine, general medicine, general surgery, ob/gyn, orthopedics, pediatrics, CCU, ICU, geriatrics, palliative care—you name it. But you really do have to put the time into all of those specialties to build those basic competencies."

"Time off?"

"One day a week, unless I've got some vacation scheduled."

He whistled. "Damn, those are some long hours."

"Yeah, but it's what I signed on for. And I love working with patients. I'm never bored, either at the ER or the family practice. Especially at the ER, you don't know what you're going to see from one minute to the next. And I get to see patients with problems in every imaginable specialty."

"Sounds kinda like being a uniformed patrol officer, except there *is* a lot of boredom between the peaks of activity."

"Not here," she said. "And this residency—these crazy hours—won't last forever."

"Bet it feels like it some days."

She laughed. "So, are you going to pick me up at the hospital?"

"No problem, but what about your car?"

"I live close enough that I usually walk to work when I'm working days. That way, I get at least some minimal cardio and call my exercise done for the day."

"Did you guys do that often? Go swimming, I mean?"

"As often as we could," she replied. "Once or twice a week, maybe. Often enough that I got into the habit of keeping a bathing suit in my locker. It's still there, although I almost took it home last week. It makes me tear up when I see it."

Shit. Why did he always have to be hurting her? "We don't have to . . . I mean, if this is too hard—"

"Everything's hard right now," she said matter-of-factly. "Waking up is hard. Brushing my teeth. Putting one foot in front of the other until I get to work. It's all hard, so we might as well be doing this stuff. You said you wanted to know what Josh's life was like, right?"

"Right."

"Okay, then. Pick me up at seven. I'll try to get out the door promptly."

"Deal."

$\approx$

With little to fill his time, Boyd was at the ER at six thirty.

He hadn't intended to be there that early. In fact, he'd planned to take his time getting there, maybe stop at the liquor store he'd seen on York Street and buy a bottle of wine to have on hand, then maybe scope out the downtown restaurants for good places to eat. But as soon as he got behind the wheel of his rental, for some reason his mind went to Dave Bradley, Josh's coworker. He remembered how uncomfortable the guy had seemed when Boyd asked to search Josh's cubicle. Had it been because allowing an outsider that kind of access might land him in trouble? Possibly. But he'd seemed relieved when Boyd found nothing, which suggested he had something to hide.

Now there was an angle he could be investigating.

So he drove straight to the hospital and settled in the ER waiting room, where he hauled out his laptop and used his Wi-Fi stick to get connected to the Internet. Tuning out the misery of the unhappy people waiting for their turn to see the doctor, he went online and started researching "David R. Bradley, reporter." He was in up to his eyeballs in all things Bradley when he became aware of Hayden standing beside him.

"Hey," Boyd said, "I'm just—"

"What the hell are you doing researching Dave Bradley?"

CHAPTER 11

"Nothing." Reflexively, he closed his laptop. "I was just poking around online."

"Like hell." Her normally full lips were pressed into a thin, stern line and her brows were drawn together over flashing blue eyes. "I saw the screen, Boyd. You're researching Dave Bradley, and I want to know why."

Damn, she had good eyesight. "Okay, you got me. That's what I was doing."

"I can't believe this! What did Josh say about him?"

"Josh?" He blinked up at her. "Nothing."

"I had it handled, Boyd. I didn't need Josh to come to my rescue then, and I don't need you to do it now." She stood there, hands on hips, radiating frustration. "Okay, so it was a little annoying when he didn't take the no-dating thing seriously at first, but he came around. I told Josh he would, and he did. Dave hasn't bothered me in . . . God, *weeks*!"

Boyd stared up at her. "Hayden, I have no idea what you're talking about. Josh never said anything about David Bradley. I don't think Bradley's name even passed his lips in our discussions, or not that I remember. And certainly not in the context of him trying to date you."

She fell back a step. "Then why are you researching him?"

Boyd shrugged. "I thought he was less than truthful with me when I was there the other day. He seemed nervous about my search of Josh's cubicle. That's all. It had nothing to do with you."

"Really?"

"Really."

Hayden groaned. "I'm such a loser. I'm so sorry I jumped all over you."

He grinned. "You can jump all over me anytime."

She blushed furiously. "Don't be nice. That was incredibly self-absorbed of me."

"Hey, don't give it another thought."

"I won't if you won't," she said.

"Already forgotten." He smiled at her reassuringly, but of course he wasn't moving Dave Bradley off his radar. Not by a long shot.

"So, are we ready to go?" she asked.

"Totally."

Killarney Lake, as billed, turned out to be little more than a pond. But Hayden was right—it was quick to get to, less than fifteen minutes from the hospital in light traffic. The sand was more like gravel, the small beach was crowded, and the water was probably shallow and tepid. But for all Boyd cared, the beach could have been crushed glass and the water leech infested. Because he was going to get to see Hayden in a swimsuit.

He deferred to her as to where to spread the beach blanket, the one he'd bought at the sporting goods store where he'd picked up the bathing trunks. She chose a spot on the grassy edge of the beach, beneath a tree.

He spread the blanket, dropped his new beach towel on it, then kicked off his sandals and peeled off his T-shirt. A glance at Hayden told him she was peeling down too, and she was doing it with the unselfconsciousness of a clinician who dealt with human bodies day in and day out. He didn't look at her fully until he'd taken a seat on the blanket.

She was in the midst of twisting all that beautiful blonde hair into a knot on top of her head. Between her uplifted arms and her position above him, Boyd caught his breath. Damn, she was hot. And she was wearing a simple navy Speedo one-piece.

Boyd had dated some knockouts in his time, women who'd worn racy bandeaus or barely there bikinis at the beach. But none of them held a candle to Hayden in her modest neck-to-thigh one-piece. How was that even possible?

She sat down on the other side of the blanket, the one closest to the tree's trunk.

"I see you picked the same side of the blanket that Josh used to."

"Did you usually sit here under this tree?"

She nodded. "If it was available."

"Then that's why he always chose this side," he said. "He was putting himself between you and the foot traffic." He gestured to a pair of young men who'd just raced past, no doubt in a contest to see who could reach the lake's edge first. "I'm betting he walked on the street side of the sidewalk too."

"Yes! He *always* did that, now that you mention it." She blinked. "I never knew. I mean, I didn't realize he was protecting me."

"He'd have done it for any woman. That's what our dad—the one who counts—drilled into us. Gentlemanly manners and all. But I'm sure he took particular pleasure in doing it for you."

They were silent for a while.

"He loved your father, you know. Your mother too. Just because he was looking for your birth parents didn't change that. He talked about Frank and Ella a lot."

"Yeah?" He drew his legs up, linking his hands together in front of his knees. "What'd he tell you about them?"

"He said your mother used to be a teacher?"

"Yeah, but she quit when we came along, stayed at home with us until we started kindergarten. Then she went back to do substitute teaching."

"Josh credited her with turning him into a reader and writer."

"I'm not surprised. The two of them were very close."

"You didn't go in for that stuff."

He shrugged. "Not a whole lot. I'd rather be out in the shop with Dad, watching him do stuff and handing him tools."

"I hear you're a pretty good carpenter in your own right."

He laughed. "I can muddle my way through your average DIY project, but nobody would call me a carpenter. Now, Dad is a carpenter."

"Josh said you do all the repairs around the house these days."

"Under close supervision, of course."

"Which you don't really need, according to Josh."

"It's good for Dad. And good father–son time." He swatted at a fly.

"Sorry about that. I think the flies are a little worse in the grass here. Would you prefer to be out on the sand in the full sun?"

He turned a jaundiced eye on the rocks and pebbles that comprised the so-called sand. "No, this is good." He glanced back at her, taking in those amazing curves and the slender neck revealed by her upswept hair. Out of nowhere, it struck him how Josh must have felt, sitting here much as he was, looking at the woman he loved. A woman who was clearly oblivious of that love, or at least the nature of it. *Poor bastard.*

"You okay?"

Her question made him realize he was staring. "Sorry, I just spaced for a second. Must be sitting here in the sun making me dozy." He shook himself as though to throw it off. "So what else did he tell you?"

"Let me see . . . I know they're both big baseball fans, and that they used to take you to Blue Jays games when you were really young."

"God, yes. We froze our butts off at that old Exhibition Stadium with the wind coming in off of Lake Ontario and loved every minute of it."

She smiled. "Josh felt cheated that you missed the only Major League Baseball game ever to be played with the field completely covered in snow."

Boyd snorted. "Yeah, that was 1977. We missed that spectacle by a couple of years. We weren't even a gleam in . . . well, *somebody's* eyes at that point."

The allusion to his unknown birth parents didn't escape her. "And you used to go to games at the Rogers Centre."

"It'll always be the SkyDome to me. We were . . . I don't know . . . ten or eleven when it opened, and we were in total awe."

"Hockey games at the Gardens too."

"Not as often as ball games. Too expensive." He brushed the persistent fly from his leg. "But we both played hockey, from Mini Mites through to Midget. And Josh played college hockey."

"He told me about your dad driving you to lots of early-morning games."

"Yep. Now that I think about it, he would have been a lot older than I am when he started taking us to hockey. Hell, he was almost thirty-eight and Ella thirty-six when they adopted us."

"That's not that old," she said. "Plenty of parents are in their thirties these days before they have their first child."

"Maybe so. But not sure I'd want to be working long hours at a construction job and still dragging kids to the rink in the dark."

"Did you ever feel they were too old for the job?"

"Honestly, I never thought about it. In fact, I never really thought about them as *old* at all until Josh died."

She blinked rapidly. "It's got to be a hard thing, to lose a child, no matter what age."

He nodded, looking out over the beach.

"Do you blame him?"

His gaze shot to her face. "Blame who?"

"Josh."

"For what?"

She shrugged. "For searching for his birth parents. For coming here. For dying."

"I do not blame my brother for dying." The words came out sounding gruff, almost strangled.

"But you didn't really approve of his fixation?"

"Not my place to tell Josh what to do. He was a grown man." He rolled his shoulders. "But it's true that I didn't really approve, because of the legal scrutiny our adoptive parents might have come under. It's also true that I didn't share his need to know. Didn't understand why he'd turn his life upside down, leave a good job, to chase after someone who doesn't want to be found."

"You might change your mind about that someday."

He glanced over at her. She'd drawn her own knees up, circling them with her arms in a subtle mirroring of his posture.

"I can't see it."

She looked up from her examination of her unvarnished toes. Very pretty toes.

"What about when you have children of your own? The medical history alone—"

"That's not something that's going to happen soon."

He felt the curiosity in her gaze as she looked at him. "No prospects in the offing?"

"Nope. Though my mother does like to point out I'm getting a little long in the tooth. She was always after both of us to get busy and make her some grandchildren. Personally, I always figured Josh would be the one to oblige, but he always picked the wrong women."

Her eyes shot wide. "*What?* He never had anything but good things to say about his past relationships."

"Let me rephrase. Not wrong in the sense of being bad or incompatible. Just not marriage minded. The two I met were really smart, terrific women. But they were just as career focused and ambitious as he was at the time."

"I can see that," she said. "That he'd be attracted to smart, energetic women."

Like you. It was all Boyd could do to bite back the words. She didn't need that burden.

They sat in silence a moment. Boyd tried and failed to keep his glance from sliding over her. *Damn.*

"How about you?" she asked. "Ever come close to marriage?"

"Once," he admitted. "A very pretty vet tech I met when I helped a lady get her injured dog to a veterinary hospital. I was maybe twenty-five at the time and crazy in love. We lived together, even talked about marriage, but eventually the job got in the way. I was still working patrol, and after one too many hair-raising episodes, she decided she couldn't live with someone whose job could be so dangerous."

She held his gaze. "Did you think about leaving police work?"

"The thought didn't even enter my head, which she pointed out. I guess maybe I wasn't as crazy in love as I thought."

"I get it, though," she said. "I'd walk away too. Being a cop was all you ever wanted to do, and no one should ask you to give it up for them. It would have been a mistake."

"Like yours?"

"Exactly. Being a doctor and helping the poor was always what I wanted to do. The difference is I let someone use my emotions, my attachment, to drag me off course. When love gets twisted like that and used to manipulate, it stays twisted. Eventually I saw that and got the hell out."

Two years. That's what she'd said the bastard had cost her. If that dumb-ass hadn't come into her life, she'd be finished with her residency and probably doing some community family practice in southwest Scarborough or north Etobicoke or some depressed area of Vancouver. "I'm glad."

She arched her back, no doubt to ease the strain of the long day, but Boyd couldn't miss what it did for that Speedo.

"Well, we know what direction I took after my little relationship side trip," she said. "What about you?"

"I've had a few more . . . I was going to say long-term relationships, but maybe medium-term is more accurate." The damned fly was back, and Boyd swatted at it again. "One was nine years older than me, divorced, and not interested in going that route ever again, which was okay by me. I enjoyed it while it lasted."

"And the other?"

The memory of Carrie still made him feel like the world's biggest failure. "She had issues from her childhood that she never could overcome. Things were good at first. I thought I could lift her sadness, you know? Bear her burdens. And I tried. But it doesn't work that way. I eventually figured she was the only one who could fix herself."

"What happened?"

He picked up a stick and started poking at the rocky soil. "She left, presumably looking for a guy with a stronger back."

"I don't know where she'd find that."

His head came up and their glances collided. His chest felt suddenly tight. "Thank you."

"You're welcome."

Leaning back on his hands, he stretched his legs out. "So you guys talked about Josh's family. Did you reciprocate?"

As a change of subject, it wasn't very smooth, but it seemed to work.

"Yeah, I told him about my parents. My dad retired early and took my mother back to Cape Breton with him. It's been quite an adjustment, after spending their entire married life in the Montreal area."

"I can imagine. Siblings?"

"Nope. I always yearned for one, though. I thought I'd like to have a sister, but these past few months with Josh . . ." She lifted her shoulders and rotated her neck as though to relieve tension. "He was like the perfect big brother."

Poor Josh would never have gotten out of that friend zone. Not that he'd be the first guy to try.

"You know, I've never had less time on my hands—an eighty-hour week is not unusual—but these past months, I've had a more active social life than I've had in years. And that was all Josh's doing."

Boyd arched an eyebrow. "Yeah?"

"By the time I'd get off, usually he'd have put in his day at the paper and maybe a few hours at his personal investigation. The man had so much energy! And he got things done in a fraction of the time it takes most of us. Anyway, he'd swoop in, pick me up, stick a smoothie or a wrap or both in my hands, and announce we were going somewhere. Just cutting out the time it took to rustle up supper freed up a ton of time. Or he'd pick something up and we'd eat together in front of the TV and talk during commercials. Or he'd just run an errand for me so I could grab a catnap. He took care of me, you know?"

He swallowed. "Sounds like he did a good job of it."

"Oh, he did. And it wasn't all so he could monopolize my time. Yes, we did spend a lot of time together, but sometimes he'd do stuff for me just so I could get to bed earlier."

Jesus, how could she not have known he loved her?

"Sorry, I got off track. You asked what we talked about. Your family, my family, our friends. Work, insofar as we could. Josh liked to pepper me with trivia questions."

Boyd laughed. "Not just you. The guy was a walking encyclopedia. Talk about developing a complex."

They were quiet for a moment.

"Yeah, we talked a lot. Endlessly, you'd probably say. But lately when we came here, he seemed more content to just *be* here, soaking up the sun without talking."

Boyd snorted. "My brother? Josh? The man who talked to his cereal box if there was no one around? And who couldn't sit still unless he had a keyboard at his fingertips or a pen and paper in his hand?"

She laughed. "Hard to believe, I know. But yeah, no mile-a-minute talking. No leaping up and dragging me off to play volleyball. He seemed very . . . I don't know. Content? Almost peaceful." She met his gaze. "I actually wondered if he'd given up on the search for your birth parents. Or, you know, back-burnered it."

"*What?*"

"Crazy, huh? The thought actually crossed my mind. More than once. But I didn't ask him about it. I was afraid he might think I was judging. He knew I totally supported his search, and not just for the medical history part. Though we never talked specifics, he knew I was a cheerleader on the sidelines. So when it seemed like he might be losing interest or impetus or whatever, I didn't want him to think I disapproved."

"I'm sure he appreciated your supportiveness."

"Yes," she said softly. "I think he did. And as it turns out, I couldn't have been more wrong thinking he'd dropped it."

"I'm thinking he must have gotten a sudden break. He probably called me immediately and left that message."

"Probably."

She stood. Boyd knew he should stand too, but he was enjoying the view right where he was.

"So, are you going to swim, or just sit around looking pretty, Detective McBride?"

"I'm gonna swim, Dr. Walsh." He came to his feet, finding himself standing close to her. He saw awareness flash in her eyes, but she turned to walk toward the shoreline.

They spent twenty minutes in the water. The lake was extremely small, and the cordoned-off supervised swim area was even smaller. When Hayden ducked under the floating cordon and started stroking toward the other side of the lake, Boyd followed. There were a few people in small watercraft—kayaks and the like—in the middle of the lake, and he kept a close eye on them to make sure they weren't a collision risk.

When they reached the other side, or rather when the water got so shallow he couldn't swim any farther, he stood. "Yuck."

She laughed. "Yeah, a little sediment on the bottom."

"A little? I'm up to my ankles." He noticed she kept paddling.

It was too shallow to tread water so she was dog-paddling. He eyed the murky water. "Are you sure there are no leeches?"

"Who said there were no leeches?"

He cursed, and she laughed again.

"You should rest before we head back," he said.

She flipped onto her back. "There. I'm resting."

"You just don't want to stand up in the muck."

"That would be correct."

He reached out and pulled her to him, just close enough so he could slide his arms under her to support her so she didn't have to kick her feet or wave her arms. "There. Now you're resting."

She allowed him to support her for maybe a minute, probably less.

"We should go back now. I'm good to go."

He released her. Once again, he let her go first, following a half-length behind. He slowed his pace, of course, but not by much. She was a strong swimmer.

Once back onshore, they toweled off, then sat on the blanket and let the sinking sun dry them further. They talked more about Josh, about previous visits to this crowded little lake and longer jaunts to the beach at Mactaquac Park. She remarked again on how active Josh used to be on those outings, and how laid-back he'd grown of late, how content to just lie in the sun.

Boyd frowned. "Do you think he was feeling symptoms? You know, heart troubles?"

Hayden, who'd been lying flat on her back with her legs outstretched, jackknifed up. "No! I don't believe that at all. I mean, we still swam the lake. We still jogged together occasionally. He didn't have any difficulty with those activities, or not that I noticed."

And she would notice. Boyd believed that.

"It's more that he wasn't . . . *vibrating* all the time," she said. "He could lie still, enjoy the sun, or have dessert and a glass of wine instead of rushing off to do something else, or engage some-one else, or find another question to be answered."

He grinned wryly. "More like a normal person, you mean?"

"Pretty much."

Her answering smile caught him right in the libido. Or maybe it was the laughter in her crystal clear blue eyes, or her sun-kissed shoulders, or those generous breasts hugged so lov-ingly by the Lycra suit. Whatever the case, he found himself lean-ing in with purpose.

He saw the flash of surprise in her eyes, followed by the unmistakable blaze of desire. Then her lids closed. The sound of the kids squealing and splashing in the water disappeared as he focused on her mouth. He was finally going to taste those full, luscious lips he'd been thinking about since he first laid eyes on her.

When he placed his hand on her face to tip it up, he half expected her to pull back.

She didn't.

He closed his lips on hers in a kiss that was almost chaste. It had to be on this public beach. But holy hell, even without their bodies touching, she packed a wallop. It was like all the pent-up sexual yearning inside her had condensed for him to taste on those gorgeous pillowy lips.

She pulled back then and looked up at him. Her brow was furrowed, but not with the recrimination he expected. Her eyes were filled with passion, yes, but also with puzzlement. As though she was waiting for some resistance to kick in.

Or, oh shit, trying to figure out why she'd shut Josh down but permitted his identical twin to kiss her.

And double shit! What was he doing? This was the woman Josh had wanted. The one his heart was set on. How could he do this to Josh? Betray him like this when he was hardly cold in the grave?

Dammit, how could *she* do this to him?

No, that wasn't fair. She clearly had no freaking idea of the extent or nature of Josh's feelings.

Her tongue touched her lip. "What was that about?"

Okay, feeling like a heel and admitting it were two different things. "Are you honestly going to deny the chemistry here?"

"That would be pretty pointless. I won't deny it or try to hide from it. And part of me wishes we weren't standing on a public beach so you could kiss me properly." Her lips twisted. "How's that for honesty?"

Her words sent a savage jolt of satisfaction through him. He clamped down on it, sensing a *but* coming. Instead of waiting for her to say it, he said it for her. "But you've got your path mapped out and don't need to take any detours. I know. And I respect that. I just got caught up." He rolled his shoulders to try to dislodge the tension tightening his back muscles.

"I know. Me too." She grabbed her towel and wrapped it around her shoulders, cloaking all but her calves and feet as she sat there. "We both loved Josh. Between that shared bond and this investigation of yours, it's brought us so close, so fast. Throw in the attraction, and those moments are probably inevitable, right?"

"Right." She was giving him a pass. So why didn't he feel better?

"Between what we know *about* each other through Josh and these talks, sometimes it feels like we know each other really well. And yet, apart from shaking your hand at the funeral, we effectively just met a few days ago."

The tightness in Boyd's back seemed to work its way through to his chest and up to his jaw. He didn't like her message, he realized. He really, really didn't like it. And that fact shocked him so much that he leapt at the out she offered.

"You're absolutely right, Doc. Your diagnosis is bang on."

"Diagnosis?" She lifted an eyebrow. "Is a prescription now required?"

He produced a smile. "I can take my medicine like a big boy. Just as long as the prescription doesn't mean we can't hang out like we've been doing."

"But I don't know what more I can tell you."

"You told me something new just this evening. How Josh seemed to mellow in those last weeks, even as he was getting closer to an answer. That has to mean something. I'm not sure what yet, but it means something."

She still looked unconvinced.

"Come on, Hayden. I know how much you loved Josh. You gotta help me out. If there's a chance someone is responsible for his death . . ." He let his words trail off.

She gave him a measuring look, and he met it straight on, letting her read the plea in his eyes.

"Okay," she said at last. "I'm not sure I can help, but I'm still in."

"Thank you." The tightness in his chest eased. Until he realized his relief wasn't just about Josh. Not just about the investigation.

He wanted to keep seeing her. As often as he could.

And it wasn't just about lusting after her, which he decidedly did—powerfully. She was so damned beautiful. Exotic.

But dammit, he *liked* her. Really liked her and respected and admired her. She was smart, held a deep well of strength inside her slim body, and was powerfully motivated to succeed but not to feed her ego. She was also kind and self-deprecating and honest. He liked her in every way. The way Josh probably had before he'd taken that irrevocable step off that cliff from like and tumbled straight into love.

He was going to have to tread carefully, lest he fall off the same ledge his brother had.

CHAPTER 12

Hayden was having a hard time concentrating on her morning newspaper.

Keeping her focus was usually not a problem. And in the ER, she made damned sure it was *never* a problem. In that environment, there just wasn't room for anything else but the patient in front of her at that moment, and the one after that, and the one after that. Yeah, some of them were colds and flus and there was nothing she could do but dispense advice and write the occasional prescription if there was a secondary, opportunistic, infection present. But even with these patients, she always had to be careful. So she'd learned to keep a laser focus from the moment she logged in until she signed out, no matter what kind of turmoil might reign in her personal life.

Even off duty, she generally had no problem concentrating. She'd just put aside whatever was nagging at her, telling herself she would give it a full fifteen minutes worry time when she was ready to give it her attention. If she couldn't come up with a productive solution in that time, she mentally moved it to the shit-I-have-zero-control-over list and let it go.

But this morning, her mind wasn't cooperating, possibly because this was the first of a rare three days off—her regular off day and two scheduled holidays. Whatever the reason, her thoughts kept sliding back to Boyd.

She'd seen him yesterday after work, but only briefly, and for a very specific purpose.

He'd texted her with his latest brain wave—the idea that Josh might have hidden the diary somewhere in her apartment. He'd met her at her place after work and she'd watched as he searched her place. He'd asked her to search the dresser drawers and bathroom vanity herself, but he'd done the rest. Just watching his search, she discovered great spots to hide things if she ever decided to take up a life of crime. Spots she'd never have thought of in a million years. Up under the kitchen sink—or more specifically, in the space *between* the double sinks—got her vote for best place to stash something. He'd felt the undersides of furniture, popped the top off the toilet tank, and even peered into her freezer. He'd also scanned the books on her bookshelf, somewhere she'd never have thought to search, yet the perfect hiding place for a journal. He'd had no luck, though.

When he'd finished, he'd taken one look at her and told her to go to bed and that he'd call her the next day. He was right. She'd hit the wall, exhaustion-wise, and was grateful Boyd had recognized it. Grateful he didn't need to be told to leave. Just a thank-you for letting him search her place, an apology for disrupting her stuff, and an order for her to lock the door behind him when he let himself out.

But it wasn't yesterday that her mind kept sliding back to. It was the day before yesterday, when they'd lain there on that beach blanket and he'd kissed her in the shade of that tree while kids laughed and squealed and splashed yards away.

She'd had a hard time getting to sleep again last night, her imagination taunting her with what might have happened if she'd encouraged it, if she weren't so conditioned to push every advance away. What would a real kiss have been like? Hard or soft? Would it have been a testing, tentative, questioning kiss, or a sweeping demand? And how would his lips have felt against hers? Cool from their swim, like the rest of their bodies? Dear God, how would he taste?

Before she finally got off to sleep around one a.m. after watching two DVR'd episodes of *Elementary*, she'd wished she'd kissed Boyd back the way she'd wanted to. Public beach or not, it would have been pretty spectacular. And if she'd just done that, she wouldn't now have to wonder what it would be like. Then she'd woken at three a.m., fully aroused from a dream in which he'd done more than kiss her, and had been glad she hadn't. If her dreams could conjure that degree of detail, imagine what could have happened had they actually made out!

Catching herself, she groaned and pushed the images away. Lord, where was her self-discipline? She was going to have to find it before tonight.

She'd agreed to take Boyd to the watering hole frequented by Josh's colleagues from the paper tonight. On a Friday evening, most of them—and some of their spouses—could be relied on to be there for the happy hour period, if not longer. Boyd wanted a chance to nurse a few beers in their company, in the hopes that they'd talk freely about Josh while they were feeling all warm and loose from the alcohol.

It had been her idea. She had joined Josh and his fellow reporters at this particular pub before, after getting off shift, and she knew she'd be welcomed. So would Boyd, for that matter. When she mentioned the possibility, he'd jumped on it. And, yes, she felt guilty about exploiting her relationship with those people by springing Boyd on them. They were grieving Josh's death too, and Boyd intended to ply them for information to assist his investigation. They'd probably never be the wiser, but that didn't salve her conscience.

Dave Bradley would be there, no doubt. Josh had told her that he never missed the Friday night ritual. Not that she was expecting to have any trouble from Dave. Once she'd finally gotten through to him that she wasn't interested, he'd left her alone. Pointedly. But from what Boyd had said, she knew he'd be paying particular attention to Dave.

And she, God help her, would be paying attention to Boyd. The more they saw each other, the harder it was getting to tune out the sexual awareness. It was starting to take on a pulse of its own. She was definitely going to have to be on her guard.

Or not . . .

Her phone rang and she reached for it. *Boyd.* Despite herself, she felt a thrill in her belly at the sight of his number. Her lips tightened, and her voice was terse when she answered.

"Hayden?" he said, after the slightest of pauses. "Did I catch you at a bad time? Should I call back?"

She pressed a hand to her temple. Her reaction wasn't his fault, and she shouldn't be taking her conflicted emotions out on him. She let go of it. "No, now's good. What's up?"

"I just got the calling record detail from Josh's cell phone carrier."

"Oh, that's fantastic!"

"I'll be meeting with Detective Morgan later this morning so we can start identifying the outgoing numbers and following up."

"How far back did they go?"

"I asked for six months. Morgan and I will have our work cut out for us."

She pushed her newspaper away and sat back in her chair. "I imagine a bunch of them are going to be me, you, and your parents, so you'll be able to eliminate a lot."

"Yeah, like eighty or ninety percent from the look of this."

"I'm so glad to hear this, Boyd. Hopefully this means you're close to finding out what Josh learned. In a matter of hours or days, you could know who your birth mother was."

"That's the hope. And if we can establish that, it'll hopefully shed light on who might not have wanted that information unearthed."

"I'm so excited for you."

"Don't get too excited," he cautioned. "If the critical contact was made in person, all these phone records might not mean a damn. Or if the contact that broke the case for Josh was an incoming call, we could still be in the dark. They don't give us the numbers for any of the incoming stuff."

"Privacy legislation?"

"Yup. It would take a court order to get them to cough up that stuff."

"Well, I prefer to believe you're going to find your answer in those records. Or maybe something that will lead to something that will let you get that court order."

"Amen to that," he said in heartfelt tones. "I'll finally be *doing* something."

She heard his frustration, knew how anxious he was at the lack of progress. "Exactly. If you're out there following those numbers, poking at stuff, tugging at strings, you never know what might come loose, right?"

"Tugging at strings?" A teasing note had crept into his voice, and her heart rate responded accordingly. "You make me sound like a kitten."

Some kitten. "Never that." Then, because the brief silence between them seemed suddenly to pulse with awareness, she rushed to change the topic. "So now that you have the phone records to focus on, maybe you want to cancel tonight?"

"No, I still want to go. There's always the chance I might learn something helpful, but even if I don't . . ."

"Even if you don't, you'll have shared a beer and probably heard some stories about Josh from his coworkers," she said.

"Yeah."

The one word, so softly spoken, made her heart do a little jump. "I'll warn you, they're natural storytellers. From the tales I've heard when I've joined them, I'm pretty sure there's some embellishment involved."

He laughed. "I believe it. Josh could spin a little anecdote into a major yarn too."

"So are you picking me up tonight, or should I meet you there?" she asked briskly.

"Actually, would you mind picking me up?"

"Sure." She forced a smile into her voice, unsure of whether playing with fire was a good idea. "No problem."

"Normally, I'd never ask a lady to be the designated driver, but—"

"But I'm no lady?"

He laughed. "I was going to say, depending how things go, I might want to have a few drinks. Keep pace for a couple of rounds."

"Of course. The more you relax and loosen up, the more they will."

"That's the theory."

"Okay. But again, these are newspaper people we're talking about. You might have trouble keeping pace with some of them."

He chuckled again. "Don't worry—I won't get sloppy drunk."

"That's a relief."

"Ever see Josh drunk?"

The question caught her by surprise. "Just once. It was very funny."

"The time he kissed you?"

"Oh, no. I mean, he'd had a few beers that evening, but he definitely wasn't drunk."

"So, tell me about this other time. I haven't seen him more than pleasantly buzzed since we were about twenty-three."

"It was kind of an accident," she admitted. "He'd come over for a mini–*Burn Notice* marathon on my day off. I made rum-runners with some Cuban rum a friend brought back for me. I wasn't drinking myself because I was taking acetaminophen for a sinus headache, and combining the two can be an invitation to liver failure."

"I see where you're going. You had no idea how strong the rum was?"

"Not a clue. But by the time the credits rolled after the last episode, I was sore from laughing."

"So did you pour him into a cab and send him home?"

She snorted. "To Sylvia Stratton's house in that condition? How heartless do you think I am? He crashed on the couch."

There was another of those silences. Instantly, she imagined what it would be like if Boyd ever crashed at her place. Somehow, she knew he wouldn't be sleeping on her tasteful beige sofa. The thought sent sparklers of excitement erupting everywhere.

Maybe she should break her rule.

Actually, it wouldn't even be breaking it, would it? She'd sworn not to get entangled with a man again until she was ready for the demands of a relationship. But if she got together with Boyd, it wouldn't be an entanglement. He'd be Toronto bound the minute his investigation was over.

"So, pick me up tonight?" he said.

"Be ready at five thirty," she said.

She'd do what she could to try to help Boyd find out more about Josh's death.

And if he made a pass at her after he'd "relaxed" with a few drinks? For the first time in years, she had absolutely no idea how she would handle that.

The thought was as arousing as it was scary.

CHAPTER 13

Boyd liked the pub—an Irish one—immediately. Its long, narrow single-story construction made it look odd, hunkered there among taller, more modern office buildings in the busiest part of the downtown core. Inside, it was dark, packed, and noisy. Advertisements for fine Scotch whiskeys covered every available bit of wall space that wasn't devoted to flat-screen TVs. As a casual spot to kick off the traces on a Friday night and get a start on the weekend, he gave it a thumbs-up.

"Hayden! Over here."

Beside him, Hayden lifted a hand to wave at Grace Morgan, who'd stood up at a crowded table to flag them down. She was more casually dressed this time but was still a looker.

"Better watch it," Hayden said dryly as they started toward

the table. "Detective Morgan looks like he's ready to march you outside."

"What?" He gave Hayden a sidelong glance. "She's a striking woman. Surely he's used to men—"

"Leering at his wife?"

"I was going to say appreciating his good fortune."

"I'm sure he is used to it. But he probably doesn't see every man who looks her way as quite such a threat."

Boyd frowned. When they had to stop to let a group of exiting patrons pass in the narrow space between the tables and the long bar, he took the opportunity to question her. "Did Detective Morgan see Josh as a threat?"

"Josh?" Her head whipped around. "Of course not."

"Why not?" As he looked down at her upturned face, he almost lost the thread of his thought. She wore a tiny jean jacket buttoned over a white blouse, but because she'd left her hair loose, there wasn't much of the jacket to be seen. Strands of glorious blonde curls fell to breast level on the front, and tumbled down her back. Her lips were slightly parted and looked so damned kissable. He forced his mind back to the topic at hand. "Grace Morgan was clearly fond of him and held him in high regard for his journalistic accomplishments. I gather they spent at least some time together, in a mentor–mentee relationship. If Ray Morgan had reason to be jealous of anyone, it would be of Josh, surely."

The single-file exodus had passed, but instead of forging on toward the table, Hayden stood there looking at him as though he were incredibly dense.

"What?" he said.

"You two might have been identical twins, but I don't imagine people mixed you up very often."

"Well, one of us had to be the evil twin, right? Isn't that how it works?"

She looked up at him, laughter in her eyes. "Not evil, just . . . edgier."

He felt his chest expand, but he wasn't sure whether it was the smile or the words.

"Come on," he said. "We'd better get over there or they'll think we're having a moment."

As they approached the table, Boyd saw Dave Bradley. He was seated near the end of the table with his back to the wall. Boyd would've liked to sit next to the guy, but short of asking someone to swap seats, that wasn't happening. All the seats toward that end of the long table were taken.

Putting his hand on Hayden's elbow, he subtly steered her to the opposite side of the table so he could at least observe Bradley.

She seemed to know what he wanted, sliding into the closest empty chair beside a man he recognized from his visit to the paper. What was the name? Toner? Tozer?

Boyd took the seat beside Hayden, which put him almost at the opposite end of the table from the man he wanted to study.

The man on Hayden's left greeted her, then leaned forward to address Boyd. "Murray Totten," he said. "Glad you could come."

Ah, Totten. He'd known it was a *T* word. "Thanks for volunteering the name, man. I know we met briefly at the paper. The memory isn't what it used to be when I first put a shield on."

He grinned. "All that writing you guys do in those little black notebooks isn't just for the court's benefit, huh?"

"Exactly."

"Yo, people," Totten said, loudly enough to get the whole table's attention. "Why don't we go around the table and introduce ourselves for Boyd's benefit."

Everyone obliged, including Grace Morgan and her husband. The only empty seats at the table had placed them across from the Morgans. After a few comments from folks about how happy they were to have Josh's brother and his friend join them, people resumed their conversations.

The waitress arrived, and Boyd ordered one of the Picaroons drafts Hayden had introduced him to on his first day in Fredericton. Hayden ordered a virgin Caesar.

When the waitress left, Boyd looked across the table at Morgan. "Anything new since this afternoon?"

The other man shrugged. "Still working the numbers. But I did send the forensics lab a when-can-we-have-the-results kind of query. That might speed things up, but you never know. If you ride them too hard, I suspect they find a reason to drop you down a notch—or ten—on their list of priorities."

Boyd nodded. "I hear you."

Grace leaned forward, the better to be heard over the din in the packed pub. "Hayden tells me you're staying in Josh's old room at Dr. Stratton's house."

"That's right," he said dryly. "And I'm guessing by the expression on your face that Josh probably told you a little about how daunting the doctor can be."

Grace Morgan smiled warmly and it was like she'd turned on a high-watt inner light. He blinked. Ray Morgan was one lucky guy. Boyd cast a quick glance at the detective, and it was plain he knew just how fortunate he was.

An unexpected lump arose in his throat. This was what Josh had been looking for, what he'd hoped he'd find with Hayden. Josh had only talked at length about his feelings for Hayden the one time, mainly because he knew Boyd had a low threshold of tolerance for emotional talk. But it had been there in the background, every time the two of them had talked about Hayden.

He cleared his throat. "Yeah, there've been some awkward moments. On the whole, I'd rather go into a domestic call without backup than run into her in the hallways."

Morgan laughed. "That bad, huh?"

"And you have breakfast with her every day like Josh did, don't you?" Hayden asked.

"That's not so bad, actually."

"I'd brave it for the coffee alone," Morgan said, then exhaled sharply as his wife jabbed him. "What? It's amazing. A special blend of organic coffee beans, freshly ground. Tell her, Boyd."

"He's right," Boyd confirmed. "It is great coffee, and she puts on a good spread. I drink her fresh-squeezed orange juice and eat the free-range eggs and bask in her approval." He shrugged.

"Josh loved those breakfasts," Hayden added. She was smiling but blinking back tears. "There were times I told him to just crash on the couch after a movie marathon, but he usually wanted to go home. He said it was to avoid the walk of shame the next day—Sylvia would inevitably leap to the wrong conclusion. But I'm convinced he just didn't want to risk missing out on breakfast."

Grace laughed. "I'm sorry—forgive me. But I was picturing Josh doing his impression of Dr. Stratton looking askance at him when he walked in the door after staying out all night."

"You mean like this?" Boyd gave his own Sylvia Stratton impression, and the two women dissolved into giggles. Even Morgan smiled.

"Joking aside, breakfast at Chez Stratton is a major perk," Boyd said. "I've stayed in five-star hotels that wouldn't measure up. And that woman is hard-core about eating organic. I think even the butter is from organically raised, grass-fed cows."

"Did she always eat like that, I wonder," Grace said, "or did she get into it when her husband got ill?"

"No idea," Boyd said. "I don't even know if the guy can eat." He looked at Hayden.

"I have no idea either," she said. "But if he's not able to take food by mouth, they probably liquefy that wonderful organic food and tube-feed him. Commercial formula has its place, but it can't hold a candle to real food, which can actually help patients heal. Whether or not Dr. Stratton switched for him, he's very lucky to have that kind of nutrition."

"As am I," Boyd said. "But she seriously thinks she can have me feeling like a new man when I leave here." He slanted a look at Morgan. "I told her it would take more than a few weeks to reverse the effects of a cop's diet."

"True that," Morgan said. He leaned back in his chair, throwing his arm casually across the back of his wife's chair. She leaned in toward him, an infinitesimal shift, but one that seemed to unite them somehow. "So, what's she do for dinner? I'm guessing lots of salmon, greens, that kind of thing?"

"I'm on my own for everything but breakfast." He glanced at Hayden. "Hayden has taken pity on me and kept me company for dinner a couple of times, but I'm gradually finding a few good spots."

"Oh, where are my manners?" Grace exclaimed. "I should have invited you to dinner by now." She glanced at Hayden. "You too, of course, Hayden."

"Accept quickly," Hayden advised. "Grace is an amazing cook. Better than anything you'll find in a restaurant here, or, well, pretty much anywhere. Josh used to actively fish for invitations, I think."

Grace laughed. "Don't build his expectations up too high. Now that Emily is crawling, I'm not quite as ambitious in the kitchen as I used to be."

Ray leaned closer to his wife. "Sweetheart, he's a cop. You couldn't possibly disappoint him, even if you were a mediocre cook, which you are not."

Hayden concurred, and she launched into a description of some of the meals she and Josh had enjoyed at the Morgans.

Listening to her, Boyd realized that while Josh and Hayden hadn't been frequent guests, they'd dined together a handful of times in the almost six months Josh had been in Fredericton. Plus Morgan had no doubt joined these Friday night happy hours with his wife at least occasionally. To think Boyd had once entertained the thought that Morgan might be dogging it on this investigation.

Then Hayden said something about one of Grace's recent articles, and the two ladies were off again.

Boyd took the opportunity to look down the table at Dave Bradley. The other man was just excusing himself. As he got up and headed in the direction of what Boyd presumed was the men's room, he excused himself and followed.

Dave Bradley looked more than surprised to see Boyd enter the washroom behind him. "Hey, Boyd," Bradley said, an unsettled expression on his face.

"Hey, Dave." Boyd crossed the small room to lean against the vanity between the two sets of taps.

A moment later, Dave approached the sink to wash his hands. "How'd you make out with your search for Josh's notebook?"

"No luck." Boyd purposely did not give ground, forcing Bradley to come closer than he was likely comfortable doing. As a tactic, it was probably pretty transparent—no one liked their personal space invaded—but he didn't especially care. "Not so far anyway. I almost have to wonder if someone else found it sooner."

"Someone else?" Bradley's gaze darted away. "Like the cops, you mean?"

"If it was a cop, it must've been a crooked one, because Ray Morgan assures me nothing like that was logged into evidence."

"Huh." Bradley dried his hands and tossed the towel. Boyd noticed a level of discomfort in the other man's demeanor.

"But I was thinking more like someone at the paper."

Bradley's face flushed. "Like me, you mean. That's why you followed me in here? To quiz me about Josh's notebook?"

"Quiz you?" Boyd unfolded his length and stood, towering over the shorter man.

"Look, I'm sorry about Josh." For a change, Bradley met and held Boyd's gaze. "I really am. But you're barking up the wrong tree. I did not take Josh's notebook. I didn't hide it or destroy it. Hell, I've never even seen it, at least not that I remember." Bradley's gaze slid away again.

Despite his general jumpiness, there was a ring of truth to the man's words. Which was probably why Boyd went on the offensive.

"So, what's this about you pursuing Hayden?"

Bradley paled. "I don't know what Josh told you, but I haven't said a word to Hayden in months. I promised your brother I'd leave her alone and I have. I don't know what more I can do." He dragged a hand through his hair. "Christ, the last time I had a sprained ankle, I drove myself all the way to Oromocto instead of going to the local ER, in case I caught her on duty and she took my being there the wrong way."

"Why were you so squirrelly when I came to your office, if you had nothing to be worried about?"

"Because I took something! All right?"

Boyd kept his face expressionless. "What'd you take?"

"Pictures." His face was so flushed now, he looked like he could have a heart attack. Wouldn't that be poetic if Boyd had to call Hayden in here to work on Dave Bradley?

"Relax, man. Just take a breath, calm down, and tell me about it."

Bradley gulped a few breaths, but he still looked like hell. "Josh took pictures of me. I was sort of following Hayden. I never meant her any harm and I'm sorry if I scared her, but I only wanted to—"

"Come on, Bradley. I've been a cop for a long time. I have a pretty good idea what you wanted." Boyd's hand itched to smack the bastard. Guys like him never saw the harm in what they did. "So Josh filmed you stalking Hayden Walsh and was holding the footage as insurance to make sure you left her alone."

"Yes." Bradley gulped more air. "He took pictures, mostly, but there was one video. When we got word at the paper that Josh had died and there would be a death investigation, all I could think about was someone finding that file with the pictures, the video, and Josh's notes."

"So you tossed his office until you found the file?"

"Yes. And I deleted it from his camera too. There was a copy on the memory card."

"How do you know there aren't other copies on his hard drive? Or in his Dropbox?"

He laughed, but it was a strangled, unhappy sound. "Because no one from the police department has come to talk to me." He scrubbed a hand over his face. "I did try to get into his laptop, but I couldn't crack the screen saver password to get at anything."

Boyd had had a little trouble with that himself, trying everything from childhood pets to name-and-birth-date combinations. Finally, he'd typed in *HaydenWalsh*, and the computer obligingly logged him in. "Then I turned up and your editor turned it over to me."

"Yeah." He let his breath out with a heavy sigh. "And I've developed an ulcer, waiting to hear they've wrapped up their investigation."

"So I should feel bad for you? Is that it?" Boyd raked Bradley with his gaze. "That's kinda what you get when you do shit like that. You'll always be waiting for the shoe to fall."

Bradley turned beet red. "I didn't do anything terrible. I just liked her, you know? But when he showed me the pictures and the video . . . it looked so much worse. Much creepier."

"It *is* creepy, Dave. When you follow someone surreptitiously or stake out their place, it's kinda the definition of creepy."

"I'm sorry." He hung his head. "I don't do that anymore, not to anyone. I swore to Josh that I wouldn't, and I won't."

"That's good," Boyd said. "And don't think about backsliding because Josh is gone. If I ever learn that you've been charged with anything remotely like this, I'll happily volunteer to testify for the Crown about this conversation of ours, your admissions about stalking Hayden, your theft of the evidence my brother compiled—the whole nine yards."

The door opened inward and Colin Parsons, the sports writer, came in.

"Boyd, glad you came tonight," he said. "Hayden too."

"Thanks, man."

Parsons nodded toward the door. "They've started telling Josh stories. You should get out there."

"I'll do that." He turned to Bradley. "We good here?"

Bradley dredged up a smile, no doubt for Parsons's benefit. "We're good."

CHAPTER 14

Two hours later, Boyd was conscious of Hayden's eyes on him as he struggled to fasten his seat belt.

"Good thing you arranged for taxi service," she said dryly.

He wasn't sloppy drunk—not by anyone's measure. But when the Josh stories had started, he'd kept the draft beer flowing. "Yeah, sorry about that. I wasn't counting on quite so much reminiscing." He finally jammed the seat belt home and leaned back.

"Did you get anything out of it?" She keyed the ignition and the engine sprang to life.

"Did I learn anything helpful, you mean?"

"Yeah."

He closed his eyes as she backed out of the parking spot and exited the lot. "I don't know. Probably not. But who knows? Sometimes you can't tell what bit of information might be the thing that trips a connection in your brain that leads you down the right path." He opened his eyes and glanced sideways at her as she braked for a light that had turned yellow. "Thanks for doing this," he said. "Tonight, I mean. Even if it turns out not to produce anything especially useful to my investigation, it was still great to hear what an impact Josh had on so many people."

"Sad, though." She flicked her gaze over to him, then returned her attention to the traffic light. "You held up better than I did."

He'd noticed tears, even as she'd smiled and laughed through the stories and shared some of her own.

"Yeah, I'm a freakin' rock."

She flicked him another quick glance, but the light had gone green and she needed to focus on traffic.

"We had an official memorial service for him," she said. "About a week afterward. With the funeral happening in Ontario and most people not being able to go, they needed to do something, you know?"

"Of course."

"But tonight was better. More relaxed. You got to hear a lot more personal stories."

Boyd smiled. "Like Josh punking Colin Parsons about the Red Sox trading a star second baseman five minutes before the paper's deadline, just to see him run."

Hayden grinned. "I think the whole newsroom appreciated that spectacle."

Boyd found himself smiling too. "Good thing the guy's got a sense of humor."

"Josh would never punk someone who couldn't take it in stride. Dave Bradley, for instance. Dave is way too serious, too literal. He's a brilliant guy, or so Josh said, but his social skills are . . . lacking, shall we say."

Boyd's mind was whirling. Hayden had insisted Dave was harmless. Maybe she was right. Maybe he was just locked in by his social awkwardness. Maybe Bradley had just tagged around after Hayden, wanting to start a conversation with her but not knowing how. Maybe each time he thought he'd finally screw up his courage and talk to her, but then wound up falling back again, afraid. Not that it made his following Hayden—or anyone—okay. Marginally less alarming, possibly, but still highly inappropriate.

"How does he manage to do his job, if he doesn't interact well with people?" he mused.

"Phone," she said without taking her eyes off the road. "I asked Josh the same question, but apparently he has no trouble with interviews so long as they're not face-to-face. He also does research, information gathering, compiling statistics, that kind of thing, to support the other reporters."

They lapsed into silence for a moment.

Well, it looked less and less likely that Dave Bradley was a credible suspect. He couldn't be ruled out, though, because he almost certainly must have been jealous of Josh's relationship with Hayden. Of course, he didn't really strike Boyd as the kind of guy who'd commit murder to clear the playing field of competition, particularly when he was clearly too terrified to put himself out there on that empty field.

Also, Bradley didn't fit with Boyd's theory that this had something to do with Josh's investigation.

At least this explained the difficulty Bradley had looking Boyd in the eye whenever they talked. Between his social challenges and the fact that he must have been squirming, wondering if Boyd—or the local PD—had found digital copies of the stalker pics on Josh's laptop, it was a wonder he'd managed to carry on a conversation at all.

A moment later, Hayden pulled into the drive at Dr. Stratton's. When she'd reached the rear parking lot, she executed a U-turn and brought the car to a stop right outside the service entrance.

"How's that for service?"

"Couldn't be better." He hit the seat belt release, but he didn't want to get out. Didn't want to go in there and spend another solitary night in the bed Josh had slept in for so many months. Didn't want to leave the warmth of Hayden's company.

If she were another woman, he'd probably make a play right now. If she wasn't Josh's best friend—hell, the woman he'd been in love with—and if she wasn't so great and smart and dedicated, he'd lean across the console and kiss her. He'd do his level best to talk her inside, where they would *not* watch TV.

But he'd already tried that, hadn't he? True, she hadn't exactly shot him down in flames. In fact, she'd acknowledged the attraction between them with the unflinching honesty he was coming to expect from her. But ultimately she'd reaffirmed her determination to avoid sexual and romantic entanglements, and who was he to drag her off that path?

He glanced at her and realized she was holding her breath. His heart jolted. Was she waiting for him to do what he'd just imagined doing? Hell, she was probably worried tonight would be a repeat of the other day at the lake, with him making a move and her having to say no.

Of course, if he started something and she shut him down, he could blame it on the four beers he'd drunk.

Except that was total bullshit. He hated when anyone—man or woman—used inebriation as an excuse.

Before he could do anything stupid, he opened the door. The dome light came on, dispelling the intimacy. "Text me when you get home?"

She blinked from the sudden change of the mood in the car. Or possibly from the sudden lighting change.

"Of course."

He climbed out of Hayden's car, gave her a wave, and watched as she maneuvered out of the driveway. When he heard her turn onto the street in front of the house and accelerate away, he dragged a hand through his hair. *Damned alcohol.*

Unfortunately, the booze hadn't dulled the grief and sorrow. On the contrary. It just laid him more bare to it. God, he missed Josh. Missed those texts that drove him crazy, the phone calls. It had been months since they'd been in the same place at the same time, but he missed that too. Their competitions, whether it was running or fishing or shooting hoops back home in their parents' driveway with that basketball net they'd never gotten around to getting rid of. And, yes, he missed looking at Josh and seeing his own features reflected back at him. His twin.

Sighing, he looked up at the old house, his gaze traveling across the second floor to Josh's room. As he was working up the fortitude to go inside and climb the stairs to that room, he saw a light flicker in the window. Not the overhead light or a lamp, but more like a flashlight. *What the hell?*

Galvanized, he unlocked the door and took the stairs two at a time. He pushed the door to his room open and hit the light switch.

Clear.

A quick check of the bathroom proved it was clear too.

Shit. He sank down on the edge of the bed. He must be losing it. He could have sworn there was someone in here with a flashlight.

A tap on his door made him leap up and started his heart pounding hard in his chest.

"Detective McBride?"

It was Sylvia Stratton. He opened the door to see her standing there with a lightbulb in one hand and a flashlight in the other. "Can I borrow your height for a moment? I was trying to change a bulb, but I'm not quite tall enough. It's Mrs. Garner's evening off, and she's staying the night with her daughter." She looked up at him with those clear blue eyes. "No doubt she has a step stool she uses for this sort of thing, but I've no idea where she keeps it. I don't like to climb on the furniture, especially with no one handy to help in case I fell."

Christ, he must have been looking at the wrong window. Got himself all worked up over nothing. How many beers had he had?

And how anal was she that one bulb couldn't wait another six hours to be replaced?

"Detective?" she prompted.

Very anal, apparently.

"Sure, Dr. Stratton." He took the bulb from her. "Lead the way."

Five minutes later, Dr. Stratton went on her way and Boyd went to his room.

Two hours later, he wished to God Dr. Stratton had a dozen middle-of-the-night handyman jobs for him to do. If he could keep his hands busy, maybe he could still his thoughts.

He'd lain there in bed, filled with memories of Josh and a deep, aching sorrow. The alcohol had long worn off, but the maudlin cast of his thoughts had not.

Eventually, the Josh memories gave way to thoughts of Hayden.

She had looked so good tonight. And not just that mane of hair, or the dip of her waist emphasized by that tiny jean jacket, or the way her skinny-legged pants hugged her curvy but athletic butt. Yeah, those things had made an impression. An indelible one he'd probably see on the backs of his eyelids when he finally got off to sleep. But it was also her quick smile. Eyes that sparkled when she laughed and grew soft when she was sad. And her formidable energy! He didn't know how she put in those long days and still had enough gas left in the tank to help him, if not with the investigation, then with his grief. She was a match for Josh in that respect.

Hell, she was a match for Josh in every respect. No wonder he'd loved her.

His mind leapt to those moments in the car. He'd talked himself out of kissing her, ostensibly to avoid being rejected. But if he was honest, he was pretty sure she would have welcomed his kiss. And maybe he wouldn't have gotten any further than that, just a few hot kisses stolen in the parking lot. Not tonight anyway. But there'd be another night and another night, and eventually she would sleep with him.

That wasn't arrogance speaking. That was their undeniable chemistry, plus her unflinching honesty. If he pressed her, he could have her.

His body responded accordingly, but he couldn't even enjoy that. A wave of guilt suffused him. Jesus, he was fantasizing about bedding Josh's girl.

Okay, so she wasn't his girl, but she was the woman he'd loved. What corner of hell would it land him in if he seduced her?

"Don't worry, buddy. I won't do it. She was yours as far as I'm concerned."

He turned off the bedside light and tried to settle to sleep.

A moment later, he sat up, grabbed his phone. There was one way he could be sure to keep that vow to his brother.

He started composing a text to Hayden.

Then he put his phone down, lay back, and looked at the ceiling. Finally, when the gray light of predawn lightened the room, he fell asleep.

CHAPTER 15

Hayden was supposed to have had the day off, but they'd run into a scheduling problem in the ER and had asked if she could come in and do an eight-hour shift. Shell-shocked as she was by Boyd's late-night text, which she'd read that morning, she'd leapt at the chance to go to work.

Josh had loved her. *Loved* loved her, as in girlfriend and boyfriend. Husband and wife. Not the way she'd loved him. Apparently he'd told Boyd as much months ago.

She'd texted back, basically saying, "I'm sorry. I didn't know," and telling him she'd been called in to work.

The ER had been busy, for which she'd been grateful. As long as she was working, she didn't have to think about it. Because the moment her thoughts did turn to it, she inevitably remembered some moment they'd shared and imagined how the things she'd said or done, or didn't do, might have hurt him.

On her lunch break, she'd phoned Boyd, thinking they had to talk before things got too weird. He'd answered, but he'd been with Ray Morgan, working on running down those numbers. He'd stayed on the line long enough to invite her to supper, offering to pick her up after work. She'd hesitated before answering, but then asked herself why. What had really changed? Nothing. Josh was still dead. Boyd was still here, and he still wanted her help and support. So she'd accepted.

As it happened, their supper plans got scrapped when they'd had multiple trauma cases roll in as a result of an MVA on the Vanier Highway. The ER had been backed up for hours, and her eight hours turned into an interminable stretch.

Unfortunately, the medical cases didn't stop showing up just because they were full up with trauma. Hayden had dealt with a suspected heart attack, a possible stroke, an uncomplicated fracture, and the usual assortment of sudden, severe pain in the pick-your-spot. So she'd told Boyd to pick her up whatever the daily special was at her favorite vegan restaurant and she'd join him when she could. She liked everything on their menu, and it was all organic.

She'd thought about asking him to meet her at her place, but she was still feeling kind of strange about that whole text exchange. By meeting him there, and by taking her own car, she could leave whenever she felt like it.

No sooner had she parked her Subaru and walked to the staff entrance when Boyd appeared.

"Wow, an escort," she said.

"I remembered what you said about Josh meeting you down here so you didn't have to run the gauntlet alone."

"Thank you. Is supper ready?" she asked brightly.

"Yep."

"Thank God. I'm starving."

He held the door for her to enter the house. "How are all your patients from that accident?"

"I only got to see two of them, both with minor injuries. Cuts and abrasions."

"Aren't you supposed to be learning to deal with the rougher stuff?" He gestured for her to precede him up the stairs.

Good. He was treating her normally. "Yeah, but when there's so much multiple major trauma all at once, it's a bit different," she said, sending a glance over her shoulder. "It was all hands on deck for the more experienced guys, leaving me to cover everything else. And believe me—that was plenty." They'd reached his room. He opened the door, and she walked in. "Would you believe I had a heart attack victim drive himself to the hospital? When will people learn to call an ambulance when they have chest pain?"

"So nobody died?"

"Not so far." She toed off her shoes, put her purse down on the coffee table, and flopped down on the couch. "One head injury went to Saint John, but the rest are being handled here. The surgeons will be busy in the OR all night, I think."

"Tired?"

"Exhausted. Well, physically. Mentally, I'm bouncing."

"I figured you'd want either a cup of hot tea or a glass of cold white wine," he said. "I've got both."

"Wine, please. I'll do tea after we've eaten."

"Coming right up."

"I should be helping." She pushed to the front of the couch and paused, gathering the energy to get up.

"No, sit and relax," he ordered. "You earned it. Working a shift from hell when you should have had the day off."

She subsided back against the couch cushions. "Did you get my text this morning?"

"I did." He pulled a bottle of sauvignon blanc out of the mini-fridge and poured two glasses for them. He brought the glasses over, set them on the coffee table, and sat down beside her. "Sorry to drop that on you in the middle of the night. I was wide-awake and thinking about Josh, and I just decided you should know."

She picked up the glass of wine and met his gaze. "Thank you for telling me."

He looked away. "I've been back and forth about what was the right thing to do. I'd made up my mind that you didn't need to be burdened with that information. But last night, I—"

"Burdened?" She put the wineglass down again. "God, Boyd, I'm not a child. And besides, if you hadn't told me, I'd never have known what a gift Josh gave me." Though she'd sworn she wouldn't cry, her eyes filled with tears. She looked up at the ceiling and blinked rapidly to stop them from falling.

"Jesus, you're right." His voice was almost a whisper. "It *was* a gift. All I could think was how it could do nothing but grieve you more."

She dropped her gaze to his face. His eyes were shimmering too.

"It's made me look at our conversations—Josh's and mine—through a different lens," she admitted. "And I can see I probably hurt him sometimes. But I'm so glad you told me."

They were both silent for a while as they struggled with emotion. She picked up her glass, took a sip of the chilled wine to ease her throat. "This actually explains some things. Like why you were so cool to me at the funeral and when you first came here. I couldn't think what I'd done to aggravate you."

"I was being an idiot. I didn't know you, except from what Josh told me, which was obviously biased and—"

"And you were understandably upset that I didn't return his feelings the way he wanted me to. And he was gone and he'd never have a chance to move on and love someone else."

"I don't blame you anymore." He sat back, his wine untouched. "I know emotions can't be ordered up, and I know you have really good reasons for not wanting to get involved with anybody."

"Thank you." She sniffed back tears. "I appreciate your saying that. And I am sorry I didn't return his feelings the way he would have liked. But I did love him so much."

"He was happy being with you," Boyd said. "I mean, he'd have been happier if you were his girlfriend, naturally, but he got so much joy out of being around you."

"Did he think that might happen, eventually? That I'd come to love him romantically?"

He dropped his gaze. "He hoped it would."

She blinked again. "I wonder now if I shouldn't have pushed him away after he . . . you know, kissed me. I should have known. And he did so much for me, made my life so much easier. I thought he was taking care of me like a brother, but—" She broke off and took another sip of wine to wash the lump from her throat. "Maybe if I *had* pushed him away, he'd have moved on, met a smart, nice woman . . ."

He shook his head. "No. He was happy being around you. And he certainly wasn't going to fall out of love with you and into love with another woman in a few months. Eventually, I'm sure he would have, but not nearly that soon." He lifted his glass and had a healthy sip of the wine. "Okay, have we cleared the air? Said all we need to say?"

Hayden almost smiled. Poor Boyd. He so hated conversations about emotion. Josh had loved to bait him about it. He'd said Boyd thought it was better to keep that stuff safely bottled up, instead of "wearing it on your fucking sleeve and winding up bleeding that emotion all over innocent people who just want not to be bled on!" It probably had something to do with Josh's abduction way back when they were children. Josh had emerged with the optimistic, caring nature reinforced, while Boyd's less trustful, closed-off nature had been cemented.

She smiled. "Yeah, we're done. We can talk about something else."

They talked some more about Hayden's hairy shift. Then she asked him how he and Detective Morgan were making out with the phone numbers.

He pushed to his feet. "How about dinner first? It's in the toaster oven under tinfoil. I shoved it in there when you called to say you were getting in the car."

She started to get up and he gestured for her to stay.

"Just relax. I'll get it."

"Thank you." She sank back against the couch cushions and sipped her wine.

He was back quickly, with a tray and the bottle of wine to top them up. "I didn't realize you were vegan."

"I'm nowhere near vegan. Not even vegetarian, although I usually only eat fish and chicken." She took the tray from him and placed it on her lap. "The thing is, I do love vegan cuisine. It's usually organic, which I like." She peeled the foil back on the hot plate to reveal a sizeable piece of tempeh crusted with pea and cornmeal on a bed of what she knew would be Thai sticky rice and a side of sautéed bok choy. The smells of garlic and ginger rose up in the curling steam. "See? What's not to love?"

He leaned closer to look. "That chunk of . . . what is it?"

"It's tempeh, fermented soy. And I bet you could learn to like it." She took a bite of the rice. "Mmm."

"Absolutely. Right along with learning to like the captors who were feeding the stuff to me. I think it's called Stockholm syndrome."

She laughed spontaneously, then coughed as she almost inhaled some rice. "God, Boyd, could you give a girl a warning when you're going to say something like that?" She reached for her wine to wash down the rice.

"Sorry." He grinned, but, again, it seemed slightly forced. Was he still feeling bad for telling her about Josh's feelings? Surely not.

As though sensing her concern, he grabbed the remote. "How about some TV while you eat?" The small flat screen sprang to life on the guide channel. "Any preference?"

She realized he was trying to divert her attention from him, but she went along with it. "How about the news?" She checked her wristwatch to see the time was about right. "I haven't seen or heard anything all day."

He tuned in to a local CBC station and she ate in silence as she took in what was happening in the world. There was also coverage of the accident that had tied up the ER.

After both her meal and the news were done, he offered to take her tray, but she insisted on dealing with it herself. "If I don't get up and move, I'll crash. Especially after that chocolate mousse dessert."

"Can you even call it a mousse if it's made with coconut milk?"

"Absolutely. I should have saved you a taste."

"Uh, that's okay."

He followed her to the kitchenette, where she rinsed the dishes and left them in the sink. She left the tray for him to deal with, since she had no idea where it went. When she turned around, he was leaning against the counter.

FATAL HEARTS

She leaned her butt against the counter too, turning her head to study him. "Are you okay, Boyd?"

He glanced sideways at her. "What do you mean?"

"Do we need to talk more about Josh? I know you don't—"

"God, no."

"Then what is it? You seem a little down."

He looked like he was going to deny it. She could almost see him doing the emotional cost-benefit analysis. Finally, he looked away, sighed, and scrubbed a hand over his face. "I'm feeling discouraged, I guess."

"Nothing with the phone numbers?"

"Not so far."

"But you can't have exhausted all those months' worth of phone records yet?"

"No, not by a long shot. But we've been through the most recent ones. I was hoping there'd be something there in the last days or week before Josh's death." He rubbed the back of his neck. "By the way, Josh did have an appointment with the car dealer to get that rear passenger door lock fixed. He'd also ordered a new two-hundred-dollar pair of high-tech running shoes with gel insoles."

She ignored that useless information. "Couldn't it still be there, but farther back? You've said yourself you don't know when a piece of information is going to click into place. Maybe that happened for Josh."

"Maybe. Or maybe the caller dialed in to Josh's phone, in which case we're shit outta luck unless something breaks and we can get a court order."

"What does Detective Morgan think?"

"He thinks I'm being unduly negative."

"Maybe he's right," she said. "You still have a lot of numbers to run down, right? And something will connect to something else and you'll be off on the right track."

"I hope so." He passed a hand over the back of his neck again, making her wonder if it was stiff. Probably tension. "I just wish I could have found that damned notebook. But I've searched everywhere I can think for it."

"And you're not learning anything from me." Saying it aloud gave her a pang of hollowness. If he had nothing to learn from her, there was no need for them to hang out, was there?

That brought his head back around again. "That's not true. I'm learning lots from you about Josh and his life here. Probably more than you or I yet know."

"Really?" The hollow feeling began to recede. "Because the last thing I want to do is waste your time. If it would be better used—"

"You're not wasting my time, Hayden. You're giving me the context I need. Yes, I knew the basics about his life here from our phone conversations over these past months, but it was a pretty bare sketch, compared to what you've told me. And, yes, I can get pieces from Sylvia Stratton and her staff and Josh's coworkers. But no one knew him like you did. And it helps knowing his life here was happy, thanks in no small part to you."

She blinked rapidly. "Thank you."

"The rest of it . . . it's just frustrating. I don't seem to be making much progress. We're stuck waiting for those reports, but at the same time, I'm fucking *dreading* them." He gave a harsh laugh. "I'm afraid the coroner's office is going to take one look at them, pronounce natural causes, and the file will be closed."

She couldn't deny that possibility, so she said nothing.

He looked off toward the sitting room, leaving her free to look at his profile. He looked tired, she realized. Lines of fatigue etched his face. Was he not sleeping?

"I can't help but think if it was me lying in the ground in that family plot, Josh would have done a better job getting to the bottom of what happened."

His words throbbed with so much emotion, Hayden felt her own throat grow painfully tight. *Say something!* "Oh, no, Boyd. No."

He bent his head, massaged his temple. "If our positions were reversed, he'd have answers."

"I don't believe that. Josh was an amazing investigator, but he wouldn't be any further ahead right now than you are. He still would've had to deal with funeral arrangements. He'd have had to help your parents through those initial days. He'd only just be getting started, like you are."

"Yeah, you're probably right," he said, but he didn't look like he believed it.

In that moment, she felt the edge of his grief as keenly as her own. Without thinking about it, she reached for his hand, lacing her fingers with his.

His head was still bent, and she saw him transfer his focus to their joined hands. Then, almost in slow motion, he lifted her hand and turned so he faced her. For a wild few seconds, she thought he was going to press his lips to the back of her hand. What he did felt even more intimate. He unlinked their fingers and pressed her hand to his chest.

The feel of all that solid, warm muscle through his shirt was somehow shocking. As was the eye contact. It was electric. She couldn't look away. But if she didn't, he would kiss her. That's where this was going unless she stopped it. She could pull back now and he'd let her go. He wouldn't say a word about it or make things awkward. But dammit, she was tired of always guarding her reactions. And God help her, she wanted to know his kiss. A real kiss this time. She burned for it.

Then she became conscious of the thudding of his heart beneath her palm.

His heart. It felt so strong, so alive.

Suddenly it seemed crucial to get closer to him, closer to his vitality. To feel alive herself.

She leaned in, brought her other hand up to his chest.

With a groan, he released her hand that he'd been pressing to his chest so he could draw her fully into his arms.

Yes! At the full-body contact, every hormone, every nerve bundle in her body joined the chorus. *Yes, yes, yes, yes.*

But despite the desire she'd seen darken his eyes, all he did was press her body to his—warm, living flesh against flesh, as though he sought only to comfort or be comforted. It was she who went up on tiptoe and pressed her lips to his. There was the slightest hesitation on his part, long enough for her to wonder if she'd made a horrible mistake. Before she could retreat, he lifted his hands to her head, holding her in place as his mouth crashed down onto hers.

The thrill that forked through her was almost painful, leaving her nerve endings feeling singed. Her heart thumped so hard, she could feel her pulse throbbing in her fingertips. And his smell! So like Josh's scent, it was comforting and familiar on the one hand and confusing on the other.

Then he urged her lips apart and his tongue swept into her mouth. The taste of him exploded on her senses. There was no echo of Josh here. Only Boyd. She pressed closer, sliding her arms up around his neck. Conveniently, that brought the aching tips of her breasts into contact with his chest. A bolt of desire shot straight to her womb. Without conscious thought, she rubbed her breasts against him.

He growled against her lips, sending another thrill zinging to her core. One of his hands fisted in her hair. He broke the kiss and urged her head backward. The arm that encircled her pulled her closer, and he bent to kiss her exposed throat. Delight shivered through her at the contrasting sensations of his hot, silky mouth and the abrading rasp of stubble. She arched against him as he explored the delicate skin, then found the sweet spot below her ear. The heat of his mouth, the warmth of his breath on her skin, the vibrating urgency of his body beneath her hands . . . Dear Lord, it was almost too much to bear. But the alternative— stopping him—was unthinkable. She couldn't even remember why she might want to.

"Touch me," she commanded.

He didn't need any more encouragement. Or a road map. He released her hair and dropped that hand to clasp one of her breasts. His thumb found the stiffened peak through the thin fabric of her bra and T-shirt, and she gasped softly.

Then his lips were on hers again, as though he wanted to take the sound into him. This time, she met the demand of his mouth with demands of her own. Her tongue tangled with his, stroking, tasting. All the while, his hands moved over her, her breasts, the dip of her waist, her ass, setting up a tingling arousal everywhere they landed.

She slid her hands under his T-shirt, gliding them greedily over his skin. She'd seen his bare chest at the beach, knew it was mostly hairless except for the dusting of hair on his pecs and the thin arrow of hair pointing south. But touching him was still a revelation. Her palms transmitted the information to her brain and to other parts of her anatomy. The smooth texture of the bare skin, the rougher texture of the haired area, the thrilling hardness of his abdomen—it was sensory overload, but she craved more.

Oh, God, she needed to get horizontal with him.

She pulled her mouth from his, her eyes fixing on his damp kiss-reddened lips. "Tell me you have condoms."

She felt the change in him immediately, but it was still a shock when he released her and stepped back.

"Oh, Christ, Hayden. I'm sorry."

He was *stopping*? "Sorry? What for?"

"For all of that." He dragged a hand through his hair. Hair that she'd already done a pretty thorough job of mussing. "You don't want to get involved with anyone—much less with your dead best friend's brother. I respect that. I respect *you*. This was . . . I'm sorry. I don't really have any defense, except—"

"Defense? Boyd, you don't need one. I'm the one who started—" She looked up at him, horrified. "Oh, crap, I jumped you. You're grieving, feeling low, and I freaking *jumped* on you. I am so sorry."

～

Boyd was so fixated on the battle to keep his hands off her, it took a few seconds for his brain to process her words. "Wait, what? You didn't jump me."

"Yes, I did." She put a hand over her mouth. "Omigod, I so totally did. You were feeling discouraged and I took advantage of that. All you wanted was comfort and I—"

He wanted more than ever to draw her into his arms. "Hayden, what just happened had very little to do with comfort. And *nothing* to do with you taking advantage of me."

"But—"

"But nothing. That was me doing what I've been wanting to do since the first moment I saw you at the hospital."

"What if I said I changed my mind?"

"Changed your mind?" His heart leapt. As did another part of his anatomy. *But holy shit, how can this be happening?* He'd specifically told her about Josh being in love with her, thinking that would somehow kill this attraction. "I'd say you're smarter than that."

"I'll ignore that insult, mainly because I haven't been very smart. Not smart at all. You've been right in front of me, and the attraction has been there, but I haven't done anything about it. The whole keeping my distance from romantic or physical entanglements—it's become such a habit. It really didn't occur to me that you're the perfect candidate."

Perfect candidate? She couldn't be serious. Could she?

"Oh, Hayden, no. I am so not a good bet."

She lifted an eyebrow. "Can I count on you to leave when the investigation is done? Go back home to your life?"

"Well yes, but—"

"Then you actually are a very good bet. Because that's just what I need."

Dear God. Had he heard that right? The hottest, most gorgeous woman he'd met in years had just propositioned him, offering a no-strings sexual relationship with a wide-open exit clause. But she was also the nicest, most amazing woman he'd ever met. And oh God, she'd been *Josh's love.* How was he supposed to reconcile that?

How could he start an affair with the woman Josh wanted to marry?

Because you want her.

"Boyd? Aren't you going to say anything?"

No. No, he wasn't going to say anything. He was done thinking too.

He reached out and hauled her to him. She made a little squeak of alarm when she collided with his chest, but he swallowed it, crushing those soft, cushiony lips beneath his in a kiss of pure, searing demand. She opened her mouth to him immediately. His tongue swept in, claiming her. And Christ, she tasted good. Heady and female and fucking fantastic. Her arms snaked up around his neck, and she clung to him. Which gave him perfect access to her back, the curve of her hips, her firm, luscious ass.

Yeah, he was toast. No way in this life or the next was he about to say no to Hayden.

Because they both needed to breathe, he pulled back and looked down at her. Her face was flushed, her eyes unfocused, pupils dilated.

"That, sweetheart, is getting jumped."

She drew her tongue across her plump bottom lip, probably to soothe it, but his cock reacted predictably.

"Isn't there more to it?" Her voice was huskier than he'd ever heard it. Sexy.

"Yes, much more. And, yes, I do have condoms."

CHAPTER 16

Boyd followed as Hayden led the way to his bedroom.

His instinct was to lift her up until she locked those long legs around him and carry her to the bed, kissing the hell out of her all the way. He wanted to fan the flames of her excitement. Instead, he let her lead the way under her own steam, giving her the chance to let the reality of what they were about to do sink in.

When she reached the bed, she turned. Her smile was tremulous. "All the times I came over here, I never even sat on this bed."

The reminder of Josh should have cooled Boyd's jets, but it didn't. He'd grown used to sleeping in the bed his brother used to occupy. "Does it bother you that Josh slept here? Because if it does, we could—"

"It doesn't."

Good. Because he didn't know how he would have finished that sentence. *Do it on the tiny couch? On the floor? Up against the wall?* Hayden deserved better.

With her eyes locked on his, she reached for the hem of her T-shirt. Clearly she hadn't changed her mind. The T-shirt came off over her head, and she tossed it aside. His eyes clapped onto the white bra cupping her breasts. It was one of those seamless things designed to make women look amazing in sweaters and T-shirts, but it was not the kind of bra he often saw. No color, no lace, no feats of engineering in the cleavage department. Basically not the kind of bra a woman wore when she knew she was going to be undressed. At least, not the women he knew. Somehow, the difference made him feel unaccountably tender toward her.

"Come here," he said.

She stepped into his arms with no hesitation, lifting her face for a kiss. It was a long, drugging one, unhurried and sensual. It was as though now the decision was made, they had all the time in the world.

But sensual and slow eventually gave way to urgency. When her hands worked their way under his shirt, he tore it off. She pressed herself to him, gasping at the skin-to-skin contact. He reached for the clasp of her bra and worked it free. She moved back long enough to let the garment fall away. He had just enough time to register the lush shape of her breasts with their rosy-pink tips before she pressed them to his chest again. And, oh Christ, they felt good.

He needed to get her naked, and he sure as hell needed to get out of his jeans. But first, he needed to locate a condom.

He pulled back. Her eyes were heavy lidded and sensual, her lips reddened. And her poor face. She was going to have some whisker burn. If he were a better man, he'd stop and shave right now. But he wasn't. He rubbed her lower lip with the ball of his thumb. "Wait here. I'll be right back."

"What?"

"Condom."

"Oh! Of course."

He ducked into the en suite bathroom, grabbed his shaving kit, and dug out a package of condoms. With one in hand and a couple more in the pocket of his jeans, he went back to the bedroom.

She reached for him, going up on tiptoe to kiss his mouth again. He had no objection to that. Then her fingers glided down his chest to find the button of his denims and unfastened it. He stilled her hand with his own.

"Ladies first."

She gave him a wicked smile. "Oh, I like that policy. Especially in the bedroom."

He turned her around so her sweet, round butt was tucked up against his hardness and reached around to find the button at the top of her jeans. He freed it and slid the short zipper down. Then he slid his hand inside her panties, his fingers finding her moist warmth. She made a mewling sound that went straight to his groin. God, she was slick!

But he wasn't finished torturing her. Not yet. Tossing the condom on the bed, he lifted his newly freed hand to her left breast. He still hadn't seen them properly, but they were full enough to fill his hand. With one hand, he delved into her wet heat, and, with the other, he teased her nipple into a tight, hard nub. Panting now, she ground her butt into him.

"Now, Boyd." The plea emerged with what sounded almost like a sob.

He released her. She immediately turned around, stripped her jeans off, panties and all, and stepped out of them. Sweet

Lord in heaven, she was gorgeous. Her hair was tousled, her lips swollen. Her breasts were beautifully proportioned, crested with rosy-pink tips that had hardened into tight buds. Her waist dipped, flowing smoothly into womanly hips, strong, shapely legs, and pretty feet. His gaze traveled back up to the apex of her thighs, where a neat thatch of golden hair hid the sweetest part. The sight hardened his cock even further. He'd never cared much for the trend of women waxing themselves bare. Maybe it was the cop in him, but he didn't want to feel as if he were bedding a prepubescent girl.

"You are so beautiful," he said. "Perfect."

"And you are so not naked."

He laughed, shucking his jeans and underwear off just as she had; then he bent to peel off his socks. When he looked up, the expression on her face made him grin.

"You're not so bad yourself."

He took her in his arms and kissed her. Then he whisked her off her feet, causing her to gasp. Smiling with satisfaction, he placed her on the bed and followed her down. He wanted to lie beside her and tease her some more. Kiss every inch of her body and bring her to climax with his mouth. But that would have to wait until he'd had a close shave. She wouldn't thank him for whisker burns on her most tender, intimate flesh.

Instead, he covered her body with his. Weight propped on his arms, cock nestled between her legs, he pressed her lush body into the mattress. She clutched at his shoulders and surged against him.

Dammit, where is that condom? He rolled away, located it, and sheathed himself in record time.

"Please, Boyd. Don't make me wait. I want you inside me."

He rolled to face her. Without encouragement, she rolled onto her side to bring their bodies into alignment.

"Kiss me."

He obeyed, taking her mouth in another deep kiss while he found her sex with his hand. Groaning, she parted her legs for him so he could stroke her. He almost groaned himself when he found how wet she was. How ready.

She pulled at his shoulders and rolled onto her back. He took the hint, covering her again with his body. Some fumbling and he was there, poised at her entrance.

"Now!"

He pushed into her scalding heat with deliberate control, but she surged up to meet him, taking most of his length. The shock of sensation stilled him. She gasped and stilled too, and the sound reminded him that it had probably been a while for her. Maybe a long while.

"Are you okay?"

She ran her hands down his flanks. "I am so much more than okay." Her hands found his butt and urged him closer. He took that as permission to move. Reminding himself she was out of practice, he pulled out marginally and rocked back into her, filling her completely. He did it again and again, setting up an insistent rhythm. It felt so good, he had to grit his teeth to keep the tempo easy. And the view of her breasts bobbing with every rocking thrust didn't make it any easier.

"Oh, yes." Her words were husky, barely recognizable as her voice. "That's good."

He liked a woman who wasn't afraid to say what she liked.

Then her hands were on his chest, his abdomen, his sides. They skated over his skin, one moment all soft palms, the next clutching with fingernails. Damn, but he wanted those hands everywhere. On his back, at his nape, in his hair . . . Before he even realized what he was doing, he'd picked up the rhythm, driving into her harder, faster, his strokes longer.

"Yes!"

She moved with him, meeting his every thrust. He felt the tension rising in her as the tempo increased. Going down on one elbow, he reached between them to part her folds wider, moving higher to hopefully give her more friction. That tipped her over the edge she'd been striving for. Her words were broken, sobbed out of her, as her orgasm rose, peaked, and rolled over her. It was all he could do to hold on and let her ride it out before his own need took over.

She held him close now. Her breasts beneath him were soft and cushioning, and their nipples had contracted into tight, hard points from her orgasm. Her breath was warm in his ear, and she was so incredibly tight as he plunged into her, her internal muscles still clenching and releasing. She sank the fingers of one hand into his hair, and he came with a muffled cry.

Arms trembling, he rested on her a moment while the world righted itself.

Goddamn.

CHAPTER 17

Hayden stretched luxuriously as she watched Boyd head to the bathroom to deal with the condom. She couldn't remember the last time she'd been so blissed-out.

She had orgasms. Regularly. The mechanics of arousal, sex, and orgasm were no mystery. She was very good at taking care of herself. She owned a vibrator and knew how to use it. But there was just no comparison between that and sex with a talented, attractive partner you could trust.

And she did trust Boyd.

No, he wasn't the kind of guy who hung around long. Even if Josh hadn't bemoaned his twin's chances of ever finding a woman he wanted to settle with, she'd have known that much. It was there for anyone to see. No doubt a lot of women had seen it and taken it as a challenge, imagining that they would be the ones to bring him to heel.

In that respect, he was the anti-Josh. But that's what made him perfect for her. Or rather, perfect for right now.

So no, she couldn't "trust" him to hang around after his investigation was done. But she didn't want him to. She *did* trust him with her body, her person. She trusted him to be a considerate lover and to be discreet. Just as it was ingrained in him to walk on the traffic side of the sidewalk, he would treat her with respect.

And best of all, she liked him. They were connected too. Their love of Josh, their grief over his loss. Though they'd only known each other briefly, she felt as though she'd known him much longer.

"You're looking pretty pleased with yourself, Dr. Walsh."

She looked up to see Boyd approaching the bed. He was still naked, and she caught her breath at the sight of him.

"Do I?" She bit her lip. "I guess I am at that."

He picked up the coverlet from the bottom of the bed and crawled in beside her. After positioning a pillow behind his head, he drew her close and tossed the throw over them.

"Good idea," she said, snuggling into his chest, her head resting on his left arm. "I was starting to feel the chill."

He made no reply, just brought his left hand up to stroke her hair. She closed her eyes and gave herself over to the moment. The lazy caress sent waves of pleasure shimmering through her. Not arousing—it would take some time before her system rebooted enough for that—but sensual.

Eventually, though, as the minutes ticked by with no sound but for the slowing beat of his heart beneath her ear, she began to worry. She tipped her head back to look at him, catching a pensive look on his face. Her stomach plummeted.

Was he having second thoughts about what they'd done? Was he wondering how to extract himself from the situation gracefully? Might as well be direct. He'd give her a straight answer.

She drew back so she could look at him. "What are you thinking about?"

"The damned telephone numbers."

She almost wilted with relief.

"I know." He grimaced. "Not very romantic talk, is it? It's just where my mind goes, every moment it can. The investigation."

"What about the phone numbers?"

He pulled her back against him. "So far, the ones we've chased down are pretty much the same players Morgan identified on his own. Obstetricians. Old ones, new ones who've taken over old practices. Most of them Morgan's already talked to, and the others he's planning to interview. The ones he's already talked to all readily admitted meeting with Josh, but none of them could help him with his quest. Only two had records of identical twin boys born around the time we were."

"I presume Morgan followed those up?"

"Yeah. One set of twins was Asian and, with the other set, one child had hydrocephalus, which led to cognitive developments."

"Oh, poor thing." She put her hand on his chest. "It must have been from injury sustained during childbirth. If it was congenital, both twins would have had it."

He covered her hand with his, stroking it. "Yes, an unfortunate complication of birth, the doctor said."

"But there are still numbers to explore?"

"Oh, yeah. But so far, we're getting stuff like the car dealer and the Running Room. Restaurant take-out numbers. A whole bunch of them were calls he made in the course of his work at the newspaper—he didn't carry a separate cell for work."

"You're scared you're going to run all the numbers and come up with nothing?"

"Yeah," he admitted. "As soon as I saw there was nothing particularly helpful in the last couple of weeks' calls, it's been hard to sustain much optimism."

They were quiet for a moment.

"You say Morgan has been chasing down obstetricians. Has he been looking at GPs too?"

His hand, which had been stroking hers, stilled. "I know deliveries by family doctors weren't that unusual back then, but a multiple birth? I thought that automatically warranted an obstetrician."

"It does. I'm sure it did thirty-five years ago too. But—"

"But if they were trying to keep the whole thing off the record, so to speak, why not use a GP? Or a midwife for that matter."

"I don't think there was a licensed midwifery program in New Brunswick at the time," she said. "But yeah, sure. It might have been a home birth attended by either a doctor or someone qualified—or holding themselves out as qualified—to attend deliveries." She tipped her head back to look at him. "Omigod. Josh might have been thinking in that direction. It was months ago, but he did ask me about midwifery back then. I told him they didn't—and still don't—have hospital privileges. We do have legislation, and I imagine privileges will come, but those births are and have been exclusively home births."

"That's good! Josh had probably exhausted the ob-gyns and turned his attention to the alternatives."

She could feel the excitement in him. He was practically vibrating with it. It made her happy to see the discouragement banished. "I hope it was a GP. They'd probably be easier to find thirty-five years later than an unregulated midwife."

"That's where I'll start," he declared. "Morgan can chase the rest of the baby doctors, and I'll start running down the family docs."

"That's a pretty sizeable pool," she cautioned.

"I just need a way of figuring out who was practicing here when we were born, then figuring out where they are—if they're still around, if they moved on, if they're dead. I'll start with the ones who are still here, and I'll reach out to them."

"Won't that take a long time?"

"Not necessarily."

She bit her lip. "It sounds like a pretty big job. And remember, Josh was an investigative journalist and it took him the better part of what?" She did the mental calculation. "Six months to get to the stage where you think he had a major breakthrough."

"I may have mentioned this, but in my real life, I'm a detective."

She rolled her eyes. "I wasn't casting aspersions. But you need to explain the fast-track scenario. How can you get to the answers any faster than Josh did?"

"I figure out who he was likely to have talked to and visit them. Give them the hard candy."

"Uh . . . hard candy?"

"Yeah. You know, I put on my stern face and say I know they talked to Josh about the circumstances of our birth and adoption, and they'd be well advised to tell me what they know before I find out through other means."

She frowned. "What if they say they don't have a clue what you're talking about, that they never heard of Josh or never talked to him?"

He shrugged. "I'll say something like, 'I guess we'll see when I get through all his notes and the boxes upon boxes of research records he left.' Then I'll watch them to see what they do."

"The imaginary boxes of research records."

"Naturally."

Suddenly, her mind was awash with possibilities, none of them good. Yes, he might shake some information loose with that approach, but, holy crap, how much consternation it would cause. And how much danger would he set afoot?

"Boyd, that could be dangerous. If someone did kill Josh over his investigation—"

"Believe me, I know," he conceded. "It could well be dangerous. But I can't see any other way."

She threw her legs over the edge of the bed and reached for her T-shirt from where it lay on the floor. She heard him sit up, felt his eyes on her as she pulled her shirt over her head.

"I can take care of myself, Hayden. And unlike Josh, I'm going in with eyes wide-open."

She reached for her jeans, pulled them on, then found herself holding her panties and bra.

"Josh would do it for me," he said, his voice soft. "If our positions were reversed, he wouldn't quit digging until he knew the answers. Even if it was dangerous."

Shit, shit, shit. He was right and she knew it.

She sighed. "I know." She tossed the underwear on the bed and sat back down. "I'm just unnerved."

"C'mere." He leaned back again and held out his arms. She went into them.

Instead of trying to kindle desire again, he just kissed her forehead and snuggled her close. His hand resumed the stroking of her hair, but she couldn't settle into it this time. She pulled away.

"We should get started."

"We?" He went up on his elbows.

"Yeah, *we*. I let Josh exclude me from his search. I don't know whether I could have helped or not, but I could have tried, at least. I won't let you do the same." She got off the bed again and started pacing. "I'm plugged into the health system better than you are, and I'll do whatever I can to help, as long as it doesn't involve divulging personal information."

He got up, found his jeans, and hauled them on. Even as pre-occupied as she was, she couldn't help but admire that fine butt and broad, muscular back.

"That would be fantastic." He scooped up his shirt and put it on. "Maybe I'll have another look from the legal end, although there's precious little to work with."

"That's right. The legal part was very murky, wasn't it? That whole thing about the birth certificates not matching up with any registered births or adoption records."

"Murky would be a walk in the park. Unfortunately, it's more like impenetrable blackout." He rubbed the back of his neck. "Maybe I could track down the Fredericton lawyer's secretary or something."

"The one who handled the adoption from this end?"

"Yeah. We got his name from the Ontario lawyer who acted for my parents."

"Why not ask the lawyer himself? Unless . . . Oh, crap, he's dead, isn't he?"

"Long dead, in fact. He perished in a fire that swept through his office one night when he'd been working late. This happened the very same year we were born. The theory was he got drunk, passed out with a lit cigarette in his hand. Of course, all his records were destroyed in the fire."

"That sucks."

"Doesn't it?"

"What about the Ontario lawyer? Didn't he have a file?"

"Absolutely, complete with an order of adoption and consent of our birth mother, I'm sure, but even if he weren't retired and in the beginning stages of Alzheimer's, he can't just give that information out. You need a court order to unseal that stuff. Josh did get a court file number, but when he petitioned the court, they didn't have corresponding records, or at least not that matched our case. Nor could the courts locate a file or record of any kind for that time frame involving twins by the name of Holbrook, our supposed surname at birth."

"Unbelievable."

"You can see why Josh concluded that it was an out-and-out illegal adoption, propped up by falsified records. It's almost like someone from this end was working right from the get-go, from the very freakin' minute we were born, to obscure the trail."

She frowned. "Could it be that you were misdirected to Fredericton? Might the adoption have happened in another jurisdiction? Nova Scotia, maybe? Prince Edward Island?"

He shook his head. "Josh checked with vital statistics in every province and territory across the country, and nothing turned up. Probably because our name wasn't really Holbrook."

Oh, shit. Of course. "Speaking of vital statistics, what about other sets of identical twins born on your birthday? Have you checked into that?"

"Not the kind of information you can easily or legally draw out of the government records. It also presumes that whoever faked the birth certificates stopped at inventing the surname. If someone was that determined to erase the trail, they probably messed with the birth date too."

"So if neither you nor Josh believed anything written on those birth certificates, why was Josh so convinced you were born here?"

"The one thing he did believe was that the lawyer who died in the fire here was the one who handled the adoption. Edward

Bowlin, Esquire, had a reputation as a bit of a fixer, which fit with a shady adoption deal. I'm inclined to agree."

"This is incredible," she said. "I had no idea. I mean, yes, I knew there were irregularities. I knew the private adoption records couldn't be located and unsealed, which is how most kids go about finding their birth parents. But either Josh glossed over that part or I wasn't paying very close attention, because I had no clue it was so crazy and convoluted."

"I'm sure it was the former. He didn't want people thinking our adoptive parents participated in an illegal adoption."

She chewed her lip a moment. "Did they?"

"Not knowingly." His answer came without hesitation. "The deal was handled between the lawyers, as far as Josh could tell."

"The deal?" She slanted him a look. "That sounds very businesslike."

"That's exactly what it was, a deal. A transaction. Frank and Ella McBride had a desperate need and the means to pay, and our mother clearly had the product."

Hayden hoped that wasn't the case, but she knew that adoptions like that did happen.

"I presume your parents must have known what Josh was doing here. I mean, he'd have to explain why he'd leave a national newspaper to come work for a tiny local one?"

"Yeah, they knew."

"Did they mind?"

"Not at all. They totally supported him. Of course, they didn't know it was probably illegal. Josh just told them there was some bureaucratic bungling involved."

That made sense. People were quick to believe in the incompetence of civil servants. "You seem to know quite a lot. I thought you and Josh didn't talk about this stuff."

NORAH WILSON

He waved a hand. "This was back in the very beginning, when he thought all it was going to take was a relatively straightforward petition to the courts. I listened every time he ran into one of these walls. Our difference of opinion arose when it became obvious the trail had been intentionally obliterated thirty-five years ago. Once he'd decided to move to Fredericton to pursue it, I told him I wished him well. Man's gotta do what a man's gotta do. But I also made it clear I wasn't going to be part of the search." He went to the window, although Hayden knew there was nothing to see out there but the dull gleam of a couple of cars parked beneath the sentinel light in the staff parking lot below. "And, yes, I am well aware of the irony. If Josh could see me right now, he'd be laughing his ass off."

"No, he wouldn't." She walked up behind him and slid her arms around him. He stiffened initially, then relaxed. "He'd be cheering you on."

"You're right. Well, for the investigation part anyway." He turned to take her in his arms.

She pulled back so she could look up at his face. "But not the having sex with me part?"

He let her go. "Forget it. I shouldn't have brought it up."

"Boyd, there's no reason to feel guilty. None. I loved Josh dearly, but he and I were never going to end up here. We're not betraying him."

"No? Then why do I feel guilty?"

"Survivor guilt. It's very common with twins. You probably feel guilty for enjoying a meal."

He frowned.

"Or laughing spontaneously at something funny, or for experiencing a sense of peace when the sun is shining on your face, or even getting a good night's sleep and waking up feeling good."

"I don't sleep so well anymore."

"I'm not surprised. Sleep disturbance is pretty common with grief. Some people feel chronically under-rested and sleep all the time, and others can develop insomnia. All you can do is work through it." She made a mental note to give him some material on sleep hygiene. There were probably a few things he could do to improve his situation.

"I ran the same route Josh did in Odell Park. Well, a longer route. Took me a little over fifty minutes, and afterward, I was almost giddy from the endorphins. And when I realized what I was feeling, I felt so shitty."

She pressed herself against him, and his arms came up around her, hugging her hard. She hugged him back. "That's probably not going to go away overnight." She leaned back in his arms. "You guys were linked from the moment of conception. You're bound to feel the grief of his loss more intensely than anyone else, and you may feel it longer than others think is appropriate. That's why you need to work actively on grieving, to make sure it doesn't rob you of pleasure and happiness going forward."

His thumbs dug into the flesh of her upper arms, but she was sure he didn't notice. "That's why I have to find out what happened to him. Otherwise, I feel like I'll be stuck here."

"You'll figure it out."

He looked down at her, his eyes darkening. "Are you sorry?"

"About *this*?"

"Yeah, about this."

"I'm sorry about a lot of things, Boyd." She laid the flats of her palms on his chest, covered now by the T-shirt he'd pulled back on. "I'm sorry—God, I'm *heartsick*—that Josh is gone. I'm sorry now that I didn't drag more details out of him about his investigation. And I am so, so sorry I didn't get a chance to say good-bye to him." She curled her fingers into the material of the shirt. "But I am very definitely *not* sorry about what we just did."

"Good." He folded her close again.

She slid her arms around him and pressed her face to his chest.

"Do you have to rush off?" he asked, his voice a rumble against her ear.

"Not really. I'm off tomorrow. Well, unless they call me in again, but I do need to catch up on sleep. Maybe in an hour?" She leaned back in his arms to look up at his face, and the way he was looking at her made her pulse jump and her breath come faster. "I don't want to meet Sylvia while I'm creeping out in the middle of the night or at dawn."

"An hour?" He threaded a hand through her hair, as though the texture of it was endlessly fascinating. "You think that's going to be long enough?"

Oh, boy! "Maybe two."

He grinned, steering her toward the bed. "That'll have to do."

This time it was a more leisurely business. Between kisses, they helped each other out of their clothes, hands and eyes exploring territory that was still thrillingly new. By the time he stepped back, desire pulsed in her like a living thing. A hungry, hungry living thing.

"God, I want to *inhale* you," she breathed. "You have no freakin' idea."

His eyes blazed. Then he bent and dug a condom out of the pocket of his discarded jeans and held it out to her. "Where do you want me?"

Excitement clutched in her belly as she realized what he was really handing her. She took the condom from him with fingers that trembled slightly. "Under me."

He lay down on the bed and scooted to the center, pushing the pillows aside so he could lie flat. She climbed onto the mattress beside him. For a moment, she just soaked up the image of him lying there, all six-plus feet of him, one hand behind his head, the other lying on his flat belly. His erection lay hard and heavy against that belly. Her breath hitched at the idea of touching him, sheathing him, straddling him, and taking him into her.

"Um, Hayden?"

She blushed. "Sorry. I got so carried away thinking about what I could do, I kind of forgot to do it."

She swung her leg over him until she straddled his waist. Twisting her hair to one side, a hand pressed to his chest for balance, she bent forward to kiss him. His hands came up to run along the outsides of her upper arms. God, how had she never noticed how erogenous that area was?

For long moments, they kissed, while his hands trailed fire over her back, up to her nape, then around to the sides of her breasts. At that, she groaned and sat up, giving him better access.

"Oh, Hayden, baby, I gotta say I love the view from here."

"I was thinking the same thing." The feel of those long, talented fingers caressing her breasts and tweaking her nipples was incredible. Watching him do it drove her arousal into overdrive.

She wriggled, conscious of his erection, which nudged her backside. The yearning emptiness inside urged her to lift up, fit him to entrance, and take him inside, but there was the matter of the condom.

But having been handed this gift, she was determined not to rush through it. She wanted to savor every minute.

She bent to kiss his mouth again, then tipped his head back to kiss the side of his neck. The taste of his skin exploded on her tongue, encouraging her to slide lower. With lips, tongue, and, yes, teeth, she explored shoulders, pecs, those amazing abs. His muscles contracted beneath her, and she could feel his tension, his excitement, coiling tighter and tighter. Then she felt his hands in her hair.

Smiling, she slid lower. His penis jerked before she could even touch it, reacting to the warmth of her breath, or maybe the tickle of her hair on his lean hip. The musky sex smell of him brought her to full arousal. She could feel herself readying for him, her sex growing slick again, internal muscles pulling her uterus up, making room to take his lovely, lovely—

"Hayden," he groaned. "I'm thinking now might be a good time for that condom."

She smiled. "Soon."

She circled her fingers around him and he bowed his hips off the bed. She bent and took the head of him into her mouth. He emitted a hiss that segued into a groan of delight. Spurred on by the sounds he was making, she took him more fully into her mouth, applying gentle suction. The breath that sighed out of him was about the sexiest thing she'd ever heard. Taste and smell and sound—it all combined to drive her still higher as she worked him with her hand and mouth.

"Hayden." The hand in her hair now urged her up. "Baby, we'd better make use of that condom, if we're going to. Otherwise . . ."

She rose up. "Sorry. I got a little carried away." She tore open the packet, removed the condom, and applied it.

"Damn, that's sexy. Your hands, so small and soft, but so sure."

She smiled. "What can I say? Doctors know their way around latex. Granted, it's usually exam gloves I'm putting on."

He laughed, but when she moved up his body and positioned herself over his shaft, there was no more humor in his eyes. Just need. Unable to deny herself any longer, she sank down on him until they were fully joined.

"That feels so good."

The words came from Boyd, but they might have come from her. She stilled, savoring that first shock of invasion, then started to move on him. His hands went to her breasts, cupping them, squeezing, rasping his thumbs over her nipples. *Oh, God!* After her brave words about taking her time, this was not going to last long. Despite herself, she picked up her pace. He dropped his hands to her hips, holding her, helping her, thrusting up to meet her. Thighs trembling, she tried to hang on, tried to hold back the orgasm. Mistaking her problem, he reached between them to stimulate her with his hand. She came immediately.

With the last tremors of ecstasy fading, she bent down and kissed him, her hair spilling around them. His arm came around her, and she found herself on her back beneath him, their bodies still joined. The demonstration of physical strength thrilled her. As did the growling sound he made deep in his throat. Then he was moving inside her, long, powerful strokes that revealed how much restraint he'd been exercising before.

She sank her hands in his hair, loving the feel of it between her fingers. Then she moved on to his nape, his shoulders, and on down to the dip of his back and his tight butt. His breathing grew harsher, his thrusts more frenzied, until he found his own release.

Afterward, she held him in her arms as his trembling weight rested briefly on her, and she felt a piercing sweetness fill her. Followed quickly by panic.

She pushed at his chest.

"Sorry." He moved away. "Didn't mean to crush you."

She hadn't minded his weight. What she'd felt was the opposite of minding. But she let him believe it, because she didn't want him to see her freaking out about it.

He brushed her hair back, kissed her on the forehead, then got up to deal with the condom.

By the time he rejoined her, she'd recovered her composure. The tenderness had taken her by surprise, that was all. She just needed to be more on guard, especially in the immediate aftermath. There was a reason they called it afterglow. Biology's little trick to bond couples into a unit suitable for reproduction and child rearing. But she wasn't a slave to her hormones. Knowledge was power.

She was not going to get attached to Boyd. Her life wouldn't allow it.

He pulled her into his arms and they lay there for a while. Hayden let herself enjoy his stroking of her hair. She even let her hand rest on his chest where she could feel his heartbeat. But she had no intention of relaxing fully into it. This kind of intimacy would have to be rationed, treated very carefully.

She sat up. "I should go."

"So soon? The hour isn't even up, let alone the two you promised me." He waggled his eyebrows suggestively, and she laughed.

"I have to call my mother."

"Where is she?" He looked at his watch. "I'm guessing points west, if you're going to call her this late."

"She's in Nova Scotia, actually. Outside of Sydney, to be specific." She started hauling on her clothes. Again. This time, taking time to put her underwear on. "But she's a night owl. Now that she and Dad are both retired, she keeps much later hours."

"Okay, I remember now. Your mom emigrated from Haiti, and your dad was born in Cape Breton, right? And they moved there after your dad retired." He got up and started dressing too. "It's pretty clear you didn't grow up there."

"What? Because I don't stay stuff like, 'G 'way wit ya,' or call everyone 'buddy'?"

"Or the use of the word *after* in that odd way."

"As in, 'I was after having a piece of that pizza'?"

"Yeah. *That.* What I'd like to know, though, is how you came to sound like a regular Maritimer?"

"I do not!"

"Yeah, you do. Where'd you go to med school?"

"Dal," she confessed.

"There you go. You must have absorbed some of that Maritime accent during your years in Halifax." He turned his T-shirt right side out and pulled it on. He really didn't need to do that on her account. "So, how often do you call your parents?"

"My mom," she clarified. "Dad won't talk on the phone. So we exchange greetings through Mom."

"I guess that lets out Skype."

"God, yes! They don't even have a computer. I keep trying to interest them in one by telling them all the things they can do online. But they say they'd rather talk to their neighbors in person instead of strangers on Facebook, or go see a real bank teller." She reached for her light jacket. "I can't argue with that, at least not as long as they're able to get out and around."

"Good point. Why settle for virtual relationships when you can have actual ones?"

Like the *actual* sexual relationship she was currently having. Much better than her relationship with her battery-operated friend.

"I should phone my folks too. They think I'm on a fishing trip."

"You told me." She could just imagine how horrified they'd be to think their son's death might have been something other than a horrible but natural tragedy. "That was incredibly kind of you, shielding them. Though they must worry about you a lot since—"

"Yeah, they do." His eyes followed her as she found her purse and dug her keys out. "These last few days, I've been checking in with them every evening, to see how they're doing, and so they can switch off the unconscious worrying. They really appreciate it, so thank you."

"Thank me? What for?"

"For reminding me that people worry. Whether I think that worry is rational or not really isn't the point. Reassuring them is."

She smiled tremulously. "You're welcome."

CHAPTER 18

Boyd found himself whistling in the shower.

Last night, he'd hated to let Hayden go. He'd walked her down to the parking lot, and that kiss outside her Subaru had been as hot and hungry as the first one they'd shared. He almost thought she might invite herself back upstairs. But she'd been right not to. They'd both needed sleep. He'd come back to his room and crashed on the bed with Hayden's scent burrowing into his brain. For a change, he'd fallen asleep quickly and slept deeply. The only thing that could have improved his slumber would be if Hayden had been there by his side.

He'd liked the feel of her in his arms, but she clearly wasn't the overly cuddly type. For which he should be grateful. No, for which he *was* grateful. This wasn't one of those situations where a woman proposed no-strings sex, then proceeded to try to hog-tie him. He respected that. He respected her. And he'd try to give her everything she'd been missing, while letting her keep her emotional boundaries.

The bigger challenge might be keeping a safe perimeter around his own heart.

He stopped whistling.

God, how long since he'd had a thought like that? A decade, at least. Since the vet tech, Laurie's defection, he'd never had to worry about his heart. The razor wire on his emotional fences hadn't lost its gleam. Yeah, he'd chosen to let it down partially now and again, but never fully. Maybe he never could.

The thought was both comforting and sad.

Thrusting away any further self-examination, he shut off the taps and reached for a towel.

Downstairs, he found Sylvia at her usual spot at the table.

"My, don't you look dashing this morning, Detective."

He lifted a hand to his chin. He'd shaved with carnal thoughts of getting between Hayden's thighs, but if it pleased Sylvia Stratton that he'd cleaned up, so much the better.

"I do like a clean-shaven man," she said.

"Well, that seals it. My holiday from shaving is over." He went to the coffee carafe and filled his mug, then held it up. "Refill?"

"Please." While he poured her a fresh coffee in a new china cup—she never refilled the old, he'd learned—she picked up the pitcher of orange juice by her elbow, poured a glass for him, and topped up her own.

"I've a special treat for you this morning. Grilled breakfast sausage. It's made locally and contains no nitrates or preservatives."

"Sausages?" He breathed the word reverently as he placed her fresh coffee within reach. "Seriously?"

"Seriously." She smiled, and for a second he caught a glimpse of what must have attracted the Senator to her. "Of course, you mustn't count on it being here every morning. It's far too fatty."

"Of course. Thank you."

Boyd piled his plate with scrambled eggs, sausage, and a baked tomato, and returned to the table. As he ate, Sylvia went back to her crossword or sudoku puzzle or whatever it was she did every morning.

When he'd cleaned his plate and drank his OJ, he helped himself to some of the homemade yogurt. He was really developing a taste for it, and he knew Sylvia would approve. He'd already heard her lecture about how gut health impacted so much more than digestion, including good immune system health. And damned if he didn't feel better. Not that he was ready to concede that dietary change could change his world. Hell, maybe it was just the great sex.

That thought started a cascade of mind pictures that he'd best not be thinking about at his host's table, so he pushed them away.

"Dr. Stratton, I was wondering if you could answer a few questions for me."

"Questions?" She arched a delicate eyebrow.

"About my birth parents. I haven't been able to find Josh's notes about his investigation. Detective Morgan is working on the case, trying to reconstruct my brother's search. I've actually been working with him these past few days."

Both dark eyebrows rose this time. "Indeed."

"I know you were one of Josh's first stops when he came to town, presumably because you were practicing here during that era and delivering babies."

"That's certainly true. I was one of Josh's first contacts here, and I did conduct a full family practice." She took a sip of her coffee. "I was so favorably impressed by your brother that by the time we finished speaking, I found myself offering him a room."

"Yes, thank you for that."

"We got on well enough over our breakfasts, although I fear your brother thought I was rigid, but that's just because I am." Her self-deprecating smile was almost charming.

"I've been known to be a little rigid myself, as Josh could have told you."

She stroked the handle of her coffee cup. "I presume you want to know what I told Josh during our first meeting?"

"Yes, ma'am. As well as any opinions you might have formed since."

"I'll tell you now what I told your brother. If someone conspired to obliterate the record of your birth, making it difficult if not impossible for you two to locate your birth mother, it's safe to say that takes money. Lots of it."

Well, duh. Of course it takes money. But whose money? "You think our mother came from a wealthy family?"

"I would bet on it." She took a drink of her coffee and placed the cup in its saucer. "It would take money to buy that dreadful lawyer's services. It would take money to falsify the documents and to hide the birth. I even suggested to Josh that it might have been a privately attended birth."

"Was that legal here at the time? Supervised home birth?"

"I hardly think legality would have been a consideration, given what happened with the birth record and the whisking away of the children to another province."

That's pretty much what he and Hayden had concluded. "I agree it would take money to do this, but I can't exactly go to all the families on the social register in Fredericton to ask them if any females among them gave birth to twins thirty-five years ago, then committed a series of criminal acts to conceal the fact and dispose of the babies."

"No, I wouldn't recommend it. People would complain to powerful people, and you'd find yourself sitting in a very hot seat, Detective."

"So what do you suggest I do?"

"I'll give you the same advice I gave your twin. Look at the physicians to the wealthy. While whoever did this might stoop to using a questionable lawyer to make a problem go away, they would never risk the life of a daughter or niece or young cousin to just any doctor."

"Why would a reputable doctor go along with something like this?"

She shrugged. "Loyalty to the family, possibly. Or a combination of loyalty and a monetary inducement. Physicians can be poor money managers and even worse retirement planners, for instance. Or I suppose it could even have been done in exchange for a favor."

Again, pretty obvious. Maslow's hierarchy of needs. What did everyone want? Since it was a physician, they wouldn't be physiological needs. More on the order of self-esteem or personal power or wealth. But he was curious what she, a doctor herself, thought a fellow doctor might want for providing such a heinous service. "A favor? Like what?"

"That would depend on what the physician wanted and what the family could offer." She drank the last of her coffee, then pressed a pristine napkin to her mouth. "It could be admittance to an exclusive club they otherwise wouldn't be considered for."

Boyd nodded. *Self-esteem.*

"Or if the individual sat on the hospital board, perhaps they could exert their influence on the physician's behalf."

Personal power.

"If the family had corporate connections, they might be in a position to provide inside information to help the physician's portfolio thrive."

And there we have it. Wealth. Financial security.

Well, that narrowed it down. *Not.*

"So who are these physicians to the wealthy? Do you have a list?"

"I made one for your brother, so it shouldn't be too hard to reproduce. And of course, I included only those who were practicing here when you were born."

"When I was supposedly born," he said. "If they went to the trouble of falsifying our names on the birth record, they might have done the same with the date."

"You were adopted as little more than newborns, correct?"

"That's correct. Our mother says we still had the remnants of our umbilical cords."

Sylvia waved a dismissive hand. "Then your actual birth date won't be far off whatever the birth record says. They couldn't have billed you as more than a few weeks old, or the developmental differences would have given the lie away. The discrepancy would have been instantly obvious to your adoptive family's physician, who presumably took over your care immediately."

"So the birth date is probably accurate, give or take a couple of weeks?"

"Precisely. As for the list, if I can't find a copy, I'll reproduce it for you."

"Thank you. That would be very helpful," he said, though he wasn't entirely sure it would help. For starters, Josh would have taken a hard look at every physician on that list. If she'd supplied it to him early on, as she seemed to indicate, his twin would have found something if there'd been anything to find. But he was touched nevertheless. Dr. Stratton could definitely be a pain in the ass. A snob and an unbending perfectionist with a spine of steel. But clearly she could be kind too. "I do think I'll have to cast the net a little wider than that, though."

"Pardon me?"

"I love your theory, but what if it wasn't my mother who came from money? What if it was my father? If my mother were of more modest roots, she might have seen a regular run-of-the-mill doctor."

Her lips thinned. "Indeed."

He decided to try his and Hayden's theory out on her, that the physician was a GP, not an obstetrician. But Sylvia being Sylvia, he went about it backward. If he just laid the question out there, she might get her back up in defense of her family physician colleagues. But if he gave her an opportunity to correct him, he doubted she could resist it.

He leaned back in his chair. "Of course, whatever GP she was seeing, it was probably only for the first part of the pregnancy. There must've been an ob-gyn involved for the delivery, since we're talking twins, which are higher risk than single births, right?"

"Ordinarily, yes," she said. "But remember, standards were different back then. And we're a very small center. Things haven't always been done as they are in bigger centers. They still aren't."

Bingo. "Oh, and here's a thought. What if it was our father who had the dough—and the reputation to protect? His focus might've been less on the health of the pregnant mother and more on getting the unwanted children shipped off as far away as possible."

"If that were the case, I hardly think he would have abandoned the young lady to substandard care." Her brows knit together in a fierce frown. "If the pregnancy were lost or the deliveries botched due to poor care, that would have been the *beginning* of the young man's nightmare, not the end. The woman might have blamed him for their loss, and rightly so, since he could have afforded the best possible care."

"Point taken," he conceded, more to humor her than anything. "Sounds like we should give the docs on your list priority."

She looked only marginally mollified by that concession, but she let it drop. "Very well. I won't be able to produce anything for you until at least tonight. Is that satisfactory?"

"That's fine," he assured her. "Are you off to church?"

"Good gracious, no. I'm off to Saint John to visit with my son, Jordan."

"He's a doctor too, right?"

"He is." For a moment, she looked like any mother, proud of her son. Then she lifted her nose a little higher. "The Strattons have been physicians for many generations."

Wow, that would be wild. To inherit your occupation, or at least the expectation of occupation. He offered up a thank-you to Frank and Ella McBride for not doing that to them. Neither he nor Josh had been attracted to construction, and God knew they'd had a close enough look at it working for their dad's company in the summers.

"And he was okay with that? I mean, did he chafe against his birthright or embrace it?"

"I believe he's happy with his life, with his choices."

"That's important." Boyd found his voice growing gruff. "We never know how long we're going to have, so we'd better be doing work we like and hanging out with people we enjoy."

"That's an excellent philosophy, Detective. Now, if you'll excuse me, I really must get ready to go." She rose, and he did too. She waved for him to resume his seat. "Sit. Enjoy your coffee, and there's more orange juice."

He sat.

She walked around the table, leaving her dishes where they were, and paused beside his chair.

"Is Dr. Walsh working today?"

Her question came from so far out in left field that it took a few extra seconds for Boyd to process it. "No. No, actually she's not."

"Feel free to invite her over. She might enjoy the spread." She indicated the buffet with a sweep of her hand. "I believe she joined your brother for breakfast at least once."

That was a great idea, actually. Then they could work together on the investigation.

Right. Like *that* was the only thing he was thinking about.

Realizing Sylvia was waiting for a response, he cleared his throat. "Thank you. That's very kind. I'll invite her."

"Good. Well, I'll be off shortly, after I've freshened up."

Ten minutes later, Dr. Stratton was out the door and gone. Only then did Boyd whip out his cell phone and call Hayden. She answered on the fourth ring, just seconds before he would have hung up.

"Did I wake you?"

"No. You interrupted my yoga routine. It took me a while to find the phone."

He had a sudden desire to see her in her yoga gear, contorting her body . . .

"Boyd?"

"Sorry. I spaced there, thinking about your downward dog."

She laughed. "You dirty dog."

"Guilty." He could clearly picture the curve of her full, luscious lips, the way she pinned that lower lip with her teeth sometimes. "Um, I was calling to see if you wanted to join me for breakfast."

"Sure. Where are we going?"

"Actually, Sylvia's place. She's going to Saint John to visit her son, and when I told her you had the day off, she suggested I invite you over."

"Really?"

He grinned. "Really."

"I can be there in seventeen minutes."

"You're welcome," he said, then realized he was talking to dead air. She'd hung up.

CHAPTER 19

She was there in sixteen minutes.

Boyd had hoped she'd still be in her yoga pants, but she'd changed. As it turned out, he couldn't complain. She wore a pair of skinny-legged jeans and a tailored navy jacket over a beige shirt. With her amazing mass of hair loose—God, he loved it like that—and her face bare except for some lip gloss, she looked both wholesome and incredibly sexy. He met her at the service entrance, pulled her inside the door, and greeted her with a kiss.

"Well, hello to you too," she said when she could breathe again.

"Sorry. Couldn't resist."

"What makes you think I wanted you to?"

The heat in her eyes sent a jolt of excitement through him. "Better do breakfast first. Mrs. Garner will be around soon, wanting to clean up after us."

The mention of breakfast refocused her in a hurry. "God, yes. Let's eat."

He led her to the kitchen. When she saw the rows of chafing dishes and the fruit and yogurt, she groaned.

"Omigod, this looks just as good as I remembered. I can't believe you get to eat this every day."

"I know," he said. "I'm not sure what Josh was paying to stay here, but I'm pretty sure it wasn't enough."

She picked up a plate. Behind her, he picked up a much smaller one.

She looked from hers to his. "You're making me feel like a real glutton, McBride."

"I've already eaten," he said. "This is dessert."

She helped herself to the scrambled free-range eggs and baked tomato and went with the fish instead of the sausage.

He took some sliced fruit and another sausage. When Hayden raised an eyebrow, he said, "What? They're locally sourced and nitrate-free. And it's the first time I've had proper breakfast meat since I came here. Don't begrudge me. Tomorrow it'll be gone."

"A special treat for you, I take it?" At his nod, her eyes narrowed. "Well, isn't Dr. Stratton being accommodating."

"Actually, she's been very accommodating." Plates filled, they went back to the table. He sat down at his usual spot, placing the saucer on top of his dirty plate. She took a seat to his right. "Coffee?"

At her nod, he got up and poured the last of the coffee in a clean mug and plunked it down beside her plate.

Between bites, she asked, "How else has Sylvia been accommodating?"

"I asked her to share what she'd told Josh when he came calling all those months ago."

She swallowed the forkful of eggs she'd been chewing before speaking. "What did she tell you?"

"She pointed out it would take a lot of money to make a pair of babies disappear so thoroughly and neatly. She thinks our mother came from a wealthy family who could afford to pull that off."

"So, what do you do with that information? Go knocking on the doors of the rich?"

He shook his head. "That'd get me run out of town in a hurry. Or at least shut out of the investigation." He picked up the glass of orange juice he'd refilled. "Dr. Stratton suggested I start by talking to some docs who would have catered to those rich families back in the day. Said she'd produce a list for me. The same one she gave to Josh."

She picked up a spoon, poured a little cream in her coffee, and stirred it. And stirred it some more.

"What?"

"I was just thinking . . . maybe it was the father's family who had all the money, not the mother's family. In which case maybe the young mother wasn't seeing the crème de la crème of doctors. Maybe she was just seeing her regular nonglamorous doctor."

He started laughing.

"What's so funny?"

"That's just what I said to Sylvia."

"You did?"

"Yep. Great minds, huh?"

"Did you also ask her about the feasibility of a GP being involved instead of an ob-gyn, given that we're talking twins and a probable primipara?"

"Uh . . . I'm not sure."

She blinked. "You're not sure?"

"Because I don't have a clue what a primipara is."

"Sorry. That's medical speak for a woman who hasn't given birth before."

"Then yeah, we talked about that too." He put his coffee down and leaned back in the chair. "She maintains that in quiet backwaters like this, things weren't always done the way they'd be done in big cities."

"So GPs might have been delivering twins?"

"She seemed to suggest it was possible. And that it might have been a doctor-supervised home birth. She felt pretty strongly that we should look at her doctors-to-the-rich list. I kinda take her point. She pointed out that if the father had lots of money, but abandoned the 'young lady' to substandard care, the babies might have suffered for it. No way he'd want that to happen. If she decided to take it out on his family, it could spawn a whole new level of scandal."

"I suppose," she conceded. "But if that doctors-to-the-rich tip was such a hot one, you'd have thought Josh would've uncovered something a lot sooner."

"I know, but I didn't have the heart to say it. I just thanked her." Boyd rubbed a hand under his chin. "Okay, so we're looking at all the family docs who were practicing here at the time?"

"Well, the ones who are still alive or for whom we can find contact information."

"If I'm looking for a doctor, I'd usually check with the College of Physicians and Surgeons. Would they keep records from year to year about who was practicing here?"

"Got it right here." She drew her cell phone out of her pocket and waggled it, looking pleased with herself. "I called Marta, the secretary from the ER, when I got up this morning to ask the best way to find that information. She confirmed that the College publishes an annual directory that identifies all doctors, what their specialty is, and where in New Brunswick they practice. She requested that information for the year of your birth, and they shot it right back at her. And now I have it."

"Great work. So now we isolate all the general practitioners who were practicing in Fredericton at the time, then compare those names against the telephone directory."

"Or against a current list from the College, which I happen to have." She reached for her messenger-bag-type purse and pulled out a small booklet. "It's last year's, actually, but that's plenty current enough. It'll show us which of those guys are or were recently still in practice."

"It's a great place to start," he said. "If we make our way through that list without hitting pay dirt, then I'll have to look at docs who've died, retired, or relocated their practices."

She grimaced. "That sounds a lot harder. No convenient telephone number or office address in the annual directory."

"Harder but not impossible," he said.

"The College could probably tell us which ones among them have died, for instance. But I'm not sure how to approach the relocation issue."

"Well, we'll worry about that if and when we have to," he said. "Let's get this other list whipped up, shall we?"

"Your room?"

"Might as well. Dr. Stratton should be away for half the day, at least."

She got up and started to pick up her dirty dishes.

"Leave them," Boyd said. "Dr. Stratton always insists they be left for Mrs. Garner to deal with."

"How does Mrs. Garner feel about that?"

"What's this?" The old housekeeper bustled into the room. "Did I hear my name?"

Hayden blushed, which Boyd thought was hilarious. "Hayden was about to tell me what a lazy SOB I am for not cleaning up after myself, and I was just explaining that Dr. Stratton prefers the dishes be left for you."

"I should think so! That's my job."

"Are you sure?" Hayden said. "It would be no trouble to load this stuff in the dishwasher."

"I'm very sure. That's just not how things are done here." Her features softened. "But thank you. I appreciate the sentiment. Now off with you." She made a shooing motion with her hands.

"Yes, ma'am," Boyd said.

When they got up to the room, Hayden turned to him. "Omigod, do you think she was listening?"

Boyd shrugged. "So what if she was?"

"We were poking holes in Sylvia's theory about your mother being from a rich family."

"Seeing as I pretty much said that to Sylvia, I don't see a problem." He peered closer at her. "Does it really bother you?"

She shrugged. "Not really. Not much anyway. It's just that Josh said she was very loyal to Dr. Stratton. Very devoted. Protective, almost."

He snorted. "Protective? I wouldn't have thought Sylvia Stratton needed protecting from anything."

"Everyone needs protecting from something, Boyd. Even if it's just from ourselves or our obsessions."

She looked so sad, and he knew she was thinking about Josh. Damn him for being an insensitive jerk.

"You're right." He pulled her into his arms. "We all could use that."

Her arms came around him and they just stood there for a few moments, fused together by their shared grief. And God, it was good to hold her. The feeling it gave him was so incredibly peaceful. As his hands stroked her thick mass of hair where it lay against her back, he felt his sorrow ease and another need start to build. He moved his hands to her upper arms, letting his thumbs rub the soft flesh there.

She pulled away and cleared her throat. "We should get at that list," she said, her eyes downcast.

Dammit. He was an asshole twice over, turning that moment of grief and comfort into something sexual.

"You're right. Let's get to it." He moved to the kitchenette, grabbed his notepad, and went and sat on the sofa. "Why don't you give me that booklet? You read off the names and I'll check the current directory. If we get a match, their name goes on this list."

"Sounds perfect." She pulled her phone out of her pocket and went to sit beside him. After finding the document, she started scrolling through.

The first few names she called were not on his list. The fourth one was. "Got him. But wait. It says he's an anesthetist. Should I toss him out?"

She shook her head. "Write it down. If it's the same guy, he probably started out as a GP, then specialized. That was a lot more common back then. We can't discount him."

"Fair enough."

Of the next flurry of names, three were in the newer directory, and Boyd carefully noted them on his pad.

"Angus Gunn," she said.

"Got him. Still here and still listed as a GP."

"Dr. Gunn . . ." she repeated. "Angus Gunn."

"Same one or different one?" He looked up from the booklet. "I've only got the one."

"Same one. It's just that the name is ringing a bell."

He zeroed in on her face. "How so? Did Josh mention him?"

"I think he phoned Josh in the days before Josh died."

Holy shit! "Gunn? Are you sure?"

"I will be in a minute. We were out for dinner when Josh got the call. He didn't have his notebook with him and needed something to write on, so I pulled out my checkbook. He used my pen to write something on the edge of the check register. I see it every month when I write a check to my hairdresser, the one merchant left in the world who doesn't take debit or credit."

"Do you have it with you?"

She was already reaching for her purse. Drawing out her wallet, she flipped the checkbook compartment open. "There." She handed it to him. "Dr. Angus Gunn. And it has a phone number."

His heart raced. This was important. He knew it. He looked down at the entry for Dr. Angus Gunn in the directory. The number didn't match the one on the directory, but that didn't mean it wasn't valid. It could have been a cell phone versus a home or office line.

He pulled his cell phone out of his pocket and punched in the number.

CHAPTER 20

Hayden held her breath while Boyd waited for Dr. Gunn to answer.

"Dr. Gunn?" His eyes went to Hayden's. "This is Boyd McBride. Sorry to be disturbing you. Am I dragging you away from anything? Good. Look, I believe you talked to my twin brother, Josh McBride, not long ago."

There was a pause. Hayden could hear the buzz of the doctor's voice, but she couldn't make out any words.

"Yes, thank you. It was a horrible shock for all of us."

Another pause.

"Good. I had hoped he had spoken to you about his investigation to find my birth parents. I never was much of a fan of the search for our parents, but after what happened to Josh, I'm sure you can appreciate the incentive I now have for finding them. The whole medical history thing."

His gaze had drifted away as he talked, but it came back to meet Hayden's again.

"Well, I appreciate that so much, Dr. Gunn. That's the best news I've had in weeks. Thank you."

Hayden's stomach fluttered. Did this mean Dr. Gunn had the information Boyd needed? Had he been involved in the birth?

"How's right now?" Boyd said.

Hayden's eyes widened. Could they really be this close? Could it really be this easy?

"I see. So when do you think your guest will be gone?" A pause. "Eleven o'clock is great," Boyd was saying. "What's the address?"

He reached for the pen and pad he'd been using earlier, which caused him to swing away from her. When he started jotting something down, Hayden craned her neck to read it. *Mitchell Street.* She knew the area, off York Street, she thought. Definitely residential. And from what she remembered, there were some huge expensive houses. The neighborhood was very well established. Not historic like Dr. Stratton's property, but not a new development either. Just about what she'd expect for a senior physician.

"You're doing the right thing. Yes. Absolutely. Thank you."

He hung up the phone and turned to face her. The expression on his face was starkly frightening.

"Boyd?"

"He knows." His nostrils flared. "He was there when we were born. He can tell me—no, he's *going* to tell me who our birth mother is." He looked at his watch. "In two hours, I'll have that information. Oh, Hayden, this is going to make all the difference in the world. Once I know our mother's identity, this whole thing is going to unravel. I know it."

"I can hardly believe it," she breathed.

"Me either. We were looking at a significant job, contacting all those people and trying to squeeze out of them anything they might have told Josh. Now, because Josh left his journal behind when you went for dinner and wrote Dr. Gunn's name on your checkbook, we just sidestepped all that . . . *whoa.*"

He seemed to lurch sideways, then reached for the back of a chair to steady himself.

"Boyd? Are you all right?"

"I'm fine." He pulled the chair out from the small table and sat on it. "Okay, actually I'm feeling a little shaky," he confessed. "It's the shock, I'm sure. That phone call knocked me on my ass, but I feel fine now."

"You're sure?"

"Very sure." He took her hand and hauled her onto his lap. She squeaked in alarm.

"Boyd!"

He met her with a fierce kiss. His hands gripped her head, fingers tunneling into her hair. Her own hands roamed his chest, delighting in the way his muscles contracted under her touch.

Before she knew what was happening, he'd stood them both up and backed her to the bed. They went down together, fully clothed, side by side. She tried to kiss him again, but he pushed her onto her back and urged her arms over her head. With one hand pinning both of hers, he lay beside her, his gaze fastened on her uptilted breasts.

"Your breasts are so beautiful."

"Are you just going to look at them?"

His golden eyes darkened, and a smile curved his lips. "Patience, sweetheart. All in good time."

He proceeded to touch her through her clothes—her midriff, her belly, the curve of her hip, the outside of her upturned arm, her unprotected sides. Everything *but* her breasts. When he finally closed a hand around one of them, she arched up off the bed.

Between the two of them, they made short work of her jacket and shirt. But instead of removing her bra, Boyd slid down her body to open the fastener on her pants. She helped by lifting her butt off the mattress while he worked them down. She'd already kicked off her shoes when they'd entered the room, but the jeans were so skinny legged that they were tricky to get off. In the end, he peeled them off so they were inside out.

He sat back on his heels to look at her. She'd worn her sexiest bra today. This one was black and lacy and made the best of her assets, which was exactly why she rarely wore it. Much as she enjoyed how it made her feel, she had a tough enough time fending off dinner invitations as it was. But she was glad she'd worn it this morning. From the look on Boyd's face, so was he. Her excitement kicked up a notch.

He splayed a big hand on her chest above her breasts, and she practically purred. But instead of exploring her breasts, that hand slid down between them, pausing to trace the tiny black bow decorating the center of her bra. Then, without touching her breasts, that hand slid right on down her belly. Her abdominal muscles contracted and quivered. Then he bent and put his mouth on her skin.

She gasped.

He looked up at her. "I wanted to do this so bad last night, kiss every inch of you, but I didn't want to hurt your soft skin with my beard. The first thing I did this morning when I got up was shave." He rubbed his now clean-shaven face across her belly, sending sparks of pleasure shooting through her.

She put her hands on his head, delighting in the feel of his sleek, shiny hair beneath her hands.

"Uh-uh," he said, removing her hands and kissing the inside of one arm. He rose up and pushed her hands above her head again. "No touching," he commanded. "If I have to tie those hands, I will."

A thrill arrowed through her at the idea of being tied up, at his mercy. But not here at Sylvia Stratton's house.

"I'll comply," she said. "Now that I know the rules. As long as you'll do the same for me another time."

"Deal."

He kissed his way down her upturned arms before turning his attention to her face. Forehead, cheek, mouth. Every new area he explored brought new delights. The warmth of his breath on her neck, the tickle of it in her ear, the nip of his teeth when she was least expecting it. Even the feeling of his fully clothed body brushing against her naked skin. Again, he skirted her breasts, touching just close enough to make them ache for more. She was dying to sink her hands in his hair and direct his mouth where she wanted it, but she'd promised not to touch him back.

Down her midriff he went again, across her flat belly. He moved lower, and she thought she might come just from feeling his warm breath between her thighs. But then he moved lower still, all the way to her feet. Each foot got a massage, which was a strange combination of arousing and soothing. She wondered briefly if he knew reflexology. Whether he did or not, he was playing her body like a freakin' violin.

By the time he'd made his way back up to her thighs, she was completely ready. But he had other ideas. With strong, insistent hands, he urged her to roll over. Then he repeated the journey from her sensitive nape to her toes. He used his calloused palms on her back, then trailed hot, openmouthed kisses over it. The curve of her butt beneath the scant material of her lacy panties seemed to hold endless fascination for him, but her arousal level had reached the knife-edge between pleasure and torture. She needed him inside her.

"Please, Boyd. No more. I need you now."

He flipped her over—with her active, eager aid. When he grasped her panties, she lifted herself so he could ease them down and toss them aside. She expected him to peel his own clothes off and locate a condom, but, instead, he moved between her thighs again. She shuddered in helpless delight at the feel of his breath on her naked skin. It took all her willpower to close her legs and reach for him.

He looked up. "What's the matter? Don't you want this?"

She ducked her head. "I'm so wet."

"I know." He pressed a kiss to her inner thigh. "And you smell like heaven. Like all things good. I can't wait to taste you."

"But you'll *drown* down there," she protested laughingly.

"Baby, if I do, I'll die a happy man."

"Boyd!"

He touched her pubic hair lightly, and that barely there sensation sent a jagged bolt of excitement through her. "So are you going to let me kiss you here?"

By way of answer, she let her thighs fall farther open.

The first touch of his tongue—a wide, silky stroke—was electrifying. She arched up, then fell back. He continued to lap at her, and she gripped the coverlet with her fingers just to hold herself together. Then he closed his mouth around her and suckled gently. She started to crest, but he backed off immediately, soothing her with words and strokes of his hand on her thigh. Then he went back to her sex, driving her up once more with his lips and tongue. Each time she hovered on the brink of climax, he soothed her down again, then repeated the process until she was wild, begging.

Finally, he stripped his clothes off, slid a condom on, and lay down with her. She pulled him on top of her, guiding him to her entrance. He thrust home, once, twice, three times, and she started to come. And come and come. The climax rolled on and on as he pumped into her. She heard her own harsh breathing, heard her incoherent words. For a second, it was almost like being out of body, seeing herself—oh God, *hearing* herself—having this fantastic, mind-blowing orgasm. Then reality pulled her back in. She could feel the deep trembling starting in him and just held on tight as he plunged toward his own release.

Afterward, he collapsed on her for just a second, then moved away. Or tried to. She closed her arms around his neck. To hell with keeping her distance. After *that* experience, she wasn't ready to let go.

He rolled, pulling her on top of him. She felt absolutely boneless, as if she were in danger of melting down around him like warm syrup.

"I didn't know it was possible to feel so good."

He laughed. "You're welcome."

She lifted her head to look at him. His face looked more relaxed than she'd ever seen it. "Next time, it's my turn to torture you."

His grin started slow, then spread like a pat of butter melting in a hot pan. *Damn, but that is one sexy smile.* "I'll look forward to it." He glanced at his wristwatch. "But right now, I'd better get cleaned up. It's almost time to head over to Dr. Gunn's."

She grabbed his arm and looked at his watch. "You've got to be kidding me! Is that really the time?"

"It is." His expression was self-satisfied. Smug, even. Which was okay by her. He deserved to look smug.

She moved off him so he could get up, then admired his backside as he strode toward the bathroom.

Her smile faded. Within the hour, he'd know who his birth mother was. If he was right that Josh had been murdered, and if that crime was committed to stop Josh's private investigation, then Boyd would be infinitely closer to the answers he sought.

Infinitely closer to leaving.

The thought caused a swell of dread, which quickly condensed into a hard, indigestible knot in her stomach.

And with it came panic. How could she be so upset about this? His leaving was not just inevitable, it was something she had devoutly wished for. She wasn't anywhere near ready for anything permanent. She had plans. Plans that had already been derailed once by letting herself get attached.

Then another thought occurred to her, and the knot in her stomach became a huge boulder. She sat up in bed. "Boyd!"

∼

Boyd was at the bedside in second. "What? What's wrong?"

"I don't think you should go over to Dr. Gunn's alone."

He sagged. "That's what you scared the crap out of me for?"

"I've got a bad feeling about this."

"It'll be fine." He sat beside her on the edge of the bed. "I've gone into much more dangerous situations, Hayden."

She slanted him a look. "Without a weapon?"

Okay, she had him there. "The guy wants to get some stuff off his chest. That's all." He hoped.

"Maybe he just said that to get you over there. If Josh's death was related to the birth investigation, and if this guy was involved in the birth . . . Boyd, he could be setting you up."

"Already thought of that. I'll tell him I set up a fail-safe. That if anything happens to me, the notes from my investigation will go straight to the Fredericton Police Force."

"You think he'll believe that?"

"He'd better believe it, because it's true." He brushed a tightly curled strand of hair back behind her ear. "I've preprogrammed a message to go to Detective Ray Morgan. I update it whenever I have something to add, and every night I push the programmed send date back by twenty-four hours. Before I go to Dr. Gunn's, I'll just update the log, indicating I'm going to meet with him to finally learn the identity of my birth mother."

"I'm coming with you."

He frowned. "I don't think that's a good idea."

"Why not? You've just said it's not dangerous."

Dammit. "That doesn't mean I want you in the middle of this. Hell, anywhere near this."

"Too late for that." She stood. "I've been helping you. And even if I hadn't been, they'd probably assume I have been from all the time we've spent together."

Shit. She had a point there. "That's not necessarily a bad thing," he said. "If Josh was murdered, the more people who know what's going on with my investigation, the less likely the murderer is to believe they can clean this up the way they did with Josh. You know. So does Dr. Stratton. And Detective Morgan, of course."

"So there's no reason why I shouldn't come along."

He massaged the back of his neck. "I'm saying having all those people know makes it marginally less risky for me to be confronting people. I still don't want to involve you directly in the investigation."

"I'm coming along." She bent to pick up her underwear. "Josh was my friend, and I'm already part of this. And besides, you could use a second set of eyes and ears. Medically trained ones. Have you stopped to consider that this truth of his that he wants to tell might be a piece of misdirection? If I'm there, I can quiz him about the details, see if he trips up."

He really didn't think this meeting was going to be dangerous. Though Hayden's point was well taken, that this could be a ploy to lure him there, she hadn't heard Dr. Gunn's voice on the phone. Boyd's gut told him this was a man who was ready—no, anxious—to unburden himself. Just the same, there was no way he was letting Hayden walk into it.

"Good point."

"I'm glad you agree, because—"

"I'll relay what he said right away, and you can tell me if it was bullshit."

"But—"

"You can wait in the car outside the house, okay? I'll come report to you as soon as we're through. If he fed me a line of crap, medically speaking, you can straighten me out and I'll go back at him, see if he wants to change his story."

"But—"

He glowered at her. "That's my final offer, Hayden."

She glowered right back. "I can't believe how high-handed you're being about this!"

"Not high-handed. *Cautious.* You're my backup, baby. If you think something's gone wrong, you can call in the cavalry. It just makes more sense than both of us going in there."

He saw the resistance drain from her and knew that he'd won. *Thank God.*

"Okay, I'll stay in the car. But you have to dial my phone and keep the line open. Otherwise, I might not be able to hear if it goes bad."

"Agreed."

Forty minutes later, they pulled up outside Dr. Gunn's Mitchell Street home. It was older and not as large as the new developments, but Boyd figured it was worth a big chunk of change. And it was extremely well maintained. The shrubs and flower beds were meticulously groomed, the grass was golf-course green, and the driveway was set with stone pavers in a herringbone pattern. In the drive sat a shiny black Lexus SUV. Clearly, there were no money problems at Casa Gunn.

"Okay, call my phone," Hayden said.

He obliged, then slid the phone into his pocket. With a quick kiss, he climbed out of the car, walked to the front door, and rang the bell. He could hear the echo of it inside, but no one came to answer. After a moment, he rang it again.

"What's going on? Why is no one answering?" Hayden's voice came from his pocket.

"Hush, he could open the door at any moment."

"But he's not."

He frowned and rang the bell again. "He said he had some company that might take an hour or two to get rid of, and to come on over at eleven. I'm sure I'm not wrong about the time."

"Judging by the 'DR.GUNN' vanity plates, that's got to be his vehicle in the drive," she said.

He leaned sideways and looked in the long, narrow window flanking the door. Nothing moved. He rapped on the door with his knuckles.

Then he tried the door. The knob turned in his hand. *Unlocked.* The hairs on the back of his neck prickled.

He turned back toward the street, meeting Hayden's gaze. "Door's open. I'm going in. Stay there."

He pushed the door open and stepped inside. "Hello?" he called. No answer.

Leaving the door ajar, he moved farther into the foyer. "Hello? Dr. Gunn? It's Boyd McBride."

He took a few more steps so he could look down the hall. "Dr. Gunn?"

A door closed behind him, and he whirled, ready to launch himself at the threat.

Hayden, he told his jackhammering heart. It was Hayden who closed the door, not a hostile.

"Boyd?" Her voice sounded scared. He focused on her face and saw that he was the reason she was scared.

"Jesus, Hayden," he said. "I wasn't expecting the door to close. Tactically, we don't do that when we enter a building. Never close off an avenue of retreat."

She looked back at the door. "Should I open it again?"

The seconds it took to open a door could be the difference between life and death, if an officer came under fire. On the other hand, this wasn't Toronto, and it wasn't like they were flushing addicts out of a crack house. Under the circumstances, maybe leaving the front door yawning open wasn't the best idea anyway.

"What you should do is go back to the car where you agreed you would stay."

Hayden hugged herself. "Something's wrong. You're inside the house yelling your head off, and he's not responding."

He turned around. "Dr. Gunn?" he called again. Then louder, "Dr. Gunn? Hello? Anyone home?"

Something *was* very wrong. Those hairs on the back of his neck that had prickled when he'd found the door unlocked went into full bristle mode. If he had a sidearm on him, he'd have drawn it right about now.

Dammit, why had he let Hayden talk him into bringing her at all? If he'd slipped out without her, she wouldn't be standing here right now.

Or maybe she would. She was a stubborn thing.

And what should he do with her now? Make her stay here in the foyer or keep her with him where he could hopefully protect her?

As he was debating the question, she brushed past him and headed toward what he imagined was the kitchen.

"Hayden!"

She turned to look at him. "His car is home and he's not answering the doorbell or our calls. He might have had a heart attack or a stroke or an aneurysm or God knows what."

Maybe. Or maybe something even worse had happened. "Just do me a favor and stay behind me. If it turns out to be a medical emergency, he'll be all yours."

"Okay."

Since she'd been heading for the kitchen, and since there was a faint sound coming from that direction, he kept going. The sound turned out to be the dishwasher in wash mode. The scent of coffee lingered faintly in the air, but it was overpowered by the smell of a cleanser. If Dr. Gunn had entertained a guest in here, he'd cleaned up very thoroughly afterward. There wasn't so much as a coffee cup or a plate or a stray crumb to be seen.

He nodded his head to indicate they would go left next, through the adjoining room. It appeared to be a formal dining room. He moved through it and emerged into an open area, which he quickly realized was an extension of the foyer. From where he stood, he could see the entryway where they'd come in, as well as the foot of a staircase.

He walked back to the entryway, calling Dr. Gunn's name again. Still no answer.

He turned right this time. The first room he encountered appeared to be Dr. Gunn's study, or so he imagined from the masculine color scheme and the shelves of books lining the wall.

When he stepped fully into the room, he realized why Dr. Gunn hadn't answered the door.

"Jesus."

"What?" Hayden moved around him before he could stop her. "Omigod!"

Dr. Gunn, or what Boyd presumed was Dr. Gunn, sat in the chair behind his desk, his body hunched forward on the leather-bound blotter in a pool of blood.

CHAPTER 21

"Stay back," he commanded when Hayden would have rushed forward.

"But he might still be alive. I need to check for vitals."

Boyd had seen enough of these scenes to know Angus Gunn was beyond Hayden's help, or anyone else's. At least on this plane of existence. He also knew she had no choice but to check. "Go ahead and check for a pulse."

She tiptoed up to Dr. Gunn's body and pressed a finger to his neck. "Nothing." She pulled her hand back and wiped it on her jeans. "He's cooling off fast too."

"Come on—let's get out of here," he said.

Her eyes widened. "We're just going to leave him?"

"We're going to remove ourselves from this crime scene before we contaminate it any further than we already have."

A patrolwoman was on-site within two minutes. Boyd stepped up to talk to her, leaving Hayden leaning against his car. He gave the officer his name and Hayden's, and explained he'd had an appointment with the doctor at eleven. When Gunn didn't answer the door, he became worried and entered the house to find the scene in the study. Of course, the officer went in to confirm the situation herself, and she emerged considerably paler. When she radioed the dispatcher, her voice was higher and thinner than it had been on arrival as she called for backup.

"Your first DB?" Boyd asked.

Her eyes sharpened. "You a cop?"

"Detective. Toronto Police Service Homicide Squad." He held out his hand.

"Constable Ellen Green." She grasped his hand in a firm shake. "Little far from home, aren't you?"

"My twin brother was the journalist found dead in his car in Odell Park last month."

"Josh McBride." She nodded. "I remember. So what are you doin' in town?"

"Carrying through on my brother's investigation of our birth parents." It was perfectly true. Just not the whole truth. "That's why I'd come to talk to Dr. Gunn, actually. I spoke to him on the telephone just this morning, and he said he knew who my mother was, promised to tell me all about it."

"Guess he had a change of heart, huh?"

"Or someone changed it for him."

At that point, two more squad cars arrived, and Boyd could hear more sirens approaching. He stood back while the officers entered the house. Mentally, he pictured what they were doing, clearing the residence room by room to ensure no suspects lurked inside, not to mention other victims or witnesses or even free-roaming pets who could contaminate the scene.

Even as they worked, more units arrived to set up perimeter containment to seal off escape routes.

Then the EMTs rolled in. Boyd knew the ambulance wouldn't be leaving with a patient, but he figured he'd let them come to that conclusion themselves. It'd be hours before the scene was processed and the body ready for transport to the morgue.

He glanced over at Hayden. She looked a little shaken still, her arms wrapped protectively around herself. He started to go to her, but a gray Ford Taurus rolled up. Boyd was relieved to see it was Ray Morgan who climbed out of the vehicle. Officer Green met him at curbside and the two of them talked for a few minutes. Then Green pointed to Boyd. Morgan thanked the uniform and headed in Boyd's direction.

"Morgan," Boyd said. "Glad to see you caught this one."

"My sergeant assigned me when he saw who the nine-one-one caller was."

Boyd nodded.

"So, explain to me how you came to be here, McBride." He glanced over at Hayden. "She with you when you found the body?"

"Yeah. She's a little shaken up, I think. I'm sure she's seen lots of trauma, but probably not in the field. I was just going to go see what I could do for her."

"Sorry, but you won't be talking to her until we have your independent statements." Morgan nodded his head toward the curb, where another sedan had pulled up. "That'll be my colleague, Craig Walker. I'll have him interview Hayden."

Boyd watched as the newcomer climbed out of the car. It was a full-size vehicle, but Walker dwarfed it. As he walked toward them, Boyd figured he probably dwarfed most things. The man was built like an NHL enforcer, and he had the mug to match.

Not battered like a hockey player's, but ridiculously rugged. This dude was going to interview Hayden?

"I don't know, Morgan. Shouldn't you do both interviews, so you can make sure our accounts match up?"

"You can wipe that scowl off your face, McBride. Walker won't be flirting with your girlfriend. He's about as taken as a man can get."

It was on the tip of Boyd's tongue to deny that Hayden was his girlfriend, but he bit it back. He didn't know how to politely categorize his relationship with Hayden. He didn't want the men thinking they were casual fuck buddies, passing the time while Boyd was here. It was more complicated than that. Deeper. Yet it was also a temporary thing, a no-strings affair. Jesus, what the hell *did* they have going on?

Morgan introduced him to the big detective.

"Walker," he acknowledged.

"McBride. Sorry about your brother. That was messed up, man that young dying."

A surge of emotion caught him by surprise. He'd thought he was done with that. He'd gotten to the point where he could talk about Josh's death without choking up. But something about the big guy's head-on reference to Josh slipped right under Boyd's defenses.

God he missed his brother.

"Thank you."

With a nod, Walker went over to interview Hayden. Boyd forced his attention back to Morgan, who was asking how they'd come to be at Dr. Gunn's. Quickly, he recounted his and Hayden's efforts to make a short list of family physicians, as distinct from the ob-gyns that Morgan was running to ground, who might have been involved with his birth, how they fixed on Dr. Gunn, and what happened when they called him.

"Dr. Gunn confirmed he was present for our births. According to Gunn, he'd already told the story once to Josh and agreed to tell it to me. We made an appointment for eleven. When Hayden and I arrived, I asked her to stay in the car. I went up to the door and rang the bell repeatedly and knocked on the door, but no one answered. However, Gunn's car was in the drive. When I checked the door, it was unlocked, so I went in. Hayden heard me calling for Gunn and getting no answer, so she came on in. Long story short, we found him dead in his study, slumped in a pool of blood. From where I was standing just inside the door, it looked like he'd bled out from a slashed artery in the forearm. Hayden got a closer look than I did, and she concurs. Radial artery, she thought."

"That's what Officer Green tells me," Morgan said. "She figured he knew what he was doing with that scalpel. Vertical slash."

"Somebody certainly did," Boyd said.

Morgan ignored that. "So, did you touch anything?"

"No. I didn't go any deeper into the room than just inside the door. Hayden did, to touch his neck. She insisted on checking for vitals in case he was still alive. She got no pulse and indicated his body had already begun to cool significantly. We backed out of the room and came out here to make the call."

As Morgan scribbled some notes, Boyd's gaze wandered to Hayden and the big detective.

"Thank you, that's good for the moment," Morgan said. "Now I want you to park it over there. Got it?"

Boyd peeled his gaze away from Hayden to see that Morgan was pointing to the vehicle he'd arrived in.

"We need to get separate written statements from the two of you before you put your heads together again, okay?"

"Understood. And if you can get me a statement form, I'll write mine right now while it's fresh, instead of standing here twiddling my thumbs."

"Okay by me." Morgan summoned Constable Green, who, together with another pair of uniformed officers, had already cordoned off the property with crime scene tape. "Can you get the man a statement form and a pen?"

"Yes, sir."

When the officer walked off toward her cruiser, Boyd said to Morgan, "You do realize this is foul play, right? I mean, shortly after Dr. Gunn told Josh whatever he told him—presumably information that included the identity of our birth mother—Josh died. And within hours of agreeing to talk to me about the same subject matter, Dr. Gunn dies."

"I'll admit, it doesn't smell good, but I haven't seen the body yet. Could we give the coroner and our forensics team a chance to form an opinion before we start leaping to conclusions?"

Boyd's lips tightened. "Of course. But while your guys are combing the place for evidence, could you look for a file that might be my mother's?"

"You didn't look around yourself?"

"I was tempted to—believe me." Boyd rubbed his temple to try to ease the headache that was starting up. "But I didn't want anything mucking up your crime scene. If Hayden hadn't insisted, I wouldn't even have let her check for vitals. Because the only thing I can think as I'm standing there is that if somebody killed Dr. Gunn, it was probably the same person who killed Josh."

"Those are two big ifs, McBride, seeing as we don't yet know for certain whether Gunn or your brother were homicide victims. But I appreciate your restraint."

Boyd shrugged. "Wasn't worth the risk of jeopardizing your case. And if there was a file there when we stumbled on the body, it'll still be there when you process the scene. But I've got a sinking feeling you won't find it. If someone killed Dr. Gunn, they'll have taken it."

"If there was a file there in the first place."

"He said he'd show it to me." He raked a hand through his hair. "And, yes, maybe that was just a ploy to lure me over here and there *is* no file. But that doesn't make a helluva lot of sense."

Morgan acknowledged the comment with a grunt. "So what you're suggesting is if there's no file to be found, someone helped him slit his wrists. But if we do find your mother's file, then he likely committed suicide?"

"I guess, yeah." He dragged a hand through his hair. "I can't see a killer leaving it. But if Dr. Gunn committed suicide over guilt about his role in our unorthodox adoption, or even over what happened to Josh, then he very well may have left the file or a note or something. He promised me information, and I think he meant it. But it's possible he may have intended to keep that promise with a paper trail, rather than a conversation."

"What about this visitor he said he was expecting? Any idea who that was?"

"None. But they might look good as a suspect. They were probably the last ones to see him alive." He rubbed at his neck again.

"If there even was a visitor."

Boyd angled a look at Morgan. "You're suggesting he made up his mind to take his own life even as he talked to me on the phone. That he made up the visitor to give him time to get it done before I came knocking."

Morgan shrugged. "One scenario is just as likely as the other right now. We need more information." The approach of a vehicle drew Morgan's attention away. "Sorry, we'll have to finish this conversation later, McBride. The coroner's here." He nodded in the direction of his car. "Remember, plant yourself over there, and no talking to Hayden until we have both your statements."

He watched Detective Morgan stride across the lawn to greet the guy from the coroner's office. The two of them made their way up the drive and disappeared into Dr. Gunn's house.

He slid his glance over to Hayden again. She was still fully involved with Detective Walker. There was nothing remotely flirtatious in their postures—just an attractive, distraught-but-composed woman being interviewed by a tall, ripped, testosterone-exuding woman magnet—

"Detective?"

He turned to see Constable Green had approached with a statement form on a clipboard.

"Thank you." He took the clipboard from her. "I'll get right to it. And maybe you can suggest to Detective Walker that Dr. Walsh be offered the chance to do the same. We're not supposed to talk to each other until you have our official statements, so the sooner the better, since we're traveling together."

"Will do."

Boyd took the pad and paper over to Morgan's car. Using the car's roof for a desk, he wrote up his statement. He found himself falling into cop speak, describing the victim as the deceased, and noting the location of the desk as being at three o'clock relative to the doorway. Not that Morgan would mind. Precise and unambiguous were what mattered.

He paused briefly when the forensic van rolled up. Two men and a woman hopped out. As he watched, they pulled on pristine white overalls, then grabbed big fishing-tackle-type cases from the van. He knew that before they entered the house, they would cover their footwear with plastic shoe covers, don shower caps, and pull on latex gloves, all in aid of keeping their own hair, fibers, and prints from contaminating the field. The bearded guy would no doubt put a surgical mask or hairnet of some kind over his face. Not as glamorous as the CSIs on TV, but then, not much about police work resembled what you saw on TV.

He went back to his statement. When he finished, he thought about handing it to the constable but decided against it. He wanted to hand it directly to Morgan if he could, so they could continue their conversation. That would give him a chance to press him for more information about what he'd found inside.

He glanced over at Hayden to see she was sitting on the street curb on the other side of the driveway, writing her own statement. *Good.*

He leaned against Morgan's car to wait. With nothing to do now, he started to get antsy. *Dammit all to hell.* He'd gotten *this close* to discovering what Josh had learned, only to have it jerked away. His gut told him someone had done this to Dr. Gunn. The timing of the so-called suicide was too convenient to suggest otherwise.

"McBride."

Boyd looked up to see Ray Morgan standing in the doorway of the house, giving him a come-here gesture. As Boyd crossed the lawn toward the house, he saw the man from the coroner's office leaving.

"What's the word?" he asked, looking at the coroner's retreating back.

"At first blush, it looks pretty convincing as suicide. The angle of the wound seems right. Even a couple of hesitation marks parallel to the fatal incision, where he started to cut, then backed off. Oh, and the pathologist thinks he might have taken some blood thinners to make extra sure, but there'll be a full autopsy. And we'll see what forensics comes up with."

Boyd digested that. "Was there a note?"

"No note, suicide or otherwise. But we did find this on the desk." Morgan held up a plastic evidence bag. Inside was a thin blood-covered file.

CHAPTER 22

Hayden had just finished answering a few questions from Detective Walker about her statement and signed off on it when she saw Detective Morgan emerge from the house and summon Boyd. When Morgan held up a plastic evidence bag with what looked to be a file in it, her breath caught in her lungs.

From her angle, she could only see Boyd's face in profile, but that glimpse was sufficient to set her heart pounding. Were the answers he sought in there? Answers Josh might have died for? Would the cops even let him see the file?

She hurried over to his side. "Is that what I think it is?"

A look passed between the two men.

"Speak freely," Boyd said. "Hayden knows what's going on."

"It is what you think it is," Detective Morgan said. "At least I think it is. It documents the prenatal care of a young woman and the subsequent delivery of male twins on April 7, thirty-five years ago."

"That's gotta be you and Josh," Hayden said.

"What's her name?" Boyd's voice broke, and he swallowed. "What's my mother's name, Morgan?"

"I've got to get direction from the department on this, and they'll likely need to get direction from legal," Detective Morgan said. "It's evidence in an active case. It's also personal health information. Thanks to the falsification or forging of your birth registration, this could take some sorting out before you're granted access."

"Dammit, Morgan, my brother died for that information. I deserve to see it."

Morgan's eyes hardened. "Your brother died. It remains to be seen how or why. You'd do well to remember that."

Boyd's jaw bulged and the tendons stood out in his neck. Hayden laid a hand on his arm, where the muscles were bunched and ready for a fight. He barely seemed to notice.

"Dr. Gunn intended me to have that information. You know he did."

"I do know that," Morgan said in a low voice. "Which is why I'm carrying this file in a see-through evidence bag."

Hayden and Boyd both dropped their gazes to the blood-soaked file. The label was clearly legible. Duncan, Arianna Lynn.

"Thank you." Boyd lifted his gaze to the detective's again. "Jesus . . . thank you."

Detective Morgan shrugged. "It was laying right there on the desk. In plain sight for Dr. Walsh to notice when she approached the desk to check the vic for a pulse, right?"

Hayden hadn't noticed much beyond the dead body of Dr. Gunn facedown in the biggest pool of blood she'd seen, in or out of an ER, but she grabbed at the explanation, for Boyd's sake. "Right."

Boyd glanced from Morgan to Hayden and back to Morgan again. "I have no words, except thank you."

"Well, you did us a solid by not screwing with my scene or snagging the file yourself. Least I could do."

"I appreciate it. Now that I have a name, maybe I can find some answers."

"Don't thank me too profusely, McBride. From my admittedly quick perusal of the file, it looks like Arianna Duncan is deceased."

Hayden drew a surprised breath, then glanced at Boyd. His face had gone completely expressionless, which she'd come to realize meant he was deeply affected.

"I see," Boyd said, his voice flat.

"I shouldn't be telling you any of this. But on the other hand, it's nothing you're not going to find out when you dig into that name. Although given the deliberate obfuscation of facts that seems to have plagued your birth and adoption, I can see you might want to give that a rigorous look to make sure there really was a young woman named Arianna Lynn Duncan and that she really is dead."

"I'll do that."

"I'm really sorry, man. I'm sure you wanted to meet her, talk to her."

"Thanks, but it's not like I didn't think that was a possibility. As I warned Josh, it's been thirty-five years. A lot can happen."

"Wait a minute," Hayden said. "The death certificate was in the birth file? That seems odd to me. Unless . . . Did she die in childbirth?"

Detective Morgan shook his head. "Not in childbirth, no, but within a few months. And here's the thing, the reason I'm telling you this—she apparently dropped dead of some kind of heart thing too."

Hayden gasped. "Like Josh? Sudden cardiac arrest?"

"Cardiac arrest, yes. That's the term I read." He looked at Boyd. "I'm giving you this information for your own safety, McBride. I know the results of the genetic testing you had done aren't back yet, but if your mother and your identical twin died of this, it's seems pretty certain that there's a genetic component."

"Yes, it does," Boyd said, in a voice Hayden thought was altogether too composed. "About the file—was there anything in it about our adoption?"

"Yeah, there appears to be a signed consent form. Also, a big flag for the nurses reminding them that the babies were being adopted, and while they could show the mother that the twins were healthy, they weren't to let her hold or nurse them."

"To prevent her from bonding with them and changing her mind," Hayden said, imagining that poor woman's grief at not being able to touch her own babies.

"Look, do you need us to hang around?" Boyd asked. Wow, he was *volunteering* to leave the scene? She would have bet he'd have to be chased off. On the other hand, he'd just been handed a lot to digest—his birth mother's identity, the fact that she was dead, all but conclusive evidence that he and Josh had both carried a genetic electrocardiographic abnormality.

"Have you given your statement, Dr. Walsh? Signed and everything?"

She nodded. "I have."

Morgan turned back to Boyd. "I'll need a minute to read yours, okay?"

Boyd handed the completed form to him.

After a few minutes, Morgan said, "Good job. Couldn't be clearer." He handed the statement back to Boyd. "If you'll just autograph it for me."

"Great." Boyd whipped out his pen and, using the deck railing for a desk, signed the statement and handed it back. "You've got my cell number if you need anything more from me."

"And I put mine on my statement," Hayden put in.

"Then I guess you can both take off. It's probably just as well you're not here when the media gets wind of this. Which should be any minute."

Oh, crap. The media. Hayden hadn't even thought of them. She most definitely didn't want to be on the front page of tomorrow's paper, standing on Dr. Gunn's lawn.

Boyd thanked the detective again and the two men shook hands. A minute later, they were in Boyd's car, driving away.

At the first red light, he turned to her. "Hungry?"

"Excuse me?"

"It's well past noon."

Hayden couldn't be less hungry. Her stomach still lurched when she thought about the scene back there in Dr. Gunn's study. But if Boyd wanted to eat, they should eat. She had the feeling that once he let this new information soak in, he'd throw himself into the investigation and would need the fuel.

"Good idea." She suggested a unique burger joint downtown that had been a favorite of Josh's. He could get a big burger while she had a turkey burger with brie and no bun. Surely she could manage that much.

He glanced over at her. "You okay? I know that was rough back there."

"I'm fine. I've seen worse in the ER."

"I'll bet."

He turned his attention back to traffic, leaving her to think about what she'd said. Yes, she'd seen worse in the ER. Sometimes a lot worse. But this had shaken her.

Not the blood, and not the fact that she'd touched a dead body. She'd seen lots of that stuff in her career to date. Rather, it was the whole tableau. Seeing blood and ravaged bodies in a clinical situation was one thing. Seeing it in the field was entirely different. It was so much worse, knowing that mere hours earlier, Dr. Gunn had been on the phone with Boyd. Gunn had probably made his decision during that very conversation. He'd probably hung up, taken out his scalpel, poured himself a whiskey or whatever had been in that old-fashioned leaded crystal glass she'd seen on the desk. Had he tossed it back and done the deed immediately? Or had he sipped it as he contemplated ending his life?

How many scenes like this had Boyd seen? A lot, she was pretty sure.

The silence stretched between them until Hayden felt compelled to break it. "It was good of Ray Morgan to share that stuff with you."

"Yeah, it was." He flicked his gaze over to her, then back to traffic. "He said from the beginning he'd share anything that pointed to a health risk for me. But I was thinking more along the lines of toxicology reports."

"Do you think they'll let you see the file or have a copy of it?"

"Eventually, maybe. But I doubt I'll see it anytime soon. There are no legal documents to back up my claim that I'm one of those twin boys and therefore next of kin with a right to see it. I wouldn't be surprised if it took a court order to make them open it up." He shot her another glance. "I'm sure Detective Morgan is of a similar mind. That's no doubt why he told me as much as he did, so I'd have enough information to start putting the puzzle pieces together myself."

She studied his face in profile. "Will you do that? Bring an application to the courts to get the records?"

"I will, but I expect it'll take a while," said Boyd. "I'll have to connect the dots, and, thanks to lost files and fabricated birth certificates, those dots are damned few and far between." He stopped for a yellow light that was about to turn red. "I was thinking about something else, though. Morgan said the file contained my mother's signed consent to the adoption. Yet thirty-five years later, people seem to be dying over it. In what world does that make sense?"

"Maybe she didn't consent, you mean?" She glanced at him. "That could explain why Dr. Gunn felt guilty enough to commit suicide over this."

"If it was suicide."

"Either way, I'd assumed he must have helped someone to obscure the trail so no whiff of scandal could come back on them. You know, put a fake name on the birth record or something. But you're right—he could have done so much more. He could have practically *stolen* you guys away from your mother."

"That's what I was thinking." He took his eyes off traffic long enough to flick her a glance. "For a doctor to help a family pull off an untraceable adoption, that's bad. Really bad. But if everyone consented, is it kill-yourself bad? Especially thirty-five years later?"

She glanced at his profile. "Okay, I'm on board with the idea he might have done something worse than help cover something up. But for the record, for some people, especially professionals, reputation is everything. The professional disgrace from an investigation could definitely be enough to drive someone to suicide. Or maybe he just felt responsible for Josh's death somehow. Maybe that guilt layered on top of the old stuff was enough to put him over the edge."

"Again, that's *if* he actually committed suicide." The light had turned green, and he accelerated through the intersection.

She swept her hair to one side. "So, before I jumped in with my speculation, where were you going with that thought? That your mother might not have consented, I mean."

"The thought occurred to me that maybe he coerced our mother's consent. She might have been manipulated or railroaded into giving up her babies. Her family, lover, physician, priest . . . they could have ganged up on her, made her sign that paper. For chrissakes, documents have been forged or altered all over the place with this case. I was just thinking, why should you trust that consent form any more than any other document?"

He braked hard, signaled, and pulled into the crowded parking lot of a Tim Hortons.

She put her hand on the dash to steady herself. "Boyd, are you okay?"

"You know those Internet sites that try to help reunite people with their birth parents?"

The sudden subject change threw her. "Um . . . yeah?"

"Josh had been combing those sites since he was old enough to register us. I used to think what a bitch she was. Not for giving us up—hell, even before I became a cop and saw some damned sad cases, I knew there were times when kids were way better off when their mothers gave them up. But what I *did* blame her for was not registering at one of those damned sites. He never lost faith that he'd find her. I'm sure he nurtured a fantasy of some fairy-tale ending where we'd get to know her and discover we had a big, happy extended family, but year after year, nothing. Then he got the lead that pointed him to Fredericton and turned his life upside down to chase it."

Hayden's heart fell. "And now it looks like your mother has been dead all this while."

"Yeah. Looks like." He rubbed his face, looking suddenly tired. "I mean, I knew that it was a possibility she could have died somewhere along the line, but it was just that—a *possibility*. Shit, she'd still be a relatively young woman if she were still alive. The far bigger *probability*, to my way of thinking, was that she was alive and well but just didn't want to connect. I guess this makes me a jerk, huh?"

"Never." She put a hand on his leg. "It makes you a good big brother. You were just trying to look after Josh, protect him from hurt and disappointment."

He snorted. "Yeah. And what a bang-up job I did at that."

"Oh, Boyd, no. Josh was a grown man. And you weren't his keeper. Whatever happened, happened. We'll get to the bottom of it. But none of it is your fault. None of it."

He turned to her. "I could have helped him more."

"You *were* trying to help him," she said simply.

He looked away. "I should go to the library and see what I can find in the newspaper archives."

She grimaced. "It's Sunday. They won't be open today. But I've got tomorrow off. I'd be happy to go with you then, do whatever I can to help."

He laughed softly.

"What?"

"This was your day off, and look what I've dragged you into. I sure know how to show a girl a good time, huh?"

"You're not allowed to feel bad about that either," she said. "You know I'm anxious to get to the bottom of this. Josh wasn't my brother, but he was my friend, and I need to know what happened to him."

"Fair enough."

Something about his voice made her look at him closely. His color seemed off. Maybe some food and a caffeine injection would fix him up.

"Hey, why don't we eat here? They have a great panini, and I love their green tea."

"Tea at Tim Hortons?"

"It's good. Come on."

When they climbed back in the car half an hour later, Boyd looked better. Hayden felt a lot better too. She'd actually found her appetite.

"Okay, so what do we do now?" she asked.

He checked his watch. Hayden had just checked her own, so she knew it was just after one.

"Actually, maybe I should go back to Sylvia's."

Her eyes sharpened on him. His color looked better than it had before, but he still looked off. "Are you okay?"

"Just tired. I think it's the yo-yoing."

"Yo-yoing?"

"One minute, we're on our way to talk to Dr. Gunn to get all the answers; the next minute he's dead, possibly murdered, and the critical information I need is out of reach again. But then it turns out that the file's there, a little blood-soaked but legible, which probably means he committed suicide. But then Morgan lets us see a name. Awesome! I finally have the necessary information to locate my birth mother. But whoops, she's actually been dead almost as long as I've been alive. So, yeah, yo-yoing. I feel like I could sleep for a week."

Hayden smiled. This was good. Not that he was exhausted, but that he'd confess to it. Or more specifically, to owning all those emotions.

"Want to come back to my place?" As soon as the invitation

was out, she wanted to call it back. He probably wanted to be alone. He'd already said he wanted to go home.

"God, that would be heaven. You wouldn't mind?"

"I'd love it. I need to unplug too. I see blood most days, but that scene . . . I don't know how you cope with that kind of thing."

"Sleep will help." He reached over and clasped her hand.

Touch helped too, which he clearly knew. When he put the car in gear and reversed out of the parking space, he did it one-handed. In fact, he held her hand in his all the way up Regent Street to her apartment building.

Inside, Hayden dropped her purse. This time, she took his hand, leading him to the bedroom.

～

He knew where Hayden was leading him but he needed to make a quick stop by the bathroom. After he washed his hands and was about to leave the room, he caught a glimpse of his face in the mirror over the dainty vanity. He looked like shit. No wonder Hayden had asked if he was all right. He was just feeling worn-out, literally, from the emotional roller coaster he'd been riding since Dr. Gunn's call. A month ago, he wouldn't have admitted that under pain of torture.

So why was he opening up to Hayden?

Because he wanted her to know him. Wanted her to really see him.

He held that terrifying truth, turned it around and around in his mind as he looked into his own eyes in the mirror. Examined it from every angle. What in the hell was that about? He hadn't felt anything remotely like this since Laurie. He'd left himself wide-open to her, and then she'd excised him from her life and sewed the wound up as neatly as she'd sutured the lacerations on that dog he'd brought her. After that, he'd pretty much let people see what they wanted to see. Never again would he be tempted to expose so much of himself. That kind of openness was for the young in the first blush of love. And in his experience, people didn't seem to notice the difference. They took what they saw and heard, extrapolated a little, and voila. They'd built their own version of Boyd McBride, one that suited their ends.

Which suited him.

So why was he feeling like that with Hayden?

Then another thought occurred to him, one that eased his mind. Clearly, it was the no-strings deal. Hayden expected exactly nothing from him. No, *better* than nothing. Her only stipulation had been that he go back to his own life when the investigation was over and leave her to hers. What did it matter if she saw behind the curtain? He would likely never see her again once he left here.

Man, he must be tired, because that thought made him feel both better and worse. And what was with all this navel-gazing? That was more self-examination than he'd done in the past decade.

Well, prior to Josh's death. A person didn't weather something like that without some soul-searching.

He glared at himself in the mirror. Screw this noise. He needed to sleep. Shit had a way of sorting itself out and falling into place when you left the brain alone to process it. That's what he'd do.

Hayden met him in the hallway. She was dressed in yoga pants and some kind of spandex-infused workout top—a comfortable layer that screamed "sleep" not "sex." As she squeezed by him in the hallway, he wondered if she had any idea how appealing she looked. Or how great she smelled. But she was right. They needed sleep. And in this strange mood he was in, avoiding sex right now might be a really good idea.

"Mind if I grab a nap?"

"Go ahead."

He had almost dozed off in the moments it took her to brush her teeth or whatever she was doing. He opened his eyes when he heard her enter the room.

"Hey, you're on my side. Push over."

"Sorry." He scooted over. "I had the other side figured as yours."

She grinned. "Because of the clock?"

"Yep."

"I keep it over there to maximize the chance that I'll actually get up rather than hitting the 'Snooze' button."

He arched an eyebrow. "Not a morning person?"

"I'm a great morning person. After I actually get up. And after I've had coffee. And a shower. And food." She climbed into bed, then climbed right out again. "Hop up. I'll pull the bedspread back so we can get under it."

He waggled his eyebrows. "I could keep you warm."

"Sleep," she said sternly. "We need to give our minds and bodies a chance to rest and reset."

She was right. He rolled off the bed and climbed back in under the coverlet. "I hope there's no prohibition against snuggling, because I could really use it."

"You are such a liar," she said, moving into his arms. "I know you're doing all of this to comfort me. That whole thing back there with Dr. Gunn—"

"Hush." He absolutely was doing it for her, but the moment she laid her head on his shoulders and nestled into his side, he felt his own burdens lighten. "Sweetheart, any time I can get you in my arms, I'm going to do it, and I'm not being selfless. Believe me."

She sighed and laid her hand on his chest. She was silent for a moment. Just when he'd begun to wonder if she'd fallen asleep already, she shifted her position. A few more fidgety moves and he felt her relax fully against him in a way a body could only do in sleep.

Feeling incredibly full of some nameless tender emotion, he closed his own eyes and reached for sleep.

CHAPTER 23

His first conscious thought was that he was right where he wanted to be. Hayden had rolled away from him in sleep, and apparently he'd rolled after her. They both lay on their sides, with his body curled protectively around hers. Her delectable ass was pressed into his groin. No, not just pressed there. She was wriggling against him.

He locked a hand on her hip and held her still. Peering around her shoulder to see her face, he called her name softly. "Hayden?"

Her eyes came open and she looked up at him. "You're real."

Yeah, real hard. And getting harder when she used that sleep-husky voice. "Yep. As real as it gets."

"I thought I was dreaming. Or I *was* dreaming. I don't know. Was I . . . ?"

"Grinding that sweet ass against me?"

She lifted her hands to cover her face.

He grinned. "Don't be embarrassed. It's the very nicest kind of dream, but I don't have a condom on me." He slipped a hand around her to cup one of her breasts and closed his mouth on the point of her shoulder. "We rushed out this morning and I left them in my shaving kit."

"Don't look at me. I don't bring men home to spend the night with me, remember?" She gasped and arched, a reaction to his fingers tweaking her puckering nipple. Or maybe to the nip of his teeth against her skin.

He grinned against the shoulder he'd been nibbling. "I don't know about you, but I can think of some things we can do that don't require a condom."

"Oh, yes," she breathed. "And it's my turn."

The fingers that had been plucking her stiffened nipple stopped. "Your turn?"

She twisted away from him, tossed the coverlet off, and sat up. "Yes, my turn. To torture you. To make you crazy." She moved up onto her knees beside him and looked down at the tent he'd pitched in the thin material of his track pants. "I can see you like the idea."

"I'm all yours, darlin'." He reached to cup her head, intending to pull her down for a kiss.

"Uh-uh-uh. No touching." She pushed his hands away. "How quickly we forget the rules."

He groaned. "Baby, I don't know if I'll be able to keep my hands off you. They seem to have developed a mind of their own when it comes to you."

Her smile was absolute wickedness. "I'll make you the same offer you made me. I can tie them up. I'm not really a dress person, but think I have some pantyhose lying around here somewhere."

His cock jerked, a fact that didn't escape her attention.

"Much as I appreciate your willingness to sacrifice your pantyhose, that won't be necessary," he croaked. "I'll be strong. No hands. Well, until you ask me to use them."

Her eyes sparkled. "That sounded like a challenge, Detective."

"It was, Doctor."

Her smile broadened, growing absolutely carnal. "Hands behind your head," she said. "Isn't that what you tell the people you're about to slap the cuffs on?"

"In bed, you mean?" He pushed the pillow off the bed, then laced his hands together behind his head, making a cradle of them.

"No!" She laughed. "I meant in the field." Then she sat back on her heels. "But now that you mention it, ever handcuff anyone during sex?"

"No."

"Too cliché, cop breaking out the cuffs?"

He should say yes and let it go, but he was finding it harder and harder to lie to her, even by omission. "No, nothing like that." He lifted his shoulders in a tight shrug, considering his hands were behind his head. "It's more that I didn't want to send any messages, subliminal or otherwise."

Something flickered in her eyes, and he wondered if he'd been a little too honest. But she just nodded.

"That makes sense, not mixing capture-and-keep messages with hook-and-release practices. Lots of guys wouldn't spare a thought for that kind of thing. I guess that's Frank McBride's influence too?"

"Indirectly, maybe, in that he always told us to be straight with people as much as possible. He didn't have any specific advice for navigating the dating waters, other than no always means no and show women respect."

Hayden blinked rapidly again. "I think I love your father."

"Hey, that's enough of that!" How had they gotten onto this subject anyway? "I thought you were going to fool around with my body, not my brain."

She grinned. "Oh I intend to get to the body, but I'm fascinated by what goes on in that mind too." She leaned over him and put a finger to his forehead. "You know the most powerful sex organ is in here, right?"

"Uh . . . I'm pretty sure that's just women."

She laughed. "Maybe so." She slid down and laid a hand on his leg. Even through the material of the pants, it felt amazing when she skimmed that hand up his inner thigh. He hissed and arched, trying to make her hand brush against his arousal.

"Would you like out of these pants?"

"You have no idea how much," he groaned.

She hooked her fingers into the waistband. "Lift," she commanded. He obliged, lifting his butt off the bed. She slid the thin material down, dragging it maddeningly against his erection.

He gasped, unable to keep the sound in. She pulled the pants down his legs, but slowly. She bent to press her open mouth to his hip bone, his thigh, his knees. Jesus, she was killing him. Finally, she dragged them off.

He flexed his feet. "Hayden, don't—"

"Touch the feet. I know. I got the scoop from Josh. To tickle the foot of a McBride man or menace him with a snake is to risk bodily injury." She glanced at his face. "I always wondered how Josh could stand in the muck of that lake and have the grasses tickle his legs."

"Hello? Totally different. Although if a snake or an eel swam by, he'd have dumped you and swum for shore."

"He would not!"

"Okay, he probably wouldn't. But he'd have wanted to."

She started kissing her way back up. Just as he'd done to her yesterday, she skipped over the part that most yearned for her touch.

"Let's get this shirt off."

"Am I allowed to help?"

She sat back on her heels. "Go ahead."

He hauled the shirt off and tossed it, then put his hands back behind his head.

"How are your arms holding out up there? Shoulders okay?"

He chuckled.

"What's so funny?"

"You're kinda sorta topping, Hayden. I don't think you're supposed to worry if my arms are getting stiff."

"I can't help it. I look at that position and think about your rotator cuffs. I guess I'm not very good at this."

"I don't know. I've got a hard-on that says different."

She glanced down at it. "You do, don't you?"

"I was wondering if it had escaped your attention."

Her laugh this time was sharp and spontaneous. "That'd be pretty hard to miss."

"Yes, very hard."

"You know what I also notice?"

"What?"

"I'm talking way too much for a woman with so many other options in front of her."

"Other things you could be doing with your mouth?"

"Exactly." She bent over him and kissed him.

With his hands out of the game, he had no choice but to let her lead the dance of tongues. In truth, he had no desire to wrest that control from her. She was so clearly enjoying it.

Out of nowhere, it struck him again how lucky he was to be the object of all her pent-up desire. And how much she'd sacrificed for her career. Celibacy was one thing. A big damned thing. But for her, probably the emotional intimacy, the need to touch and be touched, even in a nonsexual way, was the bigger part of it. It was criminal she felt she had to do that, and all to keep some guy from latching on to her and staking his claim. Like the asshole who let her sacrifice those two years of medical school so she'd have enough time for him. After that experience, he totally got why she felt she had to avoid relationships altogether. Lots of guys talked the talk, pretending to be all pro-woman, but when push came to shove, how many of them would have turned out to be just another meathead who didn't want his "woman" going off to a third world country now and again? Never mind that it was humanitarian work.

He wanted to make up for everything she'd missed out on. Starting with lying here and passively accepting the torturous, leisurely tour she was presently taking of his body.

Her mouth was on his neck, trailing fire to his ear, where she paused long enough to whisper something very dirty. The promise sent a surge of lust through him, swift and brutal as an electric shock. His head actually spun.

Her hands traversed his chest now, their touch both soft and sure. He'd never been touched quite that way before. Damned if he could figure out the difference. Then she moved lower over his abs and he forgot to analyze anything. His muscles contracted under her featherlight stroke.

"God, I love your body. Lean, toned muscle, but not too bulky. And none of this pumping up some muscle groups at the expense of function. You must avoid the usual contraptions at the gym."

He was impressed. Everyone thought the way to a great body, including most of his colleagues on the force, was through pumping iron and doing a million reps on the machines. "Yeah, I thought I'd pass on the freakishly overdeveloped upper body and the legs of a rooster."

She laughed again, trailing her hand farther down his belly. "I can see you put your focus on your core."

He sucked said core farther in. "It's *killing me* not to be able to lay my hands on you. Your body is so damned beautiful."

"It gets me around."

That it did, but he suspected she had no idea how graceful and eye-catching she was.

"I'll never have buns of steel, I'm afraid." She gave her booty a shake as evidence.

He groaned with the need to touch that delectable part of her anatomy. "Baby, I don't know any men who are looking for buns of steel. I think that must be another one of those things women want to show off to other women. Men generally like things that jiggle a little."

Then she put her mouth so close to his stomach. There was a time and a place for talking, and a time and a place for kissing, licking and—*oh, Christ*—biting! Her even white teeth had nipped the right side of the taut V of muscle leading to his groin. He hissed, but not in pain.

She soothed the spot with her open mouth. "I always thought they needed a better anatomical name for this." She ran a delicate finger along it. "Iliac furrow doesn't do it justice, but the street names are so corny. Adonis belt. Apollo's belt."

He didn't care what she called it, as long as she traced it with her mouth, all the way down to the base of his erection.

"Hayden?"

"Yes?"

"I'm dying here. Please touch me."

She laughed, her breath an agony of delight on his skin.

He groaned his relief when she did just that, taking his cock in hand. The same deft touch she'd used on the rest of him made his already hard member harder still. *Jesus!* As she studied him, he uncupped his hands from behind his head and lowered his arms so he could at least grip the sheets.

She moved between his legs, urging his thighs farther apart to accommodate her. He obliged. And, oh, God, the picture she made kneeling over him, fully dressed, pulling that glorious riot of hair to one side to keep it out of the way. Then her mouth was on him, taking the head of his cock inside her warmth.

He closed his eyes, removing that sensory input, but all that did was intensify the incredible sensation of her mouth, her tongue, her firm, sure grip sliding over him. He dug his fingers into the bed so hard he was sure he'd leave imprints in the mattress. He wanted the pleasure to never end, but she drove him relentlessly upward. Only when he felt the first signals that he was going to come did he use his hands to touch her glorious hair.

"Hayden, you have to stop. Now."

She lifted her head but kept working him with her hand. His orgasm slammed into him. On his back like this, maybe because he wasn't in control, the release was intense, rolling through him, going on and on.

"Am I still alive?"

She grinned, handing him the box of tissues. "I take it you enjoyed that?"

"I think there needs to be a new word for what that felt like." He cleaned himself up, then lifted his gaze to her, eyeing the yoga gear. "Okay, you being fully dressed a minute ago was hot, I have to admit, but right now all I see is a lot of clothes between you and your orgasm."

That drew a laugh.

"Where's your vibrator?"

Her smile disappeared so fast, Boyd had to grin. "Excuse me?"

"Your vibrator. And, honey, don't tell me you don't have one. I'm guessing it must be in that lingerie drawer that you wouldn't let me search."

She blushed, but she grabbed it and handed it to him.

Within moments, he had her writhing in ecstasy on the bed. She was so responsive, so amazing, so freaking ripe and ready, he had to pin her bucking hips to the mattress before she exploded with her own orgasm.

While she lay there in what looked like pretty profound post-coital bliss, he held her loosely. She absolutely could not afford to bond to him. And he absolutely should kiss her and roll away, tell her that's the only way he could sleep. But the soft yet solid weight of her body against his was too sweet, too perfect. Besides, it wasn't all about him. After the harrowing day they'd had, who was he to deny her that human touch, that fundamental comfort?

In silence, they both drifted off to sleep.

By the time they woke the second time, Boyd felt if not completely restored, pretty damned close. Hayden made them a late supper of gluten-free pasta in a faux cheese sauce made from nutritional yeast. It wouldn't have been his first choice, or even his *fiftieth* choice. Of course, Hayden had given him the speech about why she chose to limit her gluten. He'd also heard why everyone should eat nutritional yeast—high protein, high fiber, lots of folic acid, a day's supply of B12, et cetera, et cetera. And actually, it was surprisingly good. Any shortfall was made up by the dessert of baked custard, the kind made with lots of eggs and milk like Ella McBride made.

They'd talked about Dr. Gunn's death. He couldn't keep his thoughts from going there, but he hadn't planned to raise the subject. He figured he'd already torpedoed her day off. But when she'd raised it, they were off and running. Not that they did—or could—reach any conclusions, but it helped to bat ideas around. He couldn't wait to learn more from Morgan, whom he hoped would share what he could. The problem was, in the current information vacuum, suicide and homicide were equally plausible.

He kept picturing the scales of justice. On one side rested the suicide theory. Gunn had had some level of involvement in Josh and Boyd's illegal adoption, possibly coercing, or helping to coerce, Arianna Duncan's cooperation. He'd confessed his sins and named names to Josh, after which Josh had died or been killed. Consumed by guilt, either for the original offence or upon learning of Josh's death, or by the cumulative weight of both, he'd committed suicide. The act might or might not have been hastened, or even triggered, by Boyd's call.

Then, on the other side of the scale, he plopped the murder theory, and they balanced perfectly. Gunn had confessed his sins and named names for Josh, and Josh had died or been killed shortly thereafter. When Boyd called, the tortured doctor had seized on the chance to unburden himself, promising to share the contents of his mother's file with him. But before that could happen, Gunn's "guest" had murdered him, just as they'd probably murdered Josh.

Except why would the murderer go to those lengths to cover something up, then leave the file?

The mental scales tilted in favor of suicide.

Yet Boyd didn't entirely buy that, not at a gut level. With any luck, there'd be trace evidence at the scene that could help him refine his thinking.

When he'd said he should head back to the B&B, she hadn't protested. Nor had he expected her to. He knew putting space between them was necessary, especially after this afternoon.

On the drive back, he resolved to talk to Sylvia about Dr. Gunn as soon as he could corner her. He needed to hear what she knew about the man, what kind of practice he'd run, and whether she thought he might have offed himself over whatever he'd done to facilitate whisking Arianna Duncan's babies away.

He parked in his assigned space, climbed out of the vehicle, and hit the "Auto Lock" button. He turned and headed toward the service entrance. He hadn't traveled more than a few steps when an alarm went off. He turned toward the sound, his heart stuttering, then pounding in heavy thumps he could actually feel.

What the actual hell? It was just a stupid car alarm. Man, those bouts of insomnia must be getting to him.

Sylvia Stratton poked her head out the service entrance door. "Detective McBride, would you kindly shut off that racket before my neighbors call the police."

He pointed to his rental. "Not my car. It's the one beside it. The little Hyundai."

"Ah, that's Mrs. Garner's. I'll send her out to silence it."

By the time he reached the door, the alarm had stopped. Inside, a flustered Mrs. Garner was apologizing. "I don't know how that happened, Dr. Stratton. The keys were in the pocket of my coat in the closet."

"No worries. It happens," Boyd offered. Mrs. Garner bustled away.

"So how are you holding up?" Sylvia asked.

He blinked. How was he holding up to being surprised by a car alarm? She was looking at him expectantly. "Sorry, come again?"

"I was wondering how you're holding up. I got back from Saint John to hear that you and Dr. Walsh had rather an eventful day."

He locked his gaze on her face. "How did you hear that?" He was sure Facebook and other social networks were probably abuzz by now, but there's no way those random people could know he and Hayden had been there.

"I had a call from David Bradley."

Boyd's antenna went up. "Dave Bradley?"

"Yes. He wanted to work up background on Dr. Gunn." Her expression told him what she thought of Dave Bradley. Or perhaps just reporters in general.

"But why would he call you?" He frowned, feeling like a dull child. Maybe he'd gotten too much sleep. "Unless . . . Are you related to Dr. Gunn?"

"Goodness, no. But we were colleagues and very dear friends. He's actually the Senator's physician."

"I'm so sorry," he said. "I didn't realize." Now that he looked at her, he could see the strain in her. Her shoulders were drawn higher toward her neck, as though she were hunched in on her grief. He could understand that.

"Of course you didn't. And thank you." She inclined her head in dignified acknowledgment.

It made sense, he supposed, that they would be friends. Both Dr. Stratton and Dr. Gunn had been in practice here forever. But how had Dave Bradley known about their relationship? Of course, it *was* a pretty small town. Maybe it was just a natural assumption on Bradley's part that the doctors would have known one another. And what did he imagine he was going to get out of Sylvia Stratton, the original dragon lady? Bradley would find himself overmatched.

More importantly, had Boyd dismissed Bradley as a suspect too soon?

"Sorry," he said. "Maybe I'm being obtuse, but I guess it has been a long day. How is it that Dave Bradley would know about your friendship with Dr. Gunn?"

"I *am* related to Mr. Bradley. Distantly, to be sure, but he's been here before, at Stratton House, for a dinner party or two. That, of course, is how he knew Dr. Gunn and I were great friends. Not that I've had either the time or inclination to socialize since the Senator fell ill, but I do . . . sorry, I *did* make time for Angus. We used to have a glass of sherry or sometimes something stronger—he did bend that elbow a bit much—over our conferences about the Senator's treatment plan. As I mentioned, he was my husband's doctor."

"I guess it's been a rough day for you too," he said gently.

She inclined her head. "Thank you. I really don't know what I'll do now. I trusted Angus utterly with the Senator's life, and now I'll have to go doctor shopping." She shook her head. "I never thought I'd be in this position."

Boyd didn't know what to say to that. If Dr. Gunn had earned this demanding woman's trust, he must be of impeccable character. At least insofar as she knew. How could he have presented such a sterling face to the very shrewd Sylvia Stratton, yet have been involved in an illegal adoption, the ramifications of which were being felt thirty-five years later?

Unless . . . Had Sylvia known all along about Dr. Gunn's involvement in his and Josh's birth and covered it up? Deliberately misdirected them to protect her dearest friend?

Time to feel her out.

"I can't stress enough how sorry I am for your loss, Dr. Stratton, but I presume you've deduced why Dr. Walsh and I called on Dr. Gunn this morning?"

"I presume Angus must've had some information for you relating to your search?"

"He did."

"And now, given my decades-long friendship with him, I imagine you must be wondering if I knew that all along."

He held her now-steely gaze. "The thought did cross my mind," he admitted.

She lifted an eyebrow. "You realize that would mean I'd been misleading first your brother, and then you, in order to help Angus escape the consequences of whatever it is he might have done."

"Dr. Stratton—"

She held up a hand to stop him. "You're absolutely right to wonder. Had I been in possession of such knowledge, I might well have tried to protect him." She shrugged and grimaced, in a what-are-you-going-to-do sort of gesture. "Angus was one of my oldest friends. But as it happens, I had no knowledge of any improprieties." She clasped the strand of pearls at her throat, looking as distressed as Boyd had ever seen her. "So, what did you learn that led you to Angus?"

He thought about declining to answer, but he knew all too well how it felt to lose someone you loved and be denied answers to the most basic of questions. He knew full well how the need to understand burned in your brain and twisted your gut.

"I found a note that Josh had written, with Dr. Gunn's name and number," Boyd said. "When I called him and introduced myself, he didn't seem at all surprised to hear from me. In fact, I told Hayden at the time that he almost seemed relieved. He confirmed that he had spoken to Josh and was prepared to share with me everything he'd told Josh."

"I see." Her arched eyebrow invited him to continue.

"He said he was present when Josh and I were born, which I presume means he delivered us. I didn't get to talk to him, though, as I'm sure you know. Nor was I able to examine the file he'd laid out on his desk before . . ." He let the words trail off. "However, I did catch a glimpse of the name on the file. It seems our birth mother was a young woman by the name of Arianna Duncan."

He watched her face as he said the name, searching it for a start of guilt or a flicker of recognition. Her expression did indeed change, but not in a negative way. Instead, a faint smile touched her lips.

"My goodness, you've been successful in your search, then? Well, that is a very big consolation. Is there a reunion in the offing?"

"I'm afraid not. My subsequent research shows that she died within three months of our birth."

"I'm so sorry. You must be terribly disappointed."

Was he? He hadn't even had time to sort that out. But he made an affirmative sound. It seemed to be what was expected. He was certainly sorry that a young woman had died, possibly after being coerced into giving up her children. But he didn't have so much as a mental picture of Arianna Duncan to hang those feelings on.

"I'm sorry for your loss too." And he was. She and Dr. Gunn had had a long-standing friendship. As rigid as she could be, she seemed vulnerable now somehow.

"In truth, I'm having a hard time crediting it," she said, fingering the pearls again. "The evidence will no doubt speak for itself, but I will have to reserve judgment until I've seen that proof laid out."

"Of course." Boyd would have liked to offer some comforting thought about Gunn just having made a mistake, one that he'd paid dearly for, but he knew nothing of the man or what motivated him to do what he'd done.

She sniffed, and Boyd suspected she was fighting tears.

He put a hand on her shoulder, which felt incredibly frail for all the command presence she managed to assert most of the time, and squeezed gently. "Again, I'm very sorry, particularly if our visit precipitated Dr. Gunn's decision." He dropped his hand, part of him marveling that he'd dared to touch this seemingly untouchable woman.

"Thank you, Boyd," she said, using his first name for perhaps the second time since they'd met. She straightened her spine, which she'd allowed to relax the slightest bit. "But I hold no ill will about your visit. Much as I hate to think Angus might have made a misstep somewhere, I also have to recognize that if he had nothing to be ashamed of, your visit would have been . . . less eventful. And I know how important your search was, particularly after your brother's unfortunate death."

"Thank you."

Her eyes sharpened. "Do you happen to know how your mother died? You say she passed within months of your birth, so she must have been fairly young."

"It sounds like sudden cardiac arrest. I haven't been permitted access to the file, of course, but the detective—Ray Morgan—told me that much. He figured I needed to know it. And, yes, I appreciate this means there's probably a genetic issue."

"Oh, dear, yes! I presume Dr. Walsh has warned you against avoiding possible aggravating agents? Certain drugs can be proarrhythmic."

"She has," he confirmed. "And I'm good there. About the only thing I ever take is ibuprofen for muscle aches if I overdo something, but I won't even be taking that."

"Nothing recreational either," she warned sternly.

"Again, nothing but a beer or two. No worries."

She nodded, apparently satisfied. "Well, good night, Detective. I believe I'll fix a hot milk and retire."

"Good night, Dr. Stratton."

She turned and tap-tapped off in the direction of the kitchen. Boyd went up to his room, but he didn't go to bed. All that sleep through the afternoon and evening, though desperately needed, had knocked his circadian rhythm off.

Instead, he sat down, opened his laptop, and Skyped his parents. When his mother asked how the fishing was going, he wanted to tell her the truth. But it was too early. So he told her he'd taken the day off and driven to Fredericton for supplies. She teased him that it was a beer run, while his father speculated he'd gotten tired of ugly male mugs and had gone looking for female companionship.

Before he could stop himself, he blurted out that he'd looked up Hayden Walsh, Josh's friend. That led to tons of questions. *Will you see her again? How is she doing? It was so kind of her to come all this way for the funeral. We got the nicest letter from her afterward. Did you see the letter before you left for your fishing trip? No? Well, it was a very lovely letter.*

He told them Hayden was still very broken up about Josh but was keeping busy with work. He added that he was planning to stay in Fredericton for a few days, to visit with her longer. There was only so much fishing and poker playing a man could do. Ella expressed her approval and asked him to thank Hayden again for being such a good friend to Josh. He assured her he would. Feeling better for having told them even a tiny fraction of the truth, he signed off.

Of course, his wide-awake mind went back to the events of the day. He played it over in his head, again and again, and every time he came back to one question. Well, lots of questions, but the main one was, was it suicide?

He kept coming back to that phone conversation. Frankly, Gunn hadn't sounded like a man on the verge when they'd talked. More like a man who wanted to get something off his chest. Of course, maybe the relief Boyd had thought he'd heard was relief at having committed to a course of action, like that long-ago jumper on the overpass he'd told Hayden about.

He had to admit it did look like suicide. The detective's and the coroner's assessments seemed to support that. And what had Morgan said? The ME thought there might be an anticoagulant in the mix. What better way for a doctor to ensure success than doubling down on the blood thinners? And the angle of the cuts seemed to bear out the idea that they were self-inflicted.

On the other hand, Boyd could probably have stood behind the guy, if he was already unconscious, and with the scalpel squeezed into the guy's own grip, made a credible slash that looked self-inflicted. He made a note to mention that to Morgan, who would hopefully not roll his eyes and accuse him of being crazy.

Next question. Presuming it was suicide, what had Gunn done that was suicide worthy? Yes, the whole reputation thing. And who knew? Maybe the doctor had just been handed a pancreatic cancer diagnosis or something. Maybe he was ready to check out anyway and wanted to do it before any blemish on his career could surface.

Or . . . *Jesus Christ—maybe he'd killed Arianna Duncan!*

Boyd leapt up from the table, almost knocking his laptop to the floor, catching it at the last second.

He pushed the computer farther back on the desk, out of harm's way. His blood pumping, he forced himself to sit down and think about it.

Okay, if Gunn had killed Arianna Duncan, or caused her death somehow, that would ratchet up the guilt levels. But if he'd lived with it this long—thirty-five years—why now? Did he think his actions were about to be outed? That would be ironic, since Josh's notebook had disappeared and neither Boyd nor the police had anything to tie Dr. Gunn to Arianna Duncan, let alone tying Boyd and Josh to Arianna.

What if Gunn killed Josh?

He couldn't believe he was even thinking that. The idea was insane.

Unless it wasn't.

Maybe it made a sort of sense. If Gunn had been his mother's physician and knew she'd died of cardiac arrest, maybe he'd taken a gamble that Josh had inherited the same susceptibility. Maybe when Josh went to see him, Gunn had slipped him some noxious agent—or aggravating agent, as Sylvia had called it—in the hopes that Josh would meet the same end as their mother had.

Boyd forced himself to sit down again. *Think it through, man.*

Okay, if Gunn had slipped Josh something, surely the forensic toxicology report would uncover it. Depending on what that agent was, of course, it still might look like an unfortunate natural occurrence. But if it was some esoteric substance, or some prescription drug that couldn't be explained away, surely that would be enough to establish foul play. As long as it wasn't so esoteric that the forensic techs wouldn't even think to check for it.

But if Gunn had done it, how could they prove anything now?

And damned if that didn't leave him in waiting mode again. Waiting for the tox report. The genetic testing seemed superfluous now, but eventually it would land, no doubt confirming long QT syndrome or some other genetic problem with the heart's electrical wiring. And now they were waiting for the coroner's ruling on Dr. Gunn, either confirming suicide or suggesting something else. At this point, he hoped suicide would be a slam dunk. Only because if someone had killed Gunn, that meant a killer—likely Josh's killer—was still out there.

Whether it was the cast of his thoughts or the fact that he'd had all that extra sleep earlier, he was suddenly restless. So restless he couldn't stay in this room a minute longer.

Sylvia would be in bed by now. So would Mrs. Garner. He could creep down to the kitchen and make some of that warm milk like Sylvia had done. Or better yet, maybe there'd be a bottle of opened wine in the refrigerator or maybe a beer or two he could replace.

After easing out of his room, he closed the door softly behind him and started along the landing toward the stairs. But the sound of coughing stopped him. Male coughing, he realized. He waited to see if anyone would respond, but when no one moved in the house, he backtracked. For the first time since setting foot in Stratton House, he made his way down the hall past his own suite. At the end of the hall in what had to be a sunny corner room in the daytime, he found Senator Stratton.

CHAPTER 24

No nurse sat in the room, which surprised Boyd. He'd gotten the impression the Senator was never left alone. Of course, the rails on his hospital bed were probably rigged to alarm if he tried to crawl out, if he could even move. Hell, he was probably fully wired to alarm if his heart faltered or respirations dropped. For all Boyd knew, Sylvia's room might be as well equipped as an ICU nurses' station.

The Senator coughed again. Glancing behind him and seeing no one, Boyd entered the room. The man in the bed had probably been a big man once. Even now, he was clearly tall and large-framed, but he looked like he'd suffered muscle wasting, either from age or from his confinement in the bed, or both. Boyd moved into the pool of light around the bed.

"Sir?"

The Senator looked up and his eyes widened. Then he coughed again. Boyd glanced around and saw a Styrofoam cup of ice chips, largely melted now.

"Can you have some ice chips to ease that tickle?"

The old man gave a slight but distinct nod.

Boyd took the spoon from the cup, gathering the largest of the remaining ice chips. The Senator opened his mouth obligingly.

After a few seconds, Boyd offered him more. The old man nodded again. After a few more repetitions, the Senator declined more ice with a shake of his head.

Boyd put the cup back down. "I guess you're not able to talk?"

Another shake of the head.

"I should go. I'm not supposed to be in here. But when I heard you coughing—"

The Senator shook his head, much more vigorously this time, and his eyes begged Boyd to stay.

Boyd looked back at the empty door, sighed, and pulled up a chair. "Your wife will be perturbed if she finds me here."

The Senator nodded gravely.

Boyd smiled. "So you can't sleep either, huh? Right. You probably get way more sleep than a body can stand."

The Senator lifted his eyebrows.

"What's keeping me awake?"

He nodded.

"The same thing that keeps me awake most nights since Josh—that'd be my identical twin brother—died last month."

The old man's face suffused with obvious emotion.

"Had you met him?" Boyd asked. "He was staying here, but I thought Dr. Stratton's rules forbade visitors. Of course, here I am, right? I guess Josh might have wandered in too."

The Senator nodded.

"That sounds like Josh. He was too curious for his own good. I don't know whether he talked to you or not, but he'd come to Fredericton from Toronto to look for our birth parents. From a message he left me on my phone, I gather he'd found the answer, but, unfortunately, he didn't leave me the details. Then he died."

The Senator's face contracted.

"Are you okay, sir?" Boyd bent closer. "Should I call for someone? Your wife?" At his vehement head shake, Boyd subsided. "I'm sorry. I didn't mean to upset you. I shouldn't have raised the topic. It's sad, a man so young dying. Not that he was super young. Thirty-five, and lots of miles on him. He had a good job— he was an award-winning investigative journalist. Great career, great friends, a great life. It's just . . ." He shrugged helplessly. "It just ended too soon. And though I hate to say it, I fear it wasn't natural causes." Boyd dragged a hand through his hair. "But that's in the hands of the coroner now. We're waiting on forensic toxicology and genetic tests."

The Senator raised his eyebrows again.

"The genetic testing? That's because he died of sudden cardiac arrest. Sitting in his car after a lunch-hour jog, actually."

Boyd wasn't sure why he was volunteering all this information, but it felt good. Maybe because the Senator couldn't talk back or repeat anything. Or maybe because he seemed so interested. With the old man's eyes imploring him to continue, Boyd obliged.

"He was really healthy—fitter than me, probably, because he had a better diet. The thing is, today I found out who our mother was, but apparently she died in a similar way within months of giving birth to us and giving us up for adoption. Which makes a genetic link look pretty inescapable."

Or a killer had poisoned both of them to keep his dark deeds from the past from coming back to haunt him. But Boyd didn't suggest anything like that to the old man. He looked upset enough. In fact—*shit*—he looked to be getting more agitated by the moment. Maybe more of the ice chips—

"What on earth are you doing in here?"

The voice from the door arrested Boyd's reach for the ice chips. He swiveled to see a middle-aged nurse or personal care worker of some kind standing in the doorway, holding a steaming mug. She must have left her post just long enough to put the kettle on and brew some coffee or tea.

"Sorry, I was on my way downstairs when I heard him coughing and coughing. When no one turned up to help him, I came in and give him some of the ice chips."

The woman bustled over to the other side of the bed, put her beverage down on a wheeled tray, and turned to the Senator.

"Oh dear, he looks agitated. Dr. Stratton will be so upset."

Boyd blinked. "Surely he'll be calm by morning?"

"Just leave." She whipped out a blood pressure cuff, put it on the Senator's unresisting arm, and started pumping it up. "And please stay away. Dr. Stratton forbids anyone else being in here. I could lose my job for this."

"Sorry," he said again. "I didn't know you were downstairs or I'd have gone down and fetched you. He just sounded so—"

She took the stethoscope out of her ears and removed the blood pressure cuff briskly. She gave him a dark look. "Go."

He went.

Geez, what was wrong with visiting the old man? Okay, the subject matter he'd raised wasn't all that uplifting, but he'd have moved on to better things. The poor bastard, confined to that bed with nothing but a procession of nurses. Probably not one of them a hockey fan. No doubt the old guy pulled for the Ottawa Senators. Boyd could have razzed him about that. Everyone knew anyone with heart was a Maple Leafs fan. Well, heart and a lot of long-suffering patience. And maybe a wide streak of masochism.

And baseball. Boyd could at least read the old guy the game summaries or box scores. Hell, why wasn't there even a television in the room?

Wait, maybe there was. He hadn't really inventoried the room. But if there was one, he bet it never got tuned to the sports channel or the news feed or frickin' C-SPAN or CPAC. And that was just wrong. There was life in the old guy's eyes. He was in there.

Maybe he should ask Sylvia's permission to visit.

Right. And maybe she'd carve him a new one.

He made his way downstairs. There was no wine or beer in the refrigerator, so he warmed some milk in the microwave and drank it right there as he distracted himself by flipping through the headlines in the day's newspaper. He rinsed the cup and stashed it in the dishwasher, hoping he wouldn't incur Mrs. Garner's wrath for cleaning up after himself.

Back in his room, his brain immediately fell back into the rutted groove. Josh—natural causes or foul play? Dr. Gunn—suicide or foul play? Arianna Duncan—natural causes or foul play? And was there anything he could do besides freaking waiting on other people's investigations? Unless . . .

He brought his computer out of sleep mode and Google searched "Arianna Lynn Duncan." Nothing. He tried "Arianna Duncan" and "A. L. Duncan" too and got some hits on the latter. Unfortunately, they didn't relate to his mother. Looked like his first impression was right—the death was just too old for the obituary and news articles to go digital and get interwoven into the fabric of the Internet.

He pushed the computer away, turning his focus to Dave Bradley. His turning up was likely nothing. Sylvia had explained the family connection. Bradley was a reporter, and Dr. Gunn's death was newsworthy in this small city. Boyd didn't like it, though. Didn't like hearing the other man's name at all.

Damn, the warm milk wasn't doing anything for him. He felt manic. Anxious. Like he'd come out of his own skin if he couldn't do something.

His phone made a soft trill, announcing a text. Smiling, he reached for it, knowing it could only be Hayden. It was.

Are you as wide awake as I am? she'd written.

Instead of texting her a reply, he called her.

"I guess that's a yes," she said.

As soon as he heard her voice, the crazy, frustrated energy morphed into something else. Something he knew how to deal with.

"That's a hell yes," he said. "I was hoping to talk you into some phone sex."

She laughed. "That would also be a hell yes."

294

CHAPTER 25

The next day, Hayden directed Boyd through light morning traffic to the library, a spot she'd visited a time or two to borrow audiobooks. The staff was extremely helpful, showing them how to use the equipment. Actually poring through the material was a little laborious, but Detective Morgan had given them a time frame—July 1979. After about twenty minutes, Boyd found it.

"This is it. Arianna Duncan, aged twenty, July 17, 1979, at the Dr. Everett Chalmers Regional Hospital." He glanced up at her. "That doesn't sound right, does it? If she died of sudden cardiac arrest, that kinda precludes getting to a hospital, doesn't it?"

She shrugged. "They probably transported her by ambulance and a doctor declared her dead on arrival. Even if she was dead on the scene, she's not declared until she hits the hospital. That's where she died as far as the record is concerned."

"Jesus, twenty years old."

"Oh, that's so sad."

"Listen to this—she was predeceased by father, Robert Duncan, and mother, Gladys Duncan (née Carrier), of Saint Andrews, New Brunswick, and survived by a brother, Sheldon, also of Saint Andrews."

Hayden smiled. "You have an uncle."

"Well, I had one thirty-five years ago."

Her smile faded. She couldn't blame him for his pessimism. If Arianna Duncan was a full sibling to Sheldon Duncan, he could have long QT syndrome. And with their parents dying when they were so young—or at least when Arianna was young—luck did not seem to follow the Duncan family.

"Do you suppose they'd have done an autopsy? Would the coroner have investigated that kind of death back then?"

"Probably."

"I'll drop by and fill out the request."

She gestured to the microfilm. "In light of that obituary, do you think you need a death certificate too?"

"It's probably overkill, but yeah. I actually did it last night, at the Service New Brunswick website. Same as I did for Josh."

"Does the registrar of vital statistics check to see if there's a paper trail confirming that you're really next of kin?"

"We'll soon see." He raked his hair off his forehead.

"Okay, get that thing printed off so we can get around to the coroner's office."

There was no lineup at the coroner's office. Boyd told the front-office clerk that he was in town for a limited time and hoped to pick the report up soon. The woman assured him she would personally see that it was expedited. He asked for a sticky note, on which he wrote his name and cell phone number. Yes,

yes, of course, she'd be happy to call him when it was available. It would possibly be as early as Tuesday.

Tuesday? As in tomorrow? Hayden rolled her eyes. Josh used to get the special treatment too. Of course, for Josh, it was that crooked smile and the sparkle in his eyes. For Boyd, she suspected it was more that they wanted to tear off his shirt.

From there, they'd gone to the police station. Boyd had wanted to have a private word with Detective Morgan to see what more, if anything, he might be able to share about Gunn's death.

Hayden chatted with Detective Sean Hayes while Boyd went off with Ray Morgan to sign his statement. When he and Morgan emerged from the interview room, they bumped into someone, a tall, solid-looking man. The other guy wasn't quite as a tall as Boyd, but he managed to seem bigger somehow. And not in a bodybuilding, no-neck kind of way. He just had a sort of physicality that was hard to ignore.

Boyd stayed to talk to the big guy, but Ray Morgan came over to join Hayden. As soon as he arrived, Detective Hayes excused himself, picked up his coat, and walked away.

"I hope I wasn't keeping him from anything important," she said as she watched the younger detective's retreating back.

"Hayes?" His gaze flicked toward the exit. "Nah. If he had somewhere he needed to be, he wouldn't have stayed to keep you company out of politeness."

She lifted her eyebrows.

He laughed. "I guess you could take that a couple of different ways, but all I meant was Detective Hayes is a nose-to-the-grindstone guy. Never seen him dog it on the job. If he hung back to chat, it was because he wanted to, and it wouldn't have been at the expense of an investigation."

"Good." She glanced up at Detective Morgan. "Any news you can share about the investigation?"

"I just gave McBride what I felt comfortable telling him, which is that it's looking like a pretty cut-and-dried suicide. But, of course, he had to give me his theory about someone rendering Dr. Gunn unconscious in his chair, then approaching him from behind, positioning the scalpel in the victim's own hand, and making the fatal slash."

"You don't sound pleased."

Morgan's good-looking face screwed up in a frown. "Every thing's a conspiracy with that guy." He seemed to become aware of his frown and forced his features to smooth. "And you can tell him I said that. He won't be surprised, considering I already said it to his face."

Hayden smiled. "What's the saying? Just because you're paranoid doesn't mean they're not out to get you."

He sighed. "I know. And I plan to call the pathologist and ask him to take a real close look at the angles, see if there's anything there in the physical evidence to suggest he had help opening that artery. And the forensic toxicology should turn up something if someone rendered him unconscious."

"Will it, though? Will they look for anesthetizing agents?"

He pulled out a small black book and jotted something down. "They will now. And maybe they do it anyway. I'm pretty sure they're going to find alcohol in his system."

And possibly some cirrhosis of the liver, if what Sylvia had told Boyd was true. She seemed to think her friend indulged a little too much. Of course, by Sylvia's exacting standards, that could be one or two drinks a day. But instead of saying that, she remarked that she hadn't smelled any overwhelming alcohol smells.

"Due respect, Doc, it can be pretty hard to focus on much else when the victim is lying in a puddle of his own blood. That's pretty much all you tend to see or smell."

"True," she acknowledged. She picked up her purse. "Did Boyd tell you what we found out this morning?"

He cocked his head. "What do you mean?"

"Just that we were able to get the death certificate for Arianna Duncan, and that he's filed a request for the coroner's investigation records."

"Oh, yeah. He mentioned that. It's encouraging to see that detail, at least, seems to be as billed."

"Do you think Boyd's right? That this Dr. Gunn had something to do with helping adopt those kids out, then obscured or falsified the record to keep the truth buried?"

"I do. It's the only thing that makes sense." He rubbed his forehead. "Look, I know McBride has a whole collection of alternate theories, but he knows as well as I do that the obvious explanation is usually the one that proves to be true. It's good as an investigator to keep an open mind to other possibilities, but McBride seems to be working overtime to make this Dr. Gunn thing anything but suicide."

She tightened her grip on the strap of her purse. "You're wrong there, Detective. I'm pretty sure he's praying that it was suicide and that the coroner can establish that beyond a reasonable doubt. Otherwise, this isn't anywhere near over, and he needs it to be over. I don't even know if he appreciates how badly he needs that, but he does."

And when it was over, *they* would be over. Boyd and Hayden. He'd go back to Toronto, and Hayden would go back to life as it used to be. The idea made a hollowness rise in her chest.

When she'd convinced Boyd to embark on this relationship, she'd known it wouldn't be easy to give up. She'd still been adjusting to the loss of Josh when Boyd had come along and filled up that void to a degree. Then, by moving their relationship into the sexual realm, she'd let Boyd occupy an even bigger space.

When it was over, which could be sooner rather than later, she would be left with a hole in her life. She'd miss him like crazy. Miss the sex, miss those serious, guarded eyes.

Oh, she'd get through it. The demands of the job didn't leave much time for wallowing. Work had always been her panacea. And there was no point ruining the here and now by anticipating the loneliness to come. Instead, she would focus on enjoying as much of this as she could.

"You know, before I got the call yesterday about Dr. Gunn, I was supposed to call you and invite you and McBride to dinner," Detective Morgan said. "Grace was bummed about this coming up, since it meant canceling those plans."

"Right," she said. "We're witnesses in your case now." She offered her hand to him and he shook it. "Tell Grace we're disappointed too."

"I will. And let me walk you over there and break up that huddle. I need my sergeant back."

Hayden's breath caught as they crossed the detectives' bull pen. Both men—Boyd and Ray Morgan's sergeant—were leaning against the edges of different desks. The unknown guy sort of slouched there with his legs crossed at the ankles and arms crossed over a broad chest, while Boyd sat near the end of another desk, one leg braced on the floor, the other sort of swinging. He looked so comfortable, so at home. This was his world, or an approximation of it. Funny how little time she'd spent thinking about that.

Boyd caught sight of her then, and his eyes seemed to light up, which helped dislodge that hollow feeling.

"There you are."

"Here I am." She reached his side, then turned to look closer at the big guy.

"Hayden, this is Sergeant Quigley. He was very helpful when I came to town the first time."

"Miss." The sergeant held out his hand.

She shook it. And, oh, yeah, this guy definitely had an extra something about his physical aura. "Good to meet you, sir."

Boyd shoved off the desk. "Well, we should get out of your hair. I know you've got work to do."

"We'll keep you posted on your brother's file, McBride," Ray Morgan said. "Sarge here has put in a request to get the reports expedited, given the probable intersection with this new case. We're hoping that means the tox report, at least, should pop free a little sooner than it might have otherwise."

Boyd's gaze shot to Sergeant Quigley. "Thank you, sir. That's much appreciated."

"No problem."

Outside on the street, Boyd took Hayden's hand as they walked the short distance to where they'd parked Boyd's rental behind city hall.

"So what are you going to do with the rest of your day?" he asked when they'd climbed into the car.

"I'd made no plans." She rolled the window down for some air while the A/C got up to speed. "I was kind of wondering if there was anything more we could do on the case."

He looked over at her. "Which one?"

"Either. Both." She shrugged. "I know you must be going crazy waiting on those reports. And how about Sergeant Quigley putting that call in? I could have kissed him."

"You and me both," he said with feeling.

She grinned. "You didn't answer my question. Is there anything we can be doing?"

"I was thinking about trying to locate Arianna Duncan's brother." He pulled from his pocket the folded paper with the copy of the obituary they'd printed at the library. "I thought I'd go home, dig out my laptop, and do a little sleuthing, see if I could find this guy's address or number."

"Sheldon was the name, right? From Saint Andrews." She glanced at him. "Do you suppose he's still alive? And still in the Saint Andrews area?"

"We'll soon see."

When they got to Stratton House, Sylvia was nowhere in sight, for which Hayden was grateful. Boyd had told her about his impromptu visit with the Senator and the nurse's horrified reaction. He had no idea whether his transgression had been reported or not. Since he'd emerged unscathed from breakfast, she suspected not. As Boyd had pointed out, perhaps the nurse and Dr. Stratton hadn't yet connected. Or maybe the nurse wasn't planning to report it at all. She'd seemed to think she could lose her job over it.

They hurried up the steps to Boyd's room. He went straight to the table to flip his computer on, while she went to flop on the couch.

She glanced over at his computer and saw that he had the search engine loaded. While he worked, she let her mind drift. Naturally, it went back to last night and their playful lovemaking. His focus and intensity in bed she'd totally expected. The playfulness, not so much. It was—

"Got it!"

His declaration pulled her back. "You found him?"

"Yep. Still in Saint Andrews, according to this phone directory." He looked over at her. "Wanna take a drive?"

"Sure. But shouldn't you call ahead? Make sure he's home or that he'll see you?"

He frowned. "How far away is Saint Andrews?"

"Hour and a half, maybe," she estimated.

"Then, no, I'll risk a wasted drive. I'd rather not get into it on the phone."

"And you'd rather not risk him telling us not to come?"

"That too," he confessed.

"Okay, let's do it."

"Excellent." He pulled out his phone and plugged the contact information into it. He looked up at her. "Need to go home for anything, or can we get on the road?"

"I think I'm okay." She looked down at her cargo pants and blouse. "Unless you think I need a change?"

He crossed to the couch and picked her right up off it. She squeaked and grabbed him around the neck.

"I think you look good enough to eat."

"I'll take you up on that offer when we get back to town," she said huskily.

He put her down so she could slip her feet back into the sandals she'd kicked off. They made their escape without seeing Sylvia, although Hayden felt a little guilty about it. Boyd had said that Sylvia had been a close friend of Dr. Gunn's and was about as devastated as he imagined she was capable of getting, short of losing the Senator.

She forgot the guilt quickly, though, as they got iced coffees and hit the road. The sun was shining, it was a Monday, and she was off work.

She hadn't taken a road trip since she and Josh had gone to Grand Manan for two days. The island was rugged and beautiful. Josh had loved it. Boyd would love it too. She found herself wishing they were headed out for a weekend themselves, instead of a quick trip to visit a man who almost certainly was Boyd's uncle. Arianna Duncan's younger brother.

Her pleasure in the sunny day dimmed a little as she worried about the reception Boyd would get. She understood that this kind of thing was best handled face-to-face, but, personally, Hayden would rather have a little more notice than a knock on her door.

"Ever been to Saint Andrews?"

His question drew her from her thoughts. "Once, on a day trip with a nurse from the ER. She's a big gardener, so we checked out the Kingsbrae Botanical Gardens. Walked the beach, did some touristy stuff, had supper at a dining room at a supposedly haunted bed-and-breakfast, and drove home. It was nice."

As the miles passed, she asked him about the lake house—did it belong to his parents? Was it their usual summer holiday spot, or a casual rental? He responded that his parents did own it, but they rented it much of the year. The rental income made it affordable to keep, but it also meant there was always some repair or upgrade that needed doing. He'd launched into a story about some of the stuff renters had inadvertently left behind, including a baggie with just enough weed in it for the then fifteen-year-old twins to try their hand at rolling their first joint.

"And how did that work out?" she asked.

Boyd said nothing but gave her a glance, like *that* was a story that would never make it to her ears.

The rest of the trip passed in near silence, but it wasn't an awkward one. It was very companionable. When they reached Saint Andrews, she started scanning for the street.

Boyd spotted the street sign first—it was on his side. Less than a minute later, they were there, in Sheldon Duncan's driveway. He killed the engine but made no move to get out.

"Are you rethinking the not calling first?"

He shook his head. "Not really. And we're here now. Let's just see how it plays out."

The outside of the house was neat and tidy, but not as picture-book perfect as some of them. The walkway was lined with stones—from the beach, no doubt—and pieces of driftwood added architectural interest to a few small flower beds.

"Cute," she said, but he was too focused on the door they were approaching to respond.

There was no doorbell, just an anchor-shaped brass door knocker. He lifted the anchor and rapped it a couple of times. Hayden heard movement inside, which was a relief. It would have sucked to come all this way to find no one home. Of course, who was to say this Sheldon Duncan hadn't taken an extended vacation at a child's or grandchild's house so he could rent his place out during the lucrative tourist season?

The door opened to a glossy-haired young lady in casual capri pants and T-shirt. The child she held on her hip had matching brown hair, albeit much finer. According to the information they'd found on Sheldon Duncan, Hayden suspected either he or his offspring still lived there. The young woman in front of her looked like she might be Josh and Boyd's younger sister, or maybe their mother if they'd traveled back in time. It was those tawny-golden eyes.

Boyd noticed too. She felt him go absolutely still beside her.

The young woman searched Hayden's face first, and, when she shifted her gaze to Boyd, her eyes widened. "Your eyes . . ."

"I guess they must be a Duncan trait," Boyd said, "although I've only just discovered my mother was a Duncan."

"Omigod! You must be . . . Are you . . . ? I mean—"

"Yes. I'm Arianna Duncan's son," Boyd said. "And I'm guessing you must be Sheldon Duncan's daughter?"

"I am." She backed up, inviting them to follow.

"Is your father home?" Boyd stepped inside and looked around.

Hayden, who'd been watching the young mother while Boyd had been scanning the environment, saw her eyes darken.

"No. I'm afraid he'd not with us anymore. He died at sea years ago when his boat got tangled in fishing gear and capsized. That was nineteen years ago."

Hayden watched Boyd absorb that. "I'm so sorry. I looked him up in the phone book, and the number is still listed in his name."

"I know," she said. "Mom could never bring herself to change it."

He looked around. "Is your mother home?"

"She went across the lines with some friends for the day."

"The lines?"

"Sorry, across the border to the US. She's going to feel so bad that she missed you." The infant on her hip—a little girl, Hayden guessed, judging from that completely unnecessary barrette in her skimpy bit of silky hair—turned her head into her mother's shoulder to hide. "Can I get you a cup of coffee or tea?"

Boyd smiled at his first cousin. "Coffee would be nice."

When the woman looked inquiringly at Hayden, she said, "Yes, please. Coffee would be great."

She led them to a bright kitchen, where she kissed the child on her head and deposited her in a playpen. As she pulled out a coffeemaker and measured coffee and water, she introduced herself as Angela Wood. Her house a few miles outside town was being renovated, so she and her husband, Jeremy, were living here with her mother, Sandra, for a few months.

Boyd introduced himself and apologized for dropping in without notice, indicating he'd be happy to come back when her mother was available. He added that he'd just discovered his mother's identity within the past twenty-four hours.

"You clearly knew about your father's sister, Arianna," Boyd said. "What did your parents tell you about her?"

"I knew about her babies too—you and your brother. Mom says Dad used to talk about Arianna's children and wonder if you guys would ever find us. I don't remember any of that talk. I was only four when Dad died."

"The records got messed up," Boyd said by way of explanation for the delay. "My identical twin, Josh, spent a lot of time and energy solving the mystery."

"I'm so glad he did." She looked at the door. "Is he with you today?"

"No." Boyd's voice sounded a little strangled. "Josh died last month from a heart issue, much like our mother seemed to have done."

Tears sprang to Angela's eyes, and she covered her mouth. "I'm so sorry."

"Me too," Boyd said simply.

Angela turned to Hayden. "And you are . . . ?"

Before she could answer, Boyd apologized for the oversight and made the introduction. She noticed he introduced her as *my friend*, not *Josh's friend*. She supposed he wanted to keep it simple. There'd be plenty of time for more extensive explanations if they decided to stay in touch. Which she presumed Boyd did, given his offer to come back when Sandra Duncan was available.

"Your eyes," Angela said. "Mama always told me I looked like my aunt Arianna, and now, seeing those eyes when I opened the door . . . I've only ever seen that color in the mirror."

"These days, that's the only place I see it too."

Angela's beautiful eyes darkened. "So, have you been able to find your father?"

"Actually, no," Boyd said. "There's no mention of our father to be found in the records I've uncovered so far." He shrugged. "I guess I was sorta hoping your dad could help with that."

She grimaced. "Sorry. And, actually, even if he was still with us, I don't know if he could answer that. From what my mother has told me, both Dad and Aunt Arianna wound up going into foster care when they were in their early teens. Different families. Dad went to a local family here in Saint Andrews, but Arianna went to Fredericton. She'd have been well out of foster care and on her own when she got pregnant, I think. But Dad would still have been in the system. I don't know if they had enough contact that she'd have told him about the father. And I gather he didn't talk about it much. It made him too sad."

Hayden could see Boyd's disappointment, but he hid it quickly. By the time Angela had finished her long-winded explanation, there was no evidence to be seen.

"Yes, it must have been a horribly sad time for your dad, losing his only sister so suddenly and unexpectedly. I can relate."

"And so sad for your mother, that she didn't have a chance to know her babies, or go on to make a life for herself."

Hayden could barely swallow around the lump of emotion in her throat, but Boyd managed to answer.

"Yes, very tragic. But if it's any consolation, Josh and I went to a really great family. Our parents were terrific."

"I'm glad." Angela's eyes glittered. With her own infant now in her arms again, Hayden knew she couldn't help but feel for the woman who'd lost her babies, then her life.

They stayed for an hour, during which the baby—April Elizabeth—went to sleep. Hayden noticed Boyd glossed over some matters—the business with the adoption record, the birth certificates—and completely failed to mention others, specifically Dr. Gunn's apparent suicide. She approved. Until those questions were answered, why bring that stuff up?

Boyd did gently suggest that since it looked like the Duncan side of the family carried a genetic risk for sudden cardiac arrest, that she and the baby should probably be tested. Angela assured them she would see a doctor about it right away.

As they were preparing to leave, Angela produced her phone and asked Hayden to take a picture of the two of them. Hayden obliged, then took out her own phone and took a safety shot.

After a last-minute exchange of email addresses, Boyd and Hayden left.

He started the car, but instead of putting it in gear, he looked across at her. "Are you in a hurry to get home?"

"Not a bit. Why don't we find some food, then go for a walk on the beach?"

They ate at a little café on the main drag, taking their food upstairs where they could watch the passing tourists on the street. Just as she had the last time she'd been there, she marveled at how neat and tidy the old buildings were. And they were old. Saint Andrews had some of the best-preserved examples of colonial heritage in North America.

They also had a beach, and she sensed Boyd needed to walk. They found a place to park their car, then followed a path to the rocky floor of the bay.

"What is this body of water?"

"The Passamaquoddy Bay." She pointed to an island not far offshore. "And that's Minister's Island."

"Can we go out?"

"We could, at the right time of day. But not now. When the tide comes in, that land bridge disappears and you're stuck until the next low tide."

Their walk was cut short by the fact that the tide had started to turn. Back on the safety of the rocks, they huddled together to watch the tide pour in. Boyd sat behind her, his chest providing a backrest and his strong legs warm around hers. When she tipped her head back to look at him, he kissed her tenderly on the forehead, between her eyes, just above the brows.

The third eye kiss. She smiled, feeling the sense of well-being flooding her.

Hayden's mother used to do that to her all the time. Heck, she did it to everyone she loved, claiming it was her way of "blessing" them. Hayden wasn't sure about all that awakening psychic sight stuff, but she figured the simple acupressure applied to that point was definitely beneficial. Sort of like a tune-up to the pituitary gland.

Finally, a little sunburned and wind-kissed, they retreated to the car. At her suggestion, they stopped and bought the fixings for a seafood chowder. They talked for the first hour of the drive; then Boyd fell silent. She knew he needed time to process the reality that he had an aunt and two cousins who were anxious to bring him into their lives. As they approached Fredericton, he took her hand and sent her a smoldering look. The next ten minutes seemed longer than the rest of the drive, because Hayden knew what was going to happen when they got back to her place.

After placing the fixings for the chowder in the refrigerator, she led him to her bedroom. Despite the intensity in his eyes, he was in no rush. Slowly, almost reverently, he helped her out of her clothes, pausing to kiss each bit of skin he exposed. She did the same for him, tasting the tang of the outdoors, the sunshine and sea air. This time, she had a condom handy, but he was in no hurry to make use of it just yet. They lay down on the bed, hands arousing, then smoothing, soothing. It was a slow build. By the time he took the condom from her, she was readier than she'd ever been. For all the slow lead-up, their joining was wild, shattering, leaving them clinging together like shipwrecked souls on a beach.

Afterward, she made the seafood chowder using a Haitian recipe her mother had passed down to her. As Boyd helped her prep the ingredients, she explained that the real thing called for conch meat, but scallops, shrimp, and haddock pieces would have to do. They ate it with the last of a baguette that had already been too hard when she'd bought it yesterday, but Boyd swore it was the best meal he'd ever eaten. She was pretty sure it was all the sex endorphins talking, but she'd take it. The sex elevated everything. The so-so sauvignon blanc she'd pulled out of the fridge was way better than it had any business being for what she'd paid for it.

Then they lay down on the bed again and made slow, deliberate love. Even as she did it, Hayden knew she'd pay for it, but she couldn't stop it. Couldn't turn away from him, even though she knew she was giving him her heart. Didn't want to. The pain would come anyway, whether she opened herself these last few degrees or not.

Afterward, she held his face between her hands and kissed his forehead every bit as tenderly as he'd done to her earlier on the rocks. He tightened his arms around her, and she smiled against his skin.

CHAPTER 26

Boyd lay there with his eyes closed, savoring a feeling of peacefulness and well-being that he hadn't felt in a long time. Hayden's lips moved softly over his brow, a tender caress.

He was playing with fire. He knew it. Making love like this, letting so many barriers down, it was an invitation to disaster. It was the perfect climate for these delicate tendrils that connected them to transform themselves into lasting bonds. Unwelcome ones, at least on her part. He wasn't so sure anymore.

He'd known all of this as they'd lain so softly together in the darkness of her room. He'd been helpless to pull back, helpless to keep from taking what she so freely offered, because he'd never wanted anything more in his life.

Now he had to figure out where this left them, what it meant. For him. For her. For them.

Them. The word resonated in his brain like an accusation. He'd promised he'd go back to Toronto when this was done and let her go back to her life. And dammit, he would. If that's what she really wanted.

The trouble was, he wasn't sure that's what he wanted anymore. The job was the job. It was pretty much all he'd ever wanted to do, but that didn't mean he had to do it in the same squad, in the same division, the same police force.

His euphoric sense of well-being started to slip, eroded by the promises they'd made, the things still left unsaid. As though feeling his conflict, she pulled away. Grabbing her robe, she covered up.

"I suppose I should go." He sat up on the edge of the bed. "At the very least, I need to discover if there's any music to be faced with Sylvia. If she's heard about my visit with the Senator, she might be angry enough to throw me out."

He hoped Hayden would say that if Sylvia did that, he could come stay with her.

She didn't.

Instead she looked away. "I'm sure it won't come to that. She's much too married to her dignity."

Well, okay then. It stung for a second, but good for her. That meant her sense of self-preservation was kicking in again. And not a moment too soon.

He dressed quickly. At the door, he kissed her. Despite the distance she was trying to put between them, the kiss still held every bit of tenderness they'd shared moments before.

It didn't matter. He wouldn't stay.

It was dusk, and traffic was light as he drove back to Sylvia's, too dark to see well but too light for the headlights to be very effective. Even as he kept a sharp eye for pedestrians, cyclists, and the ubiquitous skateboarders, part of his mind worried about Hayden. But his attention snapped fully back when he met a vehicle pulling out of Sylvia's driveway just as he was signaling to turn in. Naturally, the other driver took advantage of Boyd's slowing down to gun it and shoot out into traffic, but Boyd had enough time to recognize the man at the wheel. *Dave Bradley.*

Shit, what's he doing here? From Sylvia's tone yesterday, he'd gathered she had a low threshold of tolerance for this nephew-in-law or third cousin or whatever he was to her, and even less patience for the media.

He continued around the house to the rear parking lot. Anxious to get inside and see what Sylvia had to say about Bradley, he cut the wheel and slotted the rental into his customary parking spot. Or rather, he started to. At the last second, he glimpsed an infant on the ground, partially wrapped in a baby blanket.

He slammed on the brakes and brought the Altima to a tire-dragging stop.

Oh, sweet Jesus!

He jammed the car into Park. His brain was screaming at him to leap out and see if the baby was all right, but his body wasn't ready to cooperate. His heart thundered. A wave of dizziness swamped him. He gripped the steering wheel and squeezed so hard his hands hurt, waiting for his world to snap back. At last, it did. It could have been a few seconds; it could have been a minute—he had no idea. But suddenly, his limbs were his to command again.

He leapt out and ran around to the front of the car to find—a doll. Even before he bent to pick it up, he knew it wasn't a baby. It had looked realistic when he'd caught that fleeting glimpse of it in his headlights, but not up close.

Goddammit! He'd almost given himself a heart attack over a stupid doll.

What in the hell was a doll doing in the parking lot of Stratton House?

He got back in the car, parked it properly, then let himself into the house. Instead of going straight to his room as he usually did, he went toward the kitchen to see if he could find Mrs. Garner. She was there, inventorying the contents of the spice cupboard.

She looked up at him when he entered, her expression moving from surprised to alarmed when she saw him carrying the doll carelessly by one of its arms.

"Mr. McBride?"

"I found this in the parking lot. Specifically, I found it in my parking space. And by *found*, I mean I almost ran over it. For a few moments I thought it was an actual baby."

Mrs. Garner plunked the spice bottles down on the counter and rushed to his side. "Oh, dear. The doll is mine. I bought it for my goddaughter's little girl, but I have no idea how it came to be in your parking spot. I left it locked in my car, on the backseat." She took the doll from him. "I am so sorry. That must have been unsettling."

"No biggie." Except that he'd had to peel himself off the steering wheel. "Someone probably grabbed whatever was in there and dumped the doll when they realized what it was. Although usually they like to get a little farther away before they sort through the booty and decide what to keep and what to jettison." He raked a hand through his hair. "They must have felt pretty comfortable back there. Dr. Stratton might want to check to make sure the sentinel light is coming on at an appropriate time and staying on until full light."

"Of course. I'll see that it gets checked."

"Have you got time to come outside with me now? Maybe with a flashlight, we can see if there's any evidence of a break-in. And you can check if anything else is missing."

"Thank you. I'd appreciate that." She disappeared into the pantry and came back with a flashlight, which she handed to him. "I did have some other things in the car, including a new MP3 player in there. Just a cheap one."

"Now that I'm betting they didn't dump."

He was right. The other purchases were gone. They didn't find any evidence of a break-in, but, then again, the thief hadn't had to. The car was unlocked.

"Oh, dear. I always lock it."

"Maybe your remote is acting up," he said. "The alarm did go off the other day for no apparent reason."

"You're right!"

"If I were you, I'd take it to the car dealer or to an electronics dealer and get them to replace the battery. That could be all that's wrong."

"I'll do that tomorrow," she said.

"In the meantime, you might want to call the police to report the theft."

"Oh, I don't know that I should do that. It's hardly worth an officer's time. And what are the chances they'll recover anything? The MP3 player wasn't expensive, and it would be indistinguishable from thousands of others."

"You're right that it's highly unlikely anything will be recovered, but your report helps the police track where this activity is happening. They can put out a public bulletin if there's a rash of car break-ins in a particular area."

"Of course. I'll do it."

They headed back inside. Boyd planned to go up to his room, but Mrs. Garner offered him a drink.

"Pardon me for saying, Mr. McBride, but you look a little pale," she said before he could decline. "And no wonder."

He grinned. "Well, after thinking I'd run over a baby, I guess I can use it."

He followed her back to the kitchen. She went to a different area of the cupboards and opened a door to reveal an array of bottles of hard liquor. "What would you like?"

"Any whiskey there?"

"Eighteen-year-old Scotch?"

"Perfect."

She poured him a few fingers in a glass and left the bottle on the counter. "I'll just go make that call to the police now."

He sipped the neat Scotch. Damn, it was good stuff. He lifted the glass again, this time just to smell it. There was that citrusy element he'd tasted. Man, Sylvia would probably have a bird if she knew Mrs. Garner was dispensing the stuff for medicinal purposes.

He took another swallow. Better. With one ear listening for Mrs. Garner, he leaned back in the chair, trying to persuade his tight muscles to relax. To think that an hour ago, he'd been so relaxed and replete, he'd felt almost boneless. Just like that, he flashed back to Hayden's place. Hayden under him, not being able to get close enough, deep enough. The two of them entwined on her bed, skin to skin—

"There you are!"

Dr. Stratton's imperious words from the distance of about a foot away jolted Boyd, making him almost slosh the precious Scotch.

"Here I am," he said, trying to cover his startle. "Although I'd almost drifted off there."

She looked at the cut crystal glass he held in his hand. "Mrs. Garner thought I needed a stiff drink after I just had the crap scared out of me," he offered.

She lifted an eyebrow. "How so?"

He explained about the doll in his parking space, dropped there no doubt by a thief who decided he didn't want it, that had looked for all the world like a real baby, at least at a quick glimpse.

"How harrowing." She went to the cupboard, took down a matching cut crystal glass, and poured herself a whiskey. "After ten minutes with David Bradley, I think I rather deserve a restorative too."

Okay, that answered that. Bradley must have been here to press her for more details about Dr. Gunn.

She came to stand over him. He thought about standing himself but decided against it. She was making a point with her superior position. And because he knew what she was doing, it robbed her of the intended effect. From the way her lips tightened, he figured she'd just come to the same conclusion. Nevertheless, she held her position.

"I heard about your late-night visit with the Senator."

"Yeah, sorry about that. It's just that I heard him coughing, and no one seemed to be going to his aid. I couldn't leave the poor guy like that with a tickle in his throat, so I went in and fed him some ice chips."

"I know," she acknowledged. "And thank you for thinking of his comfort. But henceforth, if you are ever in that situation again, please find the caregiver or myself and we will see to him. There will always be someone on duty, and we will never be farther than the kitchen or the bathroom."

"It was no trouble."

"But it was, Detective. Any disruption to the Senator's schedule, to his routines, is most distressing for him. I'm sure you witnessed him beginning to get agitated?"

"Well, yes, but—"

"But nothing, Detective. The Senator is my responsibility. I will brook no interference in his treatment. Just so you know, my husband had a very difficult night and a worse day, and is only now attaining some semblance of peacefulness."

Boyd was stricken. He thought he'd been helping the guy. "I didn't know. I thought he might appreciate a visitor now and again."

She held up a hand. "I'm sorry. I can't permit it. Please know that I don't make these rules lightly. It's just the way it has to be. It's better for the Senator and for all of us. And it's not as though he lacks for stimulation. I read to him every night."

"I was thinking he might enjoy some male bonding," he said, not ready to relinquish the man with the desperate eyes to his peaceful all-female existence. "We could watch a ball game on TV. Or if TV is out, we could listen to it on the radio. Baseball is great to listen to. Or you know, maybe I could just read him the game summaries or something."

"That's very kind of you," she said, "but I think we'd best proceed as we mean to go on. I'm thinking you won't be here much longer."

He blinked.

"It's true, is it not?" She took a sip of her whiskey. "You've solved the mystery of your mother's identity, and the cause of your brother's death seems much clearer, if there was ever any doubt. Given what will probably be a short stay from this point on, I really can't permit you to befriend the Senator. Much as I'm sure he'd enjoy your company, he'd only suffer the more when you leave."

And wasn't that the truth?

Mrs. Garner chose that moment to make her reappearance. "Well, that's done. The police have been notified." She drew up short when she saw Dr. Stratton standing by the table with a glass of whiskey in her hand.

She blanched, but Dr. Stratton just laid a hand on her arm. "I heard someone took property from your vehicle and left some of it as an unpleasant surprise for Detective McBride."

"Yes, that's exactly what happened. The gifts I bought this afternoon are gone, although the doll obviously was recovered." She sent an anxious glance toward the bottle of Scotch. "I thought after the scare he had, Detective McBride could use something to put the color back in his cheeks."

She nodded. "You did well, Mrs. Garner. I'd have extended the same offer in your place."

The older woman seemed to relax. "Thank you, ma'am." She turned to Boyd. "And I'm so sorry about the doll. I thought I'd locked the car. I'll get the battery changed in the remote, as you suggested, and hopefully that will do the trick."

Sylvia tipped up her glass and downed the rest of the Scotch. "I don't know about you two, but I feel I've endured enough trials for one day. I'm off to read to the Senator for a while before I retire."

As soon as Dr. Stratton left, Boyd made his own escape to his room. But Sylvia's words followed him. She was righter than she knew. If the forensics lab bumped Josh's file to the top, or even close to the top of the list, the case could all but be put to bed. It seemed like the genetics report could be more of a formality now, something that would confirm the clear familial issue. If there was anything valuable to learn, it would be from the forensic toxicology.

What if it showed nothing at all?

Boyd compressed his lips, cursing that voice in his head. Because if that happened, he'd have to accept that Josh had just . . . died.

If that happened, he'd have to go home.

The thought filled him with a dark dread, but he didn't know if that black feeling was for his failure to find some kind of justice for Josh, or whether it was the thought of leaving Hayden.

Man, he needed to crash and let sleep push his brain's "Reset" button. But first he needed to text Hayden to let her know he was in for the night. He did it quickly, before he was tempted to dial her number. Given his strange mood tonight, he should not be talking to Hayden. Her immediate thanks told him that consciously or unconsciously, she'd been waiting for it. Just like she'd done with Josh. Thank God his scare in the parking lot hadn't made him forget. He hated the idea of her worrying about him, even in a low-level, unconscious way.

He should call his parents too. He'd promised himself he'd be more faithful about that, now that his brother was gone. Except what was he going to say? How could he explain the day he'd had? *Guess what, Mom? I found an aunt and two cousins.*

Yeah, no. That conversation was going to have to wait so he could have it in person. A conversation where he fessed up about what he'd really been doing in New Brunswick these past days.

He wouldn't go into the situation with Hayden. They wouldn't approve, and they'd be right. He should have been stronger. Should have denied her. Kept his hands off her. Not that he thought for a minute that her career plan could be swept off course, no matter what she might or might not have come to feel for him. She'd never let that happen again, nor would he allow it. But it could leave her unhappier—lonelier—than he'd found her. And that would just suck.

Except these past few days had been some of the most amazing days of his life. If he had to do it over again, he knew he still could not resist her.

Physically, she was his idea of perfection. Athletic but not too much so. Strong, toned muscles blending into real feminine curves. And that hair! That curly mass of amazing, multihued golden hair. That golden skin and those blue, blue eyes. Lips so lusciously full, he couldn't look at her without wanting to kiss them. He knew he'd never find anything more perfect.

Or more perfect for him, at least.

And her mind, her spirit, her passion for her job, her patients. And, yes, in bed. He'd been lucky enough to taste that passion, and when he left, she'd go back to saving it for someone else, once she achieved what she wanted career-wise. And he'd better goddamned deserve it. He'd better be worthy of her and not turn out to be a jerk who said all the right things until he got his hooks into her.

Damn, his brain was like a hamster on a wheel. On crack.

He thought about going downstairs and snagging that bottle of Macallan's. Instead he took a long, hot shower. It took a while, but the hot water seemed to unbend him and wash away that slightly manic feeling. When he crawled into bed, all he was left with was the stuff he didn't want to think about. But happily—or not—if there was one thing he was good at, it was shoving that stuff down and slapping a lid on it.

This time would be no different.

Thankfully, his new friend, insomnia, left him alone.

CHAPTER 27

Boyd killed the Skype connection and reached for his coffee. It was stone-cold.

Angela Wood had called and explained that her mother, who was really sorry to have missed him yesterday, wanted to Skype with him. Could he spare half an hour? He'd agreed, of course, but it had turned out to be more like an hour and a half.

It had been an informative conversation. Sandra Duncan had met Arianna in school in happier days, before Arianna and Sheldon lost their parents in a car accident. Sandra was closer to Sheldon's age, and didn't really know the older girl all that well, but Arianna had been a beauty, she assured Boyd. Beautiful, shy, and very sweet.

While Sheldon had been fostered out to a local family, Arianna was not. Sheldon liked to think that because his sister was so pretty and smart, her social worker set out to make sure she had more opportunities. For whatever reason, Arianna had ended up with a family in Fredericton.

Boyd braced himself to hear that his mother had been impregnated by her foster father or foster brother, but apparently his mother had lucked out. The foster family was really nice. A stay-at-home mom with a younger daughter of her own, and a dad who was a university professor. The prof had helped Arianna make her course selections in high school and helped her apply to university. She was accepted into the nursing program and was in her first year when she got pregnant.

Boyd assumed it was a fellow student, but Sheldon's impression was that it was someone older, someone she met at her part-time job. She used to act as a hostess at an exclusive steak house in one of the hotels, to help pay her tuition.

Boyd was not impressed. A fellow student was one thing. He could understand kids getting carried away. But it sounded like his father was a rich older guy who seduced an innocent college student. What a douche.

Sandy went on to tell him Arianna had been sort of happy about the whole thing, Sheldon thought. Or as happy as an unwed woman could feel in her situation. She'd been looking forward to the babies' arrival. But then she did an about-face and said she wasn't keeping them. Sheldon saw her once after she'd given them up and was shocked by how distraught she was. He tried to get her to tell him who the father was so he could beat the piss out of him—*thank you, Uncle Sheldon*—but she wouldn't tell. She kept saying it wasn't his fault, that he didn't even know. Sheldon convinced her to see a doctor about her depression. He'd had one telephone call from her after the meds had straightened her out. She'd said she was feeling much better and was going to try to get her kids back. Then the next thing they knew, she was dead.

Boyd had felt so crappy to hear that. The antidepressants her brother had talked her into taking might have restored her mental health, but they were clearly the "aggravating agent" that caused her sudden cardiac arrest. Of course, he hadn't mentioned that. As far as he was concerned, the Duncans didn't need to know that detail. It was clear that Sheldon Duncan had felt guilty enough for not being there for his sister, never mind that he'd been a minor in the foster care system at the time.

Unless . . . Could someone have killed his mother the same way they'd killed his brother?

No, that didn't make sense. Morgan had accused Boyd of being a conspiracy theorist, but not even he could buy that one. First, someone would have to know she had long QT syndrome, which he doubted was widely diagnosed in small centers three and a half decades ago. Then they would have to give her a reason to take antidepressants. Taking her babies away would certainly do it, but he doubted that was part of a diabolically complex plot to get her to take medication. Hell, she might have had straightforward postpartum depression. It was a fairly common ailment, as he understood it. Then there was the brother who'd urged her to get those meds. Without his intervention, she might not have sought medical treatment at all.

And shit, did they even know about aggravating agents causing sudden cardiac death in LQTS cases?

But again, that went back to knowing she had it, the possibility of which he figured was slim to none.

No, her death must have been an accident. No villain could have controlled for all that.

Of course, maybe she didn't have LQTS. Maybe Josh hadn't had it either. Maybe someone could have just jammed her full of some toxic substance that would have induced cardiac arrest in anyone, regardless of their health status. Except surely a rigorous autopsy would have been done on a twenty-year-old woman and toxicological tests would have pointed to foul play, if it had been present.

Sighing, Boyd got up and dumped the cold coffee. What he really felt like was a beer. Maybe he'd walk to that pub downtown where Hayden had taken him when he first landed in town. He could almost taste that tall, frosty glass of Picaroons. He might as well eat too. It was close enough to suppertime.

Ten minutes later, with the pub in sight, his phone rang. His first thought was Hayden. No one else called him these days. But a quick look at the caller ID showed *City of Fredericton*.

That had to be the police department. Heart pounding, he hit the "Answer" button. "McBride."

"Ray Morgan here. We got the toxicological report back from the forensics lab," he said, confirming Boyd's hunch.

"And?"

"There was definitely an aggravating agent present."

Boyd couldn't breathe. Couldn't make a sound. Fortunately, Morgan didn't seem to expect anything of him and plowed on.

"Specifically, an antidepressant."

Antidepressant? The word exploded in Boyd's brain. "No way! There's no fucking way my brother was taking antidepressants. Not voluntarily anyway."

"Do me a favor and sit down, would you?"

"I'm standing on the fucking sidewalk, Morgan."

"Okay, then just chill for a second. You're going to scare the nice people if you don't dial back the volume."

He turned in a circle, phone still pressed to his ear. And, crap, people were crossing the sidewalk to avoid him.

"Okay." He stepped into an empty alley. "I'm sorry about that. I'm cool now." He pressed the bridge of his nose and leaned against the brick building. "Go on."

"The report was waiting for us this morning. Testing must have been pretty much done, and then they fired it over here when Quig asked them to expedite."

"And?"

"And when we saw he had antidepressants in his system, we started calling pharmacies. We found one where he'd filled a prescription, just over six weeks prior to his death. A three-month supply."

Boyd gripped the receiver. This wasn't happening. "Who?" he said, his voice shaking with rage. "Who was the doctor who prescribed the meds?"

"Dr. Gunn," Morgan said.

Boyd pushed away from the brick wall. "That son of a bitch. He killed Josh."

"Hang on, McBride. I don't know that it's all that cut-and-dried. Turns out Josh was a patient of Gunn's."

"What?"

"Gunn has a patient file for Josh dating back to a few months after Josh came here."

"No way was he taking antidepressants," Boyd insisted.

"You don't get these therapeutic levels in your blood because someone slipped you a single dose, or even a handful of doses. Ask Hayden. You get these levels by carefully and consciously taking a prescribed dose every day of your life."

"But it doesn't make sense. He wasn't depressed. He was happy with his life here. Hayden can tell you that."

"You can't be sure of that, Morgan. If you were being treated for depression, how many people would you tell?"

"I'm telling you, he wasn't depressed. I talked to the guy often enough. I would know."

"Would *he* know if *you* were depressed based on a weekly or twice-weekly phone conversation?"

"That's different. I can be irritable and taciturn by nature. Josh never was."

Morgan sighed. "Maybe you're right. Maybe this medical file we found at Gunn's is completely fabricated. Maybe the results of the blood work he ordered up to check on thyroid function is faked too."

Boyd was a silent a few seconds. Could Josh have been depressed? It didn't seem possible. "There's really a file?"

"Yeah. It's mostly about the depression, but there's mention of an upper respiratory infection. Do you remember Josh ever mentioning something like that?"

Dammit, he had. Shortly after he'd moved to Fredericton. He'd blamed it on all the clean air. And he'd temporarily cut back the running so as not to suck the infection deeper into his lungs before it had a chance to clear.

Could Josh really have been seeing Dr. Gunn? And could he have been depressed? How could something like that slip under Boyd's radar?

Okay, pretty easily, since Boyd never asked anyone about their feelings. But no way that little detail would have gotten past Hayden.

"You there, McBride?"

"Sorry, yeah. Just trying to work this through. And I still don't buy it, Morgan. I just don't believe it."

"Well, the coroner's office is liking it. They're anticipating the genetic report will show LQTS. If it does, it'll take them about ten seconds to declare death by natural causes due to cardiac arrest arising from undiagnosed long QT syndrome, brought to light by the presence of an aggravating agent, to wit, this antidepressant with the long-assed name. But obviously, no one's about to go out on that limb without the results of the genetic tests."

"What about you?" Boyd asked. "What do you believe?"

"I believe this medical record bears a little more scrutiny. For one thing, all the consultations seem to have been at night, at Dr. Gunn's home."

"What the hell?"

"Yeah, I know. Odd. I suppose it could be they'd formed a friendship. Everyone knows what a friendly guy Josh was. Or it could be Josh cultivated Gunn as a source of information about what was going on inside the health system. Gunn was active on some provincial committees and task forces. So, on the one hand, you can kinda see how that sort of relationship might have evolved. On the other, it seems convenient that the home visits make it impossible to cross-check the appointments against the receptionist's appointment log."

"Yeah, that's pretty damned convenient, all right." Boyd swore. "Okay, tell me this—why commit suicide then? If Gunn really had this relationship with Josh, and he legitimately pre-scribed the antidepressants, and Josh voluntarily took them and then died of an unfortunate accident, where's the big guilt problem?"

"I don't know," Morgan conceded.

Boyd's mind was racing toward another possibility. A bone-chilling one.

"Or shit, maybe Gunn somehow knew long before Josh did that Arianna Duncan was his mother. If that's the case, he might have suspected Josh inherited the LQTS that likely killed our mother, in combination with those antidepressants. Maybe he set Josh up. Befriended him, convinced him he needed medication, then sat back and waited for the same thing to happen to him as happened to his patient, our mother. Maybe he killed Josh."

"Jesus, there's a horrifying thought."

"Yeah. That would make it premeditated murder."

"I get the premeditated business," Morgan said, "but, technically, I'm not sure it's murder. Even if you could prove malicious intent, that he prescribed drugs *hoping* they'd kill Josh, it probably wasn't a sure thing that your brother would die as a result. Manslaughter, more likely. And hell, if Gunn didn't have absolute proof that Josh had LQTS, maybe it wouldn't even warrant that. Maybe it's criminal negligence. Or administering a noxious substance. And for any charge to stick, you'd have to be able to prove mens rea, that he prescribed the stuff with a guilty mind. It would be up to the prosecutors to figure out."

Boyd was in no mood to debate the finer points of a possible charge against a man who was already dead.

"You said there were hospital reports in the file? Lab work?"

"Yeah, to monitor levels of this antidepressant in his blood."

"Can you confirm that they're real? Josh would have had to go to the hospital or a clinic to have his blood drawn, right?"

"Presumably. And we'll look into that. I'll also have a personal conversation with the pharmacist who filled the script, see if he or she remembers Josh."

"Good idea," Boyd said. "Make sure it was actually Josh who filled the prescription. And couldn't you also cross-check the appointment dates with Gunn's Medicare billings? Josh was fully covered by provincial insurance, so you'd think Gunn would have billed for the consultations."

"I thought of that," Morgan said, "but when I thought about it, I could see why he might not have billed. For the office-based practice, I'm pretty sure he'd have clerical staff to do the billing for him, but if the consultations and the records were at Gunn's home, they wouldn't naturally feed into the billing stream unless Gunn took the trouble to do it himself. For a few bucks here and there, he probably wouldn't have bothered."

Damn. "Makes sense, I guess. But it wouldn't hurt to know one way or another."

"Already on my to-do list," Morgan said. "I just wanted to point out that by itself, that information might not carry much weight."

"Thanks," Boyd said.

"So now that you're up to speed, can I count on you to be cool? Sit on the sidelines for once and let us do our jobs?"

Boyd dragged a frustrated hand down his face. What choice did he have? "Sure. I'll stay out of your way. Just . . . get to the truth, okay? I need the truth."

"We'll do our best. Hang in there, McBride."

Boyd pocketed his phone, then hauled it right out again. He had to call Hayden.

CHAPTER 28

Hayden had just finished dealing with a guy with a blocked salivary duct, and she was still smiling at his reaction to her solution.

He was probably pretty good-looking under normal circumstances but not tonight. The poor guy had been terrified when his face suddenly ballooned while he was eating Chinese food. Of course, he'd freaked out, thinking it was an allergy, and his girlfriend had rushed him to the ER. The expression on his face when she'd handed him a WARHEADS sour candy had been priceless. She'd explained he should keep sucking sour candies to stimulate saliva production until the stone yielded to pressure and got flushed out. She gave him instructions to return if that didn't resolve the problem, since surgery was occasionally required.

She was just about to move on to the next patient when Marta, the ER secretary, grabbed her. "I've got a caller for you—Boyd McBride. Says it's important."

Her smile disappeared. Could the tox report be back already?

She followed Marta back to the desk and picked up the phone. "Boyd? What's up?"

"Sorry to bother you at work, but I need your take on this. And you didn't answer your cell."

"You heard from the police?"

"Yeah. The tox report is back. They're saying Josh had an antidepressant in his system." He named the drug. Not the most commonly used one, but not rarely used either.

"How much? I mean, was it a ginormous overdose or a little bit or a normal therapeutic dose?"

"That last one," he said. "The kind of levels you have in your blood when you've taken it every day for weeks or months."

"No." She rejected the idea instantly. "Josh was not depressed. He was not under a doctor's care for clinical depression."

"That's what I told Morgan, but he pointed out men aren't all that forthcoming about their mental health."

"But I'd have seen something. Sure, I know men can present different than women. They don't tend to seem sad. But they do tend to get irritable. Biggest clue—they lose interest in pursuits they used to find pleasurable. I didn't see that in him at all. Or fatigue or sleep disruption. He seemed . . . normal."

"Is there any other medical reason someone might take antidepressants?"

"In some circumstances, but none that apply to Josh."

"What kind of circumstances?"

"They can be very effective for chronic pain. Certain antidepressants are also used for smoking cessation and as a sleep aid. But I know Josh didn't have chronic pain and wasn't a smoker.

As far as I know, he didn't suffer from insomnia either. Besides, antidepressants tend to have side effects that men aren't keen on."

"Like what?"

"Loss of sexual desire."

"You don't think . . . ?"

"What?"

"What if he knew the meds would curb sexual desire? Given, you know, what I told you, do you think—"

"Oh, God, I hope not." That would be too cruel. If he'd taken antidepressants to dull his desire for her, and that led to his death . . .

"No," Boyd said. "No. We were right the first time. He wasn't depressed."

She wanted to believe that. Desperately. "Wait, he didn't even have a doctor here, thanks to the shortage of family physicians. There's a waiting list a mile long. How would he even get a prescription? It's not the kind of thing they're going to hand out at an after-hours clinic."

"Morgan says he had a prescription that was filled at a downtown pharmacy about six weeks before his death."

She gripped the telephone receiver tighter. "And who wrote the prescription?"

"Dr. Gunn," Boyd said.

"Wait, *what*? That doesn't make sense. You said he'd been taking it for weeks, but he'd only just met Gunn."

"The cops say Gunn has a medical file for Josh. That he'd been seeing Gunn since shortly after he got here, probably when he had that upper respiratory bug."

"Um, he saw a doctor for that URTI—me. I advised him on over-the-counter medications for his cough, told him to rest more, cut out the running, and take lots of vitamins C and D. I even made him chicken soup."

"Then how do you explain the file?"

"It's got to be faked, Boyd. I know Josh didn't know Dr. Gunn. Remember that night he got the phone call and wrote down Gunn's name on my checkbook? He asked me what I knew about him, what kind of practice he had, and I filled him in. At the time, I figured he was interested because of his work at the paper where he covered health issues, so I told him about some of the committee work Gunn had done for the Medical Society and the Regional Health Authority."

There was silence on the other end of the line as Boyd digested that.

"I'm telling you, Boyd, Josh didn't know Gunn, and he sure as hell wasn't clinically depressed." She closed her eyes and pressed a hand to her now throbbing temple. "But now that you say he had that drug in his system, some things make sense."

"Yeah, like him dropping dead."

Hayden winced. "Yeah, that too. But remember what I said about how he seemed to mellow as the summer wore on? More content to sit and sunbathe at the lake and not so insistent about needing to be go-go-going all the time." She bit her lip.

"Well, if he didn't know Gunn and he wasn't voluntarily taking the drug—a point on which we both agree—then who was giving it to him?"

"What about the people at work?" she suggested.

"Dammit. Dave Bradley."

"What? Dave Bradley? No. Why would Dave Bradley give a noxious substance to Josh?"

"He liked you," Boyd pointed out. "He liked you so much, he was following you and taking pictures of you."

Her heart thumped. "What?"

"Josh noticed what he was doing and gathered evidence, which he then used to make sure Bradley cut it out."

"You're kidding me!"

"Not even close. I discovered it when I pressed Bradley early on about his shifty behavior. I thought he might know something about Josh's death, but after he broke and told me about the other thing, I realized he was just freaking out, thinking I'd found digital copies of the incriminating pictures."

"I can't believe this!"

"Believe it. By the way, the first thing Bradley did when he heard Josh was dead was ransack Josh's cubicle to recover the stalking photos before the cops found them."

"Omigod. I thought he backed off because I finally got through to him."

"Josh got through to him in the only way a man like that understands."

"Okay, so Dave Bradley is creepier than I thought he was. But what makes you suggest he might have been involved in giving Josh antidepressants? That doesn't make sense. To set Josh up like that, he'd need not only the general medical knowledge but the *specific* medical knowledge about how your mother died. Plus he'd have to know Arianna Duncan was Josh's mother."

"I don't have any answers," Boyd said.

"Also, Dave Bradley couldn't have done it. He'd only be able to slip Josh the antidepressant on weekdays. If you're on a therapeutic dose of antidepressant, you can't miss two days. I'm not sure about this antidepressant, but with some of them, after missing a couple of days, you'd have to back off to the introductory dose or at least a lower dose and work back up."

"Like I said, I don't have all the answers. But I do know Bradley is related to Sylvia Stratton somehow. And he's been coming around Stratton House, evidently to pry background information out of Sylvia about Dr. Gunn after he died."

"We're back to Angus Gunn, who knew how Arianna Duncan died and who also knew that Josh was Arianna's son. I just don't know how he could have delivered the antidepressants to Josh over that stretch of time."

"Oh, Jesus Christ!"

"What?"

"It's *Sylvia*. Sylvia Stratton was the only one in a position to administer the drug every day. Maybe she did it for Gunn. They were old friends."

Hayden caught her breath with a gasp. "Boyd, do you know what you're saying? This is Sylvia Stratton we're talking about. And you're saying . . . You're suggesting—"

"That she helped Gunn commit murder? Yes, I do believe it. Although Ray Morgan thinks murder would be a hard charge to make stick, no matter who did it. But think about it, Hayden. It's the only thing that makes sense."

"Sense?" Her laugh came out like a sob. "None of this makes sense. Why would she do that to Josh?"

"I don't know. Maybe Gunn had something on her, something that—"

He broke off so suddenly, she thought his cell phone had dropped the call. "Boyd? Boyd, are you still there?"

"Shit, Hayden, maybe Gunn did know something and Sylvia decided he had to go. And by making it look like suicide, she makes him look guilty of orchestrating Josh's death."

"I can't keep up." She pressed her temple. "The longer we speculate, the uglier it gets."

"Look, I've gotta go. I walked downtown for supper and now I've got to haul ass back to Stratton House."

"Don't," she said. "Don't go back there alone. Call Detective Morgan. Tell him everything you just told me."

"I'll do that right now."

"Okay."

The line went dead.

"Everything all right?" Marta asked, coming back up to the desk.

"I don't know," she said honestly. "I need to think for a minute." She met Marta's eyes. "Any problem if I take my break early?"

"Good by me. And let me know if I can help."

"I will."

Hayden headed straight for the break room. She needed to sit down and think about this. She had the ominous feeling there was a gigantic cartoon anvil hanging over this situation, and she needed to figure it out before gravity kicked in and the anvil dropped, crushing . . . *Omigod, Boyd!*

If Sylvia primed Josh to die from sudden cardiac arrest, she had to have been doing the same thing with Boyd over the nine days that he'd been here. All those free-range eggs and fresh-squeezed juice and organic fair-trade coffee—she'd bet her bottom dollar that it was spiked. Probably not with the same drug. That would be too obvious. But there must be dozens of pharmaceuticals that could put someone with latent LQTS in danger. And once the pump was primed, all that would be needed was a shock or a startle.

She grabbed her phone and called Boyd's number, but the line was busy. He was probably on the line with Detective Morgan. Thank God for that, at least.

He said he'd walked downtown. How long would it take him to get back to Stratton House? Not long. If he ran—oh, God, she hoped he didn't run but knew he would—ten minutes, maybe.

And would he really wait for Ray Morgan?

No, of course he wouldn't. This was Josh's life they were

talking about. He wouldn't shy away from confronting Sylvia. She might be an imperious freaking dragon, but she was a tiny woman in her sixties. Probably late sixties. Unless he calmed down enough to reason it through and realize she'd been drugging him too, no way would Boyd postpone confronting her.

She'd reached the staff room, but instead of entering it, she turned and hustled back to the desk. "I have to leave," she called to Marta. "It's an emergency. I'll explain later."

CHAPTER 29

The run back to Stratton House did nothing to cool Boyd's rage. Nor did the fact that he still couldn't get through to Ray Morgan.

He stood outside the service entrance of Stratton House, key in one hand, phone in the other.

He should wait until he could reach Morgan. Hell, he should wait for Morgan to arrive on the scene. But he wasn't going to.

He'd tried Morgan's cell first, of course. A couple of times. But it just kept routing him to voice mail. Then he'd tried the switchboard, who'd transferred him to a phone that rang endlessly.

He dialed the station again. This time, he told them Morgan hadn't picked up and could they put him straight through to his voice mail. They did.

"Morgan, I tried to reach you, but I guess you must be off checking your hair or trimming your cuticles or something. I wanted to tell you I think I've figured this thing out. I'm pretty sure it was Sylvia Stratton who slipped the drugs to Josh. It's so freaking obvious. She's the only one who saw him every day, and she had the perfect delivery mechanism, that sensational free B&B breakfast. I still don't know why, but I aim to find out. And . . . uh . . . you might want to come over here."

He ended the call and shoved the phone into his pocket. He let himself in and went straight to the back of the house, where he knew he'd find Sylvia in her study.

She looked up at his entrance, her eyebrows shooting up into her hairline. "Detective, to what do I owe the pleasure?" She pushed away from her keyboard. "I take it you didn't encounter Mrs. Garner, or she'd have reinforced that I don't entertain guests back here."

"The forensic toxicology report on Josh came back today."

"Did it?" She leaned back in her leather chair. "I should have thought Dr. Walsh could help you sort through it, but if you require my help—"

"Why did you do it?"

"Excuse me?"

Boyd felt the reins on his rage start to slip. "Why did you kill my brother?"

Her eyebrows shot up again. "My dear boy, I can't imagine what you're talking about."

"The antidepressants. I know you went to a lot of trouble to make it seem as though they'd been prescribed by Dr. Gunn, but I know for a fact that Josh never met Dr. Gunn until days before he died. Hayden can confirm that positively. But you and Gunn were cozy. I'm thinking you had a role to play with my mother too. The birth, the adoption, the obliteration of the trail. I know it. Don't goddamn sit there and deny it."

She sighed and pressed a hand to her forehead as though he'd given her an inconvenient headache. "Okay, yes, I did it."

He'd been prepared for anything but a flat-out admission. And now that it was out there, an undisputed fact, he felt totally gutted. Dizzy.

"But why?"

"You are as blind and stupid as that brother of yours, Detective. I eliminated Josh not because of who your mother was but because of who your father is."

Who in the hell would make Sylvia Stratton kill— "The Senator."

"Congratulations. You reached the correct conclusion in a matter of weeks, where it took your brother months."

His father was the Senator. *Oh, my God.*

"He knew about the Senator?"

"He suspected. You see, I knew where he kept that diary of his. I usually managed to snag it every few days to read about his sleuthing efforts."

Rage flared anew. "You destroyed the diary."

"I did. Unfortunately, you weren't obliging enough to keep a record of your own investigation lying around. I had to resort to a listening device in your room."

His room? The room where he and Hayden had made love?

"Yes, I can see it's sinking in. I heard the two of you. I always suspected that girl's morals left something to be desired. I'm sure she got up to the same thing with your brother."

He let Sylvia's disparaging words roll off his back. Clearly, she was trying to infuriate him. He needed to stay focused, figure this out. Why was she telling him all of this? Unless—

She opened the top drawer to her desk and pulled out a snubnosed revolver. It looked small, but he didn't doubt it was deadly.

On the other hand, seriously? She was going to *shoot* him? She was a poisoner.

"Put that away, Sylvia." He felt as though he had to raise his voice over the rapid, painful hammering of his heart. "You're a stealth killer, not a shooter. That's far too messy."

"You're right. Mostly. But I think I proved I don't mind a bit of blood with Dr. Gunn."

So she *had* killed the poor bastard.

"I did, however, give him a little anesthetic beforehand. Something that clears the system very quickly, not that they're apt to look for it anyway. Not with so obvious a suicide."

Oh shit. It finally clicked. She'd surmised Arianna's long QT syndrome. Her success at killing Josh proved her suspicion correct and that he'd inherited it. Which meant Boyd also had it. So, naturally, she'd primed him for cardiac arrest too. The same orange juice or scrambled eggs or whatever she'd used to deliver the drug to Josh, she'd also used on him. His pulse leapt and staggered.

Shit, shit, shit.

He needed to keep her talking. Morgan would get that message anytime and come racing over. Hopefully.

"So how are you going to deal with me, hmm? You're waving that gun around and I haven't obliged you by dropping dead."

"No, you haven't. As I said from the beginning, you're a tougher customer than young Joshua."

"How did you kill him? Was it the exertion of the run?"

She smiled. "No. You two were far too fit for that. I used a snake."

Boyd felt the blood drain from his face. "A snake?"

"Yes. Your brother was kind enough to regale me with tales of your shared phobias over breakfast one day."

He glanced around, trying to see if she had a snake stashed somewhere. That might just do it. He was fucking terrified of snakes.

Keep her talking.

"So, what? You put a snake in his car?"

"In the thermal bag, right beside his water bottle. It was just a tiny, harmless snake, hardly big enough to qualify, but it did the trick. He probably arrested the moment his hand touched it."

She was crazy. Batshit crazy.

Keep her talking.

"Then you slipped back and liberated the snake?"

"Obviously."

"And you were trying to do the same to me."

"Of course. Mrs. Garner's car alarm. The doll. But you've proved nothing if not resilient."

"Then how do you propose to kill me without using that gun?"

She smiled. "I thought I'd save the gun for Hayden."

"*What?*"

"You've dragged her too far into this, Detective. Josh was clever enough to keep his investigation private, but you've been leaning on her this whole while."

For the first time, real terror took serious root. He'd thought he could handle Sylvia, but he hadn't counted on her targeting Hayden.

"You'll never get away with it."

"Of course I will. There was a break-in. You suffered a cardiac arrest trying to defend me and Hayden."

"But Hayden's not here."

"You think I can't get her here?"

"But Mrs. Garner . . . she'll know there was no break-in."

"Perhaps the burglar will shoot her too."

Jesus. The woman was genuinely crazy. She'd kill *Mrs. Garner?*

Of course she would. She'd already killed her longtime friend.

Fuck!

"You don't need to do this. Hayden . . . she doesn't know enough."

"But, Detective, you just told me that she knew for certain Josh and Angus hadn't met until very recently." She got up and walked around the desk to stand a few feet away.

Oh, Jesus! He'd sealed Hayden's fate.

"That's right." Sylvia cocked the hammer on the little revolver. "She's as good as dead, and it's your fault."

Boyd's world whirled. He was as good as dead.

He had to take her out before she could get to Hayden. And if he couldn't get the gun from her, maybe he could at least force her to shoot him. If the gun went off, the nurse upstairs with the Senator would call 911 and Sylvia's plan would fall apart.

He lunged at her.

CHAPTER 30

Hayden found the service entrance door wide-open. That would be Boyd's work. What had he said? Never close an avenue of retreat? That suited her fine. She didn't want to wheedle her way past Mrs. Garner. Or muscle her way past, if need be.

She followed the sound of a female voice and almost blundered on Mrs. Garner in the kitchen. She was working at the counter, but she had the telephone receiver wedged between her neck and shoulder as she carried on a conversation with what had to be a relative.

Hayden backed quietly out of the room, then ventured down the hall toward the rear of the house. This time, she heard a male and female in conversation. Boyd and Sylvia.

"You've dragged her too far into this, Detective," Sylvia was saying. "Josh was clever enough to keep his investigation private, but you've been leaning on her this whole while."

Were they talking about *her*?

"You'll never get away with it."

"Of course I will. There was a break-in. You suffered a cardiac arrest trying to defend me and Hayden."

Oh, God. No, Boyd. Don't listen. Don't let her get to you.

"But Hayden's not here."

"You think I can't get her here?"

"But Mrs. Garner . . . she'll know there was no break-in."

"Perhaps the burglar will shoot her too."

Hayden's stomach lurched.

"You don't need to do this. Hayden . . . she doesn't know enough." His voice was fading alarmingly.

"But, Detective, you just told me that she knew for certain Josh and Angus hadn't met until very recently." Sylvia appeared in Hayden's line of sight as she came around the desk holding a gun.

"That's right." There was an unmistakable cocking sound, just like in the movies, and Hayden knew Sylvia had pulled back the hammer on the revolver. "She's as good as dead, and it's your fault."

Hayden had to cover her mouth to keep any noise from coming out.

Then Boyd lunged at her, arms grappling for her, but it was more of a staggering lurch. Sylvia leapt back. There was a crash, and Boyd hit the floor and lay there, unmoving.

Oh, God, no! He'd arrested—Sylvia had killed him!

Sylvia moved with calm fluidity to stand over Boyd's body.

"You were a fool, Boyd McBride. As big a fool as your brother, and almost as big a fool as that mother of yours. She thought she could take Lewis from me by *becoming pregnant*?" As Sylvia continued to rant, Hayden realized this was her chance. Maybe her only chance.

She glanced around for a weapon. There, on the bookcase inside Sylvia's den, was a brass heron bookend.

Please be heavy. Please be heavy.

She stole into the room and picked up the bookend. It was very heavy, and the bird's slender craned neck proved to be an excellent handle. She lifted it high and swung it at Sylvia's head. The old woman went down harder than Boyd had, and it occurred to Hayden she might have smashed the woman's skull. Frankly, she didn't care.

She flew to Boyd. And oh, God, he *had* arrested. No pulse. No respirations.

She dug out her phone and dialed 911, quickly giving the details to the dispatcher. Then she dropped the phone, knelt, and delivered thirty chest compressions. She paused to give him two breaths, then resumed chest compressions. Two more breaths. She checked for breath and pulse. Nothing.

Dammit, she needed a defibrillator. But the ambulance was probably ten minutes away.

Unless . . .

After giving him another thirty compressions and two breaths, she leapt up and raced for the stairs, taking them two at a time. Josh had always said the Senator's sickroom was as well equipped as any hospital room. She sure hoped he was right. A nurse jumped up as though to defend the old man when Hayden burst into the room.

"Defibrillator!" Hayden shouted. "Where is it?"

The nurse pointed. Hayden grabbed the portable unit and ran downstairs. "I need your help," she called over her shoulder. "Come on!"

She could hear the nurse right behind her as she thundered down the stairs.

"Omigod, Dr. Stratton!" The nurse hurried over to her employer and bent to check her vitals. "She has a pulse."

"Over here!" Hayden commanded. "We have to resuscitate him."

The nurse didn't question the order for a second. She was at Boyd's side and starting CPR while Hayden got the defibrillator set up. The nurse paused to allow Hayden to stick the pads to his chest.

"Clear!" Hayden said.

The nurse backed away and Hayden hit the "Shock" button. He arched up, then sagged back to the floor.

The nurse bent over Boyd to resume compressions, stopping to allow Hayden to give the rescue breaths. They kept that up for two minutes. The nurse checked for a pulse and shook her head.

"Dammit, Boyd, do not die on me! I'll never forgive you if you do this."

The defibrillator was back at full charge.

"Clear!"

She hit the button, and again Boyd arched up and sagged back.

This time, Hayden did the compressions herself, as well as the rescue breaths. At the two-minute mark, she pulled back and let the nurse check him again. She looked up at Hayden and smiled. "He's back."

"Oh, thank God." Hayden dumped the defibrillator controller and leaned over him. He was breathing but still unconscious. She stripped off her hospital coat, rolled it up, and slid it under his neck.

In the distance, she heard sirens.

~

Ray Morgan was the first on the scene, and Hayden gave him the *Reader's Digest* version. But when the paramedics arrived, she turned her attention to them. She recognized them from the ER—Doug Trammel and Susan Barclay—and they recognized her.

"What do we have here, Dr. Walsh? Looks like two victims."

"This one actually arrested." She gestured to Boyd. "There was a portable defibrillator on site, and I used it to get him back."

The female paramedic had already taken his pulse and was strapping a blood pressure cuff on him.

"He almost certainly has hereditary long QT syndrome. It's been silent his whole life, but over the past weeks, he's been given a proarrhythmic drug. I'm guessing it's an antidepressant, but they need to screen for anything remotely proarrhythmic—antihistamines, decongestants, antibiotics, everything. He's going to need beta-blockers, sodium channel blockers, and a quick ride to the ER."

"Perfect," Doug said. "We've got this." He glanced over to where Dr. Stratton still lay on the floor under the close eye of Senator Stratton's nurse and Detective Morgan. "There's another bus on the way for the second vic, but maybe I should take a look."

"That's Dr. Sylvia Stratton," Hayden said. "And she's no victim. She's the one who tried to kill this guy, Boyd McBride, after which she apparently was going to kill me."

"No way!"

The nurse, who'd been following all this, spoke. "I'm a registered nurse and Dr. Stratton is my employer. Her vitals are fine. I can keep an eye on her until the other crew comes."

"Well, all righty then," Doug said. "We'll just focus on Mr. McBride."

"Good plan."

As it happened, the second paramedic team arrived just as they were moving Boyd out.

"Can I go now?" Hayden asked Detective Morgan. "They're taking Boyd."

He grimaced. "I'm going to need you for a bit. Is there anything you can do for McBride if you go?"

She took a deep breath. He was right. "No."

"Then I'll ask you to hang in here to answer a few questions while we get this mess dealt with." He gestured to Dr. Stratton, who was now receiving the full attention of the paramedics.

She nodded.

Within the next few minutes, Sylvia regained consciousness. Of course, she immediately tried to get up, and the paramedics had to restrain her. After they'd checked her out and determined she needed to be evaluated at the hospital and probably kept for observation, Ray Morgan stepped in to announce he was placing Dr. Stratton under arrest for attempted murder. Hayden watched with satisfaction as a uniformed cop, at the detective's direction, quickly handcuffed her to the gurney.

Sylvia glared at the constable, then turned her attention back to Ray Morgan. "Did you say *attempted* murder?" Sylvia craned her neck, clearly looking for Boyd's dead body. "I was quite sure I'd actually succeeded."

"You did, ma'am," Morgan said cheerfully. "But Dr. Walsh here resuscitated him."

Then he proceeded to read Sylvia her rights. In typical arrogant fashion, she declared the whole thing both unnecessary and tiresome. Understandably, the detective persisted.

As they raised the gurney and prepared to wheel her out, Sylvia's mask of composure finally slipped. "The Senator!" She looked around, locating the nurse. "Miss Shepherd, you'll stay with my husband until you're relieved?"

"I will, ma'am."

Sylvia fixed her eyes on the detective. "You must call my son immediately. Nurse Shepherd has the number. He'll come and take over his father's care until other arrangements can be made."

"You can call him yourself, Dr. Stratton. I'm sure we can afford you that opportunity, perhaps at the hospital."

Her mask was back in place now. "I'd rather not speak with Jordan right now. He won't be sympathetic. But he will step in to see to his father."

"So be it." The detective tapped the gurney and addressed the paramedic. "This officer is going to accompany you and take custody of Dr. Stratton on arrival."

A moment later, the room was emptied enough for the CSIs to come in. Morgan paused to get the phone number for Sylvia's son from the RN and called him. He wasn't immediately available, so he left an urgent message. Then he took Hayden's unresisting arm and drew her toward the kitchen.

"Where's Mrs. Garner?" she asked. At Ray's lifted eyebrow, she clarified, "The housekeeper."

"She's being questioned by one of my colleagues." He gestured for Hayden to sit at the kitchen table. "I'll make this as quick as possible. I know you want to join Boyd."

He was true to his word. It took perhaps half an hour for Hayden to relate the conversation she'd had with Boyd, his epiphany that it had to have been Sylvia. Then her headlong rush from the hospital when she realized what Boyd was likely too upset to think of—that Sylvia had poisoned him too.

Morgan laughed when she recounted finding the service

entrance door ajar, per tactical protocol, but they both sobered when she pointed out that fact probably made the difference between her getting there in time to help Boyd or not. No delay while she waited for Mrs. Garner to answer the door and while she tried to explain why she needed to be directed to wherever Sylvia was.

And she related the tail end of the conversation between Boyd and Sylvia that she'd overheard. By the time she described the sound of Boyd's last-ditch lunge at Sylvia even as he must have been losing consciousness, and his body hitting the floor, she was sobbing. Usually, it helped her keep emotion at bay to think about the physical processes that were going on. Not this time. She imagined Boyd's heart going into v-fib, ventricles quivering uselessly, unable to pump blood to his brain. Then within seconds—unconsciousness. Within minutes, death. She couldn't hold it together anymore.

Detective Morgan let her cry a moment. Then he handed her a crisp, clean handkerchief, which she used to dry her tears. Also useful in helping her conquer the tears? She'd reached the part in her tale where she clubbed Sylvia over the head with the brass bookend.

"You clocked her pretty good, huh?"

She laughed, wiping away the last of her tears. "They teach you how hard to press a scalpel to get through various types of tissue, but they don't tell you how hard to hit someone to knock them out. The way she went down, I thought I might have killed her, but I didn't have room to think about anything but Boyd. So I kicked the handgun farther under the table, then started CPR. But then I realized they might have a defibrillator upstairs for the Senator. I think I about scared that nurse to death when I tore in there, demanding the defibrillator."

"She helped you with Boyd?"

"Thank God, yes. She did CPR while I got the defibrillator ready. And she kept going with the compressions between shocks."

A uniformed cop approached to interrupt them. "Thought you might like to know that Detective McBride is conscious and very much himself."

"Oh, thank you! That's such good—" *Oh, shit.*

"What?" Morgan asked.

"I need to call the ER. I kind of ran out on them after my conversation with Boyd. I tried to call him to alert him to what I figured Sylvia had done, but his line was tied up, so I left and raced down here."

"He was likely trying to reach me," Detective Morgan said, "but I was on the line with the hospital establishing that Josh McBride's blood work was definitely faked."

Hayden pulled out her phone. "I should call Marta and make sure they found someone to cover for me. As it was, I was covering for someone else."

"Go ahead," he said. "In fact, you can take off now. I'll need to sit down with you again, maybe a couple of times. I have a hunch this is very complicated and far-reaching. I just can't figure out why people needed to die, just to cover up a shady adoption."

"About that. From what Sylvia said after Boyd arrested, I think the Senator is their father. That's why she wanted to get rid of them. I think she'd have been satisfied if they had just dropped the investigation and gone home, but neither McBride was built that way, I guess."

Morgan let out a whistle. "Okay, that puts things in perspective. I'm guessing that's what this whole thing with Dr. Gunn was about. Dr. Stratton was trying to deliver up a bad guy for Boyd so he could lay the blame somewhere and go home, mission accomplished."

Hayden groaned. "Yeah, I am going to be seeing a lot of you, aren't I?"

"Yep." He laughed. "Now why don't you go hang with the guy you really want to see. Officer Gordon will be happy to give you a lift."

CHAPTER 31

Physically, Boyd felt fine. Well, a little banged up from hitting the floor, and his chest hurt like he'd been kicked by a mule, which they said was from the CPR. But all in all, he felt way better than a guy who'd been recently dead deserved to feel. And so far, everything was looking good. For a while, there'd been talk of shipping him to the Heart Center in Saint John for an ICD—an implantable cardioverter defibrillator—but they seemed more comfortable after they'd heard his history.

He was grateful now that he'd had that exhaustive workup done in Toronto after Josh's death. They'd relaxed a smidge when they confirmed that he'd had every possible test less than two weeks ago at the Toronto Heart Centre—he'd even worn a monitor for two solid days—and they'd found no identifiable electrocardiographic abnormalities. They unbent a little more when they learned he'd lived an active life and managed a demanding job without any symptoms until Dr. Stratton had started lacing his food with some kind of drug to make him vulnerable.

The consensus now seemed to be that with the beta-blocker and the something-something blocker they were giving him, he should be fine.

He could have told them that.

All he really wanted right now was to see Hayden. Dying had a way of helping a guy sort out his priorities. Especially when it afforded you a chance to have an out-of-body chat with your dead twin.

"Boyd!"

He looked up to see Hayden framed in the doorway.

"There you are." He smiled. "I was beginning to think I'd lost you to that dandy, Ray Morgan."

She laughed, but as she moved to his bedside, he saw she was dashing away tears. "I think he's taken."

So are you. Now I just have to figure out how to make you see it.

He cleared his throat. "I hear Sylvia is just a few doors away, shackled to her bed."

"Yeah, she's going to have to get used to being locked up." She wiped away another tear. "All I can say is thank God it happened at Sylvia's and that portable defibrillator unit was there. And the first time when it didn't work—God, you scared me." She sat on the edge of his bed.

He pulled her down and kissed her forehead, then tipped her face up and kissed her mouth. "Hayden, darlin', I had to come back. You said you'd never forgive me if I didn't."

She pulled back. "You heard that?"

"Heard it. Saw it. Until you hit me with the juice that second time. That must have jerked me back in. I don't remember anything after that. I really was out of it once I came back."

"Boyd McBride, are you telling me you had an out-of-body experience while you were clinically dead?"

He shrugged. "I know. I never gave much credence to that stuff. And there was no big beckoning light. Mostly, I just saw you working over me and that nurse who kept getting between us."

She laughed and swatted him. "That nurse was trying to keep some minimal circulation going so we didn't resuscitate a profoundly brain-injured version of you."

"I know. I just like to hear you laugh."

She pushed her hair back from her face. "So you're saying no to an ICD, I hear?"

"For now," he said. "But I'm happy to revisit the decision if I have any symptoms. And I'll take all the drugs they tell me to take and avoid all the ones I have to avoid. I won't take up training for an Ironman triathlon. I'll go to all the doctor's appointments I need to, do the stress tests, wear the monitor. In short, I'll be the perfect patient. And if I do all that and have so much as a flutter, or if I find I have anxiety about it, I'll be the first one at the doctor's office saying I want the ICD."

"Sounds good." She reached for his hand and linked it with hers. "Do you remember your confrontation with Sylvia?"

"You think I could forget that?"

"Well, you did lose consciousness. People often lose memory of whatever happened immediately before they black out."

"I remember everything." His face took on a somber expression. "We did it, Hayden. We uncovered Josh's murderer."

"And you found an aunt and two cousins. And, omigod, a father! The Senator is your father. I heard Sylvia gloating about not letting Arianna steal Lewis away from her with the old pregnancy trap."

Boyd felt a flare of rage at that, but he quickly dialed it back. He was under orders not to sweat that stuff anymore. From Josh.

"Yeah, seems like a proper introduction will be in order. I just wish the guy could communicate. I'd ask him how a guy his age got involved with a girl our mother's age, and then let her fend for herself when he got her pregnant."

"I expect you'll find that Sylvia managed that too. She probably ran the poor girl off before she could . . ."

"What?" Boyd asked. "Finish what you were saying."

"Sorry, I just thought of something else. Jordan Stratton is your half brother."

Boyd blinked. "You're right. I hadn't even thought of that yet."

"Yeah, lots to talk about. And this case is so convoluted. Ray Morgan is going to have you living at the police station while he debriefs you."

"Yup." He ran his thumb over the back of her hand. "Lots for us to talk about too."

He saw the anxiety leap in her eyes, felt it weigh down the air between them.

She dropped her gaze to their linked hands. "You must be anxious to get home."

"I will need to go back soon, to tell Mom and Dad about what happened to Josh, what I've really been doing in New Brunswick."

"And about this." She gestured to the monitors.

"I wish I didn't have to, but yeah. I imagine it'll be making national headlines, if not international ones. It's just too juicy."

"When will you leave?"

"As soon as the doc clears me to travel and the cops have had a chance to extract everything I know or think I know."

"A couple of days?"

"Probably."

She drew a deep breath. "You can stay with me if you like. Dr. Stratton's house will be a crime scene for the immediate future."

Boyd felt a pang at that. Here she was offering to do the thing she'd had enough sense—enough self-preservation—to avoid doing before. Letting him move in. He hoped that boded well for him.

"I'd like that," he said. "They're going to keep me tonight, but as soon as they spring me, I'd love to go to your place."

"Good. I've already arranged to take a few days' leave, so we can spend whatever time Ray Morgan can spare you together."

She ducked her head, and her glorious hair fell forward again. Where had the elastic gone that she usually used to pull her hair back? That's when it struck him—she was trying to cover up her tear-ravaged face.

She looked up at him and smiled brightly. Too brightly.

"Hayden, do you think a man's promise should survive death?"

"*What?*"

"Because I made a promise to you that I fully intended to keep at the time, but now I don't know if I can do it."

Her eyes rounded. "What are you saying?"

"I promised that I'd get out of your hair when this thing with Josh was done. But now that the time has come, I don't want to."

She just looked at him blankly.

"I want us to be together," he added helpfully.

"I told you, Boyd. I'm committed to my residency here. I can't go traipsing off to Toronto."

"I'm not asking you to."

"So, what? We try to do the long-distance thing?"

"Not that either." He heard the pace of his own heartbeat picking up on the monitor and took a calming breath. It wouldn't do to have a nurse barge in right now. "I was thinking I could relocate."

"Here?"

He laughed at her tone. "Yeah, here. You've got over a year left on your residency, right?"

"Fifteen months."

"So I'm thinking I could get a job. If the PD doesn't want me for such an indefinite stint, I can—I don't know—get a PI license or do security or, shit, hang out with the Senator."

"What about after, when I've finished my residency?"

"I'll go where you go."

"What if that's Haiti?"

"You mean the Doctors Without Borders thing?"

She put her hands on her hips. "Yeah. *That* thing."

"So you'd be gone for a few weeks here and there. You really think I'd begrudge that?"

"Boyd, the minimum commitment is nine months."

He felt his face go slack. "Nine months?"

"Yes." She looked so miserable.

"Then I'll go with you."

"To Haiti?"

"To hell if I have to. But yeah, to Haiti. Actually, Canada has a commitment to the UN to help train local police in a number of countries, including Haiti. It's called International Police Development, and is administered by the RCMP, but all kinds of forces take part in it. But even if that didn't work out, I could go as a civilian volunteer."

"You would do that?"

"In a heartbeat." Then he hastened to add, "One of those effectual ones where everything is synced up and blood actually gets pumped, not one of those v-fib sons of bitches."

She grinned, and this time it looked real, not like that horrible bright smile earlier. He must be making headway. Then her smile faded.

"What if you can't go? What if there's no program or no money or what if your parents are ill and need you?"

Ah, here we are. This was the test. Much as he'd worry about her and fret for her safety and miss the hell out of her, he would never try to stop her. Yes, it could be dangerous. Kidnap of aid workers for ransom was pretty much business as usual in some of those countries. But his job was dangerous too, and he wouldn't want her telling him he couldn't do it.

"Then I would learn to give good phone sex. And make Port-au-Prince my new vacation hotspot. And you would probably have to be really patient with me asking about the security detail."

She blinked rapidly, which he took as a good sign. "Why would you do all this? Why complicate your life like this?"

"Josh was right. I have been an emotional coward. I still am. But not anymore. Starting right here, right now. I love you, Hayden Walsh. I want to spend my life with you, wherever that turns out to be."

"You love me?"

"Of course I love you. And I'm not looking for someone to be at my side with those defibrillator paddles. I'd just get the ICD if I was worried about that. Which I am not."

"I love you too, Boyd, but—"

He chuckled.

She looked at him indignantly. "That's funny?"

"Josh said you wouldn't make this easy for me."

"*Josh?*"

"Yeah, I kind of talked to him. And by *kind of,* I mean I know it was probably me having a conversation with myself while out of body, and Josh was a projection of my own mind. But it felt like he was there. I told him I needed to get back, because now that I'd found you, I couldn't lose you."

"Josh? Omigod." She clamped a hand over her mouth and her eyes flooded again.

"Or my oxygen-deprived brain's projection of him. Whatever the case, it was comforting. He was happy, peaceful. Like maybe death isn't the lonely, cold, dark place I imagined it to be."

Tears streamed down her face, but she was smiling. "That makes me so happy. You have no idea."

"I'm not saying it *was* Josh. I don't know if I believe in that woo-woo stuff."

She grabbed some tissues and blotted the tears, then blew her nose. "I choose to believe it. It's so comforting."

"Then you'll also be comforted to know he says he'll come back and kick my ass if I do anything to hurt you."

Her laugh was choked with emotion. "What about . . . Did he say anything—"

"He still loves you. He'll always love you. But he says it's different there. And, yes, he knows I love you and he's good with that."

She sniffed. "Really?"

"Really," he said. "Now, can we get back to the part where you said you love me too?"

She tossed the tissues and sat down on the edge of the bed again. "It's true. I tried not to. I tried really, really hard. I kept telling myself you'd be leaving soon—that I wanted you to leave so I could get back to my normal life, but I couldn't help myself."

He took her hand. "Does this mean you'll release me from my promise?"

"It does." She bent to kiss him and he caught the back of her head and held her mouth there, giving her all the tenderness in his heart. She pulled back a moment later to give them both a chance to breathe.

"But don't go thinking you can get away with that again," she said sternly. "No dying to get your way."

He laughed. "I wouldn't dream of it, baby."

EPILOGUE

Boyd looked out over the crowd assembled to watch him and Hayden take their marriage vows. He'd always thought that if or when he got married, it would be one of those city hall civil ceremonies. Hayden would have been good with that, but he'd wanted to give her a beautiful, intimate wedding.

And, yeah, okay, he'd wanted the world to watch as the most extraordinary, strong, kind, brave, beautiful woman pledged to love him. Well, everyone in *his* world anyway. A world that had grown enormously in the past year.

He glanced to his left where his best man, fellow Fredericton City Police Detective Ray Morgan, stood. Of course, Morgan looked like he'd stepped straight out of the pages of *GQ* in his charcoal-gray tux. The man had actually sat down with Hayden and Boyd to pick the tuxedos. Grace Morgan had been terrifically helpful to Hayden too, in picking out gowns for the attendants.

Morgan adjusted his tie and raised an eyebrow.

Boyd lifted a hand to his own tie to find it slightly askew. Leave it to the clotheshorse to notice that millimeter by which it was off. He adjusted it. Morgan gave him a barely perceptible nod.

The organ's tempo changed slightly, and his half brother, Jordan, entered the church with Hayden's grandparents and guided them to their seats. His groomsmen were doubling as ushers, given how small the gathering was. Boyd had felt a little weird asking Jordan to do it, but he hadn't been at all insulted. Not much of Sylvia in that one. He was much more like his father, thank God. A year after the two of them met, Boyd still didn't feel like they were true brothers, and maybe he never would. On the other hand, the only bar he had to measure sibling relationships was being one half of identical twins. Probably most sibling relationships didn't measure up to that. And to Jordan's credit, he was a good man and a decent fisherman. He was also endlessly grateful that Boyd didn't hold his mother's heinous actions against him.

As Jordan made the stately walk to the back of the church again, Hayden's mother came in on the arm of his other groomsman, Detective Craig Walker. Now those men—Ray and Craig and a few of the other guys—felt more like brothers than his half brother did. But family was family, and he was grateful for all of it.

Hayden's mother shot him a smile that outshone even the beautiful, shoulder-baring dress she wore. Hayden had said the dress was designed by one of Haiti's hottest designers, Jean Yves Someone-or-Other. Boyd knew nothing about fashion, but even he could see how the garment brought together, with surprising harmony, the colors of the sea and earth of Evelyn Walsh's native Haiti. Of course, like her daughter, Mrs. Walsh could have worn a burlap sack and still looked fantastic. Evelyn's skin was slightly darker than Hayden's, and she had brown eyes and short-cropped, tightly curled dark hair. She possessed the strong European facial features indicative of her mixed heritage. And when she smiled like she was doing right now, Boyd could totally see Hayden in her. He smiled right back.

He let his gaze sweep the crowd, lighting with pleasure on Frank and Ella McBride. Beside them sat the Senator. He had an aide beside him who helped with his mobility issues. His recovery had been remarkable, perhaps because he'd never actually had a stroke. At least not initially. As it turned out, he'd gotten an anonymous tip that his first love, Arianna Duncan, who'd disappeared from his life without explanation, had given birth to twin boys before she died. Boyd's money was on Dr. Gunn dropping that dime. Wherever the tip had come from, Lewis Stratton had hired a private investigator to try to find Arianna's boys, but Sylvia had found out. She'd started poisoning him immediately. What she passed off to the doctors as a stroke was a toxic metabolic issue created by drug intoxication. She'd carefully managed him from that point on, keeping him minimally conscious. He could talk quite well now, and he had done so at length with the police.

Behind them sat Boyd's aunt Sandra, her daughter and son-in-law, Angela and Jeremy Wood, and their now toddling baby girl, April.

So much family. And now he was about to acquire some more. He glanced back at Hayden's mother and the various aunts, uncles, and cousins in the pews behind. It was easy to see where Hayden got her passion and humor from. If he and Hayden had kids, he hoped they inherited all of that. Of course, there was a chance they could inherit his LQTS, which would suck. They hadn't made any decisions, but Boyd had made it clear that he was a fan of adoption if she didn't want to risk it. Kids were still a ways off, though. She'd yet to do her first stint with Doctors Without Borders, or DWeeB, as he liked to call it, if only to get a rise out of Hayden.

She actually had a few months left on her residency. And to Boyd's surprise and delight, she'd recently announced that she'd accepted the recruiter's offer to come back to Fredericton after her months in Haiti. One of her rotations had introduced her to a collaborative practice on the Northside, and she'd been totally sold on their multidisciplinary approach. It wasn't Toronto or Vancouver, but her experience there showed her there were plenty of people who needed her services. People who were marginalized by poverty, illiteracy, mental illness, addiction, and countless other reasons.

Boyd had kissed the hell out of her, then dragged her out house shopping. She'd wanted a house with a huge interior wall big enough for his beloved panoramic art installation, but he'd shaken his head. The feeling that he used to get from looking at that picture he now got from looking into her eyes, only it was a million times better. He'd since sold both the condo and the art to the same buyer. Their life was here, at least for the moment, and give or take a few DWeeB bumps.

The organ music changed again, jolting him back to the moment. Hayden's maid of honor, Courtney Clark, a friend from Hayden's high school days in Montreal, was coming up the aisle on Jordan Stratton's arm. She looked gorgeous in an elegant gray gown. She took her place with a smile for Boyd.

Next came bridesmaid Gayle Ballard, one of Hayden's friends from med school, on the arm of Craig Walker. Dressed in a slightly different but identically colored gray gown, she looked a little dazzled by the size of her escort. But Boyd knew Craig was as happily married as the rest of them. There must be something in the water in Fredericton.

Boyd smiled at the next pair. Grace Morgan, looking as classically beautiful as ever, on the arm of Tommy Godsoe. Tommy was a former police K-9 handler turned K-9 breeder and trainer, and he and Boyd got on like brothers from other mothers.

Then every eye in the house was on the double doors as Hayden came through on her father's arm.

His breath caught at the sight of her. The dress she wore was beautifully simple, and it hugged her curves lovingly. Her gorgeous hair had been twisted up, but not in the loose, sexy thing she usually did with it. This was smooth and sleek, and as lacking in ornamentation as the clean lines of the dress. If this was Grace's influence, he approved. It gave her a classic, timeless look. And her face . . . God, he loved that face.

He got an elbow in his side. "Breathe, McBride," Ray Morgan murmured. "If you faint, everyone'll think you died."

Man, drop dead once and they never let you forget it. "Isn't that getting old for you, Morgan?"

"Nope."

Hayden and her father had reached the chancel steps and Michael Walsh took his daughter's hand and placed it in Boyd's. "Take care of her, son."

"I will, sir."

As her father moved to take his seat, Boyd whispered to Hayden, "Are you ready for this?"

There it was, that light in her eyes, the one he never tired of seeing. The one that made him feel like he could do anything, take on anything.

"I'm ready."

As they turned to face the minister, Boyd swore he could feel

Josh with him, feel his approval and that warm, cocooning peace. Then the sensation was gone.

The minister was talking, but Hayden was staring at him, wide-eyed. "Josh?" she mouthed.

He gave her a slight nod and mouthed, "Yeah."

Smiling as though she felt the same sense of benediction he did, she faced forward again.

ACKNOWLEDGMENTS

To Staff Sergeant Matt Myers, of the Criminal Investigation Division of the Fredericton Police Force, my deepest gratitude. Matt keeps me on the straight and narrow with respect to police procedural elements, including gently correcting me when I fall into American terminology/concepts in my Canadian setting.

I am also deeply indebted to Dr. Stephen MacLean, who was the perfect consultant for this project. Not only is he an MD with a wealth of experience staffing ERs (my heroine is a medical resident working largely in an emergency department), he is also a film producer/writer with a deep feel for story.

I definitely had a dream team in Dr. MacLean and S. Sgt. Myers, and I wish to emphasize that any mistakes I've made or liberties I've taken are entirely my own.

Thank you, too, to my editor, JoVon Sotak, and the amazing team at Montlake Romance.

To my agent Cori Deyoe, thank you for always being in my corner.

A big thank-you to my family for their patience during the deadline craziness.

And for their unflagging support and encouragement, thank you to so many writer friends, particularly my homies, Heather Doherty, Lina Gardiner, Kate Kelly, Barbara Phinney, Linda Hall, and Lori Gallagher. And out there in the wider world, thank you to the awesome Pamela Clare, Bonnie Vanak, Alice Duncan, Alice Gaines, Jan Zimlich, and Mimi Riser, to name but a few. Also, the amazing authors of Rock*It Reads. Last but not least, a shout out to the Wet Noodle Posse, who've been wielding those wet noodles—and sharing their support and knowledge—for eleven years.

ABOUT THE AUTHOR

Photograph by Studio 16 Digital Photography, 2013

Norah Wilson is a *USA Today* best-selling author of romantic suspense, including *Every Breath She Takes*, *Guarding Suzannah*, *Saving Grace*, and *Protecting Paige*. A native Canadian, Wilson lives in Fredericton, New Brunswick, with her family. Visit her website at www.norahwilsonwrites.com.